ALL
FALL
DOWN

CARLENE THOMPSON

ALL FALL DOWN

DOUBLEDAY LARGE PRINT HOME LIBRARY EDITION

ST. MARTIN'S PRESS ❧ NEW YORK

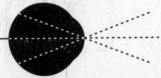

This Large Print Book carries the
Seal of Approval of N.A.V.H.

To my agent, Judith Weber,
for advice, patience, and encouragement

I would like to thank my family for their technical advice and unflagging support. I would also like to thank Ashley, for her years of love and devotion.

Prologue

She forced her eyes open. At first all she saw was a blur of stars against a sky black as death. Then a face loomed over hers. "Still awake?" it asked.

She was lying in a tangle of weeds. They brushed her face, tickling, irritating. She raised her head slightly. "Please . . ."

"Please what? Please leave you alone? I can't. Not now."

Tears gathered in the corners of her eyes. Oh, God, was she having a dream? No. In dreams, her heart beat faster. Now it was slowing, beating in hard thuds growing farther and farther apart. The tears overflowed her eyes and ran across her temples into her thick black hair.

Suddenly she remembered when she was five years old and had sneaked out of her room one night to visit the house under construction next door. She hadn't been interested in it until they told her the place was dangerous and she must *never* go there. Immediately it assumed an unconquerable allure. After creeping down the stairs while everyone watched television in the den and then scampering out the back door, nearly tripping over the untied shoelace on her Keds that peeped out from beneath her long nightgown, she had tiptoed around the building site, heady with her own daring, not admitting that she was a little disappointed by the unexciting conglomeration of boards and wheelbarrows and some big piece of machinery they'd used just that day to dig a hole Grandpa said would be a basement. She peered down into the huge hole, trying to picture it all stuffed with old furniture and books like the basement at her house. But it didn't look like much. Besides, it wouldn't look like her basement even when it was done— Grandpa had said the new people were going to make it a "rec room," with Ping-Pong tables and "a lot of other foolishness" for their teenaged kids.

Bored almost immediately with her daring night journey, she decided to liven up the event by seeing how far out over the hole she could lean without getting dizzy. She took a step, tripped on the loose shoelace, and plunged forward into the freshly dug basement. Her surprised scream emerged as a thin squeak before she hit bottom, the air knocked out of her. As she lay on her back, her right leg agonizingly twisted under her, broken, her head swimming from a concussion, she had looked up at the stars—stars just like the ones she was seeing now—and cried because of the pain and because she was afraid no one would ever know how sorry she was that she'd done something bad, so bad God might make her die for it.

But she was seventeen now, and this time she *knew* she was dying. Grandpa wasn't around to come looking for her in the next hour when they discovered her bed was empty. No one would come. No one could save her.

Panic washed over her. "Can't do this," she slurred to the face so near hers.

"I have to. I'm *going* to."

She raised her head. She was having trouble breathing, although her emotions still raged. "Goddamn you! Hate you!" she spat.

"What happened to that sweet, soft-spoken girl we all know and love? Maybe you're just showing your true colors, eh?" Pause. "Besides, I don't *care* how you feel about me, so save the little breath you have left."

She shuddered, her legs jerking convulsively. They weren't bound, but she'd lost muscle control. They jerked once more, then settled limply on the cold ground. They no longer felt like part of her. She groaned before her head fell backward, hitting the ground with a soft thud.

"That's better. You don't want to fight me right up to the last minute, do you?"

She tried to speak. She tried to say, "Please don't do this. I don't deserve *this*." But only "please" and "this" were intelligible around a tongue suddenly too big in her dry mouth.

A sigh came before the voice filled itself with businesslike concentration. "It's getting late. We'd better get on with it now."

Her right wrist was raised. The serrated edge of a kitchen knife gleamed in the moonlight. "I wish you were asleep for this, I really do. But you're so damned *stubborn*. You won't even go to sleep when you're supposed to."

For an instant it was all there—plans for

college; high school football games viewed on crisp autumn nights; Grandma's loving face; her adored cat, Taffy, that had vanished when she was seven; her new car; his warm hands moving over her lithe body; Aunt Joan's beautiful violet eyes.

Then it all vanished into an almost surreal vision of the knife skimming across her skin. Her wrist opened. Warm blood gushed down her arms, steaming slightly in the chilled night air. Her throat worked, but all that emerged was a whimper. She tried one last time to raise herself up on one elbow, but the effort was too much. She collapsed helplessly into the creeping vines, her chest heaving as she fought for breath.

Despite her fading heartbeat, her mind still functioned, although with dreamy sluggishness. So Grandma had been right, she thought in dull surprise. Grandma always said evil in your soul would turn on you like a vicious animal. Her intent had been evil—she knew all along it was. It violated everything she'd been taught about the sanctity of life. But she wasn't the only one whom evil would turn on—not the only one.

A hand clasped her left arm and raised it

to meet the knife. In the resignation that comes from total despair, she stopped thinking and gazed up at the beautiful whirl of spinning stars. Then she closed her eyes.

1

Blaine Avery smiled at the golden retriever capering before her. "Sure you *really* want to go on this walk, Ashley?" she teased. The dog barked and turned in a circle, her nails tapping on the polished oak floor. "Full of beans now that you're back home, aren't you?" Blaine laughed, bending down to rub the dog's ears.

Ashley growled the way she always did when she wanted a walk. "Okay, I'll stop chattering and we'll be on our way." Blaine stood up. "But don't forget, this is our first walk in the woods for a long time. I'm not up to chasing you, so don't go wild on me."

The dog marched to the door and shifted impatiently from side to side. Blaine drew a windbreaker over her light blue sweater, and as soon as she opened the French door, Ashley shot out into the mid-November sunshine. "I said, take it easy!" Blaine called, but the dog was already streaking across the wide terrace toward the woods a couple of hundred feet beyond, looking back and barking repeatedly as if to say, "Hurry up!"

"I guess I can't blame her." Blaine sighed, picking up her own pace. Six weeks ago, she had developed a serious case of pneumonia. After spending a week in the hospital, she'd moved into her sister, Caitlin's, home in town to recuperate. She had come back to her own house yesterday morning, but a deluge of rain during the afternoon had kept her and Ashley inside. Now it felt good to be outdoors, walking across the lawn toward the woods as she had so many times with the dog and her late husband, Martin.

Martin. Blaine closed her eyes, shivering as she drew the windbreaker tighter. She was a slim five-foot-nine with long auburn hair and light gray eyes that gazed alertly from a face whose high cheekbones stood out more than usual since Martin's death. The past several months had been hard for her, but looking up at the lemon-colored sun in a clear sky made her feel almost like her old self. Maybe the grief and the trauma of the recent past were beginning to fade, she thought.

Ashley had disappeared into the shadows of the woods, and Blaine hoped the dog wouldn't run helter-skelter for the next two hours. She didn't like leaving Ashley in the woods at night. Besides, Martin's daughter, Robin, would be home from the Sunday matinee soon, and Blaine wanted to fix her something nice for dinner. Maybe baked chicken with lemon sauce, one of her favorite recipes. Of course, Robin would probably just as soon have a pizza. And she probably would not appreciate anything special Blaine fixed for her. Tension had always vibrated between the two of them, and it had grown worse since Martin's death. The time they had spent at Caitlin's house had helped—Robin seemed, in a cautious way, to like Cait and her family— but now that Blaine and Robin were home again, she felt the old awkwardness returning.

Blaine told herself she was letting her mind wander too much, though, which was a bad habit with her. Sometimes she would find she'd walked nearly a mile without noticing one thing around her. But she couldn't let that happen today. She had the dog to look after.

"Ashley," she called as she entered the woods and followed the path Martin's father had carved out fifty years ago. Every year it was cleared to make walking in the woods easier for the occupants of the house. "Ashley!"

The dog barked nearby, then came crashing through the undergrowth toward her. "Look at you!" Blaine laughed. "Ten minutes and your beautiful hair is full of leaves and twigs. You're a mess!"

Ashley barked again and took off, refusing to stay on the path. On hot summer days she loved to swim in the creek flowing through the property. Blaine only hoped the chill of the water would keep her out of it today. She didn't want to have to give the dog a bath as soon as they got home.

Blaine walked slowly, savoring the atmosphere. In the top of a hickory tree a red squirrel rattled nuts. The needles of the towering hemlocks had begun to fall, and their light brown cones were maturing. Soon they would be dropping their seeds, which reminded her that she would have to refill the bird feeders Caitlin's husband, Kirk, had made and hung in the woods two years ago, when five inches of snow had fallen and remained for weeks. She spotted one just ahead, hanging from an elm, an elegant little structure shaped like a Chinese pagoda and painted lacquer red with elaborate black-and-gold trim. "I designed these especially for you," he'd told her proudly. "Five of them. Signature pieces. No one else will have one like them."

"Blaine! Where are you?"

Blaine jerked at the sound of her younger sister's voice. "Cait, I'm up here."

In a moment Caitlin ran up to her, her short orange hair tousled, the freckles standing out on her nose. She looked seventeen instead of twenty-seven. "What are you doing here?" Blaine asked. "Checking up on me?"

Caitlin's lovely amber eyes, naked of makeup, twinkled at her. "Of course I'm checking up on you. You promised to call me every day, and I haven't heard a word so far today."

"You are ten times worse than a mother."

"Well, our mother isn't around anymore, so I get to be what I want. Why didn't you call me?"

"I've just been busy. Unpacking, reorganizing, you know."

Caitlin nodded. "Getting adjusted to living in this house again." She plunged her hands in the pockets of her denim jacket. "I tell you, Blaine, I don't think it's a good idea for you to be here. I think you should just sell the place."

"It's not mine to sell. Martin left it in trust to Robin, remember?"

"He left you half of Avery Manufacturing, I do remember that. You're a millionaire. Why don't you move?"

"Because Robin can't live here alone, her mother is dead so she has no one else to go to, and she's had too much upheaval in her life this past year for me to make her give up on the only home she's ever known." Blaine smiled reassuringly at her sister. "Don't worry. I'll put the ghosts to rest."

"*The* ghost, you mean. Martin's ghost. But don't be too sure he's going to rest easily. I can feel him every time I walk into that house."

"Where do you come up with lines like that? Books?"

"Well, I *do*. Some of my friends think I'm a little bit psychic."

"I think you have an overactive imagination."

Caitlin sighed. "Okay. I'm sorry I brought up something painful. I'm rambling as usual, and I know I can't budge you on this issue, although I don't think you're as brave about coming back to this house as you pretend." Blaine didn't meet her sister's eyes because, as usual, Caitlin knew exactly what she was feeling. "What I really came out here to see," Cait went on, "is how you feel today."

"I'm *fine*."

"All right, don't take my head off. You look good."

Blaine took a deep breath and forced herself to relax, wishing she hadn't taken her discomfort at the memory of Martin out on her sister. It had been almost a year since the car accident, and six months since his death. It was time to put the past where it belonged. "I'm sorry I snapped at you."

"That's okay." Cait grinned. "I deserved it for prattling on about ghosts. I talk before I think." She peered into the trees. "I guess Ashley's on her maiden voyage."

"And doing great. Too great. I can't keep up with her."

Caitlin laughed. "She'll wear out pretty soon. Isn't Robin home today?"

"She's at the movies. I'm glad—she's been spending too much time immersed in schoolwork and her piano."

"You were the same way. Always studying, always determined to make something of yourself in spite of all our disadvantages."

"Yes, but Robin doesn't have any disadvantages. She doesn't need to be so driven to succeed."

"Just be glad she's motivated. A lot of kids aren't." They fell into step and Caitlin asked, "Seen any deer?"

"With Ashley around? Certainly not. They must sense she's back and ready to give them a good chase."

"Robin told me a funny story about a deer out here." Blaine looked at her questioningly. "It seems that she was with Rosalind Van Zandt, and they were only about four. All at once there was a rustle and then this white tail flagging away from them. That's how Robin described it. They both thought it was Bambi and went shrieking back to the house to tell Martin. He went right along with them and said Bambi was a movie star who deserved the very best, so he put out a salt lick for the deer."

"That sounds like the Martin I fell in love with," Blaine said, smiling. Then her smile faded. "She never tells me stories like that."

"I'm not her beautiful young stepmother. She never felt that she was competing with me for her father's love."

"We weren't competing."

"*We* know that, but we're not oversensitive teenagers. Underneath, I think she likes you."

"She tolerates me. That's it."

"So why not send her to her mother's parents?"

"Because they live in Florida and this is her senior year of high school. Besides, they've never asked to have her and she's never asked to go to them."

"That's strange."

"Not really. They were middle-aged when Robin's mother was born, and they're very old now. They live in a retirement community. They wouldn't know what to do with a lively teenager, and Robin would feel buried alive living with them. Anyway, she's always wanted to stay here."

"Well, as long as the two of you manage

to get along, I guess there's no harm in your staying together, although I *still* think you're making a mistake by moving back into this house."

"Caitlin!"

"Okay. I've said my piece." She winked at Blaine. "And when did you *ever* do anything someone told you to?"

"Dad always taught us to be independent."

Caitlin rolled her eyes, the buoyancy leaving her voice. "Yeah, and look where it got him. Mom left, he couldn't hold a steady job because of his drinking, and he died broke and sick in that sagging shack downtown because he wouldn't let either one of us help him."

"Cait, are you trying to bring up every painful memory in my life?"

"It's true. You always romanticize him, but—"

"I *don't* romanticize him," Blaine said tightly, "but I don't try to make a tragic figure out of him, either. He was *happy* with his life. And he was a good father. We had a lot of good times, Cait. You can't deny that."

"Yeah, we did. We just didn't have any money, any security, any dignity—"

Footsteps pounded on the path behind them, and they both whirled to see Robin. "I saw your car in the driveway, Caitlin," she said, panting as she slowed down. Alarm showed in her eyes. "No one was in the house and I thought maybe something was wrong. Then I realized the two of you must be out here. Nothing *is* wrong, is it?"

"Not a thing," Blaine said lightly, wishing Robin would stop panicking at every variation in routine, but after Martin's horrible death, she well understood the girl's anxiety. She, too, fought it every day.

"We're supposed to be taking a restful walk," Caitlin said tartly. "Actually, we're quarreling."

A smile flitted across Robin's face. During the two years of Blaine's marriage to Martin, Robin had seemed at first bewildered and later amused by Blaine and Caitlin's constant bickering, and Blaine had realized how strange she and Cait must sound to Robin. Having no brothers or sisters of her own, Robin seemed unaware of the frequent, harmless spats between siblings, especially two loving but equally strong-willed, outspoken sisters. "We'll save round two for the walk back home if you'll join us," Blaine said.

Robin nodded, assuming a false air of nonchalance to hide her earlier alarm. "Okay. It's a nice day for a walk."

And you would never have come along if it were just the two of us, Blaine thought unhappily. But Robin's coldness toward her was just one more thing she would have to learn to accept. It had been bad enough when she married Martin, but much worse during the past few months. Still, Robin was Martin's only child, and Blaine was determined to do the best by her that she could, even if it meant enduring the girl's poorly disguised hostility and occasional veiled insults.

"How was the movie, Robin?" Caitlin asked.

"Great. I think Kim Basinger is really beautiful. I might bleach my hair blond like hers."

Blaine looked at Robin's long, glossy dark brown hair. "You touch that perfect hair and you'll regret it." Robin's eyes flashed at her, seeming to mistake her words for a threat. "I only meant that you have great hair. I don't think you want to mess it up with chemicals."

"Yeah. You might end up a carrottop like me," Caitlin added.

Robin relaxed and laughed. She really is lovely, Blaine thought. Slender and fawnlike, with those huge dark eyes. If only she knew how pretty she really is. But self-confidence was not one of Robin's strong points. She was always comparing herself with her more blatantly striking friends, like Rosie Van Zandt.

As they ambled on, Blaine noticed the sugar maples, whose leaves varied from yellow to burnt orange to crimson and cranberry-red. After she graduated from high school and moved to Dallas to attend college and later to teach, she'd missed the beautiful autumns of West Virginia. When, following her father's death four years ago, she'd returned to Sinclair, West Virginia, it had been October, and the trees had turned the hills into patchwork quilts of color. She'd told everyone she had decided to stay in Sinclair to be near her sister, but Caitlin wasn't her only reason for remaining. The lure of the mountainous land that sloped down toward the Ohio River and where she'd grown up had been almost irresistibly strong, and she'd never regretted her decision to move back to Sinclair. Not until Martin's death, at least.

As if the thought of death had manifested itself in symbolic reality, she looked up to see two carrion crows flying overhead. "I hate those things," she muttered. "Miniature vultures."

Robin glanced up absently. "They aren't too appealing, but I guess they're necessary."

Abruptly Blaine became aware that it was getting darker. The points of light slicing through the leaves to shine on the moist path below were blurring. She glanced at her watch. Five-ten. A little early for the light to be fading, but it was.

"I think we'd better head home now," she said.

"So soon?" Cait asked. "Don't you want to walk to the end of the path as usual?"

"No. I'd like to get dinner started."

"I hope we're not having anything fancy," Robin said, dashing Blaine's visions of chicken in lemon sauce. "I'm really in the mood for a pizza."

"I *knew* it! Actually, that sounds pretty

good to me, too. We'll go to Village Pizza Inn. Do you and Kirk want to join us, Cait?"

"No, thanks. I have a roast in the oven, which is probably burning to a crisp, since Kirk will never remember to check it."

Blaine laughed. "So you might be joining us after all." She paused, then called, "Ashley!" The woods were silent. "Ashley, come on, girl!" Again there was no sound.

Blaine whistled and was glad finally to hear an answering bark. Only it wasn't just a bark of recognition. It was a volley of barks. Had Ashley cornered a ground hog? The three of them stood still, listening. No, there was something different about the barking. It held a note of alarm Blaine had learned to recognize after owning the dog for years. "Something's wrong," she said.

Robin whistled for the dog she loved almost as much as Blaine did. No response except the distant, frantic barking. She and Blaine exchanged a look, then began to run along the path with Caitlin trailing behind. "Ashley, come here!" Robin shouted.

The barking continued, but the dog did not come. She was up ahead and off to the right, Blaine decided, stopping to listen again. "She's at the creek. Maybe she tried to swim and can't make it back up the bank. We've had so much rain, it could be crumbling."

Blaine plunged into the undergrowth, feeling her running shoes sink slightly into the dark, loamy earth still spongy from Saturday's downpour. Usually she didn't veer from the path, frightened she might step on a snake. Even now she imagined a sleek head rising to bury its fangs in her leg. Could a copperhead bite through jeans? she wondered, stopping once more to listen.

This time she heard Ashley tearing back and forth through the vines along the creek, barking hysterically. At least the dog wasn't drowning, but something was terribly wrong. Blaine started off again and in her alarm screamed as a chipmunk raced across her path. She slipped on the mossy ground, colliding with a holly, and felt one of the points on its leathery leaves scratch her face. Caitlin caught her arm to keep her from falling. Then they skirted the tree and immediately spotted the dog.

Ashley had stopped running and stood at the creek's edge beside a weeping willow whose spiny, naked yellow limbs drooped desolately into the water.

"Has she found a dead animal?" Caitlin asked barely above a whisper.

"Maybe," Blaine said doubtfully. "Ash, come here."

The dog looked at her but refused to come. Instead she sat down solidly on the creek bank, staring determinedly into the water. Although she had never been trained as a hunting dog, the retrieval instinct was strong in her. A dead animal was a source of curiosity for the dog, one which she usually picked up and delivered at Blaine's feet like a gift. But she wasn't merely curious now, and she was making no attempt to retrieve whatever it was, as she would a piece of game. A sickening sense of déjà vu filled Blaine when she remembered another time Ashley had acted this way.

Cautiously the three of them approached through the dying undergrowth dank from yesterday's rain. A vaguely ripe, nauseating odor rose from the creek, and Blaine suddenly thought of the carrion crows they'd seen flying away from this direction. Her stomach tightened as perspiration popped out on her forehead. She wanted to turn and run away from this lonely, darkening spot. But she *had* to see. No matter what it was, she had to see it.

Robin reached the dog's side first. She knelt and touched Ashley's head, murmuring, "What is it, girl?" Then, slowly, she looked into the water. Her back went rigid as her hands dropped limply to her sides. "Blaine," she said in a voice gone childish with fear. "There's . . . there's something in the water."

Blaine's breath turned shallow as she and Cait picked their way hesitantly to the creek bank and looked down. Something floating. Something . . . no, *someone.*

Blaine bent down, peering into the water. Caught in the jutting roots of the old willow was a body. "My God," Cait murmured.

Blaine stared. Abruptly, the world seemed to grow unnaturally quiet, just like the figure dressed in blue jeans and what once must have been a white sweater, now muddy brown from the dirty water.

"Blaine?" Cait quavered.

But Blaine couldn't take her eyes off the floating figure. A bluish right hand, wearing a large, familiar diamond-and-opal ring, was entwined by two willow limbs and stuck up in the air, as if waving to someone on the opposite shore. Extremely long black hair floated gracefully on the dark, rippling water, surrounding a startling white face torn by fish and bird bites.

"It's a woman," Blaine said quietly as Cait leaned over her shoulder, peering at the figure.

Caitlin screamed before slapping a hand over her mouth. Blaine glanced back at her. Cait's face had turned so white that the freckles stood out like dots of brown ink, unnatural and garish. Strangely, her scream did not set birds squawking in the trees. All was silent, as if in reverence of death.

Robin licked dry lips. "That ring. That hair." Blaine's breath stopped, and sourness filled her mouth. Robin leaned forward, nearer the floating body. "Her eyes are gone," she said in an eerie, vacant voice. She turned her head slowly, gazing at Blaine. "It's Rosie, and her beautiful eyes are gone." Then Robin turned her head and threw up into the dense, creeping vines along the creek bank.

2

1

Blaine choked back her own nausea and rushed to Robin, holding her shoulders until the retching stopped. Keeping her eyes averted from the body, she pulled the girl to her feet. "We have to go back to the house and call the police."

Robin looked at her wildly. "I can't just *leave* her here!"

"You have to," Blaine said, surprised by how controlled she sounded. "I'm not leaving *you* out here. It's getting dark."

"But Rosie . . ."

Robin shuddered violently, and Blaine shut her mind to the horror. "Cait, help me," she said to her sister, who still stood with wide, terrified eyes and her hand over her mouth as if she were stifling back more screams. "We have to get back to the house."

Caitlin had always responded to the

sound of authority in Blaine's voice, and now she snapped out of her shock and rushed to Robin, supporting her left side while Blaine wrapped an arm around the girl's waist and propelled her away from the creek. With Ashley trotting ahead, they stumbled through the vines to the path. It's so quiet, Blaine thought. It is so frighteningly, unnaturally quiet in these woods. And it's such a long way to the house.

As Robin cried, Blaine and Caitlin half led, half carried her toward home. Long shadows now fell across the path, and the trees seemed to lean menacingly close, like sentient creatures in a child's nightmare. Blaine's heart thudded painfully, and her eyes darted left and right, probing the dimness of the woods. She felt as if a presence were everywhere, watching them, playing with them, waiting until they'd almost made it home before striking. Even Ashley seemed to feel it, staying close, her ears perked for any threatening sounds as she occasionally growled softly. When they finally reached the open expanse of the lawn, Blaine almost wept with relief.

By the time they staggered through the French doors, Blaine felt as if knives were slashing her chest. Too much strain after just recovering from pneumonia, she thought, fighting to keep both Robin and Cait from noticing her pain. The girl's sobbing had subsided to intermittent whimpering, and she wasn't leaning so heavily on Blaine as before.

When they entered the living room, Robin headed for the couch, but Blaine steered her down the long hall, through her bedroom to the bathroom. While Robin stood by limply, Blaine got a towel and a washcloth from the linen closet and turned on the cold water. "I want you to wash your face, then go lie down for a few minutes. You look like you're going to faint." She was relieved when without argument Robin bent over the sink. As she splashed water on her face, Blaine walked back to the living room and sank down on the couch, forcing herself to take slow, spaced breaths until the pain in her chest began to dull.

"Are you all right?" Cait asked, stopping her pacing through the living room long enough to hover over Blaine.

"I'm okay. Just breathless."

"I'll get you some water."

"Yes, please." Blaine reached for the telephone. "I have to call the police."

"Do you want me to do it?"

"No," Blaine said, recalling how Cait had a tendency to garble information when she was nervous. "Just get the water. I'll take care of it."

A deputy in the county sheriff's office answered.

"This is Mrs. Avery. There's a body in my creek. You have to send someone," she blurted, thinking she sounded ludicrously abrupt. Maybe Cait should have made the call after all.

There was a pause before a young man said, "Just slow down, ma'am. Now, this is *who?*"

"It's Blaine Avery. Martin Avery's wife, out on Prescott Road."

"Oh. Mrs. Avery." Blaine recognized the voice of a young deputy named Clarke whom she'd met during the investigation of Martin's death. He sounded excited. "Would you repeat that information, please?"

Blaine forced herself to speak more slowly. "There is a body on my property. In the creek. I believe it's Rosalind Van Zandt."

"Just a minute, ma'am." Abruptly the receiver made a thunking sound in her ear, and she heard him say loudly, "It's Blaine Avery on the phone. Says she found a body! Claims it's Rosalind Van Zandt!"

In a moment a deep, calm male voice came on the line. "This is Quint." Blaine stiffened. Logan Quint, the sheriff. They'd met in grade school, dated as teenagers, and she had thought of him as her friend until that awful day in late May when he'd come to the house after she arrived home to find Martin dead. "What's this about a body?"

"Robin, Cait, and I were walking my dog in the woods behind the house when we discovered a body in the creek. Or rather, the dog did." Her control was breaking. She caught her breath and added weakly, "I think it's been there a while."

She expected a barrage of questions, but mercifully Logan said, "I'll be right out."

Blaine felt a sob rising. "Please hurry."

"I will. In the meantime, Blaine, I want you to stay in your house. Don't go back in those woods."

2

The sun had disappeared and only a faint rose blush hung above the trees as Logan Quint and Chief Deputy Abel Stroud sped along Prescott Road toward the Avery house five miles out of town.

"Hell of a thing, isn't it?" Stroud commented. "First Martin Avery, now the Van Zandt girl, if it really is her."

"She was reported missing two hours ago, and Robin Avery was one of her closest friends," Logan said. "Blaine said Robin was with her when she found the body, so if Robin says it's Rosalind, I think we can be pretty sure it is."

"I just don't understand why you didn't call me when she was reported missin'."

"Like I said, I've only known about it a couple of hours. Her aunt said she was supposed to be in Charleston for the weekend visiting a cousin. When she didn't return by midafternoon, Miss Peyton got worried and called the cousin. Rosalind hadn't been there at all. That's when she called me, and Clarke and I have been trying to contact Rosalind's friends to see what they can tell us, although we haven't had much luck. None of them seem to be home."

"Sunday matinee," Abel said. "My girl, Arletta, goes every week. Most of the kids do. Not much else for them to do around here on a long Sunday afternoon."

"I guess not. In my day we went to the Dairy Queen."

"That's the difference between your day and mine. We *worked* on Sunday afternoons. Always somethin' to do on a farm."

Logan groaned inwardly. He'd heard about Abel's childhood on the farm until he could hardly keep from thrashing the man every time he launched into another interminable story of hardship and responsibility. If Abel were to be believed, by the time he was ten years old he'd been running a twenty-acre dairy farm single-handedly.

"Sure is a coincidence, though," Abel went on, luckily too diverted by the present drama to dwell on his youth. "Of course, if it turns out the Van Zandt girl was murdered, too, Blaine Avery's gonna be in one hell of a fix."

She certainly would be, Logan thought. Just six months ago she'd called him in hysterics to report that her husband had killed himself. And that's exactly what it looked like at first. Logan had found Martin

Avery slumped in his wheelchair on the terrace. A small, slightly stellate hole appeared in his right temple, indicating a contact wound. Later, the M.E. reported traces of gunpowder on Avery's right hand.

But Logan was bothered by the fact that Avery's Smith & Wesson Combat Masterpiece had been lying near him, not clutched in his hand, as was the case in most suicides by gunshot. Then the next day he'd discovered a slug from the Smith & Wesson lodged in a young maple tree about thirty feet away from the terrace. The slug had not been there long, which the condition of the wood surrounding it indicated, yet Blaine and Robin both claimed they'd never fired the gun and that when Avery had slipped into depression after being paralyzed from the waist down when his Ferrari was crushed by a hit-and-run driver, the weapon had been kept in a locked gun cabinet whose key Blaine had hidden in the lining of her jewelry box. The key, however, was found in Avery's desk drawer. Although it was possible Avery had found the key earlier, the only time he had been left alone was the Saturday afternoon of his death. Therefore, he would have had no earlier opportunity to fire the gun without the shot being heard by someone else in the house, leading Logan to conclude that the gun had probably been fired twice on Saturday. Perhaps Avery had taken a wild shot before he put the gun to his temple, Logan thought. The only problem was that five unspent cartridges remained in the gun's six-cartridge cylinder, and it was unlikely that the man would have replaced the missing cartridge before killing himself.

The prosecuting attorney was certain Avery had been shot, the gun placed in his hand and fired to leave gunpowder residue, then another cartridge inserted in the cylinder to make it appear the gun had been fired only once. Unfortunately, Avery's beautiful wife—eighteen years his junior, rumored to be involved with Avery's good-looking young doctor, Richard Bennett, and slated to inherit half of Avery's ten-million-dollar estate, including his controlling shares in Avery Manufacturing, one of the biggest boat-building companies in the eastern United States—had no alibi. She claimed she had left home around twelve-thirty for a shopping trip to a nearby mall. Since Avery's private-duty nurse, Bernice

Litchfield, was to arrive at one o'clock, Blaine said she had not worried about leaving her husband alone for less than half an hour.

Bernice Litchfield, however, swore she'd received a call from Martin Avery at a quarter to one, telling her his wife was taking him out for a drive and they would not be needing her services that day. Robin Avery had been with Rosalind Van Zandt from ten until four, helping decorate the school gym for the prom to be held that night, so she could not verify at what time her stepmother had left, or if she had left at all. Nor could anyone at the mall remember waiting on Blaine Avery. The investigation had been grueling, one that would have crushed a weaker woman, Logan thought. But in the end, to the prosecuting attorney's great chagrin and Logan's relief, there had been too many questions about when the shot was fired into the tree, and no hard evidence against Blaine. There had been nothing but suspicion.

"Her family never did have a good name," Stroud was saying dolefully. "Her daddy wasn't worth salt."

Logan tried to keep his voice neutral. "Jim O'Connor was okay."

"Oh, I know he had an agreeable way about him. You couldn't help likin' him just to talk to. But he was a lazy welfare bum. I can't tell you how many times I found him lollin' down in the park drunk as a lord. No wonder his wife took off and left him. Kind of a shame about those girls, though. She shoulda taken them with her. It had to do somethin' to them, being deserted by their own mama and raised by a do-nothin' like O'Connor."

"I think they turned out all right."

"I guess Cait's a good girl. Married a good, steady guy—Kirk Philips. He and his daddy got that woodworkin' business."

"I know that, Abel."

"They do good work, too. Then Cait started that day-care center." Logan felt his hands tightening on the wheel at Abel's habitual insistence on telling him the history of people he'd known most of his life. "She seems to be doin' okay with that place. I hear there's a waitin' list to get kids in there. Most folks seem to think a lot of Cait. And Blaine . . . well, she's a looker, I'll give you that," Stroud continued as they pulled into the Avery driveway. "But she's trouble. I'm tellin' you, Sheriff, the woman is pure trouble."

"I'll keep that in mind," Logan muttered, wondering if Stroud was right.

3

After Blaine hung up the phone, Caitlin called Kirk. Blaine heard her trying to soothe him, telling him she was fine and that she wanted him to stay at home with their four-year-old daughter. "Don't come out here," she ordered. "The excitement and the policemen will upset Sarah. I'll be home as soon as I can get away." Then she went to check on Robin while Blaine remained immobilized on the couch. She drew up her knees, hugging them to her chest as she stared at the French-style masonry fireplace, its mantel decorated with polished brass and copper ornaments gleaming in what was left of the sun. She swallowed a few times, controlling the sobs, and in a few minutes she was aware of her breathing calming, but she was very cold. Against her will she closed her eyes, and the body's white, bloated face floated before her.

Something touched her leg and she jumped, her eyes snapping open to see Ashley sitting in front of her. Twigs had caught in the long hair on the dog's ears, making it stand out. She looked as frightened and frazzled as Blaine.

"Come with me, girl," Blaine said. The dog trotted behind her into the kitchen and waited patiently while Blaine fixed Ashley a bowl of water and considered pouring herself a shot of Scotch, then decided it wouldn't be wise to have alcohol on her breath when the police arrived. Instead she poured a glass of orange juice and sat down at the kitchen table, worrying.

What if the body came loose from the tree roots and floated away before Logan got here? But it couldn't float far in half an hour. This was just a little creek swollen by Saturday afternoon's rain, not a river with a swift current, although two miles away the creek did flow into the Ohio River. If the body hadn't gotten trapped in the tree roots, it would probably be well on its way to the river.

Ashley had flopped down in exhaustion under the kitchen table, but she perked her ears a few minutes later at the sound of a car in the driveway. Then she scrambled up and barked her way to the front door. The bell chimed. Blaine opened one of the double doors to see two men standing on the porch.

"Evening, Mrs. Avery," the taller one in uniform said.

She and Logan had become very formal in the past few months. "Please come in." Ashley reluctantly stood aside, although she looked with suspicion at the two men, almost as if she knew their presence spelled trouble. "You made it out here in record time."

"That's what the red light on the car's for," Abel Stroud piped up. He'd been a deputy for as long as Blaine could remember, and she'd never liked his self-important aggression. Even his looks offended her. Right now the thin, graying hair he carefully combed over a bald crown with hair tonic was drying out to stand in dirty-looking wisps, and he'd gained at least ten pounds since she'd seen him in July. Zipped into a too-small jacket, he resembled a sausage stuffed into casing. His cheeks were flushed with excitement, his pale blue eyes darting everywhere. But there was something Blaine had learned during the investigation into Martin's death—Stroud was not the fool he often pretended to be. And that made him dangerous, because for reasons she didn't understand, he didn't like her. She felt he'd been disappointed when she hadn't been arrested for Martin's murder.

"You think you've found Rosalind Van Zandt," Logan Quint said, looking at Blaine.

Blaine had been unaware of Robin slipping into the room and was surprised to hear her say evenly, "It *is* Rosie, Sheriff. I knew immediately from the long black hair it was Rosie."

Robin was wrapped in a white terry-cloth robe, her eyes huge in her blanched face. Caitlin went over and put her arm around the girl's shoulders.

"She was reported missing a little over two hours ago," Logan said. Cait had turned on a couple of lamps, and their soft light played over his features. Blaine noted the changes in the face she had once known so well. At thirty-two, Logan had an air of robust health and vitality that was tempered by lines of fatigue around his mouth and sadness in his dark eyes. His hair was as dead black as ever, though, and the Iroquois blood passed on to him by his mother showed in his prominent cheek-bones and aquiline nose.

"Rosie was supposed to be in Charleston," Robin said. "Instead she was lying out in that horrible creek—" She made a strangled sound, and Cait stroked her wet hair.

"Did she tell you she was going to Charleston?" Logan asked.

"Yes. She said she was going to visit her cousin Amanda."

"Did she do that often—go away to visit Amanda?"

"Maybe three or four times a year. They were pretty close. There was a rock concert in Charleston Friday night. She said she and Amanda were going to it and then she'd spend the weekend, since her aunt didn't like her driving at night."

"Do you know Amanda?"

"Sure. She's the same age as Rosie and I. She's a really neat girl. I've spent the week-end at her house, too. There are six kids in the family. Amanda's mother never cares whether there are a couple of extras."

"But Rosalind didn't invite you to come along this time?"

Robin hesitated. "No. But then, she knew I had to help Blaine move back in here."

"You didn't *have* to help," Blaine said. "I could have managed our stuff just fine on my own. I didn't know anything about the rock concert."

Robin waved a hand in dismissal. "It doesn't matter. She didn't ask, anyway. Besides, I don't even like the group that was playing."

"I see," Logan Quint said. Then he added, "Mrs. Avery, I suppose you'd better come with us to the woods to show us exactly where the body is."

"Of course." Blaine inwardly quailed at the thought of having to go back into those woods, but she wanted to appear strong for Robin and Cait. "Rob, will you be all right here with Caitlin for a little while?"

Robin nodded. "Yeah. Sure."

"Maybe Blaine would rather I go with you and let *her* stay here," Cait said.

Blaine shook her head. "No. I know the woods better than you do."

Stroud looked impatient. "Well, we'd better stop all this talkin' and get goin'. It's almost dark."

"He's right," Logan said. "And I think I hear the emergency squad."

He went to the front door, and Blaine looked out the front windows to see an ambulance and another police car pulling into the driveway. He glanced back at Blaine. "Is it a long walk to where you found the body?"

"The way I went this afternoon, yes. But unless the body's floated away from the tree, we could get much closer to it by going back down Prescott Road and turning onto the access road at the south end of the property."

"Access road?"

"There's an oil well back in the woods. Trucks use that road about every two weeks to reach the storage tank. The well isn't far from the body."

"Good. Let's go."

Blaine and Abel Stroud got in the sheriff's car, and while Logan was talking to the drivers of the ambulance and the patrol car, Blaine caught Abel studying her closely in the rearview mirror. "You feelin' okay these days, Miz Avery?"

"I'm fine."

"I heard you had a pretty nasty case of

the pneumonia. Out of your head for a while, weren't you?"

"Yes, because of my fever, but I'm all right now. I'll be starting back to school tomorrow."

"That's what my girl, Arletta, told me. You remember Arletta, don't you?"

Oh, *did* she. "Yes," she said without expression.

"You know, she was real hurt over that grade you gave her in English last year, but I told her, 'Hell, honey, don't anybody out in the big world care a thing about Shakespeare, so don't you worry one little bit about it.' " So I've been put in my place, Blaine thought. Annoyed, she shifted her gaze out the window and didn't answer. But Abel wouldn't give up. "Takin' that class over in summer school didn't sit too well with her, though."

"I'm sure it didn't."

"Didn't sit too well with me, either, her wastin' a whole summer on a lot of impractical silliness."

"Abel, Arletta didn't flunk a course in Shakespeare, she flunked grammar. *Basic* grammar. And I don't think learning to write intelligibly is a lot of impractical silliness."

"Well, now, don't get on your high horse." Stroud craned around to look at her, his wide forehead puckering in mock concern. "You *sure* you're feelin' all right these days? You seem pretty tense to me."

"I just found the body of my stepdaughter's best friend on my property," she snapped. "Wouldn't *you* be tense?"

She caught Stroud's half smile and could have kicked herself for letting him bait her the way he had done all through the investigation into Martin's death. He was always careful not to do it in front of other people, though. She wondered whether he did it for fun or because he hoped to goad her into slipping and admitting something he thought she was hiding.

She was relieved to see Logan striding to the car. "Okay, we're ready," he said.

Daylight saving time made night fall uncomfortably early, Blaine noted. At six o'clock, the sky was already violet. In thirty minutes it would be black. She hoped she would be able to lead them right to the body and not lose her bearings in the woods. She had never been in them after dark, but she knew the location of the old willow. Surely the darkness wouldn't completely destroy her sense of direction.

They turned right, onto the narrow, graveled access road, the ambulance and second police car following them. As they jolted over potholes, Blaine knew she would need to have new gravel spread soon. A lot had been lost in Saturday's deluge. Maybe she would have it done next week, before bad weather set in. Then she thought how odd it was that your mind could fill itself with trivialities in the face of disaster. Maybe that was its means of self-protection.

They slowed as they reached the beginning of the woods. "Car parked up ahead," Logan said.

Blaine leaned forward to see a red Toyota Celica convertible pulled to the side of the access road. She was very familiar with the car—it had been a gift from Rosalind's aunt on her seventeenth birthday.

"That's Rosie's car," she said.

They stopped and got out to look at it. The car's tires were sunk about an inch into drying mud. "Look how clean the car is," Logan said. "Someone parked it here before the storm yesterday. Otherwise, hitting those potholes even at a low speed would have splashed mud all over the lower half of it. Besides, it's plastered with dead leaves brought down by the rain."

Stroud nodded. "Haven't you spotted this car before, Miz Avery?"

"No. It's so far back it can't be seen from the main road, and I haven't been out here since I moved back yesterday morning. The truck hasn't been here to pick up oil for over a week, either."

"I guess that explains why it hasn't been found," Logan said. "Anything in there?"

Stroud pointed a flashlight beam into the window. "Empty." He removed a handkerchief from his pocket and tried the door. "Locked."

"We'll look it over better later. Right now I want to get to that body."

They started up again, going deeper into the woods. It was much darker here, with the trees crowding close to the road. About five hundred feet into the woods stood the oil well. Blaine remembered how disappointed she'd been when she first saw it, rising only about seven feet high; she'd pictured the towering rigs she had seen in the movie *Giant*. Martin had laughed. "I'm not running a big oil company here, sweetheart.

Just one little well that brings in a few thousand dollars a year." Near the pump stood a tall, pale green storage tank where the oil was kept until a truck came to collect it. Immediately beyond the well the road ended.

"We'll have to walk from here," Blaine said.

The three of them climbed out of the car. The ambulance attendants walked behind them, carrying equipment Blaine didn't care to see. Maybe a gaffing hook. And certainly a body bag. The deputies had more flashlights, and Abel Stroud carried a camera.

The big flashlights put out yellowish beams in the dusk, lighting the winding path. No one said anything—the only sounds were those of twigs snapping under their feet, small animals scurrying through the underbrush, and a night breeze rustling hauntingly through the dying leaves on the trees. Blaine stopped. "Down there." She pointed to the left. "There's a big willow on the creek bank."

"Lead the way," Logan said.

Blaine drew in her breath. "You want me to go back there?"

"I don't want us wandering around on the

creek bank for ten minutes looking for the willow tree. The light's almost gone as it is."

She glared at him. The tree was huge— they couldn't miss it, and what difference would five minutes make? Was Logan trying to make this as hard as possible for her? If so, his gaze didn't waver guiltily, and she felt Abel Stroud's little eyes watching her closely with what she thought was amusement. Well, she wouldn't give either Logan or Stroud the satisfaction of seeing her cower on the path like a terrified little girl. "Follow me," she said, her voice hard-edged as she tried to cover her fright.

"Wait a second." Logan pressed one of the flashlights into her hand. It felt heavy and only slightly warmed by his touch.

"Thank you," Blaine said coldly.

They plodded into the undergrowth. The creek ran just short of one hundred feet from the path, but Blaine felt as if they were walking through miles of withering vines covering muddy earth that sucked at their shoes. She was scared out in the woods Martin had loved so well, leading these men to Rosalind's body. Oh, God, her aunt would have to formally identify her, Blaine thought in horror. Joan Peyton. She had been the guidance counselor at the high school since Blaine was a student. Joan had moved in with her parents, Ned and Edith Peyton, after finishing graduate school in the early seventies. She was devoted to her family and devastated when Ned Peyton died of cancer a year ago. But it was Rosalind on whom she had doted, Rosie, the daughter of Joan's sister, Charlotte, who had been killed in a chartered plane crash in Brazil when Rosie was ten months old. Rosie was the center of Joan's world, and while her death would be bad enough, seeing her body in this condition would be a nightmare from which Joan would never recover.

Blaine was suddenly freezing, although the temperature was around forty. Above her head two bats darted and swooped. She cringed, even though she knew they were more interested in catching insects than in tangling themselves in her hair. Still, she shifted the flashlight to her left hand and with her right twisted her long hair into a loop and stuffed it down under the collar of her windbreaker. In the distance came the unsettling, trembling call of a screech owl, its whistle running down the scale like the sound of doom. Blaine couldn't help thinking that in the Egyptian system of hieroglyphics, the owl symbolized death, night, and cold. Should she tell Abel Stroud that? she wondered with nervous facetiousness. He'd think she was crazy.

As if he knew she was thinking of him, he asked sharply, "We gettin' anywhere *near*, Miz Avery, or are you lost?"

Blaine gritted her teeth. "We're near, Abel."

They finally arrived at the creek bank, and Blaine spun the flashlight to the left. The beam picked up the willow. She took a few more steps forward and shone the light downward. Rosalind's stiff hand with its rigid fingers swayed as the night breeze shifted the willow limbs. She appeared to be waving a macabre hello, while the black holes where her eyes had been seemed to burn through Blaine. "There," Blaine said roughly, quickly shifting the light away from the ravaged face.

She stood back while two brawny young men went to work with gaffing hooks. Logan leaned forward, grabbed the willow limbs, and with surprising force tore them loose from Rosalind's arm. Blaine turned away as, with a great sloshing of water and muttered warnings—"Be careful! She's stiff as a board. Don't lose her!"—they dragged the body up on the bank. Vaguely Blaine was aware of Logan kneeling to examine Rosalind. "Fish and birds been at her eyes," Abel Stroud said. Blaine repeatedly swallowed to wash down the hot water flooding into her mouth at the thought of Rosie's missing eyes. She was determined not to be sick in front of all these people. Then Abel exclaimed, "Well, goddamn, will you look at that!"

"Blaine," Logan said, "I want you to come here and look at her."

Damn him! she thought. What's the purpose in *my* looking at her? But she closed her eyes briefly, then turned around and took a couple of steps closer.

The girl rested among the weeds, her rigid legs splayed. One foot wore a white leather running shoe, the other only a muddy sock. Her lips were bluish, her face dead white except for the red bite lesions where muscle showed through. Her hair lay in filthy strings.

"That's Rosalind," she said weakly.

Logan nodded. "I know. But I want you to look at something else. I wouldn't have seen this if I hadn't pulled her arm loose from the tree." He rolled back the sleeves of Rosalind's grimy sweater to reveal deep, vicious gashes in both her wrists. In one gash rested a silver bracelet with *Rosalind* engraved in beautiful script.

3

"Suicide," Abel Stroud pronounced.

Blaine stumbled away from the body. "I don't believe it."

"I know," one of the ambulance attendants said sadly. "It's hard to believe a young kid would kill herself. I've got a girl about this age myself."

"If she hadn't gotten caught in the tree roots, she would have sunk, and we might not have found her for weeks," Logan said. He looked up at Blaine. "I'm going to take you home now. We have a lot of work to do here."

Blaine nodded, beyond speech. They trudged in silence through the vines and down the path back to the sheriff's car. Logan muttered curses as he struggled to turn the car around on the narrow access road with the ambulance and the police cruiser so close behind and trees on either side, and Blaine realized he was more shaken by what he had seen than he'd appeared at first. But then, Logan had always been reserved, his feelings revealed only by small, unconscious gestures. The thought floated away, though, as they sped over the access road, the car spitting gravel behind it, and headed back toward the main road.

Finally Logan spoke. "When Abel said 'suicide' back there, you said you didn't believe it."

"How can I believe that girl committed suicide *here*, just six months after Martin shot himself?"

"Maybe that's why she chose this place—because there had already been one *suicide* here." Blaine heard his emphasis on the word *suicide*, but kept quiet. "I just can't understand why the dog didn't find her before now."

"Stop playing cat and mouse with me, Logan. The police have watched my every move for months, and you know very well the dog and Robin have been with me at Cait's house for five weeks since I had pneumonia. Ashley wasn't brought back here until I came yesterday morning, and I kept her confined in the enclosed side yard or in the house until we took our walk a couple of hours ago."

"That explains it. But why did you stay at Cait's so long? It doesn't take five weeks to get over pneumonia."

Blaine gritted her teeth, resentful of having to explain herself once again to the police. "I needed some time away from this house. I wish Robin and I could have gone somewhere this summer, but there were so many questions about Martin's death. You people put me through hell."

"Look, Blaine," Logan said evenly, "I know you've been furious with me ever since the investigation into Martin's death, but I was only doing my job."

"With a great deal of gusto, it seemed to me."

"And what was I supposed to do? Go easy on you so everyone could say I was protecting a woman I was once involved with?"

"When we were teenagers? You actually think people even *remember* we dated way back then?"

"They remember, all right. They remember everything around here, especially the Indian and Jim O'Connor's daughter. We were considered a colorful couple," he said dryly.

"I don't think colorful is quite the word they used."

"It doesn't matter. Those days are long gone. Besides, there's no point in going into a tailspin over the investigation of Martin's death now. You were never even charged with the murder."

"Only *suspected*. That was enough. Half the town has already tried and convicted me. I'm surprised they even let me keep my job at the high school."

Logan sighed. "Okay, let's drop this for now."

"That's fine with me," Blaine snapped, annoyed by the tremor in her voice. She had thought the nightmare was over, but it seemed to be starting again. She was scared. All evidence to the contrary, Blaine had always believed Martin committed suicide. She'd lived with him—she'd known the depth of his depression. And who would murder Martin? But the police believed someone had, and she'd been the prime suspect. Now another death had occurred on this property, but Blaine was certain *this* one was not a case of suicide. She knew with a bone-chilling certainty that someone had killed Rosie. And here she was in the middle of things again. What she needed was a few comforting words, a sign of confidence in her good character, but Logan appeared to be carved out of stone, a lawman to his very bones. She felt as if she hated him at that moment as he drummed his fingers thoughtfully on the steering wheel.

"You knew Rosalind Van Zandt. Did you ever get any indication she might be suicidal?"

"No," Blaine said firmly, trying to swallow her hostility and shock and be as accurate as possible. "She was beautiful. Outgoing. Very bright."

"I know all that. She was one of those kids who has their picture in the paper every week for doing something outstanding, like being the county fair queen or heading up the student council drive to collect money for the homeless. How about boyfriends?"

"Nothing serious that I know of. Joan was pretty strict with her. The only guy I've seen her with is Tony Jarvis."

"Tony *Jarvis!* I thought you said Joan Peyton was strict."

"I know they seemed like an unlikely pair, and I don't think Joan was too pleased about their friendship, but from what Robin told me, their relationship was casual. They mostly got together to work on music for Tony's rock band. Tony wrote the music, and Rosie did the lyrics."

"Are you sure that's all it was?"

"No, I'm *not* sure. Rosie spent a lot of time at our house, but she didn't confide in me about her romantic life, and Robin and I aren't close. That's all I know. Maybe Robin would tell you more."

"Okay, what about Rosalind's background? How did she feel about her parents' deaths?"

"She didn't even remember them."

"I was in high school when they died. I remember the hubbub caused by their accident, especially since Joan was the guidance counselor at school and had to take some time off, but I don't remember the details."

They'd turned into the driveway and Logan had switched off the engine, but he obviously did not want to go into the house until he'd finished questioning her. Blaine settled back against the vinyl seat and took a deep breath as she dredged up the story she hadn't thought about for many years. "Rosie's father was an engineer. He went to Brazil to build a bridge. Charlotte, Rosie's mother, came here for a visit with Rosie right after he left. Rosie was a baby. Then Charlotte decided to go on to Brazil alone, and a month later Joan was to take Rosie down. Except that in the meantime, Charlotte and Derek, her husband, were killed in a plane crash. I've always thought that was one reason Rosie and Robin got to be such good friends—they'd both lost their mothers when they were very young. Robin was only one when Gloria died, you know. And, of course, Martin was a good friend of the Peytons."

"Did he know Charlotte well?"

"Yes, I think so. He knew Joan better, though. She was closer to his age."

"Did Martin ever meet Rosalind's father?"

"If he did, he never mentioned it. Rosie said her parents were married in Boston, her father's home. I don't think he got along too well with the Peytons, and he didn't come around much."

"Why didn't he get along with them?"

"I have no idea, Logan. I don't think Rosie

knew, either. Maybe they thought he just wasn't good enough for Charlotte, or maybe they weren't happy that his work took him all over the world and therefore took Charlotte away from them. They were crazy about her, but they hardly ever saw her after she got married, or so Martin said once."

"Did Rosalind talk about her parents' deaths?"

"Not really. One time she showed me pictures of each of them. Her father was really handsome. Charlotte wasn't a beauty, not like Joan. She *did* wonder what they'd been like, especially her mother. Rosie said Charlotte couldn't possibly be the paragon everyone claimed she was." Logan threw her a sharp look. "Oh, she said it with amusement, as if she fully understood how people aggrandize the dead. But there didn't seem to be any emotional scars because of her parents' deaths. She was so young when the accident happened, and her aunt and her grandparents adored her. She certainly wasn't starved for affection."

Logan nodded. "I see," he said reflectively. Blaine glanced at the moon hovering clear and sharp-edged over the house. How different it looked from the way it had the other night, when fog diffused its light to a creamy glow.

The other night? Blaine thought, stiffening. What night? What exact night had she taken a drive out to the house? Thursday? It must have been Thursday. But it wasn't, a clear, frightened voice said in her head. It was Friday, the night when Rosie had told her aunt she was going to Charleston.

"Blaine?"

She whipped her head around. "What?"

"I asked if something was wrong."

Tell him, her conscience said. But caution won out. "Nothing is wrong beyond the obvious."

"You just seemed to blank out on me for a minute."

"I'm cold and tired and overwhelmed. This is all so awful."

Her voice, her very wording, sounded unnatural, and she knew Logan noticed, but he let it go. Instead he glanced toward the big picture window at the front of the house where Robin stood peering out at them. "I have to question her, you know."

"Yes. Unfortunately, I know the drill," Blaine said.

Robin gazed at them with an almost frightening calm when they came inside. The hair around her face had dried, but she still wore the white robe, her feet encased in ragged, fuzzy slippers. She looked like a frightened child. Cait and Ashley stood protectively beside her.

"Did you find Rosie?" she asked Logan.

"Yes."

"What happened?"

"Her wrists are slashed. It looks like suicide."

"Oh, no!" Cait whispered while Robin blinked at him a couple of times, her face motionless. But Blaine saw her fists tightening in the pockets of her robe.

After a moment of silence, Cait said in a thin, strained voice, "I've already put on a pot of coffee. I think Blaine needs it. Do you want some, Logan?"

"Yes, that would be fine. I've got a few questions to ask Robin, too."

Logan didn't seem taken aback by Robin's unnatural calm. He's seen it before, Blaine thought, last May when her father died.

Blaine and Logan followed Cait and Robin to the kitchen. The three of them sat

down at the glass-topped table while Cait
began pouring coffee. Blaine noticed that
Cait's hands were shaking. Her own felt
numb.

As Cait set the cups on the table, sloshing more than a little coffee into the saucers,
the doorbell rang for the second time that
night. "I forgot to tell you," Cait said. "Rick
called. He said he'd come right over."

Before Blaine could rise from the table,
she heard the door open and Rick call,
"Blaine? Robin?"

"We're in the kitchen," she answered.

Richard Bennett was the town's only orthopedist and had treated the broken shoulder Martin had also received in the accident
that left him a paraplegic. Rick had been a
good friend of Martin's long before his marriage to Blaine, and after Martin's death he
had remained a friend to her, one of her
steadfast supporters when so many people
in town thought she might have killed her
husband.

Cait was already fixing a fourth cup of
coffee when Rick walked in. His dark brown
hair with its streak of premature gray along
the right temple was slightly tousled, his
hazel eyes sharp beneath dark brows drawn

together in a frown. He looked tired and alarmed, his normally youthful, jaunty manner gone. "Are you three all right?" he asked in a voice gravelly with fatigue.

"We're not physically hurt, if that's what you mean," Blaine said. "I guess Cait told you earlier what's going on."

"I just happened to call to see how you were settling in." His face looked ashy beneath the remains of a summer tan. He glanced at Logan. "Rosalind Van Zandt is dead? It was really her out in the creek?"

"I'm afraid so."

"Good Lord." Rick let out a long, slow breath. "I was just at her house an hour ago, checking on her grandmother. Chronic congestive heart failure, not to mention a broken hip. Joan told me Rosalind was missing. She was frantic, but then, she's so overprotective I didn't really take her panic too seriously. What happened to Rosie?"

"They say she committed suicide," Blaine said.

"Suicide!" Rick burst out. "That's crazy!"

"Her wrists were slashed," Logan said.

"*Slashed* . . ." Rick gaped at Logan, his jaw slackening. "Are you sure?"

"Kind of hard not to be. The cuts were extremely deep."

Rick walked slowly across the kitchen and sat down at the table, reaching over to cover Blaine's hand with his. "Why didn't you call me?"

"Everything happened so fast, Rick," Blaine said, flushing at his proprietary manner. Although she felt in desperate need of friendliness and warmth at the moment, she couldn't forget that rumors had swirled in the spring about her and Martin's handsome young doctor. Some who later believed she had murdered Martin claimed an involvement with Rick was part of her motive for wanting her paralyzed husband out of the way, and although Blaine knew Rick had more than a professional interest in her, she wished he wouldn't be so blatant about it in front of Logan. She kept her voice cool. "Naturally I called the police first. Then I had to go back out there with them."

"I wish I could have been here to go with you, or at least to stay with Robin."

"Well, you couldn't know if no one called you, so don't worry about it. Anyway, Cait was here, thank goodness. Why don't you take off your coat?"

Rick looked down at his camel's hair coat almost as if he weren't aware of having it on. He stood and shrugged out of it to reveal khakis and a white sweater. It was a familiar outfit, his favorite when he wasn't at his office or the hospital, but it looked more rumpled than usual. "You say she cut her wrists?" he asked incredulously. Logan nodded. "And she was in the creek?" Logan nodded again. "But that doesn't make any sense. Why would she slash her wrists, then throw herself into the creek?"

"Maybe she just fell in. We'll know more when we've had a chance to look the area over in the morning."

"God. Who's going to tell Joan?"

"I will," Logan said. "Just as soon as I talk with Robin."

The girl had gone into a deep study of the riverboat engravings hanging on the wall opposite the table. Blaine had thought Logan would take her out of the room to question her, but he remained seated. "What do you think about all of this, Robin?"

Robin continued to stare at the engravings for a few moments, then she turned, her eyes blazing. "What I think is that Rosie didn't kill herself any more than my father did."

Cait dropped the cup of coffee she'd been pouring for herself. She let out a soft cry, then grabbed for a wad of paper towels and began energetically wiping up the spilled coffee.

"Then what *do* you think happened to Rosalind?" Logan asked calmly, ignoring Cait's obvious shock.

"How many alternatives are left, Sheriff? It certainly wasn't an accident."

"So you think she was murdered."

Robin nodded. Then, abruptly, she stood and walked to the window. Sensing trouble, Ashley ambled over and nudged Robin's hand. Robin whirled, knelt, and hugged the dog so fiercely Ashley yelped in surprise. "Why does everybody die? My mother, my father. Now Rosie!"

Still clutching her sodden paper towels, Cait made a movement toward her, but Blaine stopped her with a glance. She knew too well that in times of angry distress, Robin didn't want anyone playing mother.

Robin rose and looked out the window toward the dark shadow of the woods again. "She was the prettiest girl in school, you know. And the smartest. Other kids went to her for tutoring."

Blaine sipped her coffee. She could feel the hot drink bringing warmth back to her veins, although her hands were still icy. So far Logan had not touched his own coffee as he watched Robin closely. Blaine was worried about her extreme pallor, and she was glad Rick was here, but Logan hadn't looked pleased when he walked in.

"Robin," Logan asked, "do you have any idea who might have wanted to kill Rosalind?"

Robin shook her head. "No."

"Then why did you say she didn't kill herself?"

"Because she just wouldn't do that. She wasn't the type."

Blaine saw Logan's eyes flicker. Clearly he didn't believe generalizations about the "type" of person who commits suicide, but he didn't challenge Robin. Instead he asked casually, "Did you notice any changes in Rosalind lately?"

Robin paused, and for a moment Blaine thought she wasn't going to answer. "Yeah, I noticed changes," she said finally. "Late in the summer she started acting funny."

"Funny how?" Logan asked.

Robin turned around, her wide eyes far away in thought. "Jumpy, closed off. I couldn't count on her for anything. She was always making excuses not to do things, or just not showing up. I thought maybe it had something to do with—" She broke off, color staining her cheeks.

"You thought it had something to do with the nature of your father's death," Blaine said.

Robin nodded, and Blaine felt the familiar misery rising within her. As if Martin's death hadn't been bad enough, the girl had also endured the intensive police investigation, the newspaper headlines, the avid curiosity of a bored, small town eager for a scandal.

"But there were other things," Robin added. "About a week after school started in the fall, I walked into the typing room there and saw her writing a letter. I could tell it was a letter because it had the address and return address written in block style. She practically tore it out of the typewriter when she saw me looking at it and stuffed it in a folder. I didn't see who it was addressed to." Robin looked away. "It was after that

that she started avoiding me almost completely."

"Maybe it was a letter to a boyfriend," Logan suggested.

Robin shook her head. "Rosie loved beautiful stationery. If she was going to write a letter to a guy, she would have written by hand on her pretty paper."

"Maybe it was a note to Tony Jarvis."

"She saw him every day—she didn't need to write to him. Besides, this was a *letter,* not a note. I said that."

"So you did," Logan said easily. "How serious were she and Jarvis?"

"Not serious at all. They were friends. She met him when he did work at the Peyton house and helped with old Mr. Peyton."

"Maybe there was more to the relationship than you knew."

"She never told me if there was."

"Did she tell you everything?"

"Does anyone tell another person *everything?*" Robin asked defiantly.

Logan seemed oblivious of her hostile tone. "She was wearing three pieces of jewelry. One silver hoop earring. Familiar with it?"

"Sure. She wore those earrings a lot. Where was the other one?"

"We haven't found it yet. Then there was a diamond-and-opal ring."

"That was to be a birthday gift to her mother, but she died before Mr. and Mrs. Peyton could give it to her, so they saved it for Rosie. She's been wearing it for a couple of years." Robin looked down. "I always told her opals were supposed to be bad luck, but she just laughed. She wasn't superstitious."

"Are you?"

"A little, I guess."

Logan smiled at her, not in derision, but as if they had something in common. For the first time Robin seemed to relax slightly. She even smiled back.

"Okay, so much for the ring," Logan went on. "What about the engraved bracelet?"

Robin frowned. "Engraved bracelet? You mean like an identification bracelet?"

"Yes. It was also silver and engraved with the name *Rosalind* in professional script. It looked expensive. You sound like you've never seen it before."

"I haven't," Robin said slowly.

"Do you think it's the kind of thing Tony Jarvis would buy for her?"

"Well, not really. I don't know anyone who wears those bracelets. They're kind of old-fashioned, you know?"

Logan nodded. "Could it be something a family member gave her?"

Robin shrugged her shoulders. "I can't say. I only know I've never seen it."

"All right. Was there anything else, Robin? Anything that could have been worrying Rosalind or made her start avoiding you?"

"I can't think of anything."

"How about her general circumstances? Her life at home, for instance."

"She was sad when her grandfather died last year, but he'd really suffered for a long time, and she was kind of resigned to it. She said she was glad he was at peace. Her grandmother is almost totally out of it now—you know, senile, but before she got so bad, Rosie got along fine with her. And she was close to her aunt Joan, although Joan's—Miss Peyton's—rules and curfews were starting to get on her nerves. She said her aunt treated her like she was fourteen instead of seventeen."

"But there was no serious trouble between them?"

"Not that I know of."

"How about school?"

"Rosie was looking forward to our senior year. She was in dozens of activities. She was even going to try out for the school play. And she had applied to Radcliffe. That's where her aunt went to college. I know she would have gotten in."

"What about you, Dr. Bennett?" Logan asked suddenly. "Did you notice anything different about Rosalind?"

Rick looked startled. *"Me?"*

"You're treating her grandmother at home, aren't you? Isn't that what you said when you came in?"

"Yes, so I did. Mrs. Peyton is in and out of the hospital. Joan has an R.N. there—Bernice Litchfield, the same woman who looked after Martin—but when Mrs. Peyton is home I go by to check on her. But I didn't meet Rosalind there—I met her here, when I was treating Martin and Rosalind was visiting Robin. That must have been when, Robin? March? April?"

"March, I think."

"Anyway, the girl was usually out during

my visits to her home. All I can say is that she seemed pleasant. Friendly. Always on the go. Other than that, I didn't get much of an impression of her."

"Except that she was so pretty," Robin said. "Everyone noticed that."

Rick smiled. "Well, sure. She was beautiful. Looked a lot like her aunt."

"Is there anything else you can tell me?" Logan asked Robin.

Robin shrugged. "Nothing."

"Well, you've got the night to think about it. I'll want to talk to you again tomorrow. Maybe you can come up with something Rosalind said that's important."

Robin's voice hardened. "What's the difference? She's dead now. Nothing she said is going to bring her back."

"But if she *was* murdered," Logan said slowly, "you might know something and not even realize it."

Robin looked at him shrewdly. "You don't think she killed herself, either, do you?"

"I try not to speculate," Logan said in a carefully professional tone.

Much later, as Blaine dozed in bed after Logan, Cait, and Rick had left and Robin had finally fallen into a restless sleep, she was startled when the phone rang. The digital clock by her bed glowed 12:00 in brilliant red numbers. Fumbling on her night table, she found the receiver and lifted it on the fourth ring, automatically alarmed by a call at 12 A.M.

"Hello." Nothing. "Hel*lo*." The silence spun out. "Is someone there?" Someone *was* there—she heard a quick intake of breath. Her heart began to thud, not in fear but in anger. How many cruel, taunting calls like this had come after Martin's death? So many that she'd begun to cringe every time the phone rang. Since then the number had been changed. It was even unlisted. But here was another call in the night, loudly jerking her out of the safe oblivion of sleep that had temporarily blotted Rosie's mutilated face from her vision.

She was pulling the receiver away from her ear when the noise started. A soft, sexless laugh. Then music. She paused, suspending the receiver over the phone cradle. Hang up, she told herself sternly. This is some kind of sick prank. Hang *up*. But morbid fascination forced her to press the receiver to her ear again. The song had ended. A long, empty moment followed.

Then she heard a faint hissing before simple piano music played in the background as the song began again and children's voices crooned in a coldly haunting monotone:

> *Ring around a rosy,*
> *A pocket full of posy;*
> *Ashes, ashes,*
> *We all fall down.*

4

"I wasn't sure we were going to see you today."

"I wasn't too sure, either," Blaine said, turning away from her mailbox in the main office to face John Sanders.

John paused, as if searching for the right words. Obviously they wouldn't come. "I couldn't believe what I heard about Rosie," he said simply.

"It was horrible."

"She was found on your property?"

Blaine nodded. "In the creek." She glanced around, noticing a couple of other teachers creeping nearer, listening avidly. She had known questions about Rosalind were inevitable, but she didn't feel like discussing the circumstances of Rosie's death with people she didn't know well. John was different—they'd been instant friends since she started teaching at Sinclair High almost four years ago. He was warm, funny, and one of the few people who seemed to understand that she'd held onto her job partly from love of teaching and partly to squelch rumors that she'd married Martin Avery for his money. "How about walking with me to my room?" she asked.

"Sure." John took her arm almost protectively and led her away from the rapidly growing gaggle of teachers who suddenly couldn't stop staring into their mailboxes while their ears seemed to vibrate toward Blaine.

Perhaps the handsomest man Blaine had ever seen off a movie or television screen, John was in his late twenties, tall and slender yet well muscled, like a dancer. Always carefully dressed, today he wore a beautiful golden-brown tweed sport jacket, and his brown hair curled over his pale yellow shirt collar in back. His features were classic, from the Grecian nose to the wide, mobile mouth, but it was his smoky blue eyes that grabbed people's attention and held it. The female population of Sinclair High was constantly developing crushes on him, the most blatant member right now being Kathy Foss, the school's scornful, platinum-blond head cheerleader. For a girl with average intelligence, she showed an amazing facility with sexual double entendres while in John's classes. John had once told Blaine he didn't know whether to be embarrassed, insulted, or fascinated by the girl's inventiveness.

"The police were back searching the woods this morning even before I left," Blaine said.

"Searching for what?"

"Sheriff Quint said Joan helped Rosie load a suitcase Friday afternoon before she left. Also, Rosie had her purse with her and she was wearing a jacket. None of those things were found. The purse and the jacket could have been lost in the water, but probably not the suitcase. There wouldn't be any reason for her to lug them out to the creek before she . . . died. Anyway, I'm sure the police will be talking with you about Rosie," Blaine said.

John looked at her in surprise. "Why me?"

"Because you and Rosie were close. You were always talking together."

John nodded. "She was a smart kid and we had a lot of the same interests. She wrote poetry, you know. I was encouraging her to send some of it in for publication."

Blaine smiled. "If you don't mind my saying so, that sounds a little stilted, like you're trying to hide something. Everyone knows you and Rosie didn't just discuss her work. You were friendly."

John raised an eyebrow. "Just *how* friendly does everyone think we were?"

"Well, not *that* friendly, I don't think, but more than just student and teacher."

John sighed. "You're right. She was a great girl. Outstanding, and I don't mean just her looks. She was perceptive and extremely intelligent."

Blaine looked at him askance. He sounded so artificial, and for the first time she noticed he wasn't quite as well groomed as usual. He'd nicked himself shaving a couple of times, and a drop of blood now showed on his shirt collar. Apparently he hadn't noticed it.

"Rosie *was* perceptive and intelligent," she said, catching his inquiring look when she didn't answer him immediately. "She was a lot like Robin in that respect, except she didn't have Robin's inferiority complex, which has only gotten worse since Martin's death. She is *so* closed off, John."

"I know, but I can't help you there. Robin doesn't have much to say to me. Rosie, on the other hand, was an extrovert. I enjoyed talking with her about a lot of things."

"In any case, the police will be questioning everyone who knew Rosie."

"Even though it was suicide?" Blaine hesitated. A line appeared between John's eyebrows. "It *was* suicide, wasn't it? That's what I heard."

"Just between you and me, I'm not sure. She didn't seem suicidal to me."

"She didn't?"

"No. Did she to you?"

"No-o-o." Blaine looked at him searchingly. "What I mean is, she didn't seem depressed, but she was pretty high-strung lately."

"Did she have problems?"

"She never mentioned any, but she seemed a little . . . unpredictable. She didn't always have her homework done, which was a real switch for her, and she talked a lot in class. Nervous chatter, really, but it wasn't like her."

John let go of her left arm and shifted his

books to his right, looking distant and troubled as they made their way up the crowded staircase to the second floor, where they both taught.

"What do you think was wrong with her?"

John drew his lower lip between his teeth for a moment, as if he were hesitating. "Frankly, I wondered if she was on drugs."

"Drugs! Rosie?"

"I know it sounds ridiculous, but she *did* change, Blaine. Fast."

"Maybe there's another explanation. Maybe she was in love."

"With Tony Jarvis?" Blaine grew quiet, wishing she hadn't brought up the subject of love, which would naturally lead to a discussion of Tony Jarvis. "I know she saw him last year, but I never thought her feelings for him ran that deep." His frown deepened. "But one of the poems she quoted . . . well, never mind. I'm probably overanalyzing. That's a bad habit with English teachers."

"Yes, it is. It probably doesn't mean anything."

"But the poem she quoted was something from *Sonnets from the Portuguese,*" John persisted. "I think it was the third one: 'Unlike are we, unlike, oh princely Heart!' "

"So?"

"So there's something else in the sonnet about a 'chief musician' and a 'wandering singer.' Jarvis *is* a musician and a singer. I guess I'd better mention that to the police, especially since you don't think she committed suicide."

Blaine felt her mood sinking even lower. During high school she had been friends with Tony's eldest sister, Sandra, and she remembered Tony well as a darling young child. Something in her still felt protective toward him, even though she knew he'd been in minor trouble several times over the past few years. And now because of her, John was going to tell them about a poem that could hint at a deep involvement between Tony and Rosie. Nice work, Blaine, she thought angrily.

"I said I didn't know if Rosie committed suicide," she repeated.

"I *know* what you said. I also know you." John gave her a halfhearted grin. "I can read your eyes, Ms. Avery."

"That's scary."

"Should be. There are depths and depths behind those beautiful gray eyes."

Never in all the years she had known

John had he flirted with her, but once in a while he gave her a compliment. "Maybe there's nothing behind those eyes," she said with a bitter edge. "Maybe I'm just trying to look mysterious—you know, live up to my reputation as the Black Widow of Sinclair, West Virginia."

Lockers were banging furiously as students gathered their books. "I never told you how much I admired you for coming back to school this fall after Martin's death," John said, diplomatically not mentioning the murder investigation and ignoring her sarcasm about the cruel nickname some local townspeople had given her. "And here you are again, the day after you must have gotten the second biggest shock of your life."

"I guess I'll just keep coming back until they tell me to go home. I don't have much else, John, besides a lot of money I don't deserve and a stepdaughter who doesn't like me."

"You have a sister and a niece who love you, not to mention one of the world's greatest dogs that adores you. One day I'm going to kidnap Ashley from you." He smiled, then grew serious. "*And* you have a good friend, Blaine. Don't forget, you can always count on me. And I'm not just saying that, like so many people do in a time of crisis. I *mean* it."

"Thanks, John." Blaine felt tears starting in her eyes. Luckily, the bell rang. "Great. My first day back and *I'm* late," she said shakily.

"They'll forgive you. In fact, I've heard they have a little surprise planned for you. But don't let on you've been warned." With that he winked at Blaine and strode down the hall to his own classroom.

The surprise was a dozen long-stemmed yellow roses. For the second time in five minutes, Blaine was so touched she thought she was going to cry when Susie Wolfe presented them. "From us to you," she said with her usual lack of eloquence for which a Farrah Fawcett smile always compensated. "We were going to get red, but Robin said you like yellow. Dean said you must be from Texas, whatever yellow roses have to do with Texas."

"It's a song, airhead," Dean Newman said from the back of the room.

"Drop dead," Susie replied absently, which broke up the class. Susie and Dean had been dating and arguing since ninth grade.

"They're beautiful," Blaine said. "I don't know how to thank you."

"Give us all As," Dean volunteered.

Blaine threw him a droll look. "In homeroom?"

"That's all he could ever get an A in," Susie said. Hoots from the class. "Do you really like them?"

"I love them. They were almost worth getting pneumonia for."

"Well, don't do it again," Dean said. "Do you know how expensive roses are? I offered to pull some stuff out of my mom's flower bed, but nobody'd go along with me."

Susie made a face. "Oh, he did not. It was his idea."

"Well, I appreciate your thoughtfulness *and* your extravagance. Right after my first class I'll find a vase."

"Got one." Susie went back to her desk and returned with a plastic vase already filled with water. "You can put them in something pretty when you get home, but this will get them through the day." After she handed Blaine the vase, her expression grew solemn. "Mrs. Avery, do you mind if we take up a collection for flowers for Rosie?"

The earlier bantering spirit in the room died. Blaine looked from one face to another, seeing emotions ranging from curiosity to horror to desolation. Last year a male student had sent his car off the road while trying to avoid a deer and crashed into a tree. His death had been a shock, but he had not been well known to most of the students, and he had died instantly. The most popular, beautiful girl in school supposedly committing suicide, her body lying in a dirty creek for two days before being discovered, was so much more dramatic and shattering that Blaine understood why the students now felt emotions far deeper than the regretful sadness they'd felt for the boy.

"Of course, Susie," Blaine said, grateful for her simple but tender heart. She had always liked the girl, and wished more of the students possessed her genuine sweetness. "We'll put you in charge of handling money and ordering flowers for this classroom."

After the collection, Blaine barely had time to take roll call before the bell for first period rang. She spent the next three class periods trying to orient herself, determining what the substitute teachers had covered so far. Except for the first week after her accident, she had sent weekly lesson plans to the school as a guide for the substitutes, but they invariably changed things around to their liking, emphasizing what they preferred, ignoring what they didn't like. That was only natural, Blaine thought. But it meant she had a lot of backtracking to do to satisfy her own standards.

At noon she opted for a sandwich in her classroom instead of going to one of the three strategically placed fast-food restaurants with some of the other teachers, who would undoubtedly want to discuss Rosie's death. As she ate the dry cheese sandwich on which she'd forgotten to add mayonnaise that morning, she thought of the call she'd received last night. She had discovered Rosie's body over six hours earlier, and in a town the size of Sinclair, it didn't take long for word to spread. Obviously someone had decided to scare her, maybe a teenager. Still, "Ring Around a Rosy" had been a particularly frightening choice. The repetition of the word *Rosy* obviously held the greatest significance, but Blaine couldn't forget the meaning of the song, one that had become popular during the bubonic-plague years in seventeenth-century England. The *rosy* referred to the *bubo*, or the plague sore. The *posy* was the packet of herbs people wore, hoping to ward off the illness. The *ashes* were the burned mattresses and bedclothes of those who had died of the plague. *We all fall down* was a reminder of death's inevitability. No matter what precautions were taken, the illness was relentless. More than 150,000 people had died during the plague's reign.

Suddenly she was very glad that this morning she'd told Logan about the call, even if it was only politeness that had prodded him to ask her several questions rather than simply dismiss it as the work of a crank. It hadn't felt like another crank call, though. In fact, the echo of those lyrics on the old record still made her feel cold: "Ashes ashes/We all fall *down*." Blaine shivered in the overheated classroom.

During her fifth-period American Lit class, she couldn't keep her eyes off Tony Jarvis. Although she was used to his lounging inattention and constant smart-aleck remarks that drove most of the teachers wild, she couldn't help noticing that today his handsome, olive-skinned face was tight and expressionless, his dark eyes distant in thought. For once he made no occasional sardonic cracks about how you wouldn't want to meet Edgar Allan Poe in a dark alley, or that Rip Van Winkle had probably fallen asleep for fifty years because some English teacher forced him to read Washington Irving stories. He was silent and sullen until Blaine read Poe's "Annabel Lee" aloud in class. In the middle of the poem, Tony grabbed up his book bag and stormed from the room, leaving everyone staring after him. A few minutes later, even with the classroom windows closed, she and the students could hear his Harley revving up noisily in the parking lot before he tore away from the grounds.

After school, exhausted and still shocked by Tony's behavior, Blaine forced herself to drive to the Peyton home. She parked in front, noting about seven other cars parked in the big driveway and down the street, and looked at the pristine white Colonial house where Rosie had spent most of her life. "I think Grandpa was trying to re-create Tara," she'd told Blaine once. "Can't you just see Joan and my mother sweeping down that spiral staircase on their way to senior proms? And, of course, Joan had her picture taken, tiara and all, standing halfway down it when she was Miss West Virginia. She looked *so* beautiful."

Blaine was very familiar with that picture. It had been in the paper when she was a child, and she had cut it out and taped it to her mirror, hoping that someday she would grow into a young woman as lovely as Joan Peyton. In her opinion, she never had, although careful makeup and lighting could make her look striking. Joan, however, had been a natural beauty who didn't need all the props.

Blaine took a deep breath and started up the walk to the pillared front porch. This was not a call she wanted to make. God only knew what shape Joan would be in, and perhaps old Mrs. Peyton hadn't even been told. Her health hadn't been good since her husband's death from cancer a year earlier, and Rick said the constant pain from the broken hip that refused to heal had debilitated her mentally as well as physically. Still, Blaine had always admired Joan. She couldn't let any more time pass without offering her condolences and her help.

The door was opened by a heavyset woman with broad, rather Slavic features. She wore a white uniform and a hat pinned carelessly too far to the right. She looked rumpled and upset, her eyelids swollen from crying.

"Blaine Avery." She stared at Blaine, making no move to usher her inside. "It's been months since I've seen you."

"Hello, Bernice." Blaine tried to ignore the woman's barely concealed rudeness. She had been passionately devoted to Martin, and certainly not one of Blaine's supporters during the investigation into his death. She had even suggested to the police that probably only under duress had Martin called her, telling her he was going out for a drive with his wife and wouldn't be needing her services on the afternoon of his death. Blaine had not forgotten the woman's damning attitude and insinuations, but she was determined to disregard her. After all, she was here to comfort Joan, not to confront Bernice Litchfield.

"I've come to see Joan."

"Plenty of other people here." Bernice's face suddenly contorted. "Poor little Rosie."

"Yes." A chilly breeze ruffled Blaine's long hair, and she was beginning to wonder if Bernice was ever going to let her in the house. She could hear a hum of voices in the background.

"You *found* her," Bernice said.

"Yes."

"She was on your land."

Blaine stared at her coldly. She could simply walk back to the car, or she could face the hostility and suspicion in the eyes boring into her own, as she had so many times in the past few months. She stood still.

Bernice took a breath. "Susie told me how hard the kids at school are taking this."

"Susie?"

"Susie Wolfe. My granddaughter."

"Of course. I forgot that you're related."

"I told you often enough. I guess you weren't listening."

"Of course I was listening," Blaine said with increasing impatience. "I've just had a lot on my mind lately. The family connection didn't come to me immediately."

"Well, Susie's mother is my daughter,"

Bernice said, standing stolidly in the doorway. "We're very close. I talk to her almost every day on the phone. She's a sweetie, that girl is."

"Yes, I'm very fond of Susie."

Bernice beamed at the compliment, temporarily forgetting her enmity toward Blaine. Then her face clouded again. "It was so awful about Rosie, but when I think of such a thing happening to Susie . . . well, I just can't imagine . . . Not that Susie knew Rosie real well or anything," Bernice added hastily. "She hardly knew her at all."

Which is a blatant lie, Blaine thought. The police know that, so don't expect them not to question Susie like they're questioning all of Rosie's friends. Or did Bernice's lie have a deeper significance? Blaine stiffened. Did she believe Blaine had something to do with Rosie's death, and was she trying to shield her granddaughter from a killer?

Suddenly furious, Blaine was turning to walk back to the car when she heard someone say, "Who's there, Bernice?"

Joan's voice. "It's Blaine Avery, Miss Peyton."

Joan came to the foyer. She stared at Blaine for a moment, then with a small cry enfolded her in her arms. "Blaine, I'm so glad you've come."

Surprised by Joan's unusual effusiveness, Blaine found herself chattering out an unnecessary excuse. "I'm sorry I couldn't get here earlier, but today was my first day back at school, and after all the weeks I've missed, I couldn't ask that another substitute be found on such short notice."

"I understand. Don't apologize." Joan held Blaine away from her and smiled weakly. The years had been kind to Joan Peyton. At forty-four, she had thick, glossy black hair that was undoubtedly touched up a bit, drawn into a neat French twist with the front waving slightly over her high, nearly unlined forehead. Even now, in her awful grief, she still looked tall and elegant with her broad, swimmer's shoulders and firm body kept in shape by daily laps around the indoor pool she'd had built ten years ago. Blaine had always thought she had the bearing of a queen—a real queen, not a beauty queen. She wore a gray cashmere sweater, a matching skirt, and low-heeled shoes. Although she was alarmingly pale, only the redness in her remarkably beautiful violet eyes showed that she'd been crying, and her pink lipstick was askew, as if it had been applied by a shaking hand.

"People are in the living room," she was saying, "but I'd like a few minutes alone with you. Would you come into the library with me?"

"Of course."

"Bernice, you won't mind running up to check on Mother again, will you?"

"Certainly not. That's my job." Bernice gave Blaine a final, sour look and plodded heavily up the graceful sweep of staircase.

"Just ignore her, dear," Joan said, steering Blaine into the library. "She's so moody."

"She doesn't like me."

"I apologize for her rudeness, and normally I'd dismiss her for treating a guest in this house that way, but there aren't many private-duty nurses around here, so beggars can't be choosers. We had her for Daddy last year, too." She turned. "Do you want something? Coffee? Tea? A drink?"

Blaine sat down on a leather wing chair placed in the only shaft of sunlight cutting through the dimness of the room.

"No, Joan, I'm fine."

"If you don't mind, I'll have a small brandy. I know Mother wouldn't approve of my drinking in front of the mourners in the living room—most of them are her friends. I assume Rosalind's friends will be dropping by later."

And where are *your* friends? Blaine wondered briefly as Joan poured a snifter of brandy, took a sip, and wrinkled her nose. "Quince. I absolutely hate this stuff, but Mother loves it. In private only, of course. Oh, well, I guess it's as good as anything for calming the nerves."

"Why don't you ask Bernice for a tranquilizer?"

"So she can tell everyone I had to be sedated, just like Mother? No, thank you."

"I'm surprised more people from school aren't here," Blaine ventured.

"I guess they will be, later. Most of them will want to go home and rest before coming to offer condolences. Frankly, I'd prefer they just stay home. Oh, I know that sounds awful, but times like this are the very worst for the family to have to entertain people, especially when so many are just curiosity seekers, not real friends like you." Which wasn't exactly true, Blaine thought. It was Martin with whom Joan had been good friends. Blaine had never been much more than an acquaintance and a colleague at work. "But I know you understand exactly what I'm talking about," Joan was going on. "You've been through it all."

Once again Joan's memories were inaccurate. No one had come by to comfort her and Caitlin when their father had gone to bed in a drunken stupor and died in his sleep from a leak in a gas stove. And no one except Joan had come to the home after Martin's brutal death. Everyone had been too daunted by the police swarming through the house and around the lawn. But Blaine saw no point in correcting Joan's recollections.

Joan took another sip of brandy, lighted on a chair opposite her for a moment, then quickly rose and began pacing around the room. "I keep prattling because I don't know where to begin," she said, twisting the wide silver bracelet she always wore. "Your Ashley found Rosalind."

"Yes, I'm afraid so."

"In the creek. My beautiful girl lying out there in that filthy water for God knows how long. Was it awful? I mean, did she look—" She gasped. "Oh, God, what am I going on about that for? I know how she looked. Her face, at least." Joan took a deep, shaky breath, getting control. "I suppose I should be glad she was caught in those roots and didn't sink. Bodies don't surface for days, you know. That's what Logan Quint told me. If not for those roots, it might have been spring before she was found . . ." She made a shattered motion with her hand, her voice breaking. "Blaine, I thought she was in Charleston."

"I know."

"She said she wanted to visit her cousin Amanda. You know she did that a few times a year. This particular trip *did* seem a little sudden to me, but I didn't put up an argument. Mother has been impossible the last few weeks—I thought Rosalind just needed a break. She didn't even feel free to invite people to the house anymore. We never knew when Mother was going to throw one of her colossal tantrums. A young girl shouldn't have to deal with someone in Mother's condition. I should have put her in a nursing home."

"Joan, we can spend our whole lives thinking of what we *should* have done, but it's useless. You were doing what you thought was best for your mother. Lots of people don't adjust well to nursing homes, and I know Rick Bennett thought your mother was one of those people. He thought she was better off at home. And you *certainly* shouldn't blame yourself for letting Rosie go on her weekend trip."

"That's what everyone keeps saying, but I do." Joan rubbed her forehead distractedly. "I asked Rosalind to call when she got to Amanda's. She fussed a bit, but agreed. And a little over an hour after she left, around five, she *did* call. That's when I should have known."

Blaine frowned. "You should have known what?"

"That she was lying. The call didn't sound right."

"How?"

"There was background noise—traffic. It flashed through my mind that she was calling from a pay phone, but when I asked, she said Amanda's mother had the window open. She didn't sound as if she was telling the truth, and besides, Amanda lives on a fairly quiet street. I should have called right back to verify her story. It's just that Rosalind had been complaining lately about my being too strict, too protective. Oh, not

making a big thing out of it, but dropping little remarks here and there. So lately I
haven't been checking up on her as much
as I always did. And look, just *look* what
came from my carelessness!"

She was speaking much faster than
usual, her voice high and tight. She set
down the brandy snifter and began wringing
her hands. Blaine stood up, taking those
twisting hands in hers. Close up, in the
bright light streaming through the library
windows, she noticed with a start the small
wrinkles around Joan's eyes and lips. She'd
always thought of Joan Peyton as ageless,
like a beautiful portrait. "Joan, you have to
stop this. Rosie was seventeen, and this
isn't the nineteenth century. Girls that age
need some freedom. Believe me, I've
learned that from Robin. I'm only thirteen
years older than she, but customs have
changed even in that short a time. Besides,
Rosie had never given you any trouble, any
reason to doubt her. She was the model
child."

Joan's eyes filled with tears. "Yes, yes,
she was. So easy to love, to trust. I just
don't know—" Her voice broke. "I just don't
know what could have happened. Do you

know? Do you know *anything* about what could have caused Rosalind to do such a thing?"

"No, Joan," Blaine said carefully. "And neither does Robin."

"I thought she was happy." Joan's knees sagged and Blaine led her to a chair, where she sank down and looked beseechingly up at Blaine. "What am I going to do? How am I going to get through every day of the rest of my life after this . . . this *thing* that's happened to my baby? Because she was like my own, you know. Like my very own."

Blaine hesitated. Should she tell Joan that *she* didn't believe Rosie had killed herself? No, certainly not. Now was not the time for her to offer theories that were probably wrong. Instead she put her arm around Joan's shoulders. "I guess now I'm supposed to say that time heals all wounds."

"And does it?"

"No."

Joan managed a weak smile. "You've always been brutally honest, even when you were a child. Why, I remember one day when your father was here doing some yard work. He brought you along." Joan's voice had taken on a tone of rambling, which she never did. Blaine listened patiently, knowing Joan's reminiscences were the result of grief and shock. "I was twenty and absolutely full of myself. I came outside dressed in my best bikini and began lounging seductively around the pool. I thought I looked just like Elizabeth Taylor. But you, young lady, marched your six-year-old self right over to me and said, 'You're real, *real* beautiful, Miss Peyton, but all that black stuff around your eyes makes you look like you got in a fight.' "

Blaine's face reddened at the memory. "What a brat."

But Joan shook her head in amusement. "I stormed upstairs, looked at myself in the mirror, and decided you were right. I've never worn heavy eyeliner and false eyelashes again. They made me look like a clown. And the very next year I became Miss West Virginia." Abruptly her smile faded. "But I understand what you mean about time not healing all wounds. You were speaking of losing Martin, weren't you?"

"Yes," Blaine said hesitantly, thinking that she wasn't referring so much to his literal death as to the death of his spirit, which had occurred the night of the car wreck.

"Martin was terribly unhappy, Blaine. I know what people in town said—that such a vigorous, outgoing man would never take his own life, but it was because he *had* been so vigorous, athletic, commanding, that he couldn't adjust to being trapped in a wheelchair for the rest of his life. All his sense of achievement and self-esteem vanished. He couldn't have people telling him he could have been a professional tennis player anymore. He couldn't stride around Avery Manufacturing giving orders in that Orson Welles voice. After all, I visited Martin several times after the accident. I *know* how he felt. I told the police that."

"Yes, you did. In fact, you're the only person besides me who said he was suicidal."

"Well, Bernice and Robin certainly knew it. But Bernice, of course, thought Martin Avery walked on water, and since she believes suicide is a sin, she wouldn't admit she knew how he felt. And poor little Robin." She shook her head. "I just don't think she could acknowledge that her father wanted to die. But Martin called Bernice and told her not to come that day, and he called here, asking if Rosalind and Robin were back yet. He sounded relieved when I said they wouldn't be finished decorating the gym for at least another hour. Obviously he wanted to be alone that afternoon. He *knew* what he wanted to do."

And is that why he started that violent fight with me that afternoon? Blaine wondered. Did he know I'd never leave him alone otherwise? Did he know he could drive me from the house? Blaine felt chilled at this evidence of Martin's deliberation, but she kept her voice steady. "I can understand Robin's reluctance to believe her father wouldn't want to die and leave her."

Joan frowned. "Under normal conditions, no, he would never have left his daughter. *Or* you, even if he was irrationally blaming you for the accident. That was temporary. I know you understand that." Don't be so sure, Blaine thought. "But what people like Bernice and Robin don't realize is that the severely depressed person is not thinking rationally."

Do you believe Rosie was thinking rationally? Blaine wanted to ask, but couldn't bring herself to. Asking Joan to analyze her dead niece was just too much.

Joan dabbed at her eyes with a tissue she'd pulled from her sweater pocket, and

Blaine asked instead, "Have you told your mother?"

"Oh, yes. There's no way to hide something like this. We said at first that Rosalind had gone on a trip. Mother was having one of her lucid moments and she didn't believe it for a minute. She knew from the looks on my face and on Bernice's that something was horribly wrong, so I decided to tell her the truth. She got hysterical. Thank God Bernice is here. She's been keeping Mother sedated. Earlier today, though, she woke up and seemed to think it was my sister, Charlotte, who'd just died instead of Rosalind. Isn't that amazing? Charlotte's been gone for over sixteen years."

"Your mother is so sick, Joan, and this has been a terrible shock."

"I know. It's just incredible to me the way the senile mind works. She can't possibly go to the funeral."

Joan paled again at the word *funeral*, her eyes straying off, and Blaine asked quickly, "Is there anything I can do to help with the arrangements?"

"No. Everything is already taken care of. Except for the exact day of the service, that is. Do you know they haven't released Rosalind's body?"

Of course they were doing an autopsy, Blaine thought, but she wasn't going to point out that gruesome fact to Joan, who had obviously blocked it from her usually sharp mind. "In the meantime, you *will* let me know if you need anything, won't you?"

Joan nodded. "I will, Blaine. And thank you for being such a good friend to Rosalind. She idolized you, you know."

Blaine was astonished. *"What?"*

"Oh, yes. I'm sure she never said anything to you, but I know she did to Robin. And to me. She thought you were wonderful."

"Look, Joan, I know Rosie liked me, but idolized me? I don't think so. Especially after this summer."

Joan shook her head. "She never believed you killed Martin, Blaine. She was adamant about it. Absolutely adamant."

Blaine glanced around the mahogany-paneled room with its marble fireplace and shelves full of leather-bound books, not wanting to ask the question ringing in her head, but unable to stop herself. "Is that when she and Robin drifted apart? When

Rosie insisted she didn't think I'd killed Martin?"

Joan looked puzzled. "Well, dear, I don't know. I do know they hadn't been seeing as much of each other as usual, but whether or not it had anything to do with that . . . well, no, I'm sure it didn't. You know how young girls are—always spatting, getting upset because they like the same boy, developing different interests. For heaven's sake, you don't think Robin believes you killed Martin, do you?"

"No, no, of course not," Blaine said hollowly.

Joan's forehead puckered. "Blaine?"

"Never mind, Joan. I'm just being silly. And I think you're wrong about Rosalind. She was going off to Radcliffe and devoting herself to her education just the way you did. After all, you were her real role model."

"I wish that were true," Joan said sadly. "I wish it were true, because I'm a survivor. I guess my little Rosalind wasn't."

5

1

"Who gets the last slice of pizza?" Robin asked.

"You do," Blaine and Rick answered in unison, then laughed. "You're a growing girl," Blaine added.

"What you mean is that I'm the only one who didn't fill up on beer," Robin said.

Blaine looked at her glass. "I don't think half a glass of Heineken counts as a fill-up."

Robin looked at her censoriously. "That's your second beer, but who's counting?"

"Apparently you are," Blaine said, abashed that she'd downed a whole beer without even realizing it. "I guess I'm just so tired my memory's going."

Rick picked a piece of pepperoni off his plate and fed it to Ashley, ignoring Blaine's frown. Ashley took the pepperoni in her mouth, careful not to bite Rick's fingers and just as careful not to look at Blaine, who usually didn't allow doggy junk food. "Couldn't sleep last night?" Rick asked.

"Actually, I was really drowsy when I went to bed. Then I got a strange phone call around midnight."

"I didn't hear the phone," Robin said.

"You were asleep."

"Not at midnight."

"Robin, I checked on you at eleven and you were asleep."

"But I woke up later. I looked at the clock. Ten till twelve."

"Well, I looked at the clock, too. The call came exactly at twelve. Besides, the phone in your room has a different number. It didn't ring."

Rick held up his hand. "Ladies, could you finish this fascinating debate later? I want to hear about the phone call."

"Yeah, who was it?" Robin asked.

"No one. At least no one spoke. They just played a record. A strange record." Blaine hesitated. "A child's song, 'Ring Around a Rosy.' "

Rick and Robin stared, Robin's pizza-laden hand freezing halfway between her plate and her mouth. "Are you kidding? *Rosy?*" Rick finally managed. Then he rolled his eyes. "Of course you're not kidding. God, that's sick."

"I know," Blaine said softly. "It really shook me up." She looked at Robin. "Do you know anyone who might have an old recording of that song?"

Robin slowly put down her pizza. "It's not exactly on the Billboard charts. But there is one possibility." Rick and Blaine looked at her expectantly. "Caitlin's day-care center."

"Robin!"

"I didn't say Caitlin played it," Robin returned hotly. "I just said she might have a copy of it, and people are in and out of that place all day."

"Of course. You're right," Blaine said more calmly. "I'm sorry I bit your head off. I'll check with her tomorrow."

"Did the person speak?" Rick asked.

"No. There was only the music. Then there was silence."

"You mean the person hung up?"

"No. Everything just got very quiet, but someone was still on the line. I'm the one who finally hung up."

"Did you tell Sheriff Quint about the call?" Robin asked.

"Yes, when he was here this morning. He

seemed interested, but not overly concerned."

Robin shrugged. "I guess he wouldn't be, considering your number was Crank-Call-Central all summer."

"You have such a charming way with words," Rick snapped. "Will you lay off Blaine for just one evening?"

Robin's lips tightened in irritation, and Blaine glanced at him. His burst of temper was unusual; he'd always been very kind, very gentle with Robin. Then she noticed he didn't look much better than he had last night—tired and worried. He'd been working especially hard lately, and he'd no doubt had to deal with Mrs. Peyton's hysterics today, and now Robin's sarcasm.

Robin suddenly rose and began clearing the table. "I'm going to my room and study," she said, her voice shaking slightly.

Blaine reached out and put a hand on her arm. "I'll clear up later, Rob. You go ahead."

Robin nodded and left the kitchen.

Blaine sighed. "I'm so worried about her, Rick."

"*Worried?* Annoyed, impatient, exasperated I could understand. But worried? *Why?*

She seems to be handling this whole thing remarkably well."

"*That's* what worries me. She's handling it *too* well. She hasn't cried since we found Rosie, and she insisted on going to school today."

"Would you have been happier if she'd stayed here by herself all day, sobbing?"

"No, although it might not have been much worse. As you can imagine, Rosie was the main topic of discussion with the students. I just wish Robin would show a little more emotion. She's so self-contained."

"Too self-contained, if you ask me personally. Professionally, I'd say she's a young lady of delayed reactions. Let her coast for a while in peace, Blaine. It'll hit her later, and then she'll really need someone."

"The person she'll need is her father. But he's not here, either."

"*You're* here. And I'm here, too. Or rather, I would be if you'd let me into your life."

Blaine looked into his hazel eyes now faintly rimmed with dark circles, and at the slightly crooked nose Rick told most people had been broken in a car wreck, but which Blaine knew had been broken when he was a first-year medical student and fainted at his first sight of a cadaver in a gross anatomy class, cracking his nose against the concrete floor. "It's a common reaction," he'd told her defensively when she'd burst into uncontrollable giggles at the story, "but the general public doesn't know that, and I don't want my practice jeopardized because people think I'm a wimp."

She reached out and touched his cheek. "Rick, you know how much your friendship means to me."

He groaned. "Oh, God, spare me the you're-a-nice-guy-but speech."

Blaine laughed. "I wasn't going to say that. I was just going to point out that Martin has been gone such a short time."

"Six months. And before that he gave you five months of hell."

"Rick!"

"Well, he did. Look, Blaine, he was my friend, but he changed after that accident. He blamed you."

"I was driving."

"Because he'd had too much to drink at the New Year's Eve dance."

"But it was snowing, and he always said I couldn't drive worth a damn on snow, particularly in his car." She sighed. "I guess he was right. If I hadn't slammed on the brakes when I saw that other car coming at us, we wouldn't have gone into that spin and his side wouldn't have been rammed."

"No, yours would have been." Rick squeezed her hand in his. "Blaine, you did the right thing."

"No, the right thing would have been to call a cab."

"Sure. This town has five cabs, all of which were tied up. I know because *I* tried to call one. Besides, Martin wouldn't have waited. He was getting belligerent the way he did every New Year's Eve and Fourth of July when he had too much bourbon. If you'd insisted on waiting for a cab, he would have wrestled the keys away from you and killed himself or someone else in the car. He was in *no* condition to drive, and you couldn't help it because someone went through a stop sign and rammed the car. The accident was *not* your fault."

"I guess not. I only wish they could have found that driver."

"You think retribution would have made you feel better?"

"I like to think of it as justice. What kind of

person would leave us in that crumpled car in the snow?"

"A scared person. Someone who's never been found and probably never will be. So stop thinking about it. You're not helping Martin. All you're doing is tearing yourself up every day."

"Okay, Rick," Blaine said wearily. "You've been giving me this pep talk at least once a week for nearly a year, and believe me, it *does* help, but as for our seeing each other . . ." She shrugged. "Even if Martin hadn't died just six months ago, you know all the rumors that floated around about us."

"To hell with rumors. We know they aren't true."

"Yes, but there are other people to consider here. People like Robin."

"I knew her before you married Martin, and she's always liked me."

"I know she does. But only as a family friend. She's not ready to accept my seeing someone else yet."

"So you're going to let a resentful seventeen-year-old girl run your life?"

"No, but I am her stepmother, whether she likes it or not. I'm responsible for her, and I don't want to cause any more stress in her life than she's already feeling. And don't forget, there's your ex-wife. You've only been divorced for eight months."

"Ellen wants me to be happy."

"Is that why she told everyone you forced her to divorce you last March because of me?"

"She did that to cover up. Reputation is very important to her. She didn't want anyone suspecting that *she* was the one who wanted out for another man."

"Whatever her reasons for telling that story, it was a very popular theory."

"So was your being involved with John Sanders."

"That is ridiculous. John and I are just friends."

"*Good* friends."

"Oh, Rick, stop it."

"I will if you'll stop being so obstinate."

"Fine, if you'll stop being so pushy."

Rick grinned. "Don't mince words, Blaine. Just say what you think."

"Don't joke around about this. You *are* being pushy." She leaned forward, so close she could smell his Gray Flannel cologne. "Look, Rick, I think you're a wonderful man. You've certainly been a good friend to me.

But I can't think of anyone romantically right now."

"No one?"

"*No* one."

Rick raised his hands in resignation. "Okay, then. That's the last time I'm going to suggest marriage. *This* week, that is."

Blaine broke into laughter. "You are impossible."

"And relentless."

"*And* exhausted. If you don't go home and get some sleep, you're going to lose those good looks that make you the most popular doctor in town."

"Sink me, madam, what a thought!" Rick said in a horrible imitation of Sir Percy Blakeney's English-fop accent from *The Scarlet Pimpernel*, which they'd watched on television a few nights before. "Very well, I'll bow to your wishes tonight, but I'll be talking to you tomorrow." He leaned over and gave her a quick peck on the cheek. "Sweet dreams, pretty one."

2

Half an hour later she finished loading the dishwasher. Within minutes after Robin had gone to her room, the house had begun to throb with vibrations from her powerful stereo. Blaine stopped to listen. Led Zeppelin, "Ramble On." The music had nearly driven Martin crazy, but Blaine liked it, another testament to their large age difference. Although it would have taken torture to make Blaine admit the truth to anyone but herself, she had often felt more on Robin's wavelength than Martin's. When she married, her sister had predicted this, but Blaine hadn't listened. And much to her relief, their differences in outlook had never caused serious problems. Maybe if their marriage had lasted longer, they would have.

It was ten o'clock before she got the kitchen cleaned, and after taking a long, hot bath, she decided on bed. She felt tired to the bone and her head had begun to ache. She took two aspirins and climbed between sheets printed with pink roses.

Ashley stretched out on her plaid doggy bed beside Blaine's own king-sized bed, which Blaine had occupied alone for nearly a year since Martin's accident. Before that awful night, how different things had been. Against her will, her mind drifted back to the beginning of her relationship with Martin Avery.

It had been an unusually hot Saturday night in May. The town was holding its bicentennial celebration down by the small, man-made lake, where the reconstruction of a fort destroyed in the eighteenth century would begin on Monday morning. The fact that the reconstructed fort would be located nearly a mile from where the original had stood, or that it would be surrounded by a man-made lake and approached by brightly colored paddleboats, didn't seem to bother anyone except the diehard historians, who said the whole thing would look more like something in Disneyland than an authentic fort. Blaine held the same opinion, but because the woodworking business owned by Caitlin's husband, Kirk, and his father was to be largely responsible for the inside detailing of the fort, the two men had been asked to speak at the celebration. For this reason alone, Blaine had agreed to attend. A day of hot dogs and potato salad and speeches in the hot sun was not her idea of a good time, but she guessed it beat sitting alone in her apartment watching old movies on cable TV.

She had lived in Dallas for almost eight years, since her mother, trying to make amends for deserting her daughters years before, had extended an invitation for Blaine to live with her and her second husband while attending Southern Methodist University. Blaine hadn't wanted to go, but her father had insisted. "This is a great opportunity for you. And don't forget, there's Caity to think of. I don't like to seem conniving, but your stepfather is very comfortable in the money department. You might not only be helping yourself, but also be paving the way for Caity to find a better life than I've ever provided." And so Blaine had left her father, her sister, and Logan, the only three people she loved, and gone west. Unfortunately, the uneasy truce between Blaine and her mother had not lasted for long, and Blaine had started her sophomore year living in a dorm, supported by grants and loans, too ashamed to come skulking home. What would her father think? That she hadn't even made an effort for Cait's sake? Logan was long gone, hurt by her desertion. And, of course, people in Sinclair would say she hadn't come home by choice, but had been forced to come home because she'd failed in the beautiful school in the big city. By the time she'd finished college, Cait was married and happy, so Blaine had stayed in Dallas, taking a job in computer sales she hated when no teaching positions opened up and payments on her school loans came due.

She had returned to Sinclair three years later to attend her father's funeral, and impulsively decided to abandon the lucrative, if disliked, sales job for a temporary position at Sinclair High School so she could be near Caitlin and her two-month-old niece, Sarah, for a while. She enjoyed her job at the school, which finally allowed her to do what she'd trained to do in college, and she loved Caitlin and her family, but if she had expected things to be different for her in Sinclair than they had been when she was young, she was wrong. The town was bad luck for her, she often thought. Nothing had ever gone right for her here. Of course, part of the trouble was just that Sinclair had a population of only six thousand. There wasn't much to do or many people to meet. Still, at twenty-six, she was alone except for Cait, her old school friend Sandra Jarvis, who was now married and had three children who kept her too busy to do much of anything, and John Sanders, with whom she occasionally spent an evening, although he went out of town most weekends. There was no romantic interest in her life, and although finding a husband was not one of her priorities, she did want to marry and have a family of her own someday.

Hell, she thought dismally as night closed in on the celebration and she wandered down to the dock with Sarah, sleeping peacefully in her arms while Cait helped other respectable matrons of the town dish up homemade ice cream before the fireworks display started in half an hour, she would be satisfied now with just a man who was neither involved with someone else, like John, nor married and trying to have an affair, or with one who wanted to do more than sit in a local bar drinking beer after beer as he told her about his hunting and fishing exploits. She had been a fool to renew her contract at the school and the lease on her apartment for another year, she fumed silently. What on earth had she been thinking of? she wondered. Her attachment to Cait and Sarah? Well, she couldn't live on that forever. It was time to leave Sinclair and start her own life again. Instead she was trapped for another year, and she had no one but herself to blame.

She slipped off her shoes and sat down on the dock. Sarah squirmed and whimpered in her arms, then relaxed again into openmouthed baby sleep. Blaine smiled into her oblivious face. "I wish you were mine," she whispered. Sarah blew a saliva bubble. Blaine sighed and dangled her bare feet off the dock into the lake water. The water was so cool. If she were alone, she would take off all her clothes, slip into the water, and swim her depression away. But she was surrounded by hundreds of people.

"You look like you could use this."

She jerked her head around to see a man in the semidarkness. His face was lean, tanned, smiling. Even his blue eyes smiled at her. Martin Avery. Everyone in town knew Martin Avery. "What did you say?" she asked stupidly.

"I said, you look like you could use this." He held out a bowl of homemade ice cream. "Of course, it would be better with some Drambuie or Grand Marnier on top, but such delights are not being served tonight." Blaine stared at him in surprise, and he laughed softly. "Here, let me hold the baby while you eat."

"Thank you." He set the bowl of ice cream beside her, perched himself so close to her on the dock she imagined she could feel the warmth his golden-tanned arms gave off, and deftly took the baby from her. Sarah started to wail, broke off in the middle as if reconsidering, and went back to sleep.

"This is very nice of you, Mr. Avery," Blaine said, digging into the ice cream.

"It's Martin. And it's not so nice. I remember you so well when you were a youngster. You used to come to my house with your father and work like a little demon right beside him. He got paid, but you didn't."

Blaine felt her cheeks flame at the memory of those days, one in particular when she was thirteen. Gloria, Martin's delicately beautiful wife, had come out, stopped her as she was raking up grass her father had just mown, and said, "I have some old clothes of mine I don't wear anymore. They're out of style, but I'm very small and you're a big girl for your age, and you certainly look like you need them."

Mr. Avery had been sitting on the deck, and he lowered his newspaper, staring at them both with his clear, electric-blue eyes. Humiliated, Blaine had said, "Thank you very much, Mrs. Avery, but I have all the clothes I need."

Later, as she and her father were leaving, they'd passed an open window. Blaine could hear Mr. Avery nearly shouting, "Why the hell did you offer that girl your old clothes?"

"I was only trying to help," Mrs. Avery had shot back. "Good Lord, she looks like a ragamuffin, like some orphan out of Dickens. You don't resent my being generous, do you?"

"I don't resent your being generous. I *do* resent your being cruel, and that's exactly what you were doing. You've got a lot more tact than to tell the kid she looks like she *needs* your old clothes. You mortified her."

"Oh, don't be ridiculous," Mrs. Avery had said. "That girl should have been grateful. Her problem is that she's got a lot of pride her kind doesn't have a right to."

"Her *kind?* Jesus, Gloria, maybe you'd have been happier living on a plantation in the old South. Then you could have gone around humiliating the slaves every day . . ."

Mrs. Avery had burst into tears. "Don't

talk to me that way! I'm getting pains in my chest. I've always had a bad heart. I'm not supposed to get upset, and here you are yelling at me because you think I was tactless to some little nothing of a girl *you're* defending because you think she's *pretty*. They don't come too young for *you*, do they?"

Blaine's father had bowed his head while Blaine fought hot tears of embarrassment as they moved past the window. A few months later, when Gloria Avery died of a heart attack, Blaine felt tremendous guilt because of that summer day when she'd wished the woman dead.

And now, all these years later, Martin Avery was serving her ice cream on the dock and holding her sister's baby. Blaine suddenly couldn't think of anything to say to the man, but luckily he kept talking, as if he understood her discomfort. "The fort's quite a project, but it ought to bring in a lot of tourists. This town needs something to stimulate the economy."

"Yes." Blaine glanced at him out of the corner of her eye. He looked slightly older than he had when her father had done his yard work, but he was still slim, golden-haired, and blue-eyed, with intense magnetism and energy. She suddenly thought of him leaping over a tennis net in triumph at Monaco or coming in first in the Grand Prix. The privilege he'd been reared with seemed to circle him like an aura, even as he sat on a splintery dock holding a baby whose diaper was undoubtedly wet by now. "The only thing thriving in town at the moment is Avery Manufacturing," she remarked.

"That's right. But we can't support a whole town."

The ice cream was much richer than what she bought in the store and so cold it made her teeth hurt in a pleasant way. She hadn't eaten homemade ice cream since she was a child.

Martin Avery looked out over the water. "I was sorry about your father."

Blaine swallowed quickly. "Thank you. And thank you for the flowers. There weren't a lot at the funeral." She immediately regretted the last remark, thinking it sounded self-pitying, but the man didn't look uncomfortable.

"I was out of town, or I would have come," he said easily. "I always liked your dad."

She stared at him. "You did?"

"Sure. Sometimes, when you weren't along, he'd share a drink with me after he finished the yard work. He was a smart man, Blaine."

"Yes, he was. Very smart," she said stiffly, then added, on a warmer, more intimate note that surprised her, "He just couldn't channel his intelligence."

"We all have our weaknesses."

And what weaknesses could you possibly have? Blaine wondered, turning her eyes back to her ice cream. He seemed perfect, bigger than life, a character out of a movie. How could he possibly understand that Jim O'Connor had been a man driven by dreams that his lack of education and his alcoholism had never allowed him to accomplish? And yet she felt Martin *did* know.

"I hear you're doing an excellent job at the school."

"I try. But who keeps you apprised of my performance?"

Crinkles appeared around his eyes when he smiled. "I'm on the school board."

"Oh, I forgot."

"I'm glad you've decided to stay. My daughter, Robin, will be starting Sinclair

High next year. I'd like to think of her having you for English, although her strong point is music."

"You won't be sending her away to private school?"

He shook his head. "No. I was shipped off to private school when I was young, and I resented it terribly. All my friends were here. Besides, Robin is all I have."

"Why didn't you ever remarry?" Blaine asked, immediately horrified at the bluntness of her question.

Martin, though, threw back his head and laughed. "Just as direct as your father was." The baby kicked, opened her mouth, and let out a piercing cry. Blaine finished her ice cream and set the bowl aside, then reached for the baby, who settled back into her arms with only minor fussing.

"Sorry about that," Martin said.

"It's okay. I'm surprised she's as quiet as she is, considering how noisy it is around the lake. I suggested taking her home, but Cait wants her to stay and see the fireworks."

Martin frowned. "What is she, six months old?"

"Seven. And I know—it's silly. She'll either

ignore the fireworks or be frightened half to death by them, but Cait can be stubborn."

Blaine stuck a pacifier in the baby's mouth, and Sarah fell quiet again.

"I haven't met the right woman," Martin said.

"What?"

"You asked why I haven't married again after Gloria. I was just answering your question."

"Oh. I'm sorry I asked something so personal. I feel like a fool."

A welcome breeze drifted through the night air, lifting her hair from her neck. Something nibbled at her toes, probably one of the few fish recently dumped into the new lake, and she kicked, then lifted her bare legs from the cold water, tucking them under the full skirt of her sundress.

"Would you have dinner with me, Blaine?"

She looked into the electric-blue eyes. They were smiling, but they were also sincere. Incredible as it seemed, he wasn't joking. She swallowed. "I'd love to, Mr. . . . Martin," she said.

Seven months later, on December 15, Blaine's twenty-seventh birthday, they were married. They honeymooned in the Caribbean and returned in time for Christmas. Martin's Christmas presents to Blaine had been a golden retriever puppy and a white Mercedes. She was delighted with the dog, but claimed the car was far too grand for her to drive to Sinclair High. Martin, however, insisted. She was beautiful, she was brilliant, she was meant to have the best. She'd brought love and youth and excitement back into his life. And their life *was* exciting, with surprise trips, parties and cookouts, endless bouquets of yellow roses, beautiful clothes, and the passionate love of a man she'd admired since childhood. She felt like a princess. Except for Robin's coolness toward her, the next two years had been idyllic, and only hours before that fateful New Year's Eve party, which Blaine still couldn't think about without a shudder, she and Martin had decided to have a baby.

Now it was all gone—the happiness, the security, the love—all snatched away because someone had sped through a stop sign on a snowy night and plowed into Martin's Ferrari. Blaine turned onto her side, forcing her eyes shut. "Don't think about it," she said aloud. "Don't think about what you've lost or how Martin came to hate you, or you'll go crazy." Down the hall Robin's stereo still throbbed, and Blaine concentrated on the music, finally floating to sleep with the music of Heart.

3

Blaine pulled into the driveway, turned off the engine, and took a deep breath. Was she ready to face Martin? He'd told her his paralysis was her fault. Finally he'd actually said what she knew he felt. And when she'd argued with him, told him they should have taken the Bronco to the dance instead of his fast, flimsy sports car, he'd grown furious, shouting invectives and hurling a heavy glass ashtray at her. Not at her, she realized now, nearly three hours later. He'd hurled it in her direction, just to frighten her, just to vent his anger. So she'd stormed out. But she shouldn't have done that, no matter how he'd provoked her. Martin was in no mental condition to be left alone, even for a short time.

The front door was locked. Blaine was puzzled. Bernice never left the door locked, and she was due to arrive twenty minutes after Blaine had left. But then, Bernice's car was not outside. Maybe a friend had driven her. Maybe she'd taken a cab. Or maybe she'd not come at all, a damning voice inside Blaine's head said. Maybe something had happened and Martin had been alone all this time.

Fear rushed through Blaine, cramping her stomach muscles. She used her key to open the front door. Inside, the air conditioner hummed in the big, quiet house. It was unusually hot for late May, as hot as it had been the May when Martin came into her life again. On a couple of days the temperature had reached the nineties. Maybe the weather moved in three-year cycles, she thought irrelevantly.

She walked into the living room, her glance flying to the pile of dark blue glass lying on the pale oak floor, remnants of the ashtray Martin had thrown. She should have cleaned up the mess before Bernice came. But if the woman had come, she would have picked up the glass. Bernice was not here, had never been here today.

"Martin?" Blaine called tentatively. "Martin, where are you?" The house was too quiet. Not even Ashley was around to greet her. Her breath quickened. Something was

wrong. The house seemed to throb with trouble. She stood totally still in the living room, listening, feeling. Trouble. Then she heard the whining behind Martin's closed study door. With growing dread she opened it, and Ashley burst out, circling her legs, barking in agitation. "What is it?" Blaine asked, her voice edged with fear. "Where's Martin?" She looked inside the study. It was empty, but the stench of something burning filled the air. Blaine walked to the metal wastepaper basket beside his desk and saw the charred remains of two leather-bound books—Martin's journals, she later realized. The journals he'd obsessively written in the past few weeks had been reduced to scorched covers, the pages consumed by fire.

While she stared at the still smoldering books, Ashley bounded to the French doors. She barked and whined until Blaine followed her, watching as the dog stood on her hind legs, the nails on her front paws tearing at the sheer voile curtain panels. "Stop that!" Blaine commanded. She ran to the dog, forcing her away from the doors. Then she saw Martin, slumped in his wheelchair on the deck.

Slowly she walked outside. The smooth boards of the sun deck were hot beneath her thin-soled shoes. It must be ninety today, she thought distantly. Martin shouldn't be out in this heat. Maybe he'd fainted . . .

*Then Ashley went to him, licking his limp hand. Blaine glanced down to see a familiar revolver lying on the hot boards beside him. But that wasn't possible, she thought. She'd locked the gun cabinet and hidden the key in her jewelry box. But there was the gun, shining and deadly in the afternoon sun. Chills raced up and down her arms in spite of the heat. There was the gun. **There was the gun,** her mind screamed. Finally she raised her eyes. They focused on the ragged, blackened hole in Martin's right temple as the world filled with brilliant sunshine and the shrill, monotonous buzzing of seventeen-year cicadas in the trees beyond.*

"No!" Blaine jerked awake, drenched in cold perspiration. Ashley had jumped up on the bed and was licking her face. "I'm all right, girl," she mumbled, stroking the dog and sitting up. During the weeks at Caitlin's house the frequency of the dream had lessened, and she'd hoped it would soon disappear. But she'd had the dream three nights in a row, ever since she'd come home, and she knew the trauma of that awful day in May was too firmly embedded in her sub-conscious to fade so quickly.

Shaking, she threw back the covers and glanced at the clock on the bedside table. One-thirty. The house was deadly quiet. And cold.

She climbed out of bed and shrugged into a light silk robe that did nothing to ward off the chill. Somewhere under the bed were the delicate slippers she seldom wore, but tonight the polished oak floors chilled her bare feet, so she found them and slipped them on. Then she flipped on the bedside light, but there was nothing. So her sensa-tion of cold wasn't only from the familiar dream. The electricity had gone off, which wasn't unusual. According to Martin, they'd had electrical problems in this house for years.

She crept into Robin's room, tripping over Ashley, who kept stopping in front of her, assuming a listening stance. "It's okay, Ash. The house is just creaking because of the sudden drop in temperature," she whis-pered. Robin was sound asleep, but she was uncovered. Blaine pulled the down comforter up to her chin and tiptoed from the room.

"Flashlight," she said to Ashley. "It's in the kitchen."

They stumbled down the long hall and through the living room and dining room. When they reached the kitchen, Blaine automatically flipped the light switch, but the room remained in darkness. "Great," she muttered. "Forty degrees on a pitch-black night, and we don't have heat or light." She felt her way over to the drawer beside the stove and withdrew a flashlight. The battery was weak, and it gave out only a faint light. "Oh, no," she moaned. How many times had Martin warned her about keeping fresh batteries in the flashlights? How often had he advised keeping candles handy? All his good advice had gone unheeded. And it was so *cold*. At this rate, she and Robin would both have sniffles in the morning.

Then she had a thought. What if the problem lay with the circuit-breaker box? One time not long after she and Martin had married, the electricity had gone off, and when it came on, the surge flipped half the breakers. Maybe the same thing had happened. It was worth checking out.

"Downstairs to the breaker box," she told Ashley. The dog whined and cocked her head. "Well, if you're scared, you can stay up here."

As if sensing the challenge, Ashley raised her head and trotted to the basement door. She stood at it firmly, though, staring back at Blaine with what seemed like defiance. The dog had always been frightened of the basement and usually could be coaxed only about halfway down the steps. Martin had been amused by Ashley's stubborn, irrational aversion, but tonight it was getting on Blaine's nerves. She sighed. "Look, Ash, I don't like the basement, either, but I have to go down." She took hold of Ashley's collar and tugged. "Now *move*."

She opened the door. Ashley barked twice. "I'm not going to argue with you." Blaine knew how silly she sounded, but she'd always talked to the dog as if it were human. Sometimes she thought it was. Partly. Like now, when Ashley reluctantly turned around and, to Blaine's amazement, led the way down.

Martin had just completed plans for converting the large, bare basement into a game room two weeks before his accident.

Afterward, Blaine didn't have the heart to proceed with the project, and Robin didn't seem interested, so it remained empty except for boxes and discarded furniture. Even the washer and dryer were off the kitchen in a separate laundry room.

Although the basement wasn't damp, it seemed deathly cold to Blaine in her thin robe. Ashley stopped at the foot of the wooden stairs leading to the big main room, gazing into the darkness. Then she made a couple of huffing sounds in her throat. Blaine almost tripped over her again, and for an instant she felt the same creeping sense of dread she had at the creek bank. Her hand shook slightly, and she had an impulse to run back upstairs and lock the door. But apparently Ashley, for all of her caution, decided nothing was wrong, because she finally stepped off the stairs and looked back at Blaine.

"Now you've frightened me, Ash," Blaine said shakily. "You've got me thinking about finding another dead body. But there can't be anything down here. After all, the outside door to the basement is locked. The whole *house* has been locked for weeks."

Nevertheless, Blaine hurried as she

crossed a dark corner of the basement, then turned off into a smaller room housing the furnace, water heater, and circuit-breaker box. She opened the box and quickly found the thrown breakers. She snapped them back to the On position. The ceiling light Blaine had automatically turned on when she entered the room blazed.

"What are you doing down here?"

Blaine jumped and turned to see Robin standing in the doorway. "The electricity went off. I came down to check for thrown breakers."

"Judging by the arctic temperature, the one controlling the furnace is a guilty party."

"Is that what woke you? The cold?"

"I heard noises. Must have been you and Ashley."

"Well, everything should be okay in a minute." Right on cue, the furnace hummed to life. "Thank goodness that was so easy. We'd never get anyone out here at this time of night. Let's go back upstairs," Blaine said. But neither Robin nor Ashley was listening. Ashley was sniffing something on the far side of the furnace, growling low in her throat.

Robin started, and Blaine felt a dark wing

of fear flutter inside her. "It's probably a dead mouse."

"We've never had mice in this house."

"I don't believe that. This house is fifty years old," Blaine argued.

She was suddenly overcome with panic. She felt perspiration popping out on her hands, and when neither the girl nor the dog moved, she said shrilly, "Robin, let's get out of here."

Robin ignored her and went over to stand beside the dog. Her forehead puckered; then she said in a small, frightened voice, "Blaine, come here."

Blaine hesitated, then forced herself closer to the dog and Robin and peered behind the furnace. After taking a sharp, startled breath, she bent and drew out a tan suede jacket, a small brown purse, and a navy blue suitcase. Gingerly she lifted the suitcase's identification tag and read aloud, "Rosalind Van Zandt." She raised her eyes to Robin's. "My God, this stuff is Rosie's, and it's been hidden."

6

1

For the second time in less than two days, Blaine called the county sheriff's office. Twenty minutes later, when Logan Quint pulled into the driveway, she was already in a jogging suit and had turned on every light in the house.

"It's you!" she said, opening the door before Logan had a chance to ring the bell. "I expected a deputy. Do you work twenty-four hours a day?"

"Sometimes." Blaine noted he was wearing ancient jeans, a sweatshirt, and a pair of scuffed boots. His sleepy eyes and sloppy clothes said he'd been awakened by a call and had dressed in a hurry. "Actually, I left orders that I was to be informed of any developments in the Van Zandt case, no matter what the time. Show me what you've found."

Would it kill you to smile just to make

Robin and me feel a little calmer? Blaine thought angrily, but he looked aloof, almost taciturn. Annoyed, she led the way to the basement, where Robin waited as if she thought the suitcase might vanish if it wasn't watched.

"How did you happen to come across this stuff?" Logan asked.

"Ashley, once again. The electricity went off and I went downstairs to check the breakers. The breaker box is in the furnace room. Ash found the stuff almost at once, behind the furnace."

"What makes you so sure these items belong to Rosalind?" he asked as they descended the stairs.

"The identification tag is on the suitcase. And Robin and I have seen Rosie carry that purse and wear the jacket."

When they entered the small furnace room, Logan paused to look at Rosie's things sitting in front of the furnace; then he drew on thin rubber gloves he'd carried in his back pocket. "I don't want to disturb any fingerprints," he explained. "Of course, I'll make allowances for yours, since obviously you've touched the stuff."

"We shouldn't have," Blaine said.

"It's a natural reaction." He looked at the suitcase. "I'd like you two to stay while I go through this. I may need some information."

Blaine looked at her stepdaughter. "Robin?"

"I want to stay. I knew more about Rosie's things than anyone except her aunt."

Logan knelt and pulled the suitcase to him. "I'll dust for fingerprints after we've searched it," he said.

"Why are you so concerned about finger-prints?" Blaine asked suspiciously. "I thought you said she committed suicide."

"I said that's what it looked like." He snapped open the lid. Inside, everything was neatly folded and compartmentalized. How like Rosie, Blaine thought with a catch in her throat. She was always so neat.

A pair of black wool slacks and a white silk blouse—not quite as trendy as the clothes some of the girls wore, but expensive and definitely Rosie's style. Panty hose. A pink, lace-trimmed Christian Dior night-shirt and matching robe. Three pairs of underpants. An underwire bra, a silk slip. A blow dryer and a curling iron. In one side compartment a box of Allerest, a travel bottle of Revlon shampoo, a toothbrush, tooth-

paste, mascara, blusher, and gray eye-
shadow; in the other, white Isotoner house
slippers.

"You recognize all of this, Robin?" Logan
asked.

"Yes, aside from the toiletries. The
makeup is Estée Lauder, though. That's the
brand she always wore because they don't
do animal testing."

Logan moved on to the purse. Brush,
compact, lipstick in a pink tone, a ballpoint
pen, and a roll of cherry Lifesavers lying in
the bottom of the purse; driver's license,
Social Security card, library card, and three
one-hundred-dollar bills in her billfold. Logan raised his eyebrows at the money. Four
keys on her pewter sea horse key chain.
And one key tucked away in a zipper compartment of the purse.

"House key, locker key, and car key," he
said thoughtfully, holding up the key chain.

Robin nodded. "And that fourth key on
the chain is the Peytons' garage key. I've
seen her use it."

"I see." He lifted the fifth key, which had
been concealed. "And this? Another key to
the Peyton house?"

Robin frowned. "I don't think so," she

said slowly. "It seems to me Rosie had only one key to the house. That always bothered her. Her aunt waited up for her when she was out, you see, and Rosie had to come in through the front door, so Miss Peyton could see her from the living room."

"That sounds pretty quaint."

"I told you Rosie was overprotected."

"Maybe Joan Peyton would know what that key belonged to," Blaine suggested.

Logan studied the key. "I have a feeling she wouldn't."

Blaine looked at him. "What do you mean?"

Logan gazed at the key as if it were a crystal ball, his narrow, strong-boned face looking even more angular in the light from the stark overhead bulb, his dark eyes more hooded. If I were a romance writer, I'd describe those eyes as enigmatic, Blaine thought irrelevantly. But right now her inability to read Logan's expression was more unnerving than intriguing. Suddenly he seemed severe and relentless, just the way he had last night when he'd driven her home after they located Rosie's body.

"Logan, what is going on?" Blaine asked when he didn't answer the first question. He stared fixedly at the floor for a moment, as if carrying on an internal debate, then raised his head.

"I'm going to tell you some things we don't want generally known yet," he said abruptly. "We just found out this information late this afternoon, and Rosie's aunt was informed a few hours ago, but you might know more about this than she does."

Blaine and Robin stared at him. "Go ahead," Robin said in a voice that sounded dry and far away.

"We sent Rosie's body to the state medical examiner's lab in Charleston for an autopsy, and they did a rush job, partly because of the nature of her death and partly because of her family's clout in this state. Anyway, she'd been dead forty to forty-eight hours when you found her, although she hadn't been in the water that long. I found a place a few feet up from the willow where the bank had collapsed. I think she must have been lying there and fell into the creek during the storm Saturday. She hadn't exsanguinated from her slashed wrists, in spite of her time in the creek, probably because the water was so cold. The blood analysis revealed the presence of an opiate.

Unless they know what they're looking for, though, they can't identify specific products. Anyway, because of the great amount of blood she'd lost, they couldn't say how much of the drug she'd ingested, but it was a hell of a lot. It was administered intramuscularly. Those kinds of injections require longer needles, which sometimes break off. Part of the needle was still embedded in the muscle of Rosalind's left arm. I found a syringe with a broken needle out in the woods this morning."

Blaine swallowed. "Her grandmother is on medication for a broken hip. Could Rosie have taken some of Mrs. Peyton's medicine?"

"No. They tested for those drugs. Nothing matched." Logan paused, looking at Robin intently. "The autopsy also revealed that Rosalind was carrying a two-month-old fetus."

Blaine's jaw sagged. "Rosie was *pregnant? Did Joan know?"

Logan didn't take his eyes off Robin. "She says she doesn't believe it—that there must have been a mistake in the autopsy. But there was no mistake. That's why I'm asking you, Robin. Do you know who the father was?"

Robin shook her head mutely.

"My God," Blaine breathed.

"Wait a minute," Robin said slowly. "You said the needle was in her *left* arm?" Logan nodded. "Rosie was left-handed."

"That's what the medical examiner said, based on the bump raised on her left middle finger from holding a pen." Logan finally raised his eyes. "It doesn't imply she administered the injection herself, does it? Besides, a few things looked odd even before the autopsy. The night we pulled her out of the creek, I found a lot of bruising on her arms, and one of her pierced earrings had been ripped from her earlobe."

"What about the fish and the birds that had been at her?" Robin asked. "Could they have done the damage?"

"They bite. They don't hit, especially on the temple. The M.E. found massive bruising there. A concussion."

Blaine stared at him, knowing where he was heading. Robin said, "She'd been in a struggle."

Logan nodded. "Another odd thing was that even the next morning I couldn't find the knife that had slashed her wrists. It could have gone into the creek, of course, but it seems more likely it would have been near the syringe."

"And you didn't find her suitcase, purse, and jacket," Blaine said faintly.

Logan's eyes bore into hers. "Exactly when did you move back here?"

"Saturday morning, around ten o'clock. I'd planned on staying with Cait until Sunday, but I decided the extra day would give me more time to get ready to go back to school."

"When you came back, did you discover any signs of someone having been in the house?"

"No."

"Nothing was out of place?"

"Not that I remember. Of course, I hadn't been in the house for several weeks, but Robin came out every few days to practice her piano, and Kirk, my brother-in-law, came here once a week to check on things." Blaine took a deep breath. "Logan, there's something I haven't told you. I was here Friday night."

"I thought so."

Blaine was so surprised she drew back. "You *thought* so?"

"Yes. Your car was spotted heading in this direction."

"Who saw me?"

"Abel Stroud. I live on Prescott Road, too, about a mile south of you, toward town. He was dropping by to bring me something, and he saw you driving from this direction around eight-thirty. There aren't too many white Mercedeses in this area, you know. You're kind of conspicuous."

"Why didn't you mention it?"

"I was waiting for you to."

"I'd forgotten it until Sunday night, after we'd found Rosie's body and I learned she'd left home Friday."

"Did you come into the house?"

"Yes, but only for a few minutes to turn up the heat, since I was planning to move back the next morning, and to put away a few groceries."

"Did you see anything unusual?"

"Nothing. No lights in the house. And no cars."

"Any car parked back on the access road where Rosie's was couldn't be seen from Prescott Road or your driveway."

"No, I guess not." Blaine realized her hands were shaking. She'd been terrified to tell Logan about that night. But he'd already known and hadn't even questioned her about it. So why did she still feel so uneasy?

Logan turned to Robin. "Are you sure you didn't know about Rosalind seeing anyone but Tony Jarvis?"

"I'm sure. I mean, I'm not sure she wasn't, but if she was, *I* didn't know it."

"And that relationship was casual."

"Yes. Her aunt wouldn't let her date him, just let them be friends at school. Besides, he saw other girls. I don't think Rosie would date a guy who was going out with other girls, do you?"

"I didn't know her, Robin."

"Well, she wouldn't."

"Are you sure?"

Blaine felt that Logan was badgering Robin, who was looking paler by the moment. Angered, she forced down her uneasiness and said, "Can you forget the exact nature of Rosie and Tony's relationship for a minute and answer the big question for me? Except for Robin's and Kirk's visits to this house, it's been locked up for weeks.

So how did the things Rosie took with her on Friday afternoon get in here?"

Logan stood. "Come upstairs with me."

Blaine and Robin exchanged a quick, apprehensive glance, but they followed quietly. Even Ashley trailed along. When they reached the front door, Logan opened it, locked it, then inserted the key he had found in Rosalind's purse. The lock snapped open.

"Good heavens," Blaine gasped.

Logan looked at Robin. "Did you ever give Rosalind a key to this house?"

Robin shook her head. "No."

"Are you sure?"

"That's not the kind of thing I'd forget."

"I know."

Robin looked at Logan levelly. "Then you're insinuating that I'm lying. Well, let me tell you something—I *don't* lie."

"Even to cover up for a friend?"

"No, not even to cover up for a friend." She hesitated, uncertainty flickering in her eyes. "But there is something," she said slowly. "I never gave Rosie a key of her own. But there was a time, after Blaine collapsed at school with pneumonia, when Rosie had my key to this house. I was at the hospital, and Rosie offered to come out here to get a robe and some toiletries for Blaine. I gave her the key then so she could get in."

"And she returned it?" Logan asked.

"Yes, but she could have had a duplicate key made. It wouldn't take very long at the hardware store. It's near the hospital."

Logan held up the key. "You might be right. This is a fairly new key."

"But why?" Blaine asked. "Why would Rosie do such a thing?"

"Because she needed a rendezvous spot. You and Robin weren't going to be living here for a while, and it's isolated, so she didn't need to worry about prying eyes."

Blaine stared at him. "Of course. It was the perfect place for an affair."

Logan nodded. "It was also the perfect place for a murder."

2

"Joan! Joan Ma-*rie!*"

Joan Peyton opened heavy eyes and peered at the man-tailored watch she wore even when she slept. Two-ten. She hadn't gotten to sleep until after twelve, and she hadn't slept at all the night before. "Joan!"

"Coming, Mother," she called, tossing off the sheet and padding on bare feet to the bedroom across the hall. "What is it?"

The withered figure raised itself up slightly in bed. "Come closer. I can't see you."

Joan stepped closer. "Would you like me to turn on the lamp?"

"No! It's too bright." The voice that had once ordered servants around with a rich contralto imperiousness was now high and sandpapery. But it was still imperious. "I'm cold."

"Cold! The thermostat is turned up to seventy-five. I can't even stand a blanket, and you have two over you."

At that moment Bernice Litchfield walked in, her stocky figure wrapped in a robe splashed with huge, vivid pink flowers, her faded blond hair bristling with brush rollers.

"Why, Mrs. Peyton, you shouldn't have disturbed your daughter," she said in the fondly scolding tone she often used with her patient. "You know I'm right in the next room."

"You didn't answer when I rang the bell."

Bernice's face had the swollen-lidded look it acquired when she was having one of her headaches. A flush of embarrassment spread over her broad features, shiny from a greasy night cream, but Joan had the feeling her mother had never rung the bell for Bernice at all. Her expression was petulant, the way it always was when she thought Joan wasn't paying enough attention to her.

"I want an afghan," she whined. "Joan, get me the afghan downstairs in the sitting room. The blue-and-white one I knitted last year." The blue-and-white afghan had been knitted over twenty years ago, but time no longer had meaning to Edith Peyton.

"I'll get it," Bernice said hastily.

Joan shook her head. "Never mind. I'll get it," she said with a wink to Bernice, which had become their signal for "Try to calm her down."

Bernice started to leave for the bathroom, where Edith's medicine was kept, but the old woman reached out and grabbed her hand. "You stay here till she gets back. I don't want to be alone. There's death in the air tonight."

"Oh, now, Mrs. Peyton," Bernice said, sounding as if she were talking to a three-year-old as she sat down on the bed. "What a thing to say."

"Cold-breathed, bone-rattling death!" Edith insisted.

Bernice looked appalled. "She's always had a flair for the dramatic when she's annoyed," Joan said. "I'll be right back."

She found the afghan on the living room couch, catching sight of herself in a big, gilt-edged mirror on her way out. Her hair hung, shining and thick, to her shoulders, but her face was the color of eggshells and, without lipstick, her lips looked thin and dry. Five years ago they hadn't looked that way, even without artificial color. The years and the deaths take their toll, she thought, trudging back up the stairs with the afghan. "Here you go, Mother," she said, spreading it over the shrunken figure. Even Edith's head appeared to have shrunk in the past couple of years, as if she'd fallen into the clutches of a headhunter. "Are you comfortable now?" she asked solicitously as Bernice slipped out of the room.

"Talk with me a while, sweetie pie."

"Okay. I'll stay until Bernice gets back."

"No. I want you to sit up with me till morning. I'm afraid of the dark."

"Mother, I've had very little sleep."

Edith's sagging eyelids opened wider in

anger. "Well, just get the hell out, then! Go on, get out! Forget about your mother! You'll think twice about being so selfish after I'm gone!"

Joan was used to these sudden transformations. One minute Edith was a sweet, fragile old lady whose failing memory made your heart break. The next she was a sharp-tongued termagant. Joan could hear Bernice moving around in the bathroom, searching through the myriad bottles of pills for something to help her mother sleep. Relief would be coming soon.

Joan sighed and walked to the window, gazing far across the lawn at the converted stables facing the alley that housed the family cars. The hedge along the alley had grown so tall, cars could come and go without ever being seen from downstairs, but from the second floor she watched a cat slink across the asphalt and pounce. It grappled with something for a moment, then ran off into the brush with its prize. "What would you like to talk about, Mother?"

Her mother's head whipped back toward her. "Where is Charlotte?"

"Charlotte is dead. She's been dead for a very long time."

Edith's right hand, corded with almost grotesquely prominent veins, plucked nervously at the afghan. "No, I didn't mean Charlotte. That's not right. The other one. The child."

"Rosalind."

"Yes, Rosalind! That's who I meant. Where's Rosie?"

What was taking Bernice so long? Joan wondered as she moved away from the window and sat on the bed, taking Edith's cold, bony hand. "There's been a tragedy, remember? Rosie is . . . gone."

In the moonlight streaming through the open curtains the old woman's face crumpled. "You mean dead. Rosie killed herself." Joan looked at her, surprised she remembered what she'd been told about Rosie's death. "I still can't believe it. She was so beautiful."

"Yes, Rosie *was* beautiful," Joan said softly. "And intelligent. And talented. And young."

"Beautiful. Beautiful like you. You're so beautiful. You've always been so beautiful, Joan."

"Thank you, Mother."

"I don't know where your looks came from. You were the most beautiful child I've ever seen. I couldn't believe two ordinary-looking people like your daddy and me produced something like you."

"That's quite a compliment, Mother."

"Do you think so? Being pretty isn't so great. It doesn't mean you're special in your soul." She cast a quick, birdlike look at Joan, whose temporary pleasure in the praise died. Her mother always had a talent for building her up only to immediately deflate her. Senility hadn't dulled the old trick. "Rosie was beautiful like you. But her personality, that was like her mother's. She had Charlotte's personality." Her eyebrows drew together. "Do you think Charlotte's personality entered Rosalind's body?"

How many times had she asked this since Charlotte's death? Joan thought. And how many times had Ned Peyton snapped at his wife to stop spouting a lot of Hindu nonsense? "I'll always miss Charlotte," Edith rambled on. "I'll *always* miss her."

Joan could hear Bernice rummaging through the bathroom closet, probably searching for a fresh package of Dixie cups.

"Everyone who loved Charlotte will always miss her, Mother."

"Do you think Charlotte and Rosalind are together now?"

"I hope so."

Edith sighed. "My Charlotte. She had such stinking luck with men. Never knew how to handle them like you did. First that Avery son of a bitch dropped her." Joan winced. Five years ago Edith wouldn't let a curse word cross her lips; now she showed an amazing facility with foul language. "Then that unspeakable Van . . . Van something or other killed her. He killed my baby."

"Mother, she never dated Martin Avery. She had a schoolgirl crush on him. And Derek Van Zandt didn't kill Charlotte."

"She's dead, isn't she? And he was driving."

"They died in a private plane crash, Mother, and Derek *wasn't* the pilot."

"I know he was! You all lied to protect Rosie, to keep her from knowing her father killed her mother. But, by God, I know the truth! That low-down bastard, that dirty son of a—"

Joan stood up quickly as Bernice entered

the room. "What *took* you so long?" she shrilled.

Bernice tensed, looking as if she thought Joan was going to fly across the room and slap her. "I'm sorry, Miss Peyton. I couldn't find—"

Joan took a deep breath, regaining control. "Oh, never mind. I'm just tired. You're here with the pills now. That's all that matters."

Edith's expression changed from rage to suspicion. "What kind of pills?"

"Your Valium," Bernice said.

"What's that?"

"It's a pill to calm you. You take them all the time."

Edith's face set. "I have never had radium in all my life," she said emphatically.

Bernice gave her a placating smile. "It's Valium, not radium. How about trying one tonight? And look, I've brought your water in one of those pretty patterned cups you like."

"The ones with the pink tulips on the side?"

Dear God, Joan thought. Was this the woman who, even on the sly, had once sipped brandy only from delicate crystal snifters?

"That's right, Mrs. Peyton. Beautiful pink tulips. And after you take one of your pills, I'll sit here and hold your hand until you've gone to sleep."

"All right. But I'm telling you, I've *never* had one of those pills." Her scratchy voice went on relentlessly. "I'd remember if I'd had one. I remember everything, although people think I don't. They love making fun of me. Like to think I'm crazy. Hell, crazy like a fox, that's what *I* am, and don't you forget it!"

Bernice practically crammed the pill into Edith's mouth and watched her gulp water like a drooling baby. "My hip hurts," Edith whimpered after she'd swallowed the pill.

Bernice shook her head. "Sorry, but you've already had your pain medicine. Just relax, and in a little while you'll feel much better."

"I want Joan to stay with me."

"Joan is awfully tired, Mrs. Peyton. Why not let me—"

"I want Joan!" Edith shouted with shocking force.

Joan and Bernice both recoiled. "It's all

right," Joan said tiredly. "I'm not sure I can go back to sleep now anyway."

For the next fifteen minutes Joan held Edith's hand while she babbled about a dance she'd attended when she was sixteen. She'd worn pink silk and had pink rosebuds pinned in her hair, and her dance card was full. In fact, men were fighting over dances with her! She was light on her feet, an angel in motion. Everyone said so.

But Joan wasn't listening to the tale she'd heard hundreds of times throughout her life, a tale that grew more glamorous and romantic with each telling. Instead she was thinking about Rosie. Suicide, they said. As if a girl like Rosie would commit suicide! The idea was preposterous. Joan had pretended to believe it, not saying a word to anyone about murder. At this point people would claim she simply couldn't accept what Rosie had done to herself. But surely the police couldn't believe for long that Rosie had taken her own life. The autopsy would show *something*. It had to. Besides, Logan Quint was a smart man. He had to see that something was wrong about Rosalind's death. She was counting on him. But if no one pursued the matter, she would do it herself. She would fight the verdict of death by suicide for as long as it took, until at last everyone would know that someone had wanted Rosie dead.

7

1

"Kathy, you were late for class both yesterday and today." Kathleen Foss, the school's voluptuous, platinum-blond head cheerleader, snapped her gum and looked at Blaine with maddening impassivity. "Five minutes late yesterday and ten today," Blaine continued. "I'm supposed to send you to the office for tardiness, but I don't like treating you like a child. I thought we could work this out together."

Kathy had always reminded Blaine of a china doll—just as silver-and-white pretty and just as empty-headed. She looked at Blaine with flat eyes turned azure by colored contacts. "Yeah, okay, well, I won't be late anymore."

Blaine didn't know what she'd expected—uneasiness in the face of her displeasure, gratitude for her benevolence in not sending Kathy to the office? She got neither. Kathy was totally indifferent, although she did look paler than usual. Blaine peered at her, noting that her makeup had been applied with the usual precision, but the pink blusher lay on waxy skin.

"Kathy, are you feeling all right?"

The girl looked slightly startled, the first animation she'd shown in two days. "Sure, I'm fine. Why? Do I look bad?"

"A little wan."

"A little wand?"

"*Wan*. It means pale."

"Oh. Well, no, I'm okay. Are you done talking to me?"

Annoyed, Blaine flared, "Yes, but you're not supposed to be chewing gum in school. Spit it out immediately."

Kathy looked at her as if she were crazy, and she felt ridiculous. Unlike some of the teachers, she couldn't understand why it was all right for teachers to chew gum and smoke in the building, but not for students. They weren't young kids. Nevertheless, she said nothing as Kathy raised manicured fingers to her mouth, took out her green gum, and dropped it with elaborate ceremony into the wastebasket. "Okay. *Now* can I go, *Mrs*. Avery?"

Blaine sighed. "Yes. But don't be late again."

When Blaine had first started teaching, she imagined herself establishing a good rapport with all her students, motivating even the most apathetic to develop some appreciation, if not love, of literature and composition. But as she watched Kathleen leave, she realized those dreams had been totally unrealistic. Some people could never be reached by a teacher, Kathy Foss being a prime example. For her, school was merely a showcase for her sexy young body and her athletic skills. In twenty years, she would remember being head cheerleader as the high point of her achievements and probably talk about it until her friends and family could recite verbatim all her stories for her.

It was the noon hour, and as she ate another dry sandwich in her classroom, Blaine thought about the night before, about finding Rosie's suitcase and her secret key to the Avery home.

Logan had studied Blaine, his expression changing. How had he looked? Blaine mused. Earnest? Grim? Accusatory? "Blaine, you haven't thought Rosie committed suicide since the night we found her, have you?"

Blaine had regarded him steadily. "No. I told you I didn't think she'd killed herself, and I couldn't understand why you didn't see it, too."

"I did."

"Then why did you play games with me in the car, acting like you thought it *was* suicide?"

"Because I couldn't say with certainty it wasn't, and if it wasn't, I needed you to tell me everything you could about the girl's mood without the issue of murder clouding your recollections." Blaine blushed, realizing he was thinking about her past, when she'd once been suspected of murder.

Obviously noting her discomfort, Logan said briskly, "Why didn't you believe the suicide theory?"

"The unnecessary depth of the cuts on her wrists, for one thing. Also, I told Robin to think about anything significant Rosie might have said, and I did the same. During the past couple of years, I've been around the girl a lot, too. She never mentioned anything that hinted at suicide. But she did talk a lot about the future. She said everything was going to change for her once she got out of this little town. Someone that optimistic about life doesn't suddenly kill themselves."

"But you haven't seen much of her since late in the summer. That's three months when something *could* have changed drastically for her."

"I know that, Logan. But I couldn't get something else off my mind. Rosie had a suitcase with her when she left. Why would she pack a suitcase to lug around with her before she killed herself?"

"She was supposed to be spending the weekend in Charleston with her cousin. She would have taken a suitcase to look convincing."

"Why bother telling that lie about Charleston? She could have made some excuse about going out just for the evening. By the time she was found on this property, she would already be dead. I know that when Robin and Rosie were kids, they played in the woods, but over the years Rosie had developed an aversion to them. She was always asking me if they didn't bother me, looming so close to the house. I just can't believe she would go out in them at night to kill herself."

"Unless she was messed up on drugs."

"She wasn't taking drugs," Robin said vehemently. "Oh, I know she'd been acting a little strange lately, but believe me, she was afraid of drugs, and she was especially terrified of needles."

Logan looked at her with interest. "I didn't know about the fear of needles."

"I saw her pass out one time just getting a routine blood test," Robin said.

"You didn't mention all this when I questioned you this morning."

Robin shrugged. "I didn't know she'd been drugged. I never even thought about it."

"Well, I can tell you one thing, fear of needles aside," Logan said. "Rosalind Van Zandt did not come to this house, give herself a massive overdose, hide her purse, suitcase, and jacket behind your furnace, lock all the doors, then walk nearly a quarter of a mile to the creek and slash her wrists to the bone. Considering the amount of opiate in her system, she couldn't have walked far. She might have been carried, but that's a long way to carry a hundred-

and-twenty-pound girl. It's my bet she was probably lured or coerced out to the woods and drugged near the creek."

"Then it was her murderer who put those things behind the furnace," Blaine had said. "But why?"

"Maybe something spooked him. Hell, it could have been you coming into the house that night. He might have been hiding in the basement and managed to get out the back door, locking it behind him, but not wanting to risk lugging Rosie's stuff out with him." Blaine pictured Rosie dying in the woods while she was blithely driving around, even coming into the house, so near, and felt sick. "The killer probably thought he could retrieve Rosie's things the following night. Only you came home the next morning."

"How could the killer hope to retrieve her things the next night when all the doors were locked?"

Logan looked at her solemnly. "Blaine, if Rosalind was killed by the father of her baby, he might have his own key." She went cold all over and Logan added, "You'd better get your locks changed tomorrow."

"Sure. I will," Blaine said faintly, rubbing a hand across her rigid neck muscles. Her head was beginning to ache, pain pounding through her temples.

"How do you think it happened, Sheriff?" Robin asked. "Do you think Rosie was planning to run off with her lover to get married? Maybe they were supposed to meet out here, but at the last minute he decided not to go through with it. Rosie might have gotten hysterical and he blew up—"

"And proceeded to shoot her up with the opiate he carried around with him just in case he got mad? I'm afraid not, Robin."

"Then it was premeditated."

"You're damned right it was," Logan had said with quiet fury. "And to top it all off, the bastard had the gall to try to make it look like suicide."

"Murder made to look like suicide," Blaine said aloud in the classroom, her stomach tightening. "That's what the police thought about Martin."

"If you weren't being such a recluse since you came back, you wouldn't *have* to talk to yourself."

Blaine jerked, startled out of her memories of last night, and looked up to see John Sanders standing in the doorway.

"Hi, John. Why aren't you eating out with everyone else?"

"I had a few papers I thought I'd catch up on. Mind if I come in for a few minutes?"

Blaine motioned to a chair beside her desk. John sat down and crossed his legs ankle over knee. "You still feeling pretty shook up over Rosie?"

"Yes, of course I am. I've been avoiding the lunch crowd because I don't want to go into the details," she said pointedly.

"I don't blame you." Blaine's faint hope that her hint had been taken died when he lowered his voice conspiratorially. "I heard today that it definitely wasn't suicide."

"Who told you that?"

"Arletta Stroud, campus liaison to the county sheriff's office."

"That girl! Honestly. She tells everything she knows. But her father shouldn't have told her to begin with. Not yet."

"Why not? They're pretty certain, aren't they?"

Blaine put aside her peanut butter sandwich, knowing she wouldn't be able to finish it now. "I don't know, John. I think the police are just speculating."

"And Rosie's suitcase and purse were in your house?"

"Arletta didn't leave out much, did she?"

"It's her only way of getting attention. Well, did they? Find those things, I mean."

"I'm not sure I should be talking about this."

"Everyone knows, Blaine. Arletta's been talking her stupid head off all morning."

"Arletta's always talking her stupid head off. That's why she never picks up anything in class." She sighed, stuffing the remains of her sandwich back in its plastic bag. She didn't want to talk about the murder anymore, but she had to remember that John had liked Rosie, too. Naturally he was curious. Besides, she trusted him as a confidant. "Yes, the purse and suitcase were hidden in my basement."

"Strange as hell. Arletta also said Rosie was pregnant."

"Oh, no. I was hoping no one would find that out."

"Faint hope. Joan will be even more crushed than she is now when this news gets around." He shook his head. "Any idea who the father was?"

"No, not a clue."

"How about Tony Jarvis?"

"Maybe. Robin doesn't think Rosie's relationship with Tony was sexual, but who knows? I don't want to believe Tony had anything to do with this."

"Don't forget that the summer before last, Jarvis did a lot of odd jobs around the Peyton home. Mr. Peyton was dying then, and Rosie told me Jarvis even helped the private-duty nurse shift the old man in his bed and do some of the heavier tasks involved with caring for an invalid. Rosie got to know him then and she liked him. I didn't understand it—he didn't seem like her type."

"He's handsome and sexy and talented."

"And that makes him every girl's type?"

Blaine shrugged. "I don't know. But I certainly can't imagine Tony getting a girl pregnant and then murdering her."

"Oh, I forgot. You've always been partial to our rebel without a cause, haven't you?"

"Yes. Tony's oldest sister and I were best friends in school. I remember him when he was little."

"Well, don't forget he got busted for drugs a couple of years ago."

"One marijuana cigarette when he was fifteen."

"Still, considering that Rosie was drugged before she was murdered—"

"Good Lord!" Blaine exploded. "Arletta threw in that detail, too?"

"That and a few she probably made up. But don't get so mad. It's true, isn't it?"

"Yes." Blaine sighed, thinking someone ought to put a muzzle on Arletta *and* her father.

"God, how awful," John muttered. "Poor Rosie."

She reached for her purse and fished inside for the aspirin bottle. "I've got a pounding headache." He looked concerned as she gulped down the pills with some of the coffee she'd brought in a thermos. "It must be tension. The shock of finding Rosie and all. These should fix me up. In the meantime, could we talk about something besides Rosie?"

"I guess dead, pregnant girls aren't exactly appropriate topics for lunchtime conversation. I'm sorry."

"It's all right."

"Subject closed, then," he said, looking at her with those mesmerizing, long-lashed smoky blue eyes. "You get to pick the next subject."

"Okay. How's Sam?" she asked, referring to his often-mentioned girlfriend, Samantha.

"Talk about nonsequiturs!" John raised his hands over his head and stretched. "Sam is fine. Talked to her last night, as a matter of fact."

"Does she have any intention of leaving Columbus and coming here to live?"

"Are you kidding?" John laughed. "No way. She loves her job at the hospital *and* the city. And since, unlike our dear Arletta, you can be discreet, I'll let you know I've applied to some Columbus schools for a job."

"John, I think that's great!"

"Well, I'm not expecting much. The job market is tough for English teachers right now, but at least I'm trying. Sam's happy about that."

"Are you going to spend Thanksgiving with her?"

"Yes. Leaving next Wednesday right after school. And believe me, after that grilling Quint gave me about Rosie, I wish it were tomorrow."

"He was really rough on you?"

"It was practically bright-light-and-rubber-hose time." He smiled. "Well, I do tend to exaggerate. It wasn't quite that bad, but he seemed unduly suspicious." He hesitated. "Blaine, I know you don't want to talk about this, but did you emphasize my friendship with Rosie to him?"

No, she didn't want to talk about it, but John seemed almost obsessed by the subject. "I hardly mentioned your relationship with Rosie."

"It wasn't a *relationship*. It was a *friendship*."

Blaine looked at him searchingly. "Okay. Your *friendship*. I didn't say much about it."

"But you *did* tell him."

"Tell him what, John? That you seemed to know her better than any of the teachers here except for me? Yes, I did say that much."

"I guess that was enough," he said dourly.

"What was I supposed to do? Lie?"

"It wouldn't have hurt."

"John!"

"Oh, I didn't mean that." He leaned forward to let his hands dangle between his knees. Blaine grew still.

"I think you did mean it. What has you so upset, John?"

"If a lot of rumors get started about Rosie and me, I could lose my job."

"I thought of that, and that's why I stressed to Logan that you were helping Rosie with her writing. I in no way implied there was anything romantic going on, and neither did Robin."

He grinned, although his eyes remained solemn. "Okay. Sorry again. It's just that in a town this size, you have to watch your back all the time."

Blaine frowned, but he was looking out the window, his expression worried.

2

A crowd gathered in the hall.

"So my dad says her wrists were cut *real* deep." Arletta Stroud held up her left wrist and made a violent slashing motion, then repeated the pantomime on the right, grimacing horribly. "But even then not all her blood drained out."

"Arletta, you're a real ghoul, you know it?" Dean Newman said, turning to walk away. "C'mon, Susie."

Arletta looked off as if thinking, her small eyes squinting beneath hair she teased straight up in front and lacquered into place. "Jeez, maybe she was still *alive* when he left her! Maybe she was still conscious when the animals came and began taking great big old bites out of her!"

Kathy Foss suddenly turned white and sank to the floor.

"She's *fainted!*" someone shouted.

General milling broke out as Susie Wolfe bent over her. "Dean, go get someone," she called, lifting Kathy's bleached head and laying it on her lap. "Mrs. Avery's door's right there, and I think she stayed in for lunch today."

Dean Newman, his brown eyes both alarmed and excited by the sight of the imperturbable Kathy lying in a helpless heap, strode down the hall to Blaine's door. While he rapped, Arletta began subtly easing out of the crowd. Everyone was so intent on Kathy, no one noticed her inching guiltily toward the girls' rest room. She had just disappeared when Blaine's door opened. After a quick consultation with Dean, Blaine rushed to Kathy, John following closely behind her. She knelt, took Kathy's pulse, then glanced up. "Did someone go for the nurse?"

Students looked at one another blankly, and Blaine reminded herself that in high school, the school nurse didn't elicit the awe she did in grade school. Probably a lot of the kids didn't even know there was a school nurse. "She's on the second floor, next to the counselor's office. Someone go. And *hurry*."

She didn't like Kathy's extreme pallor or the icy hands she now chafed in her own, feeling like some school matron in a Victorian novel trying to revive a swooning hothouse flower of a girl. "What happened here?" she asked the faces peering down at her. "Was Kathy sick this morning?"

Susie Wolfe shook her head. "She seemed okay in first period. Even at lunch. Kind of quiet, but okay. Then Arletta was telling us about Rosie being murdered."

"Arletta?" Blaine said sharply.

Instantly everyone began looking around. Dean said, "She must have taken off."

"Let me guess," Blaine said. "Arletta was describing Rosie's death in the most graphic terms."

Susie nodded. "She was being pretty

gross. She was talking about animals eating her before she was even dead."

"Oh, for heaven's sake," Blaine muttered. The mild language didn't express the disgust she was feeling for Arletta, but she couldn't let her true dislike of the girl show in front of all the other students.

John leaned down and touched Kathy's face. "I think she's getting some color back."

"But she's still so cold."

"What on earth is going on?"

Blaine looked up to see the school nurse hovering over them. "Kathy seems to have fainted."

The nurse pushed aside the gaping teenagers and leaned over Kathy. She took the girl's pulse, then held a tiny vial under her nose. Kathy's face twitched, and she turned it away. The nurse passed the vial under her nose again, and this time Kathy's eyes fluttered open. She looked wildly around her. "Rosie!" she cried, grabbing the nurse's arm. "Rosie, I was there. I *saw* . . ."

8

1

Blaine pulled up in front of a cheerful yellow, white-shuttered, rectangular frame building. Behind a chain-link fence stretched a neat lawn with a swing set, a natural-wood activity cube complete with cargo rope climb and sandbox, and a cedar playhouse. Black script on a white wooden sign near the door read "Caitlin's Day Care." Blaine opened the front gate, carefully closed it behind her, and went to the front door, shivering slightly. The white-gold sun that had warmed the day earlier had vanished behind a cloud, throwing the day into lavender gloom. Dry leaves rattled in the trees as the wind picked up, and overhead, Blaine saw a formation of Canadian geese flying south. According to the calendar, winter wouldn't officially arrive for a month, but to Blaine the season had already descended.

As soon as she opened the door, though,

all thoughts of winter vanished. The room was carpeted in a warm golden indoor-outdoor carpet; the walls were lined with shelves holding bright coloring and story books. Above the shelves hung pictures of Disney characters. Multicolored blocks lay scattered in one corner, a puzzle with huge, vivid pieces in another. Caitlin sat on a white plastic chair with about eight children ranging in age from three to five gathered around her. On her lap sat a wide-eyed child no older than eighteen months.

"So who can tell me what happened on the first Thanksgiving?" Cait asked.

One little boy with hair like corn silk solemnly volunteered, "The Indians came and taught the pilgrims how to square dance."

To her credit, Cait didn't crack a smile. "Well, not exactly, Doug."

"I know, I know!" another little boy piped up. He had an angel's eyes and a devil's smile. "The Indians brought mean turkeys that ate up all the pilgrims!"

Cait frowned. "Now, Jack, you know that's silly. Turkeys don't eat people."

"They *do*," Jack insisted, glancing around to make sure all eyes were fastened on his five-year-old self. "My daddy told me about how this one Thanksgivin' when he was little the turkey got right up off the platter and bit his sister's nose off!"

Six little faces crumpled in giggles while the beautiful, sensitive eyes of a girl of around three filled with tears. "You mean I'm gonna get my *nose* bit off at Thanksgivin' dinner?"

"Oh, Sally, of *course* not," Cait said firmly. She glared at Jack. "You tell your sister that's just a story."

"But it *isn't*," Jack insisted with injured dignity. "Sal, you know how funny Aunt Dot's nose looks?" The little girl nodded fearfully. "Well, that's what happened. Grandma didn't cut the turkey's head off, and that ole thing got right up off the platter and—" Jack stood, opened his mouth wide, and snapped his teeth together. Sally shrieked. Three children fell sideways, laughing uncontrollably. Jack bent double in his glee. The baby began to howl.

"Need some help?" Blaine asked.

Cait whipped her head around. "Oh, Blaine! Can you really stay a while?" Her hair was pushed back as if she'd run her hands through them repeatedly, and her shirt hung out from her slacks on the right side. "My assistant had to go to the dentist this morning for a root canal," she said. "Maybe it's just the approaching holidays, but as you can see, they're all a little wound up today."

"Sure, I can stay." It was only four o'clock, and most of the mothers wouldn't be arriving until after five. From the look of Cait, she'd never last that long. "Robin's going over to Susie's after school to study for a test and have dinner, so there's no meal to worry about."

"Thank goodness," Cait murmured.

Blaine shrugged out of her coat and looked at the children with feigned excitement. "I've got an idea! I'll tell you a story, and you draw a picture of what I'm telling you."

"We're only s'posed to do what Miss Cait tells us," Jack announced, looking truculent.

Cait gave him a long stare. "*Do* it."

Jack frowned darkly. Cait had already told Blaine that Jack was both the most precocious and the most maddening child who had ever been enrolled at the center, and he wasn't easily intimidated. At the same time, he wasn't used to the steel in Cait's voice, either. He blinked at her a couple of times before looking back at Blaine. "Okay, but we're *sick* of nursery rhymes."

Me, too, Blaine thought, remembering hearing "Ring Around a Rosy" over the phone. "I won't tell you nursery rhymes. Just get paper and your crayons, then do your very best."

All but the baby scrambled to assemble their art paraphernalia, then settled down, looking at Blaine expectantly as she struck a dramatic pose and said in a ringing voice, "This is 'The Tale of the Three Golden Apples.' "

Most of the children began industriously drawing misshapen gold and yellow orbs. Her niece, Sarah, the image of Caitlin, attempted to draw the three beautiful young women who sat on the riverbank making wreaths of flowers. Jack, predictably, drew the terrible dragon with a hundred heads that kept watch under the golden apple tree.

At five-thirty, when the last of little coats had been buttoned, prized crayon drawings shown to tired but admiring mothers, and Sarah sent back to Cait's house next door to watch *Mr. Rogers*, Cait turned to Blaine, her face drawn with fatigue. "You saved my life."

"I'm glad I could help, but I've never seen you so strung out over the kids."

"Our enrollment nearly doubled this year. Thank heaven half of them go home at noon. Also, I've never handled a whole day alone with them. And Jack, of course, equals about five kids instead of one. I'm glad he goes to school next year." She sighed. "Besides, I guess I'm still shaken over Rosie—not sleeping well, that kind of thing. I didn't know her very well, but seeing her that way . . ." Cait shuddered.

"Finding a body like that is something you never forget."

"I guess you're an expert. I'm *so* sorry it had to happen again."

"You and me both." Cait didn't say anything about Rosalind's things being found in Blaine's basement. Apparently the news hadn't reached her yet, and she looked too exhausted to be hit with any more shocks, so Blaine made her voice casual. "Caity, do you have a recording of 'Ring Around a Rosy'?"

One of Cait's red eyebrows went up. "Has your taste in music changed lately?"

"No. I just wondered."

The amusement left Cait's face. "No, you didn't just wonder about a thing like that. What's going on?"

"Don't give me a hard time. I'm tired, too. Just answer the question."

"Okay. I've got dozens of records, but I don't remember that one."

"Are you sure you don't have it here in the center?"

"No. When I opened this place, people gave me things, including records. I know I didn't buy a copy of it, and we never listened to it. The kids prefer songs from shows like *Sesame Street*. But you're welcome to go through the record collection and see for yourself."

Fifteen minutes later, Blaine had studied every record and tape in the day-care center's collection. "Nothing," she said, sitting cross-legged on the floor. "It's not here."

"You got another crank call, didn't you?" Cait demanded. She stood over Blaine, hands planted firmly on her hips, and Blaine had a sudden image of their mother standing over her in exactly the same position when one frigid February evening an eight-year-old Blaine had brought home a stray mixed-breed puppy and tried unsuccessfully to hide it in her bedroom in a wooden box on which she was sitting. Unfortunately, the puppy wouldn't be quiet. Within ten minutes the dog was on the street again, and Blaine had lain sobbing in bed until eleven, when her father, returning from a local bar and wondering what all the commotion was about, had retrieved the whimpering, frightened puppy from under a nearby tree and slipped it into Blaine's bed. Jim O'Connor spent the night on the couch for his trouble, and his wife hadn't spoken to him or Blaine for a week, but the puppy had stayed.

"You got another crank call," Caitlin repeated. "Blaine, answer me."

"How did you know?"

"I didn't think you'd suddenly become overwhelmed with a desire to hear 'Ring Around a Rosy.' Besides, I may not be Sherlock Holmes, but I can certainly make the connection between *Rosy* and *Rosie* Van Zandt."

"Okay." Blaine got to her feet. She was two inches taller than Cait and the added height often served to restore her sense of control in the face of her sister's sometimes disconcerting mimicking of their mother's aggressive mannerisms during an argument. "Someone *did* call and play that record several hours after we found Rosie. And before you say any more, let me tell you that I've already reported the call to Logan and had Call Trace put on my phone."

Cait at first looked troubled, then annoyed as she realized the significance of Blaine's search through her record collection. "You didn't think *I* made that call, did you?"

"Oh, Cait, of course not. But it was a child's song, and as Robin pointed out, dozens of people are in and out of here every day."

"Not *dozens*." Cait's face eased. "But a lot. It was a logical assumption that the record might have come from here, I guess. But I don't know who would do such a thing. The mothers of the kids are nice."

"Probably many of the people who called and accused me of murdering Martin seemed nice, too."

"I still say you shouldn't be in that house."

Blaine rolled her eyes. "Cait, Logan has a patrol car going by every hour."

"A patrol car? What for? It was suicide, wasn't it?" Cait watched Blaine turn and brush imaginary dirt from the back of her skirt. "Well, *wasn't* it?"

"No, it doesn't look that way," Blaine said reluctantly. "I mean, they're not sure, but—"

"That does it! You and Robin are coming back to my house."

"No, we're not. You and Kirk have put up with us enough—first with Kirk and coming out to the house all the time to help with Martin when he first came home from the hospital, then trying to get him used to the wheelchair, and later when I stayed with you when I was sick. Besides, you two need your privacy."

"We do not. We've been married for six years."

Blaine smiled. "Oh, well, in *that* case, Robin and I will bring sleeping bags and camp out in your bedroom."

"Sounds like an interesting idea to me," said a masculine voice.

Blaine looked around to see her brother-in-law in the doorway. He wore jeans and a plaid shirt, his sandy hair cut short, his gray eyes laughing in a face that might be called rugged if not classically handsome.

"Will you two stop making jokes!" Cait said hotly. "Kirk, the police have decided Rosie Van Zandt was murdered."

Kirk immediately sobered. "Murdered!"

"That's what they *think*," Blaine said. "They're not sure."

"I told her she and Robin should come back and stay with us."

"Maybe that would be a good idea," Kirk said.

"We're all right at home," Blaine insisted.

Caitlin told her husband, "She thinks they would be in the way of our privacy. Maybe she didn't notice, but when she was sick, you were hardly ever home in the evenings."

Blaine looked away, feeling uncomfortable. One of the reasons she didn't want to return to Cait and Kirk's home was the subtle tension she had noticed between them lately. Although she didn't know what was wrong, she knew that her and Robin crowding in on the couple wouldn't help.

Kirk shrugged. He was tall and heavily muscled, both from manual labor and from the weight training he'd done since high school. "We had some big orders, Cait. We were working late every night. But I'm home on time every evening now. I could look after everyone."

"Thanks, Kirk, but it really isn't necessary. We have a new security system, and as I told Cait, the police are watching our place pretty closely."

"The police?" Kirk seemed taken aback. "Well, I guess that's natural if they suspect a murder was committed on the property."

Blaine nodded. "Apparently a cheerleader at school, Kathy Foss, knows something about it, but she's not talking."

"You didn't tell me *that!*" Cait exploded.

"And I shouldn't have said anything now." Blaine could have bitten her tongue. "Anyway, Robin and I are okay. And your house *is* too crowded for all of us. We've already found that out. If you'd just let me loan you the money to buy that house on Townsend Street you both like so well . . ."

Cait's chin set. "You know we won't take a cent of your inheritance, even as a loan. But stop trying to change the subject. I don't know how you can even think about staying in that house after all that's happened."

"I have to go, Caity." Blaine put on her coat.

Cait sighed gustily. "Stubborn."

"Just like my sister."

"All right, if you're determined to go back to that spooky place, go right ahead."

"Thank you. I will."

"Kirk, can't you say something to change her mind?"

"I never try to change the mind of an O'Connor woman. It's hopeless."

"A wise man," Blaine said.

Cait managed a halfhearted smile. "Okay, I give up. But I'll ask the children tomorrow if any of them have a recording of 'Ring Around a Rosy.' "

Blaine leaned down and kissed her sister's cheek. "Thanks, kid. And don't worry about me."

"I just wish I didn't have to," Cait said softly as Blaine headed for the door.

2

Blaine glanced at the glowing digital numbers of the car clock. Six-fifty. She had forty minutes to drop off the pager Rick had left at her house last night and get to school for the talent show rehearsal.

She sighed, wishing she'd let someone else take over the direction of the talent show. She was already adviser of the student council and director of the senior-class play. Considering her recent illness, everyone on the faculty would have understood if she'd relinquished one activity for the year. But she'd wanted to prove she was fine again and willing to take on her share. Since Rosie's death, though, she'd felt drained. She did not need the talent show on top of everything else.

Blaine pulled up in front of the one-story brick apartment building Rick had moved into after his divorce. The porch lights glowed warmly against the night, and she went up the curving walkway littered with a few leaves brought down by a cool breeze. Rick opened the door of apartment number five, wearing a white terry-cloth robe, his wavy hair wet as if he'd just gotten out of the shower. "Blaine," he said with his warm smile. "This is a terrific surprise."

"Been looking for this?" she asked, holding up the pager.

"For about an hour this morning. Then I remembered where it was."

"And you didn't come to retrieve it because you wanted to lure me to your place."

Rick broke into laughter. "How well you know my evil intentions. Actually, I was just too tired to stop by your house for it this evening. I figured I'd survive without it until morning." Blaine handed him the pager, which he took, then grasped her wrist and pulled her into the apartment. "I have a Dutch apple pie fresh from the bakery. How about having a piece with some coffee?"

"My favorite pie fresh from the bakery," Blaine said in exaggerated suspicion. "What a coincidence."

"Not a coincidence. Careful planning. I knew you'd bring me the pager."

"That's what I thought." Blaine glanced around the dismal, cramped apartment, wondering as usual how Rick could stand it after living for four years in the big, beautiful Cape Cod home that now belonged to his ex-wife, Ellen. "Did you have a hard day?"

"Yeah, it was a long one," he said, "but nothing a good night's sleep can't fix. Now back to the original subject. How about I put on some coffee and we can each have a piece of that low-calorie pie?"

"Wish I could, but I've got to be going. I'm supervising the talent contest, and re-hearsals begin tonight at seven-thirty."

Rick tapped his forehead. "You've only mentioned that about ten times and I still forgot."

"Hard-working doctors are allowed to for-get important things like high school talent contests."

"Did you talk Robin into entering?"

"I don't know. As of this morning, she hadn't made up her mind. She's so shy."

"She'll have to get over that if she wants to perform publicly."

"She knows that. I hope she comes. I've scheduled a slot for her."

Rick looked at her closely. "Blaine, are you all right? You look kind of washed out."

Blaine forced a smile. "It's been a long day for me, too. I guess you heard the po-lice have decided Rosie Van Zandt was murdered."

"Yeah, I heard it at the hospital right be-fore I came home. The local grapevine doesn't miss much, you know. Maybe it would be best for you to move back in with Cait for a while."

"Oh, no, not you, too."

"You've already had this conversation with Cait, right?"

"Right. Rick, the house on Prescott Road is my home. I just got resettled. Besides, Cait's house is really too small for me and Robin *and* Ashley. The weeks I spent there after my accident were pretty uncomfortable. Also, I don't like horning in on them. Cait was very gracious, but I could tell Robin and Ashley and I were in her way."

"I understand, but aren't you afraid in that big house?"

"A little uneasy," she admitted, "but I'll get over it." She sighed and let Rick drape an arm around her shoulders. "You know, it was terrible to think of Rosie killing herself, but it's even worse to know she was murdered. And, of course, the students are in an uproar about it. One girl fainted when she heard the news."

"Who?"

"Kathy Foss. She's the head cheerleader."

"I've seen her at the games."

"She's hard to miss," Blaine said dryly.

"She collapsed in the hall during the noon hour. A crowd gathered around her and she woke up saying, 'Rosie, I was there and I *saw*.' Something like that, which really set off the students. They talked about it all afternoon, and like a fool, I told Cait."

Rick held her out from him and peered into her eyes. "Do you think the girl really knows something?"

"Yes, but when she completely regained consciousness, she wouldn't say another word."

"That's strange."

"Not if she's afraid to tell what she saw."

"Of course. I should have thought of that myself. Attribute my slowness to fatigue and severe sugar deprivation."

Blaine smiled. "Rick, considering the amount of sugar you consume, you should weigh a hundred pounds more than you do. I thought doctors knew all about nutrition."

"We do. We just don't always practice it."

Blaine smiled again, then glanced at her watch. "I *have* to go."

"Are you absolutely sure I can't talk you into pie and perhaps something even more sinfully delightful?"

"Such as what? Watching you doze on

the couch? Because, judging by the shadows around your eyes, I think you're going to be unconscious in half an hour."

"Maybe you're right. But one of these nights, when I'm not tired and you're not worrying about what everyone in town is saying about us . . ."

Blaine rolled her eyes and laughed. "Get some sleep, Romeo. We'll talk about gossip another time."

3

The talent show was being held at the school gymnasium, and Blaine felt a rush of excitement when she saw the participants already assembled in the building, some even practicing their routines. By nine o'clock, though, she was ready to scream and certain this would be the worst talent show in the school's history.

None of the students had wanted to go first, so she'd arbitrarily chosen Susie Wolfe, who accidentally flung her flame-tipped baton into a cluster of students standing near the stage and sent them shrieking across the gym floor. No one was hurt, and within seconds everyone broke into hysterical laughter while Susie broke into equally hysterical sobbing. It took Blaine fifteen minutes to get her settled down enough to try again.

Susie was followed by Dean Newman delivering a comedy routine that made people laugh only because it was so bad. Crestfallen, he relinquished the stage to a girl who sang "Raindrops Keep Fallin' on My Head" while holding up an umbrella and doing a thunderous tap dance that completely drowned out the music. Because two members of Tony Jarvis's rock band had already graduated and were therefore disqualified from participating, Tony went solo, performing a song he'd written called "Wherever You Are." Blaine had heard him practicing the song in the empty school auditorium before her pneumonia and thought it beautiful, but tonight it came out flat and uninspired. But then, she'd heard that Tony had been taken in by the police for questioning as soon as school was out that afternoon. Tonight he looked both sullen and tense— his olive-complexioned face tight, his lips pressed into a thin line. She was surprised he'd shown up at the rehearsal at all.

She was also surprised to see Kathy

Foss, who seemed to have recovered from her fainting spell. She looked fine and did a gymnastic routine to the Eagles' song "Witchy Woman." Kathy was indisputably good, but her routine was completely out of sync with the song, which Blaine was certain Kathy had chosen because it was seductive, not because she thought it was right for the act.

Shortly after her performance, John Sanders walked into the gym. He wore jeans and a well-cut raincoat, and Blaine couldn't help smiling at all the female eyes following him as he grabbed a folding chair and sat down beside her in front of the stage. "Do we have any budding show-business geniuses here?" he asked.

"No," Blaine said softly so the other students couldn't hear. "So far it's been pretty abysmal. Even Tony Jarvis isn't performing well."

"Police investigations will do that to you."

"You haven't been through another one, have you?"

"No, but I have this sinking feeling I will be."

"Don't be such a pessimist. What are you doing here, anyway?"

"Just thought I'd drop by and see if you're okay. You seemed pretty upset earlier today. I thought you might need someone to take over."

"That was sweet of you, but I'm fine. I just wish my name wasn't going to be listed as talent coordinator."

John laughed. "Most of the people who come to these things are parents of the performers, so you don't have to worry. They always think their kids are great."

"I hope so. Can you stay until the end?"

" 'Fraid not. I'm expecting a call from Sam, and since you're okay, I'd like to go home to get it."

"Oh, well," Blaine said with mock injury. "If you'd rather talk to the woman you love than watch all these stellar performances, I guess I understand."

"I would." John's smile faded. "But if you need me later, call. I mean it."

"Thanks, John."

After John left and Blaine had sat through two more extremely bad performances, Robin climbed up to the stage. Blaine had been thrilled to see her arrive with Susie earlier, but she was less thrilled with Robin's selection. Her head bowed, her hands visi-

bly shaking, she sat down at the grand piano and began Debussy's "Reverie." Although Blaine loved the song, she knew it
was wrong for the talent show. Robin's
teenaged audience was bored, talking and
milling around the gym while Robin forged
ahead, her cheeks growing redder by the
minute. Blaine felt miserable for her and
wondered if she'd been wrong to encourage
her to enter. Although Robin would vocifer-
ously deny it, the opinion of her peers was
vitally important to her, and their disdain
could shatter her fragile ego.

She finished and fled the stage while only
three people—Susie Wolfe, Dean Newman,
and Tony Jarvis—clapped for her. As Arletta
Stroud began flouncing around the stage lip
syncing Madonna's "Like a Virgin," Blaine
glimpsed Robin slinking out of one of the
side doors of the gym.

4

Kathy lingered in the stage wing while
Robin Avery played her classical number.
God, how boring, Kathy thought. Did anybody really *like* that kind of music? Judging
from the audience, no. Kathy smiled with

satisfaction. Nothing to worry about from Robin, no matter how talented all the teachers said she was, no matter how talented Rosie had always said she was.

Kathy stiffened, suddenly cold, although she was still perspiring from her strenuous gymnastic routine. If she couldn't decide what to do about Rosie, whether or not to go to the police, she was going to go crazy—stark raving crazy. And she was going to give something away to the wrong person. In fact, maybe she already had. God, nobody had let her alone after she fainted today! That was the dumbest thing she'd ever done in her life. But when Arletta had begun describing how Rosie might have died . . . Kathy thought of Rosie and closed her eyes, shuddering uncontrollably.

Just three months ago Rosie had been tutoring her in algebra. Kathy had been prepared to dislike her. Rosalind Van Zandt was so pretty and so smart. It was humiliating to have that calm, beautiful girl watch her struggle to understand the simplest formulas. But Rosie had never acted superior, and when Kathy completed her summer school class with a respectable C to make up for the F she'd received in the spring, Rosie seemed really thrilled. Since passing the course meant she could not only stay on the cheerleading squad but also still qualify for head cheerleader in the fall, Kathy was ecstatic and insisted on taking Rosie out to the new Mexican restaurant in town. It was over seafood chimichangas that the two of them had begun a cautious friendship.

Although Kathy knew she wasn't "book smart," as her parents said, she had an uncanny ability to read people, to sense their strengths and weaknesses, to know when they were hiding something, and it hadn't taken her long to figure out Rosie had a secret. Of course, it didn't take a genius to see how she'd pulled away from Robin Avery. Rosie never said anything negative about Robin, but Kathy wasn't interested anyway, because she didn't think Robin was the problem. The fact that she couldn't ferret out the truth, though, nearly drove her wild.

Finally, one evening a week earlier, when she'd been driving home from the drugstore, she'd seen Rosie's beautiful red convertible whipping out of town toward Prescott Road, and on impulse Kathy had followed her. She'd hung back the way they did on TV shows to make sure Rosie didn't see her, and watched as she turned off onto a gravel road and drove the car way back into the woods, then crossed the huge Avery lawn and used a key to open the front door. But there was no one home at the Avery house. Everyone knew Mrs. Avery and Robin were staying in town. Puzzled, Kathy had driven up on Prescott Road, turned around, and carefully pulled her car off the road, keeping it close enough to the trees to ensure it wouldn't be spotted from the house. Then she'd gone on foot to the north end of the Avery lawn.

Fifteen minutes later—cold, bored, and worried about missing her favorite situation comedy at nine o'clock—she'd been ready to head back to her car when she saw another car pulling onto the gravel road and gliding back into the woods. A few minutes later, a man crossed the lawn just as Rosie had earlier. Kathy peered at him, cursing the night. If it weren't for the bright moon, she wouldn't have seen him at all. She took a step forward, hoping to catch a clearer glimpse of his face, and when she did she was astounded. The front door opened, and Rosie was outlined in the faint glow coming from a dusk-to-dawn light. She threw her arms around the man's shoulders, then they both went inside, and the door closed firmly behind them. Kathy clapped a hand over her mouth to keep from letting out a whoop in the darkness. Rosie and him meeting in Mrs. Avery's house! God, what nerve Rosie had. But it made sense. This place really was out of the way. And luxurious. Actually, Rosie was being pretty smart. With Mrs. Avery gone, she stood very little chance of getting caught.

Smiling to herself, Kathy retraced her steps to her car. Somehow, her estimation of Rosie had gone up even higher. This was great! But she couldn't let Rosie know she'd followed her. No, that would make her lose Rosie's friendship, and suddenly that friendship was more important to Kathy than ever.

Without turning on her lights, she started her car and drove out onto Prescott Road. She had gone only a few hundred feet when a police cruiser bore down on her, siren wailing, lights flashing. Horrified, cursing to herself, Kathy had no choice but to pull over and sit there in full view of the house. She rolled down the window and waited until the young deputy sauntered up. "Your lights aren't on," he drawled. "Didn't anyone ever tell you it can be dangerous drivin' around with no lights?"

It took him ten minutes to check her license and write a warning, on which he'd included his phone number. The whole time his lights had flashed mercilessly over Kathy's car and blazed across the Avery lawn. Less than a week later Rosie was dead, and now Kathy knew she'd been murdered, no doubt by the guy she'd met at the Avery house—a guy who would have had to be deaf and blind not to have spotted Kathy's car in front of the house that night. Maybe he didn't know the car belonged to her. It had been awfully dark that night, and she didn't have the only Honda Civic in town. In that case, she was safe. But what if she went to the police, and they questioned him and let it slip who'd reported seeing him with Rosie, then let him go for lack of evidence? That kind of thing happened all the time. She'd seen it on TV a million times. Then she'd *really* be in danger. He'd be after her, trying to get revenge, afraid she knew more than she really did.

"I'm sorry about what happened today, Kathy. Will you wish me luck anyway?"

Kathy blinked and looked blankly at the

girl standing beside her wearing a petticoat
and midriff-baring top. God, Arletta Stroud
was trying to look like Madonna! Kathy almost burst into nervous laughter, but managed to keep herself under control long
enough to say "Good luck" and watch Arletta hurry out on the stage and begin her
bouncing dance. When one of the heavy
crosses on her necklace flew up and hit her
in the face, Kathy finally broke up. While
someone stopped the music and Arletta
checked to make sure she hadn't cracked a
tooth, Kathy peeped through a tear in the
curtain to see Mrs. Avery's reaction to *that*
performance, but she was lost in the shadows back near the bleachers. In fact, it
looked like just about everyone was gone.
Oh, well, it didn't matter. Arletta's attempt to
look sexy was a scream, and she was going
to look even dumber when everyone saw
her the night of the show. Maybe her routine
wasn't all that smooth, but her costume!
Just thinking about it gave Kathy a thrill,
and she felt like looking at it right now. She
knew she'd feel better if she looked at it.
Pretty clothes always made her feel better.

She'd had it made last month and didn't
dare leave it at home, where her mother

might find it. She'd be so scandalized she'd take the scissors to it, since she'd "found the Lord" a year ago, right after Kathy's older brother had been killed in a freak accident during a Marine training exercise. Mrs. Foss had encouraged him to join the Marines and now she felt guilty. Kathy's father had explained that to her, but it didn't make her mother's new religious fervor any easier to live with. So far she'd cut up other pieces of Kathy's clothing she thought were too revealing, and the two had running battles about Kathy's bleached hair and the short cheerleader's skirt she wore. If her mother had her way, Kathy would be in something down to her ankles. It was only because Kathy's father was on her side that she had been able to stay on the cheerleading squad at all.

Kathy went to the basement of the gym, the right half, which comprised the girls' locker room. She'd expected to see at least a couple of girls changing clothes for their acts, but apparently Arletta was the last to need a costume change. They'd started her number over, and "Like a Virgin" was still blaring upstairs.

The concrete felt cold under Kathy's feet.

She should have remembered to put on shoes—she was sure to snag her tights—but she didn't want to go back upstairs, where she'd left them, along with the jeans she'd worn over her leotard. Walking on tiptoe, she passed the showers, thrown into half shadow by the weak lights burning overhead. Someday Maintenance would have to knock themselves out and put some decent lights down here, she thought. In the daytime it was okay, when light came through the windows set high in the walls, but at night the place looked weird.

It looked very weird, as a matter of fact. Kathy paused and thought about forgetting the costume and rushing back upstairs. It was cold down here. Cold and gloomy. And she'd been so frightened all day.

But you're not going to give in to that, she silently reminded herself. Three minutes. That's all it'll take to check on my costume, and then I'll get the hell out of here.

Off the main locker room was a smaller room used mostly to store majorette and cheerleader paraphernalia. Kathy pushed the door open and flipped on the light, which consisted of a dusty single bulb suspended from the ceiling. She hesitated

again. She'd been in this little concrete-
block room many times and never thought
twice about it. But tonight the room seemed
full of new shadows. "Two minutes," she
said aloud, carefully closing the door behind
her. "This will take *two* minutes, that's all.
Then I'll know no one's ripped off my costume, and I won't have to worry about it on
top of everything else."

Along the far wall was an old dresser. It
had always looked out of place in this room
filled with metal wardrobes and storage
boxes, but since the top drawer had a lock,
it was a perfect hiding place. Kathy knelt
and felt for the key, which she had taped to
the underside of the dresser. She found it
and tore it loose from its tape. The lock of
the top drawer resisted the key at first.
Maybe there was too much stickiness left
from the tape, she thought. Finally the key
turned reluctantly and she pulled out the
drawer, which creaked loudly. There lay her
costume, untouched. She lifted it out, de-
lighting in how the black sequins sparkled
even in the dull light. Cut high over the
thighs and low at the neck, it was absolutely
dazzling! She loved it. She'd be a knockout

at the talent contest. They wouldn't forget her act any time soon!

Suddenly a click behind her indicated the door was being opened. She went rigid. Probably some nosy girl trying to see what she was up to, Kathy thought, but the answer *felt* wrong. Then the door closed. An intuitive thrill of fear rushed through her body like a deluge of freezing water, and she stood rooted to the floor, absolutely unable to turn around. She'd never had this sensation in her whole life. She was quick and athletic, but now she stood immobile, eyes wide, the costume clutched to her chest. It seemed she could hear her heart thudding behind her ribs. It also seemed she could hear a second heart thudding, but not with fear.

Something furry crossed her feet with a soft, feathery movement and she dropped the costume. A mouse. It squeaked shrilly and ran on its way as Kathy finally found her voice and shrieked, involuntarily stepping back toward the door. That was when the arm locked around her neck. "I've been waiting to get you alone," a hoarse voice whispered in her ear. "I saw you come down here."

Kathy went rigid as blood drained from her face. She managed a weak scream, although her throat was constricted by a strong arm, but "Like a Virgin" boomed on upstairs. "No one can hear you. Anyway, I have to do this, so we might as well get it over with."

Mindless with fear, Kathy let her instinct take over, and she clawed the arm, then kicked backward with a strong leg. "Damn!" the grip loosened. Kathy raised her leg, preparing to kick again, but something slammed against the right side of her head. She went down without a sound. She was so stunned she couldn't move, but she was aware. She saw a figure bending over her and felt a needle jabbing into the muscle of her arm. "No! Please don't kill me," she begged, her fists clenching spasmodically. A relentless hand held her down against the cold concrete floor. The mouse, she thought. The mouse will chew on me just like the animals did on Rosie. A tear rolled down her cheek. The stinging in her arm subsided, and she knew the needle had been removed. Whatever had been injected, though, was creeping through her body, traveling along the blood vessels like some deadening, insidious vine. "Please," she muttered. "Please don't . . . Won't tell . . ."

"I know you won't. Not now you won't."

I can't believe I'm going to die in this horrible little room, Kathy thought. I can't believe, I can't believe—

She felt something cold and sharp pressing against the back of her neck. A knife. "No, not that," she said, slurring her words.

"Afraid of knives? Don't be. I'll wait until the drug takes effect."

"Hurt . . ."

"You think I'm waiting because I don't want to hurt you? I don't give a damn whether I hurt you or not, you stupid little slut. I just want to make sure you don't go running upstairs with your wrists bleeding. They might get you to the hospital before you bleed to death."

"Don't want to die . . ."

The hand was released, and Kathy was able to lift her head from the floor. Her legs and arms, however, felt leaden. She couldn't possibly get to her feet, or even her knees. Her breathing was becoming more shallow, and she felt herself drooling. Then she vomited.

"Christ! How disgusting!"

Kathy tried to keep her head elevated, but she couldn't. Her face fell back into the vomit and she choked, although she was still fighting to keep her mind focused.

She was getting very sleepy, but she was aware of the minutes ticking away. In some stubbornly attentive corner of her mind, she could almost feel them ticking away. But time wasn't helping. Time was only making everything fuzzier, more unreal. She felt as if she were floating.

The music pounded above her. On and on. If they'd stop the music, maybe she could scream. *Maybe* someone would hear her. But the music wouldn't stop.

I can't believe . . . Kathy thought vaguely one last time. I can't believe I'm really going to die like this. Then a hand lifted her left wrist and deftly drew the knife gently across the fragile white flesh and blue veins. Blood oozed out and Kathy moaned.

"I don't know why blood makes most people so nervous. It's in all of us."

"No. No, please . . ." The knife was raised again and this time it gouged, going for the artery, but Kathy barely felt it.

9

1

Arletta threw her arms in the air, flung herself to the right, and landed on the stage floor with a flat-footed thud. The music stopped, and she peered out into the darkness. "So whaddya think, Miz Avery?" She squinted. "Miz Avery, are you there?"

Blaine reentered the gym and called, "All done, Arletta?"

"All *done?* Weren't you even watchin'?"

"I stepped out to the rest room for a minute, that's all."

"In the middle of my *dance?*"

Arletta's voice, always high-pitched and twangy, now seemed to screech through the echoing expanse of the gym.

"Arletta, you started over five times. I just couldn't wait. I'm sorry. In any case, I have a suggestion," Blaine said, walking nearer the stage. "Two of the talent contest judges are older teachers. I'm not sure they'd approve of the lyrics of this song. You might do better with something else."

"But, Miz Avery, this is my very favorite song," Arletta wailed. "My very, very *favorite!*"

"Yes, but . . ." Blaine trailed off, thinking. It wouldn't matter if Arletta sang something from *The Sound of Music*—she didn't stand a chance of winning, so why not let her do what she wanted? "Okay. But how about getting rid of some of the crosses?"

Arletta's little eyes flew open in horror, and she grabbed one of the crosses as if she thought Blaine was going to tear it off her. "But this is the kind of stuff Madonna wore back when she was gettin' started. Honest, Miz Avery, she *did*."

"I know, Arletta. Despite my advanced age, I've seen some music videos. It's just that one of those crosses is going to break your nose."

"I *have* to wear these great big old crosses. To look *real*, ya know? To look like Madonna did. Please, Miz Avery? I'll practice so they don't fly up."

"It's your routine," Blaine said, too tired to argue with the girl any longer. She felt like she'd just run a marathon. "If you want to take a chance on injuring yourself, go right ahead."

"I'll be better by Thursday night's rehearsal, *honest*, I will!"

Blaine forced a smile. "All right. Whatever you want."

As Arletta took her album off the record player and went backstage to pick up her coat, Blaine slipped on her all-weather coat and found her purse, looking for the gym keys inside. Really, she was going to have to clean out her purse. It probably weighed five pounds with all the stuff she carried around.

Arletta's parting smile and pleasant " 'Night, Miz Avery" couldn't hide the resentful glare in her eyes. Blaine knew the girl thought she was picking on her. Maybe she was. There was no doubt Arletta had the same effect on her as nails scraping a blackboard, but she couldn't help being an annoying fool. She came by it naturally. Suddenly Blaine wished she hadn't mentioned the song *or* the jewelry, although if tonight's performance was any indication, Arletta would probably knock herself out onstage during the talent contest. Still, she determined to be kinder to the girl from now on. Arletta was doing her best.

Blaine glanced at her watch. Ten-ten. Had she really been in the gym less than three hours? It seemed like six. Sighing, she went downstairs to the boys' locker room to turn off the lights. Then she came upstairs, crossed in front of the stage, and descended once again to the girls' locker room. She had her hand on the light switch when a sensation of not being alone overcame her. She paused. From where she stood she could even look into the doorless shower stalls. "Anyone still here?" she called, exasperated by the high, thin timbre of her voice. She cleared her throat and said in a more normal tone, "I'm closing up now. Unless you want to spend the night locked up in here, you'd better get a move on." But the words were unnecessary. She could see for herself that the room was empty. She flipped off the light and hurried back upstairs, deciding that fatigue and the shock of Rosie's death were making her feel all kinds of prickles and chills. Still, she didn't like being in the gym alone.

She turned out the gymnasium floor lights, then moved through the lobby, where

bright light bounced dully off the metal clo-
sures hiding concession windows. After ex-
tinguishing the lobby lights, she went outside and firmly shut the glass entrance
doors, inserting her key in the lock. Normally one of the school's two janitors was
paid extra to handle the locking up, but one
was out with the flu, and the wife of the
other was expecting a baby any day and
afraid to be alone at night. Blaine shook the
door, making sure it was locked securely.

The night had turned damply cold, the
moon glimmering faintly through a shroud
of thin, ragged clouds, the stars invisible.
Blaine pulled her lined raincoat tighter as
wind rustled across the big parking lot,
picking up dead, brittle leaves and tossing
them against the school buildings and her
car. Or rather, her car and the white Honda
Civic still sitting in the lot. She frowned. Of
course, the Honda could belong to someone who had business in the main building,
but she couldn't think of who that would be.
Certainly not the principal or vice-principal,
whose cars she knew. And if she remembered correctly, Jean Lewis, the school secretary, drove a Buick.

Curious, Blaine strode past her own car

and went to the Civic. Peering through the window, she saw a three-ring notebook and a tattered geography book on the front seat. A student's car, no doubt. She circled to the front of it and stooped down to look at the vanity plate.

KATHY

Kathy Foss, of course. Blaine rose with a sudden feeling of alarm. No wonder she hadn't felt alone in the gym—Kathy was probably still there. Maybe she had fainted again and was now locked in for the night.

Blaine hurried back to the building, wondering if she should call the emergency squad. What if Kathy had hurt herself when she fell? But she was only guessing that Kathy had fainted. Maybe she was just playing a game. Maybe she thought she'd have an exciting story to tell about the terror-filled night she'd spent trapped in the big, shadowy building. Or maybe she was trying to get back at Blaine for reprimanding her earlier today for tardiness. True, such antics would be extreme, even for Kathy, but Blaine hoped one was the explanation for the girl's disappearance.

Blaine unlocked the front doors and went through the lobby, turning on the lights. Then she flipped more light switches, and the large main room of the gym blossomed with light that seemed even brighter as it reflected off the varnished gym floor. "Kathy!" she called. "Kathleen! Are you here!"

No answer came. Blaine hesitated, then went back to the pay phone in the lobby. She would call Logan. After all that had happened, he would understand her uneasiness and not spread word around town about the incident if it turned out to be nothing but a teenager's prank. She looked up his home phone number in the ragged phone book and inserted coins. They clicked back into the return cup. She put them in again, and the same thing happened. So the phone was broken. As usual.

Sighing in frustration, she slammed down the receiver. Now what? Should she take the time to drive to Logan's house? Of course not. Kathy could be in serious trouble. She would have to do something herself.

She took a step into the gym and stopped. There they were—those weird prickles in the area of her neck. In books those prickles always resulted from the character's atavistic awareness of danger, but she wasn't living a book. She pushed down the uncomfortable sensation and walked across the gym floor. "Kathy! If you can hear me, please yell."

Again nothing. She stopped in front of the stage. The girl had to be downstairs. Although Blaine had already checked down there once, she hadn't looked in every nook and cranny, and the upstairs was so brightly lit, there was no place where Kathy wouldn't be visible.

Blaine pulled the belt of her coat even tighter, as if it could give her the strength to do something she didn't want to do. But she told herself she was being silly. Going back down to the locker room was a pain, but not a cause for dread. She couldn't let nerves get the best of her when a girl might be lying down there unconscious, maybe hurt if she'd struck her head on something. Blaine walked with determination to the concrete stairs, flipped on more lights, and descended.

The locker room looked exactly the same as it had fifteen minutes ago, the showers gleaming, the big locker doors shut. "Kathy," she called again. Her voice cracked.

She drew in a sharp breath. Something was wrong in this room. Maybe those horror writers so often mention atavistic fears because they exist, she thought distantly. They must exist, because my spine feels like an icicle, and there is not one tangible thing in this room to fear. A clean, semi-well-lighted place, that's what it is. So why is my pulse pounding in my abdomen? Why do I feel like I'm rooted to the floor?

Because the air seems leaden, she thought. Because there's a weird, coppery smell down here I've never noticed before. Because I *know* I'm not alone in here.

Her breath quickening, she looked around nervously. Gray-painted concrete floor. Five white sinks along the wall. Two commodes sitting in stalls whose doors gaped open, leaving no room for anyone to hide. Open, tiled shower stalls. Long wooden benches opposite the sinks and showers. A thirty-foot stretch of massive old lockers that had been moved here when new, compact ones were installed in the main building. Nothing was wrong. Absolutely nothing was—

Blaine's heart slammed against her ribs. Lockers. The locker halfway down the line. Something was streaming out the bottom of it. Something red.

Blaine stared in amazement and horror at the red pool forming on the floor. Bigger and bigger it grew. She moaned softly. Then, powered by a compulsion she later didn't understand, she walked to the locker and opened the door. A rush of blood and the body of Kathleen Foss tumbled out, her dead azure eyes staring right into Blaine's.

2

She was hyperventilating. Her hand, slick with perspiration, slipped on the phone receiver as someone said, "Hello? Is anyone there?"

Logan's mother. Blaine recognized her distinctive voice, although she hadn't heard it for years. "Mrs. Quint, it's Blaine O'Connor. Avery. Is Logan there?" she gasped.

"Yes, Blaine. Are you all right?"

"Tell him to come to the high school."

"What's that?"

"High school. A girl's been murdered."

"What! Blaine—"

"Tell Logan. Come to the high school."

She drew a long, shuddering breath and hung up, looking at the phone as she fought for air. Thank God she had insisted on installing a phone in her car after Martin's accident so she could check on him anytime she wasn't home. Earlier, before she searched the gym, she had even forgotten it was in the car. Memory block? she wondered now. Did she associate the phone so much with Martin's paralysis that she didn't *want* to remember it? Did she recall all the times she'd called home to have Bernice tell her Martin was shut in his study, writing in the notebooks that had become his obsession four months after the accident? To Blaine, that had seemed like another sign of his deteriorating mental state—his preoccupation with those damned notebooks he kept locked in a drawer, then burned before he died. Yes, that must be it, she told herself. There was also the fact that she hadn't used the car phone since Martin's death.

Death. She squeezed her eyes shut, then

snapped them open again, checking to make sure both car doors were locked as she sat huddled in the school parking lot. Kathy was dead, just like Rosie. Judging from the amount of blood that flooded out of the locker with her body, she must have bled to death.

Feeling faint again, Blaine leaned forward, putting her head between her knees as well as she could beneath the steering wheel. It's very dangerous for me to be sitting here like this, she thought. But I can't drive in this condition, and I should wait for Logan. If only he'd hurry.

She thought of Robin alone in the big house and her head snapped up, striking painfully on the steering wheel. She picked up the phone receiver again. Robin answered on the third ring.

"Are you all right?" Blaine asked immediately.

"You mean after my riveting performance at the rehearsal? Sure. But you don't sound so good. Where are you?"

"Still at school. Listen, Robin, something has happened—"

"What?"

"I'll explain later. Now, I want you to make

sure the doors are locked and turn on the security system."

"Why?"

I can't tell her, Blaine thought. Not now. "As I said, I'll be a little later than expected, and I just want to make sure you're safe."

"Well, the doors *are* locked."

"Good. I also want you to put the lock panel on the dog door in the kitchen."

Robin paused, then spoke with an edge of fear in her voice. "Is that because you don't want Ashley to go out or you don't want someone getting in?"

"Just do it, Robin."

"All right. But I wish you'd tell me what's going on. You're scaring me."

"I have to go now."

"Blaine!"

She hung up and sat shivering as she watched the digital car clock click away six minutes. Nervous reaction to finding Kathy's body, coupled with fear of who might come bursting out of the gym after her, made her decide she couldn't sit in the parking lot much longer. If Logan didn't come soon—

A police car pulled into the lot. Blaine suddenly felt tears of relief streaming down her face. She quickly wiped them away before she stepped out of the car.

Logan jumped out of his vehicle and strode toward Blaine. "Who is it?" he asked tersely.

"Kathy Foss." As another police car flashed into the lot, she fumbled in her left coat pocket and handed him the gym key. "Girls' locker room. She was stuffed in a locker."

Logan's eyes widened slightly, but other than that, he showed no reaction. As usual in times of emergency, he was all business.

"Also, my stepdaughter is in the house alone," Blaine added. "Please have a policeman go out there and stay with her."

Logan nodded. "I will, and later I'll need to ask you some questions, but right now I want *you* to go home."

"No, I want to wait."

"Blaine—"

Too ashamed to admit she still didn't trust her driving, Blaine nearly shouted, "I want to wait!"

Logan looked thoroughly irritated. "You've always been the most obstinate woman I know! All right, dammit, get in your car and lock the doors. I'll be back out as soon as possible, and *then* you'll go home. Under-stand?"

Blaine complied meekly. Watching in the rearview mirror, she saw Logan go back to his car, obviously sending someone to the Avery home. Then he and the deputy drew their guns as they approached the gym and stepped into the bright lobby. Although she had instinctively locked the door on her way out, she had left lights blazing throughout the building.

The wind had picked up, sending the tat-tering of clouds sailing across the face of the moon. Also, the temperature was drop-ping. She started the car and turned the heater on high, although she knew her chill was only partly caused by the temperature outside.

She glanced in the rearview mirror again, then closed her eyes. I seem always to be waiting for the police to look at a body, Blaine thought. The first time was Martin. She had sat in the house on the couch, her mouth dry, her hands shaking violently as she clutched Ashley, who remained staunchly by her side. She couldn't remem-ber how many people had arrived after Lo-gan came—she only remembered their impersonal voices discussing the position of the body, the nature of the gunshot wound, arrangements for an autopsy. And then Robin had come home. Blaine physically tried to keep the girl from looking at her father, but she tore away from Blaine and ran to the deck. She let out one thin scream before she lapsed into a silence that lasted for nearly twenty-four hours.

Someone tapped on the window and Blaine nearly shrieked. Catching her breath, she rolled down the window. "Found her," Logan said, sounding exactly as he had the night they had located Rosie's body. "Tell me what happened here tonight."

Blaine swept her hair behind her ears and looked straight ahead, concentrating. "It was the first night of the talent show rehearsals. Kathy was one of the last five people to perform. Arletta Stroud was last, and she had to keep starting over. I didn't think she'd ever finish, and by the time she did, all the other kids had left. I checked around before I closed the gym. I thought it was empty. Then I came out here and spotted Kathy's car."

Logan nodded, writing in a small notebook. "So you went back in after her?"

"Certainly. I couldn't take a chance on leaving her locked in the gym all night. I thought she might be hurt."

"Hurt?"

"She fainted today. Then she woke up saying something about Rosie and being there, knowing what happened. It's all a jumble in my head right now, but I should have called you as soon as it happened."

"I already knew. Arletta called Abel this afternoon to tell him. She probably told half the town."

"Which probably got Kathy killed. Did you question Kathy?"

"No. Every time we called her house, her mother said she was out and she didn't know where she was. I got the feeling she wasn't telling the truth, so I planned to catch Kathy at school tomorrow. Blaine, if you thought Kathy knew something about the murder, if you thought she might be lying in the gym hurt, why didn't you call me or someone else at the sheriff's office? Why did you go back in there alone?"

"I tried to call, but the pay phone in the gym is broken. All other phones are in offices that were locked. And believe it or not, I simply forgot about the phone in my car."

"You forgot about it?"

"I know that sounds strange, but I haven't used it for a long time. I didn't even pay the bill this month. I guess for once the phone company was a little slow, or it wouldn't be working. I was so worried I didn't even think to give it a try." She clasped her cold hands together, aware of how lame her explanation sounded. Just about as lame as her claiming she'd decided to go shopping the Saturday afternoon that Martin died. On the advice of her lawyer, she'd never admitted they'd had a terrible fight that had driven her from the house. But she couldn't think about that murder investigation now, not when Logan was looking at her once again as if he were trying hard to believe her but couldn't. "Was Kathy drugged like Rosie?" she asked abruptly.

"Can't tell. We'll have to wait for the autopsy. But those *wrists*—" He shook his head. "Her hands were almost severed from her arms."

"Oh, God."

"It happened in that little room where the cheerleader and majorette gear is stored. Big pool of blood there. The blood that dripped between the room and the locker

was wiped up with some kind of black, sequined costume we found on a hook in the
locker."

Blaine shivered. "Logan, that's grotesque!
Why would someone drag her to the
locker?"

"Maybe the killer didn't know how late
you'd have to stay with Arletta and was
afraid you'd check the little room before you
left the gym and find Kathy before she'd
had time to bleed to death."

"If only Arletta hadn't taken so long! I
would have checked the locker room earlier—"

"And probably gotten yourself murdered,
too."

Blaine leaned forward, resting her forehead on the steering wheel. "Oh, Logan,
just today I came down hard on Kathy for
chewing gum."

"Sounds serious."

There was a trace of humor in Logan's
voice, and Blaine looked up at him. "How
can you laugh?"

"I'm not laughing, but you have to put
that incident in perspective. She probably
never gave it a second thought."

"Maybe not." Blaine sighed. "How did the killer get in?"

"One of the locker room doors leading to the outside is unlocked."

"But, Logan, *I* didn't unlock any of those doors!"

"Any of the kids could have. Maybe not the killer—maybe he just hit it lucky—but I'll need from you a list of everyone who was here tonight."

"Okay. That should be easy. Are you going to call in the state police?"

"Not yet."

"Not *yet?*"

"I do have a degree in criminal justice, Blaine, and I worked on a couple of big police forces before I came here. I know what I'm doing. I don't want any interference right now."

At that moment the ambulance pulled into the parking lot, lights flashing. A patrol car arrived about thirty seconds later. "I hate that sight," Blaine murmured.

"So do I, but Sinclair's crime lab has arrived." Logan looked at her, his dark eyes lifeless. "I have to get this area secured, and you need to go home."

"Yes."

"Want someone to go with you?"

Blaine shook her head. "I can make it alone."

"That's what you said to me twelve years ago when you left for Dallas."

Blaine glanced at him in surprise. "I can't believe you remember my exact words."

Logan stared at her for a few seconds. "Go home, Blaine."

3

It was after twelve when Logan got home. He quietly opened the door to the three-bedroom, white frame house and stepped inside, stopping to listen for a moment. The listening was an old habit he'd acquired in the early years of his marriage when Dory so often waited up for him watching television. But no sounds floated from the family room at the back of the house. Of course they wouldn't. Dory had been gone for five weeks this time, and Logan's mother, who had moved in to look after Timothy during Dory's absence, was always in bed by eleven.

Logan walked softly down the hall to his

room. He was stopped, however, by his son calling, "Daddy?"

Logan walked into the small room decorated with posters of *Star Wars* and Jean-Claude Van Damme, his son's current hero, although he'd only seen the less violent snatches of Van Damme's movies. The posters shone dimly in the glow of the night-light. Timothy sat up in his twin bed, his black hair awry. "What are you doing still awake?" Logan asked, going to sit on the bed. "Tomorrow's a school day."

"I know. But I had a dream, Daddy. Grandma told me it was important for us Indians to tell our dreams, so you want to hear mine?"

Logan smiled. His mother, called Allie although her real name was Alequippa, was a full-blooded Iroquois determined that her only grandson would learn about the old ways, even if he chose not to follow them. Timothy had embraced some of the traditions fervently, one being the belief that dreams were the universal oracle, capable of revealing the dreamer's guardian spirit, warning him about enemies, and predicting his destiny. At one time, every morning Indian mothers had questioned their children in great detail about their dreams.

"Okay, Tim, tell me what you dreamed."

Timothy crossed his arms across his thin chest, puckered his forehead, and began talking in a hushed, dramatic voice. "Well, I was out in the woods, just foolin' around. Then all at once this big gold dog came runnin' out of the trees and started barkin' at me. Its hair was all tangled, but I petted it anyways, and it seemed to like that, but when I stopped pettin' and started to go down this path in the woods, it wouldn't let me. It grabbed my jeans leg and started pullin'. I didn't know what was goin' on at first. Then I knew the dog was tryin' to tell me somethin' bad was in the woods, so I followed the dog away. We both ran and ran. And sure enough, there was a great huge *monster* in the woods! It was comin' for me and the dog saved me!"

Logan reached out and ruffled his son's hair. "Tim, that's the beginning of *Watchers*."

"Huh?"

"The book *Watchers* by Dean Koontz. Last year you found the book and brought it to your mother. She read the first part to you, but not all of it, because you got scared when the monster appeared."

"I wasn't one bit scared!" Tim said stoutly.

Actually, Tim had burst into tears at the description of the hideous monster who stalked the dog, but Logan knew how important pride was to the little boy. "Well, I guess Mommy was mistaken about you being scared. But, son, the dream *was* about a book. It wasn't a forecast of the future."

Timothy looked dismal. "Then there's no big gold dog that's gonna protect me?"

"Not that I know of."

"Shoot." The child turned to look out the window at the brown pine tree right outside. "My birthday tree's dyin'."

"I know, Tim. We'll plant a new one."

Timothy's voice piped up hopefully. "As soon as Mommy gets home?"

"Sure."

"When *is* Mommy comin' home?"

"Real soon, I'm sure."

"What you mean is you don't know. What if she doesn't get home for Thanksgivin'?" Timothy's voice rose in distress. "What if she doesn't get home for *Christmas?*"

Logan's voice tightened. "She'll be here for Christmas, son." She'll be here if I have to drag her back from New Mexico by that beautiful, long blond hair she's so proud of, he thought. "You know your mother wouldn't miss Christmas with you."

"She missed Halloween. Next to Christmas, that's my favorite time, and she didn't come."

"But we did fine, didn't we? You looked like a real Indian chief in that costume your grandmother made."

"Yeah, I did. But real Indian chiefs aren't named Timothy. I wish I had a real Indian chief's name like you."

Logan looked at him seriously. "Well, your mother and I did consider calling you Cornstalk. How would you have liked that?"

"Not too good." Timothy giggled.

"Sitting Bull was also a possibility. Either that or Crazy Horse."

Timothy was convulsed. "Ugh!"

"What's that? Indian talk?" Timothy fell on his side, laughing into his pillow.

"Actually, the Logan I'm named after was really called Tah-gah-yee-tah. Logan is what he started calling himself because white men couldn't say his name right."

"But he was a chief, just like you!"

Logan smiled. "I'm a sheriff, son, not a chief."

"But you're the chief of all the other police."

"I guess. But Logan wasn't even really a chief—just a leader."

"A leader of the Six Nations!"

"Well, of the members of the Six Nations who decided to move south from New York."

"And Logan was a friend of the white man till his *whole* family got treach'rously murdered by an evil guy. Then he seeked revenge. Grandma told me."

"Did she?"

"Yep. He didn't have any rel'tives left."

A voice rang out behind them. " 'There runs not a drop of my blood in the veins of any living creature.' " The voice returned to normal tones. "Logan said that in his most famous speech."

Logan turned to face his mother, who stood in the doorway, tall and slim in her white robe. Her hair, barely touched by gray, was pulled back into a braid that hung to her waist. She didn't look very different from the pictures taken before her marriage, when she'd lived on the St. Regis Reservation in upper New York. Logan's father met her when as a young man he'd left Sinclair and gone to New York City to do bridge construction work; there he'd become friends with one of his co-workers, Allie's brother. They'd married months within meeting and come back to Sinclair, where Allie seemed happy, although she was considered somewhat of an oddity in the town's predominantly WASP population. She smiled and came into the room. "How can anyone sleep with all this hilarity going on next door?"

"Sorry we woke you, Mother," Logan said. "I just got in."

Her dark eyes studied his. "Was it very bad?"

"Yes."

She nodded. "You get some sleep. I'll tell my grandson wonderful stories until he drifts off again."

"Thanks, Mother," Logan said.

He bent to kiss Timothy, who murmured, "Are you *sure* there's no big gold dog that's gonna save me?"

"I don't think so."

"I'm gonna ask Grandma anyway," Timothy said. "She knows more about this stuff than you do."

Logan laughed. "She knows more about a lot of things than I do, son. Good night. See you in the morning."

In his own room, Logan undressed and took a shower in the master bathroom. He was appalled to see little flecks of blood on his neck and face, flecks of Kathy's blood that had somehow gotten on him when he put the black sequined costume in the evidence bag. He was glad the light in Timothy's room had been dim. The last thing that little kid needed to see was something else to upset him. He was upset enough about his mother.

With only a towel wrapped around his waist, Logan went to his dresser drawer and withdrew the letter he'd received from Dory yesterday. It was written on scented paper, and she'd drawn a little picture of a cactus on top.

Hi, darling,
    The weather is simply glorious here in Taos. But the feeling I get goes beyond the weather. I feel that I'm among

my own kind. Writers. There is so much creativity in the air, it's positively heady.

I hope you and Timmy are getting along all right. I really hated to leave you again, but I had to for my own sanity. I want to be a good wife. I want to be a good mother. But sometimes it's so *hard*. I get so nervous. I feel that if you get called out at night just one more time when we have something planned, or if Timmy wants me to play with him or help with his homework when I'm trying to work on a story, I will simply *scream*. And I might do something worse.

Oh, I don't mean to sound so depressing. I'm feeling so much better, really I am. And I'll come home as soon as I can, darling. I'll come home when I feel strong and whole and *capable* again. In the meantime, love to you, and give Timmy a great big kiss from his mommy.

"Why don't you try coming home and giving him one yourself?" Logan muttered, crumpling the letter in his hand. Six times. Six times now Dory had declared she "couldn't cope" and taken off. But she'd never stayed this long. And she'd called before. She'd sent little cards to Timothy before. This time there had been nothing but this one letter.

He remembered when he had met Dory. The daughter of a wealthy Chicago businessman, Wilson Whitfield, she had met Logan when, on a lark, she had come with friends to West Virginia's Snowshoe ski area. Over his Christmas break, Logan had been waiting tables at a restaurant there, trying to make enough money to pay for his last semester of college, and he'd spotted Dory. Her coloring was different, but there was something about her—the way she laughed, her tall slimness, the shape of her large eyes—that reminded him of Blaine, who'd left two years earlier for Dallas. He understood why she left, but the pain of her departure had never eased. And finally there was Dory, who was entranced with him— mostly, he realized now, because she was temporarily fascinated by Indian culture, but also because she wanted to get back at her father, who'd recently divorced his loving yet unstable wife, the mother Dory adored. In return, Dory happily dashed Wilson Whitfield's great expectations of his lovely daughter's marrying into the "right" kind of rich, socially acceptable family by marrying Logan.

The first two years of their marriage had been fine—not wonderful, not what Logan had hoped for, but fine. Then Tim was born, and suddenly Dory began to act like a caged animal. They'd tried living in San Francisco, but Dory claimed she was afraid of earthquakes and longed for life on the East Coast, so when Tim was one, they moved to Miami. There she claimed she was surrounded by rampant crime, along with too many drugs coming in from the Caribbean. She didn't want her little boy raised in that environment, she said. Now she wanted the beautiful, lush hills of West Virginia, where they'd met. Life was slower and quieter there. So four years ago they'd come back to Sinclair. Six months later, she told him she felt stifled, terminally bored. He'd explained that they couldn't keep moving. That was when the arguments started, gradually escalating until Tim had begun to creep around fearfully, frequently burst into tears, and sometimes run away from home, convinced he was the cause of

the trouble. Logan had then insisted on psy-
chiatric help for Dory, and that was when
her vanishing acts began. In the last year,
Logan had finally admitted to himself that
Dory wasn't cut out to be a mother. In fact,
he didn't think she was cut out to be a wife,
especially not the wife of a cop. She needed
constant companionship, constant enter-
tainment, but not the kind that could be provided by a middle-class working husband
and a little boy.

He didn't hate Dory. He felt sorry for the
restless, unhappy spirit that wouldn't allow
her peace of mind. But how could he have
ever thought she was like the strong, determined Blaine O'Connor he'd loved since
childhood? And how could he have ever
thought she'd be a good mother, the kind of
mother Blaine was trying to be to a stepdaughter who didn't even like her very
much, from what he'd observed? "Rebound," he said aloud. "They call what happened between you and Dory love on the
rebound."

Logan threw the crumpled letter into his
wastebasket and gazed at himself in the
mirror. I look five years older than I am, he
thought. I'm tired and I'm defeated. And

now all this hell has broken loose. Dory's gone again, my son is in terrible emotional pain, and I've got two slaughtered girls on my hands. And there's Blaine. What do I make of Blaine?

He sighed, wondering what the odds were of a woman once suspected of murder finding two dead girls in less than one week.

4

A police cruiser sat in the driveway when Blaine arrived home. She went inside to find Robin perched stiffly on the couch, making uncomfortable conversation with the young Deputy Clarke they had come to know during the investigation of Martin's death.

"What happened?" Robin immediately demanded.

Blaine tossed her purse down and sank into a chair. "Kathy Foss was murdered in the gym tonight."

Robin stared at her as if she'd just said Martians had landed. Clarke stiffened, his green eyes narrowing. "Are you sure?"

"Of course I'm sure. Sheriff Quint is at the gym now. He said Kathy's wrists had been slashed."

"I've got to get there!" Clarke said, almost crackling with the electricity of excitement. "Will you two be all right?"

Blaine felt that even if she'd said no, Clarke would have left anyway. However, she nodded, and he bolted out the front door.

"I knew someone was dead," Robin said dully after he left. "I knew when you called that someone else had been murdered."

The girl's long hair was pulled back in a pony tail still damp from a shower she must have taken shortly before Clarke arrived. She didn't look at Blaine. "Robin, did you see anyone at the gym tonight who shouldn't have been there?"

"Just the contestants. And you. And Mr. Sanders."

"That's all?"

"Yes. So which one of us did it?"

"*None* of us," Blaine said.

"Yeah, sure."

Hiding behind sarcasm and flippancy again, Blaine thought. But she was too tired and too shaken to attempt to draw the girl out. Tonight *she* needed some attention, some caring, but she certainly couldn't expect it from Robin.

Ashley, who had given her an ecstatic greeting when she got home, began sniffing at her curiously. Blaine looked at her hands, which had opened the locker door where Kathy had been hidden. Without another word, she left Robin to her sullen silence and went to the bathroom, where she stripped off all her clothes, threw them in the bathtub, and stepped into the shower stall, lathering over and over, washing her hair twice, until she felt clean again. Afterward she wrapped herself in a long, warm robe, picked up her clothes using a towel to cover her hands, and threw everything into the washing machine, adding bleach to the detergent.

At last she went back into the living room, now deserted by Robin, and poured herself a glass of wine. She sat down on the couch, Ashley beside her. She'd left the draperies open on the wall of windows at the back of the living room, and as she gazed out at the chilly, dark night, she was suddenly seized with the feeling that someone was out there, staring back. She shot across the room, drawing the draperies shut with such force she set them swinging. Ashley leaped up and chased after Blaine, sensing alarm. She tilted her head, looking at Blaine. "Sorry, girl. I'm just scared. There's nothing out there, or you'd know before I did."

Fifteen minutes later, after Blaine had finished her wine and checked the locks one more time, she climbed into bed. She was utterly exhausted, so exhausted she couldn't sleep. Every time she started to drift off, the hideous image of Kathy tumbling out of the locker to stare sightlessly at her flashed through her mind and she jerked awake.

At two-twenty she decided to get up, make coffee, and watch cable television for the rest of the night. She had just thrown back the covers when the phone rang. Logan, no doubt, deciding he couldn't wait until morning to question her further about finding Kathy. She snatched up the receiver. "Hello."

Silence.

Oh, no, not again, she thought. She wanted to slam down the receiver, but a frightened curiosity restrained her. "Hello," she said again, this time with less assurance.

She could hear the needle being placed on a record. Faint scratching sounds buzzed in her ear for a moment. Then the singing started, a rich male tenor voice that even the old recording couldn't distort:

Oh! I will take you back, Kathleen,
To where your heart will feel no pain.
And when the fields are fresh and
    green,
I'll take you to your home again.

10

1

"I got another call last night," Blaine said. Logan sat in a shaft of noonday sunlight behind his gray metal desk, regarding her solemnly. She was uncomfortably aware of Abel Stroud sitting at another desk by the beige wall, listening avidly. She wished he would leave the office and find something to do in the main room, where one other officer was doing paperwork and another was on the phone. Stroud obviously wasn't going anywhere, though, and Blaine plowed ahead. "The call came about two-twenty, and it was related to Kathy's death."

"What did the caller say?" Logan asked.

"He didn't *say* anything. Just like last time, he played a record. A recording of 'I'll Take You Home Again, Kathleen.' "

"I don't know the song."

"I do," Stroud volunteered. "My ma used to sing it all the time. It says something about 'I'll take you back to where your heart will feel no pain.' Used to make me cry when I was a little guy.' " Abel immediately flushed, obviously embarrassed by this personal disclosure, and picked up a pen and started writing furiously in his notebook.

Blaine didn't know why, but she softened slightly toward the man. "That's right, Mr. Stroud. That's the song."

Logan frowned at Blaine. "And Kathy's full name is Kathleen. How many people knew that?"

"A lot. Some people, me included, called her Kathleen sometimes, and she was always listed as Kathleen Foss in the programs they passed out at the school football games. She was the head cheerleader."

Abel had recovered from his earlier disclosure of emotional vulnerability and now looked up at her in disbelief. "The sheriff didn't tell me anything about you gettin' a call after Rosalind Van Zandt's body was found. Are you sayin' that after each of the murders you got a call where somebody played music that had somethin' to do with the dead girls?"

"Yes."

He put down his pen next to a framed

school picture of Arletta, her round face smiling broadly, her hair sticking straight up. "Sounds like somethin' you saw in a movie."

Blaine gave him a steady stare. "Well, I didn't see it in a movie. It happened."

Logan tapped his long fingers on the desk. She looked back at him, for the first time noticing how his badge caught the light and flashed at her, almost like a threat. "Blaine, you found Kathy's body around a quarter to eleven and got this call about three and a half hours later. We weren't using the radios last night—I didn't want anyone picking up the news by listening to one of those damned police scanners. So even in a small town like this, not many people could have found out so soon. The call must have come from the person who murdered Kathy."

"I know." Logan stared at her, and she felt her hands fidgeting in her lap. She forced them to be still. "I've already talked with the phone company about having my calls traced. They told me I would need three successful traces before I could contact the police, but I thought in this case one trace would be sufficient."

"It would be," Logan said.

Stroud leaned back, making his vinyl-covered chair creak ominously. "Let's say, just for the sake of argument, you really are gettin' these weirdo calls."

"I *am* getting them."

"Yeah, okay. But there's somethin' you haven't considered."

"And what's that?"

"These *calls* are prob'ly comin' from a pay phone, so a trace wouldn't tell you a thing."

"The music isn't recorded on a cassette or a compact disc," Blaine said patiently. "During the calls I hear a needle dropping down on an old record. Now, I hardly think someone is dragging a phonograph to a pay phone."

"No, but they could play a tape of an old recording," Abel maintained doggedly.

"Why would they do that? Why not just play a new tape?"

Stroud shrugged. "This is your story, Mrs. Avery. You tell us."

"Just because it's happening to me doesn't mean I know why or exactly how it's being done."

"I'm glad you arranged for Call Trace,"

Logan said. "I'd need a court order to get a trace on your phone."

"I know. But something has to be done. These calls are so frightening, Logan, I can't tell you how much better I'd feel if we could find out who's making them." Blaine paused. "There's only one drawback to finding out where they're coming from."

Logan raised an eyebrow. "What's that?"

"I won't get another one of them until someone else has been murdered."

2

As soon as Blaine Avery walked out of the office, Abel Stroud looked at Logan. "Now tell me, Logan, why would the perp want to call this woman after every murder?"

"I have no idea."

Stroud looked at him appraisingly. "How come you didn't mention her sayin' she got a call after she found the Van Zandt kid's body?"

"I suppose I just forgot."

Stroud laughed. "You? Forget? You're like an elephant. You don't forget one thing, especially if it's got somethin' to do with a case."

Logan picked up his styrofoam cup of coffee and drained it. It had been poured half an hour ago and now tasted cold and bitter. "Thanks for the compliment, Stroud."

"It wasn't a compliment—just a simple statement of fact. I think you didn't mention it for a reason."

"And what would that be?"

"You don't think she's really gettin' these crazy phone calls."

Logan crumpled the cup and tossed it in a metal waste can beside his desk. "Then why would she voluntarily ask for a trace?"

"I haven't quite figured that one out yet." Stroud sucked loudly on his front teeth, a habit that nearly set Logan wild. "But I'll tell you one thing," he said finally, when Logan was just rising to leave the room. "That trace isn't gonna show up one damn thing."

"We'll see."

"Logan." The sheriff stopped in midstride, struck by the serious note in Stroud's voice. "You know I wasn't crazy about you gettin' elected sheriff two years ago, you bein' so much younger than me and all. But I'm over that. I've seen you work. You know a lot more about investigative techniques than I do. You've worked on the big police forces. You're good, *damn* good. But you're lettin' yourself get muddled this time."

"Muddled? What have I done wrong?"

"Nothin' big. *Yet.* But I can see you want to protect Blaine O'Connor."

"Why would I want to do that?"

"Oh, come on, Logan. You used to date her."

"In high school, for God's sake. Nearly fifteen years ago."

"Still, you've got a personal interest in this case."

"Even if I wanted to protect Blaine, did that stop me from pursuing every lead in the death of Martin Avery?"

"No. But you're startin' to hold back things." Stroud leaned forward. "Look, Logan, I'm not tryin' to cause trouble. I'm only tellin' you for your own good—you'd better bring the state police in *now*. Let them take over. Get yourself off this case. If you don't, you may not have this job much longer."

11

The Lord is my shepherd; I shall not want.
He maketh me to lie down in green pastures . . .

Green pastures, Blaine thought. Well, right now Rosalind Van Zandt was being laid to rest in the brown, November-dead acres of Silver Maple Cemetery. A few snowflakes— the first of the season—had begun to fall from the low pewter sky. They were big, dry flakes that landed gracefully on the shoulders of the nearly fifty mourners who had traveled to the cemetery from the funeral home. People began to surreptitiously brush at their faces, but Joan didn't seem aware of the snow clinging to her lashes and dotting her sleek black hair with white. She stared at the coffin like one entranced, her face deadly pale, her body rigid in its long-skirted black wool suit.

Yea, though I walk through the valley of the shadow of death, I will fear no evil . . .

People were beginning to shiver, and Blaine wished the minister would hurry through the verses Rosie wouldn't have wanted. She hadn't been a religious girl, not in any traditional sense, and Blaine thought it would have been far more appropriate for one of Rosie's beautiful poems to have been read. More appropriate and more personal.

What would Martin think of this? Blaine wondered. He'd grown close to Rosie in those last few weeks of his life. Frequently Blaine had seen them sitting together, alone on the terrace as dusk closed in. Although she knew Rosie had been coming to the house since she was a child, Blaine had never noticed anything but quick, almost absentminded fondness for the girl in Martin's manner. And Robin had been puzzled by their closeness, too. She'd often stood inside, watching them talking quietly on the terrace, her face expressionless. Had she felt the more beautiful Rosie was taking her father's attention away from her? Blaine now wondered. Had she resented Rosie? Or had she been merely puzzled about the new relationship, like Blaine? If only they were closer, Blaine could ask her. But she couldn't expect a straight answer now.

Blaine's eyes wandered from the freshly dug grave to two other headstones nearby. One was simple gray, without ornamentation, and read "Edward Parker Peyton, b. December 5, 1913, d. June 12, 1990." The other—cut from warm, rose-toned granite— was intricately carved with vines and flowers and stood nearly four feet tall. It read:

Charlotte Rachel Peyton Van Zandt
b. June 14, 1950 d. March 4, 1975
So dawn goes down to day,
Nothing gold can stay.

I wonder which family member chose those lines from Frost? Blaine mused. Probably Joan, although they all believed Charlotte had been gold. "The paragon," Rosie used to call her with mild rue. "I'll never measure up to her."

Once, when Bernice Litchfield was nursing Blaine's father after his accident, Blaine had asked her about Charlotte Peyton.

"Sweet as sugar, that girl was," Bernice had said fondly. "I taught her in Sunday school and took care of her when she had a tonsillectomy. She never complained about that sore throat, not once. Bore it like a little trooper. She never turned into a whiner, even though she was sick a lot and sort of accident-prone. And she wasn't smart like Joan—in fact, she had a lot of trouble all through school.

"There was no question of her going to college. And she certainly wasn't beautiful. Looking back, I can see that she was downright plain. But it's true that beauty is as beauty does. It was her darling, sort of childlike personality that made her beautiful. And the whole family thought the sun rose and set on her. Joan was a little mother hen, always looking after her baby sister just like she does Rosie. What a shameful loss Charlotte's death was! If the truth were known, it was after her death that Mrs. Peyton started acting so peculiar. Oh, it's not all senility, let me tell you. Charlotte's death knocked her for a loop. That's why I'm so glad Joan was home to raise Rosie. I just don't think Mrs. Peyton was up to the chore. But Joan's done a beautiful job. Still, none of the Peytons will ever get over losing Charlotte."

Nor would they get over the fact that Charlotte's monument did not mark a grave. Everyone knew there hadn't been enough of Charlotte's body left after the fiery plane crash to return home. Her few remains lay beside her husband's somewhere in Brazil, and the Peytons had been forced to memorialize an empty cemetery plot in the family section. That fact had always bothered Rosie. "I don't feel anything when I look at that stone," she'd told Blaine. "I guess it's because I know my mother isn't there—the little bit of her that was left was buried in Brazil with my father. Someday I'm going there to see the grave. I want to make sure it's someplace pretty, well cared for. I know my grandparents and Joan never wanted to visit the real grave—I suppose it would make my mother's death more real to them—but somebody ought to go. I guess it should be me."

Blaine abruptly became aware of Joan moving forward to lay a pink rosebud on Rosalind's coffin. At last tears had begun to run down her face, and she murmured, "Good-bye, little Rosie." Blaine felt tears pressing behind her own eyes, and Robin grabbed her gloved hand, her grip tight. Blaine glanced at her to see her mouth pressed into a straight, harsh line, her lids blinking rapidly. She looked exactly the same at her father's funeral, Blaine remembered in despair. Desolate and frantically fighting her emotions, emotions she should release. She squeezed Robin's hand and gently pulled her away from the gravesite as the other mourners began to gather around Joan, whose eyes suddenly darted around like those of a panicked animal looking for somewhere to run. I wish I could help you, Blaine thought sadly, but I have to help my stepdaughter first.

Blaine had requested a substitute for the day, and judging from the crowd of students who had been at the funeral home, she guessed there were many absences at Sinclair High today. Although Rosie had many friends, her murder, followed only days later by the murder of Kathy Foss, had whipped the student body to a high level of curiosity and horror. Probably half the people who'd attended the funeral hardly knew Rosie. They simply wanted to come to the funerals of the murdered girls. They also wanted to study afresh the woman who had found them. All during the service Blaine had been uncomfortably aware of the fascinated glances thrown her way. And yesterday the principal had told her that three parents had called the school to say their children would not be returning until all doubts concerning Blaine Avery had been relieved. After all, hadn't there been a scandal about her husband's death this summer? And wasn't it quite a coincidence that not only were Rosie and Kathy students of hers, but she'd found the bodies of *both* girls? Of course, they forget that I wasn't alone when I found Rosie, Blaine thought bitterly. Nor do they consider that anyone who'd gone into the locker room after the talent show rehearsal could have found Kathy. *I* always happen to be in the wrong place at the wrong time.

Pushing her own discomfort from her mind, Blaine glanced around to see Caitlin and Kirk coming toward them. Blaine had expected to see Cait, but not Kirk, who looked remarkably handsome in a navy blue suit she hadn't seen him wear since her wedding. "It was a lovely service," Cait said.

Robin let out a deep sigh. "I thought it was morbid. Rosie would have hated it."

Cait looked nonplussed, clearly not knowing how to respond to the girl. Blaine said quickly, "Do you two have time to come home with us for a while?"

Kirk shook his head regretfully. "No. At least I don't. Dad and I have a big order to fill this afternoon, although after this, I don't know if I'll be able to get my mind on my work."

"And I don't want to leave my assistant alone with the kids for too long. After that day *I* spent alone with them . . ."

Blaine smiled. "It wasn't so bad."

"You missed all the good parts. They were winding down by the time you arrived." She looked at Kirk. "I didn't know you had a big order for this afternoon."

"Honey, I told you. You just don't listen half the time anymore. I have to finish a cedar hope chest for Mrs. Bailey's daughter. She wants to give it to the girl tomorrow on her sixteenth birthday."

"You *didn't* tell me," Cait said again.

Kirk shook his head in an exasperated motion and said sharply, "Caity, you haven't listened to a word I've said since you opened that day-care center."

Cait looked hurt, and Blaine was a little

surprised by her brother-in-law's tone. He was certainly tense today.

"That's all right," Blaine said quickly. "Maybe we can all get together another time."

Kirk winked, as if trying to restore his usual good humor. "It's just a bad day for everyone. The last thing you need is to have your battling relatives around."

"Battling!" Cait said loudly. "What are you—"

"Caity, let's not make a scene at the cemetery," Kirk said smoothly. He took her arm, forcing a smile at Blaine. "See you later this week."

"I want to go home now," Robin muttered as Blaine stared after the retreating backs of Cait and Kirk.

The girl hadn't cried at the funeral, but she looked incredibly pale and shaken. "Sure. I'll get you there as soon as possible."

But the car wouldn't start. Blaine tried four times before someone tapped on the car window, and she looked up to see Tony Jarvis. She rolled down the window. "I seem to have a dead battery."

"That's not what it sounds like," Tony said.

"Then what could it be?"

He smiled at her. "Mind if I look under the hood?"

"Be my guest. But try not to get dirty. You look so nice."

"For a change."

"That's not what I meant."

He grinned. "I know what you meant, Mrs. Avery. I'm just kidding. Now, pop the hood release for me."

Robin sat huddled against the door, still shaken by the funeral, but Blaine noticed her heightened color and the way her eyes followed Tony to the front of the car. Their expression! She has a crush on him, Blaine thought in amazement. Shy, intellectual Robin has a crush on a guy who rides a motorcycle, wears an earring, and has his own rock band.

Blaine took a deep breath. What was she so surprised about? Hadn't she told John Sanders just a couple of days ago that Tony was good-looking, sexy, and talented? And to someone as protected as Robin had always been, Tony's scrapes with the law might seem dramatic, romantic.

"Mind if I try to start the car?"

Blaine's mind snapped back to her present problem. She hesitated, looking again into the brown eyes that were so like those of the little boy she'd once known. Then she scooted over beside Robin. "Go ahead, Tony."

She felt Robin's body tense, whether from the nearness of Tony or from sheer surprise, she wasn't sure.

He turned the key a couple of times and got the same clicking sound Blaine had earlier. "I think it's the alternator."

"Oh, no," Blaine groaned. "That means I'll have to call a garage and have it towed in. And just look at that snow."

Tony dutifully looked at the snow, which was now falling in a thick, silent veil. Then he glanced over at Robin, who stared straight ahead, trembling with cold and nerves. "Tell you what. Why don't I run you two home?"

"On your *motorcycle?*"

Tony laughed. "No, Mrs. Avery, I have a car today."

"Aren't you going back to school?"

"I hadn't planned on it."

Blaine looked out at the snow again. "Maybe I shouldn't leave my car."

"Just lock it and it'll be fine. You two won't. You know how garages are around here. Most of them don't even have tow trucks."

"We could get a cab."

"In this snow? The Sinclair Taxi Company, with its mighty fleet of five, will be booked solid. You could be here for another hour."

Blaine looked around. Almost everyone she knew had left, and Tony was right. Besides, Robin was beginning to look bad, almost as pale and depleted as she had the night of her father's death. Blaine needed to get the girl home first and worry about the car later. And Tony? He was officially a murder suspect. But did she *really* think him capable of murder? No, she didn't. That's all there was to it.

"Okay, if you're sure you don't mind," she said slowly.

"No problem. I've even got four-wheel drive today. My dad's car."

With a courtliness Blaine had never seen him display, Tony helped her and Robin from the Mercedes. When Robin slipped on the sidewalk, he took her arm, elevating her color another notch, and in spite of the awful circumstances, Blaine couldn't help smiling. As far as she knew, Robin had never been seriously interested in a boy, and Blaine had sometimes worried that Robin's insecurity had caused her to simply squash all yearnings for romance she thought she could never have. Now Blaine knew she had been wrong. The yearnings were obviously flourishing—Robin had just kept them well hidden.

Robin scrambled into the backseat, forcing Blaine to sit up front with Tony. They drove in complete silence for a few minutes until Tony asked, "Is rehearsal for the talent contest still on for tonight?"

"No. It was canceled out of deference to Rosie and Kathy. And, of course, the gym is still cordoned off as a crime scene."

"I wonder if they'll call off the whole show," he said quickly.

"I don't think so. It's a school tradition. The last time I talked to the principal, he seemed determined to go on with it."

Blaine wished Robin would join in the conversation, but the girl remained stubbornly quiet, so they fell silent again.

Only about a half inch of snow had accumulated, and they had no trouble driving the three miles out of town to the house on Prescott Road. Blaine always loved the way the house looked in snow, like something on a Christmas card with its great expanse of white-coated lawn, dormer windows, multiple-peaked roof, and fanciful cupola. When they pulled into the driveway, Blaine spotted Ashley sitting at the bay window in the living room, anxiously watching for their return.

"Told you I'd get you here in one piece," Tony said. "I'll stop by Pearson's Garage on my way back and try to get them moving on your car."

"Why don't you come in instead?" Blaine said suddenly. She was aware of Robin tensing uncomfortably. "It's one-thirty," she continued easily. "I can make us something for lunch, and you can call the garage for us."

Tony seemed as surprised as Robin and unsure of himself. "You don't have to make me lunch, Mrs. Avery, just because I brought you home."

"Well, if you're not hungry . . ."

At that moment Tony's stomach let out a resounding growl. He slapped his hand to his abdomen, looked dumbfounded, then burst into laughter along with Blaine. Even Robin couldn't stifle a smile. "I guess that answers your question," he said. "I didn't eat any breakfast."

"We all need something to eat, and certainly something to drink. Something *hot*. I'm freezing." She smiled at Tony and Robin. "Come on, you two. Let's not sit out here arguing all day."

Martin would have had a fit, Blaine thought. This wasn't the kind of boy he'd wanted for his daughter. But Martin hadn't always been right, Blaine reminded herself. For all of his confidence, he hadn't been able to see into the human heart any more than she could. All she could go on was instinct, and instinct told her that maybe Tony, whom the girl obviously admired, would be the only person who could pull her out of her shock and depression.

Blaine quickly punched in the numbers that disarmed the new alarm system, and the three of them tramped in. Ashley stood in the entrance hall. She studied Tony closely for a few moments, suspicion showing in her expressive eyes. He knelt and held out his hand to her. She stared into his face, looked at the hand, then sat down and offered her own paw in the regal way that had always made Martin laugh.

"You've been accepted by the queen of the household," Blaine said. "Very few people get this treatment."

Tony smiled, shaking the proffered paw. "She just knows I like dogs. Got one of my own. German shepherd about fifteen years old. His name's Doc. We grew up together."

"I remember him," Blaine said.

"Doc?" Robin asked, the first word she'd uttered since Tony joined them.

"Yeah. Mom bought him for me when I was three and all hung up on Bugs Bunny saying, 'What's up, Doc?' I thought it was the funniest thing I'd ever heard. Stupid, huh?"

Robin shook her head. "Not stupid. I'm sure he likes it. The dog, I mean."

"He doesn't know any better. If he did, he'd probably rather be called King or Rin-Tin-Tin or something."

"Tony, if you'll call Pearson's Garage for me, I'll fix some lunch." Blaine shrugged out of her dark coat and shook the snow from her hair, which was beginning to curl tightly from the dampness. "Any menu requests?"

"Whatever you've got, Mrs. Avery."

Blaine went into the kitchen, hearing him talking into the phone in the living room, and opened the refrigerator door. Plenty of ham. Some sliced turkey. Swiss cheese. She'd just bought a new bag of potato chips and baked a cherry pie the night before. She only baked when she was nervous and trying to take her mind off things.

"Tony called the garage," Robin said, hovering behind Blaine at the refrigerator. "They said they'd pick up the car in about an hour."

"Good."

"Can I help?"

Robin *never* offered to help with meals, and Blaine could barely suppress a smile. "I have everything under control. Why don't you go back out and talk to Tony?"

Robin made a strangled sound and Blaine looked at her in surprise. "What's wrong?"

"Can't I please help you in here?" She hung her head, her long hair falling over her face. "I can't think of anything to say. Besides, he's a murder suspect," she whispered.

"So am I, Robin." The girl blinked at her.

"You don't really think he had anything to do with Rosie's death, do you?"

"Well, I . . . I don't know."

Blaine took a deep breath. "I've known him since he was a child, Rob. *I* don't think he killed Rosie."

"You can't be sure."

"You can't be sure about a lot of things in life." The girl gave her a long, penetrating stare. "Robin, we can't just leave Tony out there. Talk to him about anything. School. Dogs. Music."

Robin sighed, then straightened her shoulders and marched back to the living room as if she were headed to the guillotine. Blaine felt slightly guilty, knowing what an ordeal this was for her, but feeling that in the long run it would be good for her. After all, it wasn't as if Robin needed time alone to vent her grief after Rosie's funeral. If Tony left this minute, she would simply shut herself in her room and sit looking at magazines and playing her electric piano until dark, which was what she'd done for more than two weeks after her father died.

Fifteen minutes later, when Blaine carried in a tray of sandwiches and cups of hot chocolate topped with whipped cream,

Robin and Tony were talking desultorily about dogs while Ashley sat gazing up into the young man's eyes as if trying to uncover a mystery. It's almost as if *she* knows he's a murder suspect, too, Blaine mused.

"Need some help with that?" Tony asked, going toward Blaine to take the tray. "Wow! Those are the biggest sandwiches I've ever seen."

Blaine smiled. "Judging by the sound your stomach made earlier, I'd say you need a big sandwich. There's also cherry pie for later."

"Great."

As they ate, Blaine asked Tony about his family. "Sandra's got another baby on the way," he said between bites. "That makes four."

"She's been busy! I've tried to get together with her for the last couple of years, but except for a lunch at her house, she's been too tied up and distracted."

Tony's look darkened. "Yeah. She worries about the whole family, too—Mom's arthritis, which is getting pretty bad. Then Jane took off a couple of years ago to be an airline stewardess. Sandra's sure every flight she's on is gonna crash."

"You can't blame her for being concerned about her little sister."

"I guess not. Then there's me. Always the black sheep. And Joe." Not *Dad*, Blaine thought. *Joe.* "She's determined to make everything okay between us again. I don't think it ever will be—I'll never forgive him for dumping Mom and all us kids five years ago—but I've got a nice stepmother. She likes me. Joe thinks I'm worthless."

"Oh, Tony, I'm sure he doesn't," Blaine said.

"Yes, he does. He only lends me his car sometimes because my stepmother makes him. She wants us to be like a regular father and son, too."

"I've forgotten how long your father's been remarried."

"Two years. I wish Mom could have found somebody nice, but I don't think she ever really tried. She was too wrapped up in us kids. Now she's got this damned arthritis. I don't think she's gonna be able to work more than a couple more years. She just never gets any breaks."

A look of unutterable sadness swept over Tony's face, and Blaine abruptly changed the subject to his rock band. Before long, though, the subject turned to Rosie.

"I was a little surprised when you stormed out of my class the other day," Blaine ventured.

Tony looked away. "It was that poem— 'Annabel Lee.' It was Rosie's favorite poem. She wanted me to write some music for it one time, but I said it wasn't my style. She was pretty disappointed. When you started reading it in class that day, I thought about how easy it would have been to make Rosie happy, but I hadn't bothered."

Blaine noticed Robin watching him with interest. "We found Rosie's stuff in the basement," Robin volunteered suddenly.

Blaine looked at the girl in shock. She's trying to get a reaction from him, Blaine thought. She's playing amateur detective. "I know. Arletta Stroud told everyone. Suitcase. Jacket. Purse." Tony cocked an eyebrow at Robin. "Do I have it right?"

"Yeah. We found all that behind the furnace. It was hidden. Why do you suppose someone would do that?"

Tony frowned. "She must have already been in this house. Oh, I know that, too. That she was meeting someone here. But that person didn't have time to get rid of her things."

"That's what the sheriff says," Blaine told him.

"It's the only thing that makes sense."

"You don't know who she was meeting, do you, Tony?" Blaine asked.

He set his pie plate down on the coffee table and looked at her with what appeared to be complete honesty. "Don't you think I'd tell the police if I knew? God, whoever it was must have *killed* her. Slashed her *wrists*. Let her lie in the water all that time." His face took on a slightly gray tone. "It makes me sick to think about it."

If you're acting, you're awfully good at it, Blaine thought. She glanced at Robin to see that the guarded expression she'd worn ever since Tony had appeared at the car window had disappeared.

"Well, I think that's enough discussion about poor Rosie," Blaine said briskly. "Tony, how about another piece of pie?"

The early-season snow had stopped by the time Tony finished his second slice of cherry pie. The sun was struggling against the grayness of the day, and Blaine felt her spirits rising slightly. If the sun could shine on this sad day, then surely the world couldn't be as dark as it had seemed since she'd found Rosie's body.

As Blaine began gathering up the dishes, Tony turned to Robin. "You know, for the past couple of days I've been kicking around this idea about the talent contest."

Robin looked guardedly interested. "What is it?"

"Well, don't be offended, but neither of us was in top form during Tuesday's rehearsal." Robin immediately turned scarlet and Tony rushed on. "I knew I'd say it wrong. I mean, you were terrific, but that classical stuff just doesn't go over with a lot of people. Most people in the Sinclair High School audience, that is. And my song isn't ready. Rosie was helping with the lyrics, but . . . Well, anyway, it's not right yet and I'm not comfortable with it. So I thought of this—why don't you and I do something together?"

"Together?" Robin echoed.

"Sure. Me on guitar and vocals, you on the piano. Unless, of course, you can sing and I don't know it."

"I sound like a dying moose when I sing,"

Robin said with such sincerity that Tony broke up.

"Okay. No dying moose onstage," he said, recovering. "But what do you think about us doing a song?"

"Well, I guess we could." Oh, no, Blaine thought. That means rehearsals together. "Do you mean something like Eric Clapton's 'Layla'?" Robin asked.

Tony's eyes widened. "Robin, you're *psychic!* That's the song I've been thinking about since Tuesday night!"

"Really?"

"Yeah. We'll have to get the sheet music for you—"

"I already know it."

Tony gaped. "You *do?*"

"Well, I don't play only classical music, Tony. I listened to the song a few times and then I played it. The piano part, that is."

"Mrs. Avery, can you believe this?" he demanded.

No, she couldn't. She believed that anything acceptable Robin suggested would have been *the* song Tony had in mind, and naturally she'd suggested something she already knew how to play. But in spite of Blaine's doubts about Tony, in spite of her fury with the girl, she was touched by the look of hope and excitement in her eyes. Blaine hadn't seen that look since Martin had died. "What do you think, Mrs. Avery? Think it's a good idea for us to do the song together?"

"I think . . . I think it's okay as long as the two of you rehearse here," she said slowly. "I don't like Robin being out at night with all that's going on."

"Well, sure, okay," Tony said. Robin cast her a look of infinite gratitude, and Blaine prayed she was doing the right thing. She didn't want to hurt either of them, didn't want to drive Martin's daughter even farther away from her. She'd already decided that no matter how angry she was, she wasn't going to banish Robin to her grandparents' home during her senior year of high school. Still, Robin seemed so young, so vulnerable, and there was a killer loose . . .

"Why don't we do some practicing while I'm here?" Tony asked.

Robin immediately stood up and headed for the piano, with Tony close behind. Ashley was quick to follow, as if she, too, were going to participate in the act.

A few minutes later Robin was banging

out the familiar chords of "Layla" when the
doorbell rang. She and Tony remained at
the piano, but Ashley accompanied Blaine
as she went to answer it. Logan Quint stood
on the porch.

"Sorry to bother you, Blaine, but I'm looking for Tony Jarvis. Someone told me he'd
brought you and Robin home."

"Yes, he did." Blaine felt as if the day had
suddenly grown darker. "Is something
wrong?"

Logan's hooded gaze revealed nothing. "I
just need to see him."

Reluctantly, Blaine led him into the living
room. Robin halted in mid-chord, and she
and Tony stared at Logan.

He nodded at Robin, then looked at Tony.
"I'd like you to come with me."

Tony stiffened, his dark eyes growing
wary. "What for?"

"Questioning."

"You've already questioned me about
Rosie's murder. This isn't about Kathy, is
it?"

"Not directly. I just need to ask you a few
more things."

Tony slid off the piano bench and stood,

his expression growing defiant. "Why more questions?"

"I think it would be better if we talked about this in my office."

"No. Something's happened and I want to know *now*, before I go anywhere."

Robin's eyes had grown huge, their earlier shining happiness vanished.

"All right, Jarvis, we'll do it your way," Logan said evenly. "Friday evening, the evening of Rosie's murder, you said you and your group were practicing out at Ron Gibson's farm until nearly seven o'clock."

"Yeah. You talked to Ron—he told you I was there."

"You also said that after you left Gibson's, you went straight home."

Tony's chin lifted slightly. "That's right."

"Gibson's farm is ten miles south of town. You should have been home by seven-fifteen to seven-thirty at the latest."

"My mom told you I got home a little after seven."

"Yes, she did. But neither of you mentioned that your father was at your mother's house, waiting for you to get in. Seems he was pretty steamed because you'd borrowed his car that day to haul music equipment and promised to have the car back by around seven. He told me you didn't arrive home until ten o'clock." Logan paused, his eyes boring into Tony's. "Want to tell me why you lied about where you were during the time when Rosalind Van Zandt was getting her wrists slashed?"

12

1

"I hope all of you finished reading *Walden*," Blaine said to her third-period Advanced Literature class. "Who can tell me what Walden Pond symbolizes in the book?"

Several pairs of eyes shifted uncomfortably, studiously looking away from her, always a dead giveaway that their owners hadn't finished the assignment. Blaine waited five seconds, smiled at them, then said, "Is someone going to volunteer an answer, or do I have to choose a victim?"

Suddenly the classroom door flew back, crashing against the wall. A couple of girls cried out, and Blaine blanched as a woman with frizzy, mouse-colored hair and blazing dark eyes stormed into the room.

"You!" she shouted at Blaine. "You filthy, black-hearted murderer!"

Blaine was so startled she took a step

backward before she said, "Who are you?" in a thin, high voice.

"Who am I? Who *am* I? I'm the mother of a girl you killed."

"Mrs. Foss?"

Kathy's mother whirled on the class, her gray wool coat flapping open to reveal faded, wrinkled slacks and a high-necked blouse with what appeared to be a large coffee stain on the front. "You see—she doesn't deny it!"

Several students gasped, and they all seemed to shrink in their seats as if ducking blows. Blaine's heart pounded in the face of this woman's wild-eyed fury, but she forced herself to take a deep breath and say steadily, "Mrs. Foss, you shouldn't be here."

"*I* shouldn't be here!" Her lips were dry and cracked. "*You*—you murdering filth!—*you* shouldn't be here! Wolf among the sheep!" She turned to the class and began to shriek, "Wolf among the sheep! Wolf among the sheep!"

From the corner of her eye Blaine saw Dean Newman rise at the back of the room and begin edging forward. At the same time, John appeared in the doorway. "What in God's name—" he began.

Mrs. Foss spun to face him. "Yes, in God's name! That's why I'm here—in God's name. To get this abomination"—her hand whipped out in Blaine's direction—"away from these innocent children. Innocent *girls*. Girls like my Kathy. My Kathy, who's going to be laid in her grave Saturday morning!"

Abruptly the woman wheeled and flew at Blaine, hands formed into claws. Blaine instinctively raised her own hands and, with a strength she didn't know she possessed, grabbed the woman's wrists and held them in a rigid grasp. Mrs. Foss screamed and fought, kicking at Blaine, trying to wrench her arms from Blaine's iron grip while her hands with their long nails opened and closed spasmodically. Dean and John grabbed one shoulder each, trying to pull her away from Blaine. "Turn her loose," John said. But Blaine's hands seemed frozen on the woman's wrists. "Blaine, let her go!" he shouted. "Let *go!*"

Blaine's hands snapped open, releasing Mrs. Foss. Immediately she began screeching again. "She's killed before! Her own husband! Now she's killing innocent young girls. You saw it—all of you saw it. She has the strength of a demon. A *demon,* I'm telling you!"

Dean and John dragged the hysterical woman toward the door. She clasped her hands around the doorframe and held fast. John at last jerked her forcefully. Her grip loosened, and they propelled her down the hall.

"She's a murderer!" the woman screamed in the empty corridor. "She's a murderer, and mark my words, the killings aren't over yet! They aren't over yet!"

2

Twenty minutes later, after repeated attempts to locate Mr. Foss had failed and Mrs. Foss was growing more hysterical by the minute, the emergency squad arrived to tranquilize her and take her to the hospital. Ten minutes after the woman had been strapped onto a stretcher and hauled away, Blaine sat in the principal's office, shaken and embarrassed.

He looked at her solemnly. "That was quite a scene."

"I know, Mr. Hooper," she said miserably,

holding a styrofoam cup of coffee the secretary, Jean Lewis, had provided.

The principal studied her, his strong-
jawed face expressionless. "Blaine, what
would you think of taking a few days off?"

She regarded him blankly. "A few days?
I've just had five weeks off. I'm fine, really."

"You don't look fine. Besides, we have
another problem here."

Blaine gave him a long, unflinching look.
"Complaints from parents."

"I'm afraid so. I mentioned this to you before. You found Rosie *and* Kathy. You have
to admit that's quite a coincidence."

She had never considered him a warm
and understanding man, but now he looked
downright hostile. "And, of course, there
was all that business about your husband.
People around here haven't forgotten it."

"No, I don't suppose they have," Blaine
said dully.

"So I really think, for your good and that
of the school . . ."

"I should get lost for a while."

"I wouldn't have put it that way, but . . ."

"But that's what you meant." She looked
past him out the window, where the last of
a few bedraggled, yellow November leaves

were giving up the fight and floating down from the fifty-year-old oak tree outside the principal's office. "Mr. Hooper, I realize you have the school's reputation to think of, but don't you realize what letting me go will look like? What people will make of it?"

"I'm afraid your troubles aren't my problem."

"I see. Do I understand, then, that if I break my contract by resigning, I won't be sued?"

He focused on a spot just above her head. "I think that's a reasonable assumption. The school board will understand."

"I'll just bet they will." Blaine set her coffee cup down on his desk. "I'll finish out the day and—"

"Well, actually, I've already called in someone to handle your afternoon classes. I think it would be best if you left school now."

Blaine stared at him. She felt tears pressing behind her eyes, but she would not break down, not in front of this cold-eyed man who'd practically fawned over her when she was married to Martin. She stood up.

"I hope there are no hard feelings, Blaine."

"Oh, no," she said coolly. "But don't expect a check from me for your alumni society this year."

The principal's eyes flickered. The alumni society was his pet project, and one to which she and Martin had always given freely. "I really don't think there's any need to get petty about this, Blaine."

"Just think of it as my being thrifty. Goodbye, Mr. Hooper."

3

Logan looked over at Tim, who sat strapped into the car beside him. "Mind if we take a detour?"

"Detour," Tim repeated carefully. "Does that mean we're goin' someplace besides home first?"

"Yes."

"Well, no, I don't care, if it doesn't take too long. We rented that movie to watch tonight, and my bedtime's nine o'clock."

"I remember."

"I could stay up later than nine to watch it, though."

"I don't think that will be necessary," Logan said as they went past their house and headed north on Prescott Road.

"Are we goin' someplace on official business?"

"Official business? Where did you get that phrase?"

"You use it all the time when you don't want me to know where you're really goin'."

"Oh. Well, yes and no. The lady we're going to see has some problems, but we're not visiting her on official business."

I shouldn't be doing this at all, Logan thought. I shouldn't say anything to Blaine off the record, and I certainly shouldn't be going to her house. But he was going, nevertheless. His need to see her after what he'd heard today was too strong to ignore.

Tim rooted around in the pocket of his wool jacket and withdrew a piece of Juicy Fruit chewing gum, holding it out to Logan in a silent offer to split the piece. Logan shook his head. "Is this lady your girlfriend?" Tim asked.

Logan looked at his son, astonished. "My girlfriend! Where on earth did you get an idea like that?"

"Mommy said you'd prob'ly have girl-friends while she was gone."

Rage surged through Logan. As if desert-ing her family weren't enough, Dory had to pour out her insecurities about "girlfriends" on her seven-year-old child. "This lady isn't anyone's girlfriend," he said, forcing the anger from his voice. "Her husband died a few months ago, and she still feels really bad about that. But that's not the point. I don't have girlfriends, Tim. I'm married."

Tim broke the gum into three pieces, then put them all in his mouth and began crunch-ing. That stick of gum has probably been in his pocket since last winter, Logan thought. "On TV married guys have girlfriends," Tim managed between chomps.

"You watch too much TV."

"Oh, well, it's only the bad guys that have girlfriends," Tim said hastily, clearly alarmed that his television privileges might be re-voked.

"Do you think I'm a bad guy?"

"No way! You're the sheriff!"

"Okay. This lady's name is Mrs. Avery. She's a friend of mine, someone I've known since I was about your age."

"Wow," Tim said, as if his father were talking about a vast and distant space of time, like the Bronze Age.

Logan smiled in the darkness. "So this is just a friendly call, got it?"

"Got it!" Tim said, still chewing furiously on his stale gum.

4

Robin lay on the couch, munching popcorn and staring into the fire crackling behind the black wire screen. "Robin, do you want to talk about Tony?" Blaine said, laying down her book, unable to bear the silence any longer.

"No. You're against him, just like everyone else."

"I am *not* against him."

"Suddenly you don't want me to practice with him."

"I think my decision is justified. The circumstances have changed."

"I'm *not* practicing with him for the talent show, but not because of anything you said," Robin announced, sitting up and brushing back her long hair. "He just doesn't feel like it with all this police harassment."

"Robin, he isn't being harassed. He lied about his whereabouts the night Rosie was killed. Logan found out about it. You can't sit there and honestly tell me you're mad at Logan for calling him in for more questioning."

Robin's eyes dropped. "I guess not."

"Have you talked to Tony since the questioning?"

"Just for a couple of minutes on the phone."

"Did he say where he was that night?"

"Driving around, but he didn't think anyone would have believed him."

Well, I can understand that, Blaine thought. I was driving around, but I don't think anyone believes me.

The doorbell rang. "Who can that be?" Blaine asked absently.

"I've got a great idea," Robin said. "Why not go to the door and see?"

"I love it when you're in these moods," Blaine returned, but the girl was already concentrating on her popcorn again.

Through the glass in the peephole Blaine saw a collection of distorted features she barely made out as Logan's. She opened the door to find him holding the hand of a little black-haired boy who grinned up at her, one of his front teeth missing, and piped, "Hi!"

"Well, how do you do?" Blaine smiled. She looked inquiringly at Logan, suddenly aware of her eyes, still slightly swollen from the tears that had come after she'd left school, and her hair carelessly pulled back with a rubber band.

"This is my son, Tim," Logan said.

"I'm happy to meet you, Tim." Blaine's mind flew. If Logan was here, it probably meant bad news. But he wouldn't bring his son with him if he had something awful to tell her, would he? "Want to come in out of the cold?" she asked.

Logan nodded. "Sure, if you're not busy."

"Not at all." The two of them stepped into the entrance hall, both carefully wiping their feet on the mat, and Blaine said softly to Logan, "Is this official business?"

Tim giggled. Logan winked down at him, then smiled, the old, heartfelt smile she remembered so well from high school. "No. It's just that I heard what happened to you at school today."

"I'm surprised the story wasn't in the evening paper," she said bitterly.

"No—they had bigger news. FUNDS ALLO-
CATED FOR NEW CHRISTMAS LIGHTS was the banner headline." Blaine couldn't help laughing,
although she'd seen the paper for herself.
The banner headline had actually been PO-
LICE STILL STALK MURDERER. "Anyway, I knew
you'd had a horrible day, and I thought . . .
well, I just wanted . . ."

Tim was looking at him inquisitively. "You
just wanted to what, Daddy?"

"Say hello," Logan answered quickly.

Tim looked baffled by this clumsy ex-
change between the adults. Blaine smiled at
both of them. "May I take your coats?"

"Oh, we can't stay. I just wanted to tell
you that Mrs. Foss has calmed down. That
situation is under control."

"What situation?" Tim demanded. "I don't
understand anything anybody's sayin'."

"You don't need to know everything," Logan said.

Suddenly Ashley appeared in the entrance hall, and Tim let out a squeal of delight. He knelt and Ashley ran to him, as if
she were his dog and ecstatic to see him.
"Daddy, *look!*" Tim said in wonder. "He likes
me!"

"It's a she," Blaine said. "Her name is Ashley. And she sure *does* like you."

Tim's little arms clamped firmly around the dog's neck while Ashley licked his cheeks. "She's the prettiest dog I've ever seen, and I've seen *lots* of dogs!"

"I know she appreciates the compliment." Blaine shifted her gaze to Logan, who was looking at his son with such adoration that Blaine felt a momentary constriction in her throat. "Logan, are you sure the two of you can't stay for a while? Robin and I are all alone, and Tim's just getting to know Ashley."

"Oh, Daddy, *please!*" Tim begged. He looked up at Blaine. "Do you have a VCR?"

"Yes."

"We got a movie in the car. We were gonna watch it at home, but we could watch it here instead, couldn't we, Daddy?"

Robin had come into the entrance hall, and although five minutes earlier her mood had been bordering on surly, her voice was warm and friendly as she spoke to Tim. "What movie do you have?"

Tim looked at her excitedly. *"All Dogs Go to Heaven!"*

"Really?" Robin exclaimed. "That's *just* the movie I've been wanting to see!"

"Me, too, me, too!" Tim squealed. "And I bet Ashley'd like it, too. Daddy, *please?*"

Blaine cocked an eyebrow at Logan. "I think you're outnumbered here, Sheriff."

Logan grinned. "Are you sure it's all right?"

Was it all right? She had come to think of Logan as her enemy this summer, and things still weren't right between them. Far from it. She was wary of him, and she sensed he was still wary of her, but something was pulling them together, something other than the recent murders. And at least he'd driven out to say a few comforting words about her dismissal from school, which was more than anyone else had done.

"It's more than all right. Robin and I would love to have you." Logan hesitated, and Blaine said in her most authoritative school-teacher's voice, "You go out to the car and get the movie. I'll put on more popcorn. Oh, and if you think your wife might like to join us, there's a phone in the living room."

"Dory's still with relatives," Logan said quickly.

Tim's forehead wrinkled. "What rel'tives do we have in Taco Mexico?"

Logan flushed. "It's Taos, New Mexico, son, and she's with some relatives you've never met. Distant relatives."

"Well, I hope she's having a good time," Blaine said, hoping she sounded pleasantly casual, although she could tell by the look on Logan's face that he'd been caught in a lie.

"Mommy's been gone weeks and *weeks*," Tim went on. Logan looked like he wanted to put a piece of tape over the child's mouth. "I didn't know she was with rel'tives, though. I thought she was writin' stories."

Logan's voice was taut. "She is. Writing. She's never had anything published. It's sort of a new hobby for her."

"Grandma's stayin' with us while Mommy's gone," Tim interrupted. "But she's at church tonight. She sings in the choir and they're practicin'." He hugged Ashley, a forlorn expression flickering over his fine-boned features. He had Logan's coloring, Blaine thought, but the delicacy of bone structure must come from his mother, whom Blaine had never met. "Grandma's neat, but I hope Mommy comes home soon. She's been gone a really long time. I'm scared she won't be here for Christmas, but Daddy says she will."

Blaine could practically feel the unbearable tension vibrating through Logan, and she smiled at Tim. "I'm sure she'll be home. You just stop worrying. We'll watch the movie and have a great time. And, Tim, you're in charge of looking after Ashley for the evening."

"Really?"

"Yes. It's a big responsibility, but I think you can handle it."

"Sure I can!"

"Good. You take her into the living room and get all settled. I'll be in in a few minutes with the popcorn. And what do you want to drink?"

"Coke!"

"Fine. We have plenty of that. Logan?"

"How about a beer?" The earlier tension that had held him rigid seemed to flow from him, and he looked tired and defeated. "I think I could use one. Or maybe two or three."

"I'm with you." Their eyes met, and Blaine felt herself growing both uncomfortable and lighthearted as she realized they were experiencing one of those moments of perfect communion they used to share in high school. So much hostility had vibrated between them for months, and now, for the first time since Martin had died, she felt as if she weren't alone. Here was someone who knew what she was thinking almost before she did—knew and, amazingly, sympathized. She had a sudden urge to lean over and kiss him on the cheek, just the way she had when she was seventeen. Disconcerted by her bizarre impulse, she drew inward, saying in clipped tones, "I don't think Tim's going to be able to wait much longer for that movie. We'd better get a move on."

Logan gave her one more soul-searching look from his dark eyes before his own expression closed into one of nonchalant social politeness. "Sure enough. Be right back with the tape."

Tim rolled with laughter throughout the movie, and the rest of them ended up laughing, too, mostly at Tim's utter delight in the antics of Charlie, the con artist German shepherd, and his sidekick, Scratchy. Ashley remained staunchly by Tim's side, as if she, too, were watching the movie, and Tim rewarded her with almost as much popcorn as he consumed. When the tape ended, Tim requested that the movie be shown again, but Logan was firm. "It's almost nine o'clock, son. Grandma will be home soon and wonder what happened to us."

"Can't we call her?"

"Don't think so, partner. It's too late."

"But then she won't get to meet Ashley."

"She'll be tired after all that singing she did at choir practice and won't want to come out in the cold again. She can meet Ashley another time."

"Will you invite us over again?" Tim asked Blaine with almost pathetic hopefulness.

"Of course we will," Blaine said, touched. "In fact, you don't have to wait for an invitation. You come anytime you want."

Robin went over and ruffled his dark hair. "And next time, mister, I'm challenging you to a popcorn-eating contest."

"You won't win!" Tim giggled. "Me and Ashley can eat more popcorn than anybody in the whole wide world!"

"I can believe that," Logan said dryly. "Considering what you ate tonight, I shouldn't have to feed you again until Monday morning."

After Tim had bidden Ashley a passionate

good-bye and Blaine had closed the door after them, she turned to face Robin. "Thank you for being nice. I didn't know how you'd react after Logan's taking Tony away for questioning."

Robin shrugged. "I was being nice to the little boy. He looks like he can use all the attention he can get."

"You think so?"

"Sure, don't you?"

"Actually, yes. He seems to miss his mother a lot."

"I don't think the sheriff misses his wife, though."

"Why do you say that?"

"I see a lot of things you don't think I see."

"What's that supposed to mean?"

Robin raised an eyebrow at her. "Just how long ago was it that you and Sheriff Quint dated?"

"Where did you hear that?"

"From about twenty-five sources. So? How long?"

Blaine realized with dismay that she was blushing. "It was a *long* time ago."

"Oh, yeah?"

"Yeah."

"Well, I guess it's true what they say about love never dying."

"Robin! What's gotten into you?" Blaine said uneasily. She didn't like the direction Robin's conversation was taking. "Logan is a married man. Besides, that's not true. It's just a lot of romantic nonsense. Love *does* die."

"Or sometimes it just gets put on the shelf for a while, but that doesn't mean it always stays on the shelf."

She turned and walked down the hall to her bedroom, leaving Blaine to stare in openmouthed surprise after her.

5

Kirk slipped into bed, settled on his side, and pulled the blanket halfway over his head, blocking out the light from the lamp near his wife's head. Cait laid down her book. "I didn't know you knew Rosie Van Zandt."

"I didn't," Kirk said after a moment.

"Yes, you did."

Kirk rolled over, looking up at his wife's freckled, worried face. "What are you talking about?"

"I was straightening the files in your office—"

"Straightening the files!" Kirk said loudly. "Cait, we have a secretary to do that."

"She doesn't do a good job."

"She does a fine job, but it's no wonder she can't find things half the time. You come in there and mess up everything."

"I don't mess it up!" Cait returned, near tears. "I'm only trying to help."

Kirk sat up in bed. "Caity, I don't need help."

"I don't think you need me at all."

Kirk rolled his eyes. "That's not true and you know it. Now what's all this about Rosie Van Zandt?"

"When I was *straightening* your files, I found a work order for a birdhouse you made for Rosalind."

Kirk frowned. "I remember now. She wanted a birdhouse like the ones I made for Blaine—you know, the miniature Chinese pagodas. She said it was to be a birthday present for her grandmother. She wanted to put it outside the old lady's bedroom window. I told her I couldn't do a pagoda because I'd promised Blaine that design was one of a kind. So we decided on a version of the Taj Mahal."

"Why didn't you mention it after Rosie was killed?"

"I forgot. God, Cait, that was months ago. Besides, what does my making a birdhouse for the girl have to do with anything?"

"It means you knew her."

"I didn't *know* her. She came in, placed an order, and a week later picked up the birdhouse and paid for it. What the hell is wrong with that?"

"Why are you so mad?"

Kirk sighed. "I'm mad about your constant questions. Why didn't I mention this to you, why didn't I tell you I met someone? I *do* tell you almost everything that happens to me. I know I told you about Rosie."

"You didn't."

"I *did*."

"I don't remember it."

"No, you don't remember much of anything I say because you're so wrapped up in Sarah and the day-care center."

"You don't want me to be a good mother?"

Kirk's voice tightened. "That's not what I mean and you know it. I just want you to

stop trying to be superwoman. You don't
have to hover over Sarah like she's a new-
born. You don't have to think about the center fourteen hours a day. You certainly don't
have to come to my shop and reorganize
everything."

A tear ran down Cait's face. "I just want to
be part of your life."

"Caity, you are the most important part of
my life. But I want a wife, someone who lis-
tens when I talk, someone who pays a little
attention to me."

"I think I do pay attention to you."

"Like tonight when you suddenly decide
I've been hiding something from you and
you pounce on me?"

"I didn't pounce."

"Yes, you did, and you do it all the time.
I'm getting tired of it, Cait. Really tired."

"I'm sorry," she said meekly.

Kirk wiped away a tear from her cheek
and kissed her. "Caity, things have been
getting worse between us for the past couple of years, ever since you opened the center. But we can start over."

"You want me to close the center?"

"No, of course not. I just want you to
leave it behind when the day is over. I want

the evenings and the weekends to be ours, like they used to be."

Cait pulled a tissue from the box on the bedside table and wiped her nose. "There's just so much to do."

"You *make* so much to do. I don't know— sometimes I think you're trying to prove you aren't lazy like . . ."

"Like my father."

"Well, yeah. That's what you thought of him."

"He *was* lazy."

"I'm not going to argue about whether or not your father was a deeply troubled man or just plain lazy. I'm talking about us. Things are going to hell between us."

"I don't think they're going to hell," Cait said slowly, "but I guess we have been drifting apart."

"That's putting it mildly."

She gave him a weak smile. "Okay. I won't devote any less time to our daughter, but from now on I won't let the day-care center play such a big part in my life."

"And you'll *stop* nosing around at my office."

"I'll stop trying to help you there, if that's what you mean."

"Whatever you want to call it." Kirk kissed her again, this time more ardently. "Everything's going to be all right, Caity," he said softly. "We're going to be just fine now."

But after they'd turned off the light and Cait lay staring into the darkness while Kirk breathed deeply in sleep beside her, she couldn't get the date of Rosie Van Zandt's work order off her mind. August 24—just a couple of weeks before Kirk had started spending so much time working late at night.

13

1

John looked at Logan belligerently. "Okay, mystery time is over. Exactly why have you dragged me here at"—he looked at his watch—"nine-twenty on a Saturday morning?"

Logan sat down behind his desk, calmly picking up a pen while never taking his gaze from John. "You said that on the night of November fifteenth, the night of Rosalind Van Zandt's death, you were with your girlfriend, Samantha Burton, in Columbus, Ohio."

"That's right. You called her and she confirmed it."

"We called the number you gave us, and a young woman *claiming* to be Samantha Burton confirmed it."

John frowned. "What do you mean, *claiming* to be Sam? I don't get it."

"We're not quite the amateurs you take us

for, Sanders. We didn't let your alibi go with one simple phone call. We checked with the Columbus police."

"Oh?"

"Yes. And we found out a few interesting things. One, there is *no* Samantha Burton in Columbus."

John stiffened. "That's crazy!"

"There is no phone listing for her."

"She has an unlisted number."

Logan looked at him deprecatingly. "Don't you think in a murder investigation I have access to unlisted numbers? Besides, the number you gave us *is* listed—to a woman named Gail Clayton."

"Gail is Samantha's roommate."

"You just said Samantha had an unlisted number."

"She does. There are two phones in the apartment."

"So you gave us Gail's number instead of Samantha's."

Perspiration gleamed across John's forehead. Abel Stroud wandered into the room and leaned against the wall, his eyes trailing over the teacher with measured leisure. "I must have gotten the numbers mixed up."

"I don't think so." Logan leaned forward,

looking at John unblinkingly. "And here's another interesting development. There's no one named Samantha Burton working at Riverside Hospital. You did say she was a nurse there, didn't you?"

John's breath was coming faster. "She hasn't been there very long. Before that she was at Children's Hospital."

"Not according to their records."

"Well, to tell you the truth, she's not working this year." John tried to smile as if he were imparting a somewhat amusing confidence. "You see, she was embarrassed about losing her job. It was because of the economy, of course, not because she isn't a good nurse. I've been helping her out financially—"

"Stop it!" Logan stared stonily at John, who had turned the color of chalk. "Don't you understand that this is a *murder* investigation? Don't you understand that Rosalind Van Zandt was pregnant, and that you and one other person are the only men she was seen with during the last weeks of her life? Don't you understand that we *know* you were lying about your whereabouts the night she was killed?"

John's right hand had begun to tremble. "Are you saying I'm a suspect?"

"That's exactly what I'm saying."

"But Tony Jarvis—"

"We aren't talking about Jarvis!" Logan shouted. John jumped, and even Stroud's small eyes opened wider. "Dammit, where *were* you?"

John drew in a long, shuddering breath before slumping in his chair. "I didn't lie," he began in a cowed voice. "I *was* in Columbus on November fifteenth."

"But not with a woman named Samantha Burton."

"No. I told a friend of mine the spot I was in, and she agreed to cover for me."

"A friend? Is that what you call your sister, Gail?"

"Oh, God," John murmured.

"That move wasn't too smart of her," Stroud commented. "Or of you."

"I guess not. I just hope Gail doesn't get into serious trouble because of what she did. Things haven't been going too well for her. She doesn't need grief over me to add to everything else. Her intentions were good." He smiled weakly. "But like they say,

'The road to hell is paved with good inten-tions.' "

Logan looked at him expressionlessly. "I'm not interested in old sayings, so why don't you stop stalling and tell us where you were?"

"All right." John's voice sounded hope-less, resigned. "I was visiting a man named Samuel—Sam—Burleigh."

"Sam Burleigh," Logan repeated slowly. "Why did you feel you had to keep that fact a secret?"

John's gaze dropped for a few seconds, then lifted again, his blue eyes blazing defi-antly at Logan. "Because Sam Burleigh is my lover."

2

"Sanders sure wasn't anxious to take that DNA test to prove if he was the father of the Van Zandt baby," Stroud announced an hour later while munching on his third Dan-ish for the morning.

"I didn't think he was going to agree at all. Your telling him Tony Jarvis was more than willing to take the test did the trick."

"Except that Jarvis threw an even bigger fit than Sanders did about it."

"What Sanders doesn't know won't hurt him. We got what we wanted, and right now that's all I care about."

Stroud began wiping his hands on an old napkin from his desk drawer. "Of course, if he's tellin' the truth about his *sexual preference*," he said in a scathing imitation of John's voice, "there's not much hope of provin' him the father, and I'm pretty sure he's tellin' the truth. That guy is just too good-lookin'."

Logan grinned, "You wouldn't be a little jealous of those good looks, would you?"

Stroud seemed affronted. "Hell, no! It's just that if he is what he says, that complicates things even more."

"Why is that?"

"Two reasons. One, this Sam Burleigh is an anesthesiologist. That means he's got access to drugs the rest of us have never heard of. And if Sanders is his"—Stroud rolled his eyes—"*lover*, through Burleigh he could have gotten the drug that killed those girls."

"Right."

"But it could also mean somethin' different."

"You mean his homosexuality might have different implications?"

"Yep. That's exactly what I'm sayin'."

He began an intent perusal of the remaining Danish in the box on his desk as if he were selecting a diamond. Logan felt a surge of irritation. "Dammit, Able," he finally snapped, "I wish you'd stop making all these melodramatic insinuations and then letting them hang in the air! Just say what you mean."

Stroud looked up. "You won't like it."

"Tell me anyway," Logan said.

"Okay." Stroud picked up the Danish. "Nobody around here knew he was funny, did they?"

"I can't speak for everyone, but I'd say the fact that John Sanders is gay isn't generally known. According to him, that's why he lied about his alibi—he was afraid he'd lose his job if the truth got out in this little place."

"He's right. Most people around here won't put up with that nonsense. I sure don't like the idea of my little Arletta bein' taught by him."

"I think little Arletta is perfectly safe," Logan said dryly. "Just because he's homosexual doesn't mean he's some kind of violent pervert."

"You got your opinions, I got mine. But back to the point. Who are just about the only two women Sanders is ever seen with? Blaine Avery and Rosie Van Zandt."

Logan became motionless and gave him a long, penetrating stare, knowing exactly where he was heading with this line of reasoning. "So?"

"So Miz Avery's husband's been gone six months, you know. And like I said, Sanders is a real good-lookin' guy. He's also single and about the same age as her. Everybody says they're good friends, but what if it was more than that? What if Blaine had the hots for him? And what if she thought he wasn't respondin' to her because of some other female, like Rosie? And then, Rosie and Robin Avery bein' such good friends and all, what if Rosie confided to Robin she was pregnant and Blaine found out? She could've figured it was Sanders's kid. Sounds to me like a pretty good motive for one of those crimes of passion."

In a flashing surge of anger, Logan

wanted to shout that he didn't want to hear any more of Stroud's half-assed theories about Blaine Avery. But he could only imagine what Stroud would make of such a flaming defense of the woman he'd once loved. In fact, he knew what *anyone* would make of it, and he couldn't let people think he was losing his objectivity about this case. So he drew a deep breath and said evenly, "Well, I guess nothing is impossible. But at this point I'm concerned about only one thing— confirming John Sanders's alibi."

"We're trackin' down that Sam Burleigh fella. They said at the hospital he *is* an anesthesiologist on staff."

"But that doesn't prove anything. Don't you see, Abel, that Sanders might be lying about his homosexuality? Sam Burleigh might simply be someone Sanders *knows*."

Abel frowned. "But Sanders would have to figure out that we'd catch on pretty quick if he's lyin'."

"But maybe not quick enough."

3

Logan left Dillard's Hardware Store and drove to the office of Richard Bennett. Bennett's office was in a new brick building with lots of windows, a roomy parking lot, and a special entrance for the handicapped. It was the largest and nicest doctor's office in town.

A young man wearing a cast from his wrist to his elbow glanced up from a magazine when Logan walked into the sunny waiting room that, as far as he was concerned, looked like a jungle with its many pots of hanging plants and flowering confections blooming on almost every table. A middle-aged receptionist with pinched, chihuahualike features and a tag reading "Miss Roush" pinned to her flat bosom told him, with a great deal of self-importance, that Dr. Bennett was with a patient and couldn't possibly see him for another hour. Or not until tomorrow. Yes, tomorrow would definitely be better for the doctor. Would he care to make an appointment?

"This is official business," Logan said, thinking he would never be able to use that phrase again without hearing Tim giggle. "I have to see Dr. Bennett as soon as possible."

"Oh, well." Miss Roush frowned ferociously. The dog image wouldn't fade, and

Logan had a sudden, absurd vision of her shredding newspapers with her teeth for fun. "As you can see, Sheriff, Dr. Bennett has someone waiting."

The teenager, bearing a sprinkling of acne and still holding the magazine, smiled broadly. "I don't mind waiting until the sheriff has seen the doctor," he said. He looked as if he were deliberately trying to appear innocent. Logan had noticed this reaction before—the frightened compulsion to look blameless when faced with a badge.

"Terry, this office closes at twelve," Miss Roush said severely. "If the sheriff takes too long, you might miss your appointment."

"Yeah, but I don't want to get in the way of police business. I could always take a morning off from school next week and come back."

"Now, wouldn't you just like that!"

"Yes, ma'am, I would," Terry replied, grinning.

"Since this young man doesn't mind a delay, I'll go in next," Logan said. Miss Roush's frown deepened. "That *is* all right, isn't it?"

"I'll have to ask the doctor." She was nearly quivering with disapproval. "Sit down, Sheriff."

She waited until Logan was safely seated, then went down the hall, her rubber-soled shoes squeaking on the polished tiles. "Scary, isn't she?" Terry said.

Logan nodded. "I'll bet no one gets past her."

"Better than an armed guard. She's got a crush on Doc Bennett. Thinks he's her property or something." He shook his head. "Jeez, can you imagine coming home to *her* every night?"

They were both snickering when she marched back to the window above her desk. "The doctor said he'll be happy to talk with you as soon as he's finished with this patient," she announced, obviously parroting what Rick had said, then added just loud enough to be heard, "Of course, this is going to throw his schedule off for the *entire* morning."

Terry snickered again, clearly enjoying the disturbance. Logan picked up a copy of *National Geographic* and began reading about a rain forest, although later he wasn't able to remember where the rain forest was located. In five minutes Rick Bennett, wearing a white coat, came to the door of the waiting room. "Hello, Sheriff Quint. Come into my office." As Logan rose, Rick glanced at the young man. "Got enough reading material there to keep you going for a while, Terry?"

"Sure. I'm glad you finally started getting *People* instead of all that educational stuff."

Rick laughed, standing aside to let Logan pass him in the doorway. They went back to his office, a large, sunny room with a beautiful mahogany desk, maroon leather couch and chairs, and not one plant. Logan immediately guessed that the plants in the waiting room were Miss Roush's touch.

"So what can I do for you?" Rick asked, motioning to the couch as he took his seat behind the desk.

"I need some information about a drug."

"Oh?"

"This morning a kid found a medicine vial a few hundred feet from the high school gymnasium, back under a bush. I'm embarrassed that we missed it when we searched the area after Kathleen Foss's death, but we did. Of course, I don't know what we can do in the way of prints—the vial's probably been there a while and the kid handled it— but we can try. Anyway, the vial was for a drug called Dilaudid. Familiar with it?"

Rick smiled. "Sure. It's a narcotic analgesic used for the relief of moderate to severe pain associated with surgery, burns, trauma, cancer—that sort of thing."

"And how is it dispensed?"

"Tablets and single- and multiple-dose ampules for injection are the most common ways. How big was the vial you found?" Logan measured with his fingers. "Then it was a multiple-dose ampule."

"What would be the symptoms of an overdose of Dilaudid?"

"Respiratory depression. Extreme somnolence that could progress to stupor—"

"So that if someone had received a massive overdose," Logan interrupted, "they wouldn't be in any shape to fight off an attack—say someone slitting their wrists."

Rick stared. "No. Of course not."

"And how long does it take for the drug to go to work?"

"Tablets or injection?"

"Injection."

"For a normal dosage, about fifteen minutes. An overdose, five to ten minutes, depending on the amount injected."

"I see." Logan wrote in his notebook. Rick began tapping his fingers on his desk. "Obviously you think the Foss girl was drugged with Dilaudid."

"That's right. Is Dilaudid ever sold on the street?"

"Yes," Rick said slowly. "We don't hear as much about it as something like crack or ice, but it's out there."

"In a place like Sinclair?"

"Well, I don't know about that, but . . . well, yes, it's possible."

"But doubtful."

"Yeah, doubtful." Rick picked up a pen and began tossing it from one hand to the other. "Sheriff, why are you asking me all these questions? I'm sure the medical examiner's office can tell you all about Dilaudid."

"Yes, but you can tell me about Mrs. Peyton. Nothing she's currently on matches what was found in Rosalind Van Zandt's bloodstream, but I wondered if she has ever been on Dilaudid for that broken hip."

"No. She's allergic to it."

"Have you ever prescribed Dilaudid?"

"Yes."

"Frequently?"

"That depends on how you define frequently."

"How many times in the last year?"

Rick frowned. "I'd have to go through my files, but I'd say about six, seven times. Maybe more."

"Can you give me the names of some of the people for whom you've prescribed the drug?"

Rick dropped the pen, raising his hands. "I don't know, Sheriff. I could ask Miss Roush to check—"

"Just off the top of your head."

Rick sighed in exasperation. "Okay. Let me think. Of course, you realize that since I'm an orthopedist, I've prescribed the drug for people with bone injuries. That's what I am—a bone specialist."

"Yes, Dr. Bennett, I do realize that," Logan said calmly, ignoring Rick's patronizing tone that said a simple county sheriff probably wouldn't understand the subtleties of medical specialties.

"All right. Well, there was Aaron Howard—tractor accident that crushed his leg. Dan Frank—cracked vertebrae from a fall. Lucky he didn't break his neck. Muriel Boyd—broken hip like Mrs. Peyton. Martin Avery."

Logan looked up from his notebook. "Martin Avery?"

"Yes. His right shoulder was badly fractured in that car wreck. Took months to heal, and he was in a lot of pain."

"So he took the Dilaudid after he came home from the hospital?"

"Yes. For a couple of months." Rick stiffened. "You're not thinking what I *think* you are, are you?"

"And what would that be?"

"That Blaine had access to Dilaudid."

"She did, didn't she?"

"It was in the house, yes."

"Did any of it ever come up missing?"

"*No!* At least, Bernice never mentioned it, and she's the one who gave the shots."

"*Would* she have mentioned it?"

"Certainly!" Rick leaned forward. "Are you implying that Blaine Avery drugged those girls?"

"It's a possibility."

Rick glared at him. "How can you sit there so damned cold and say that? You *know* this woman. She isn't capable of murdering anyone, especially not a teenaged girl carrying a ten-week-old fetus. That's downright heinous—"

"Ten-week-old fetus?" Logan said sharply. "How did you know the fetus Rosalind was carrying was ten weeks old?"

Rick blinked in surprise. "Uh . . . Blaine told me."

"I told Blaine the fetus was two months old. That's what I told Joan Peyton. I told *no one* the exact age of that fetus. How did you come up with ten weeks?"

"I . . . don't know. I must have heard it somewhere."

"From Rosalind?"

"I'm not an obstetrician, and she didn't consult me about her pregnancy," Rick said tightly.

Logan's eyes narrowed. "I'm sure she didn't consult you *professionally*."

"And what is that supposed to mean?"

"You know what it means."

"Are you saying I was the father of Rosie Van Zandt's baby?"

"Were you?"

Rick's face was growing red in his fury. "I was *not!*"

"Then I don't suppose you'd mind submitting to a DNA test to help us determine paternity."

"I certainly would mind! Why should I? I hardly knew the girl."

"Oh, yes, you did. Listen, Bennett, do you think I'm a fool? Something has been nagging at me since I found out Rosalind was meeting someone out at the Avery house. She never knew when Robin or Blaine or Blaine's brother-in-law would drop by. *Unless*, of course, the movements of those three people were monitored very carefully. Now, Rosalind was no longer close to Robin—a fact that in itself was suspicious— so the information couldn't have been coming from Robin. So who was it coming from?"

"I have no idea."

"How about someone who talked to Blaine or her family at least once a day? How about the good doctor who was supposedly Blaine's staunch supporter during the Martin Avery investigation and naturally solicitous during her illness, keeping up with her every move?"

Rick stood up, his fists clenched. "That is utter bullshit!"

"Really? Well, how about this? Robin thought Rosie might have had a key to the house made the afternoon Blaine was taken to the hospital with pneumonia, because Robin gave Rosalind the key so she could go out to the house and get some of Blaine's things. There's only one place nearby that makes keys—Dillard's Hardware Store. Unfortunately, no one at Dillard's remembered Rosalind coming in to have a key made. But today I found out something. You know old man Dillard who owns the hardware store? He keeps meticulous records of keys they make. Strange habit, one he developed a long time ago when someone was having copies of keys made at the store so they could break into houses. I asked him to do some checking for me and find out who had keys made around the time of Blaine Avery's illness. And guess whose name turned up?"

"Mine, I suppose."

"Right."

"So I had a key made around that time. That doesn't prove anything."

"You didn't have one key made, you had two made. And one of them didn't turn out to Dillard's satisfaction, so he made a third one. He tossed the second one in a drawer. He's proud of his key-grinding and keeps the few failures he has." Logan withdrew a

key from his pocket, watching Rick's face
go from red to white. "I have that extra key
right here. I tried it out a little while ago, and
although it's not a smooth fit, it still opens
the door to the Avery house."

Rick stared at him defiantly for a few seconds; then his shoulders sagged. "I'm calling my lawyer."

"Fine. But I suggest you have him meet
you down at headquarters, because that's
where you're going."

14

1

"You admit you were having an affair with Rosalind Van Zandt?"

"Yes."

Rick sat behind a table in the interrogation room, his face pale, perspiration sheening his upper lip.

"And you lost just about everything in your divorce, didn't you, Doctor?" Logan went on. "You needed money in the worst way. Rosalind didn't have any money, but Blaine does. So when Rosalind turned up pregnant, refusing to have an abortion, threatening to tell the whole town, you killed her." Logan's voice lashed through the room. "You murdered that young girl and your unborn baby so you could get your hands on Blaine Avery's money."

Rick's lawyer, a well-dressed, grim-faced man, said coldly, "That is an assumption."

"Is it? Well, I think your client killed Rosalind Van Zandt."

"No!" Rick shouted. "I didn't kill Rosie. I *didn't!*"

"Did you give Rosalind an engraved bracelet?" Logan asked.

"Yes."

"Well, that solves one mystery. Now, let's solve some others. When did you get involved with the Van Zandt girl?"

"I'd advise you not to say any more," Rick's lawyer said.

Rick didn't seem to hear him. He stood up and walked to the window, then took a deep breath. "Old Mrs. Peyton broke her hip in April. When she went home from the hospital, I started going by to check on her every few days. That's when I met Rosie. She was the most beautiful girl I'd ever seen. And she was very . . . attracted to me. She didn't make a secret of it." He turned and smiled wanly at Logan, who stared back coldly. "Anyway, in July I talked her into coming by my office. I told her I loved her and . . . well, you can take it from there."

"You told her you loved her. Did you love her?"

"Well, no. I hardly knew her. I thought she understood that it was just talk."

"Sure. Seventeen-year-old girls are very sophisticated."

"She *was* sophisticated," Rick flared. "And she was no virgin, I can tell you that."

"Did she ever tell you who her other lovers were?"

"No. But I can guess. Tony Jarvis for one. Maybe John Sanders."

"Was she still seeing Jarvis when she got involved with you?"

"No. At least I don't think so."

"Okay, get on with your story."

Rick sat down again. He looked limp and defeated. "Meeting at my office was too risky, so when Blaine got sick and her house was left vacant, I knew it was perfect. I took her key when she was in the hospital, had two copies made, and started meeting Rosie at the house a couple of times a week. Two weeks before she died, she told me she was pregnant. I'd put her on birth control pills, but I guess she'd forgotten to take them regularly. She was terrified. That's why she waited so long to tell me."

Logan's face was tight with contempt.

"I'm sure she wasn't the only one who was terrified."

"No, she wasn't. I couldn't let her have my baby, if it even *was* my baby, and I'm still not sure about that. I explained to her that she was too young, that if it got out we'd been having an affair, I'd be ruined. She knew about my financial difficulties."

"Now why would a successful doctor be having financial difficulties?"

"My divorce."

"Come on, Bennett. There are no children—you aren't even making child support payments. What's your wife got on you that forced you to make such a ridiculously generous settlement? She did get everything except the office, didn't she—the house, the Mercedes, the boat, *and* a very large sum of money?"

"How the hell do you know that?"

"I know a lot of things."

Rick sighed. "I loved Ellen. I wanted her to be comfortable."

"You are lying," Logan said flatly. "But never mind that now. I'll find out the truth later."

Rick's lips tightened. "Anyway," he went

on, "the last few months have been like starting all over again."

"Which is why you wanted to marry Blaine," Logan said. "You were tired of living in that tiny apartment and driving a six-year-old station wagon, never having money for a vacation or the extravagances you love so well."

The lawyer leaned forward. "That is *another* assumption—"

"I *care* about Blaine," Rick said.

"Oh, yes, you *loved* your wife, you *care* about Blaine, but you were having an affair with a young girl."

"You wouldn't understand."

Logan's mouth curled derisively. "I guess not. Go ahead with your story."

The lawyer frowned disapprovingly. "Dr. Bennett, don't say anything else."

"He'll find out anyway," Rick said. "Besides, I can't live with this anymore."

The lawyer sighed in frustration. "I don't know why you bothered to call me."

"I talked Rosie into having an abortion," Rick continued. "I was going to take her to someone I know out of state. We planned it for a weekend when there was a rock concert in Charleston. It wasn't unusual for her to stay with some cousin there and go to concerts, so I didn't think Joan would get suspicious. We were supposed to meet at Blaine's at seven o'clock."

"On Friday, November fifteenth."

"Yes. But at six-thirty Rosie called, just as I was leaving the office. She said she'd changed her mind. She was crying. I asked if she was at the Avery house, and she said no. I said to go there and we'd talk about it, but she refused."

"Did you go out to the house anyway?"

"No. What was the point? I was so scared of the consequences of all this that I went to a bar. Harry's."

"About what time?"

"Around seven."

"*Around* seven? Can you be more specific?"

"No."

"Then how can I be sure you're telling the truth?"

"Because Harry made a big deal about me being there for the happy hour. I usually stopped in only around nine or ten for one drink. I don't want people thinking I'm an alcoholic."

"What time did you leave?"

"I don't know. Nearly midnight. Harry closes then. He told me I had to leave. Offered to call a cab for me."

"How do I know you were there all evening?"

"Because I played pool with someone. Then Harry turned the TV on to a wrestling match. I hate wrestling, but I got so loaded I bet him on it. I won. He ended up giving me twenty dollars. He'll remember that. Besides, the place was packed. You could ask thirty people if I was there, and they'd tell you I was."

Logan rubbed his temples. "So Rosalind called you and told you she wasn't at the Avery house. But she was. Why would she lie about it?"

"I don't know. Maybe she was afraid I'd come out there and try to change her mind."

Or maybe she was making the call under duress, Logan thought, remembering that Blaine Avery had been at the house that night.

2

Logan knocked on the tall white door of the Peyton home. It opened so quickly he was sure he'd been watched through one of the sidelight windows as he pulled up in the sheriff's car.

Joan Peyton stood at the door, her smile failing to mask the apprehension in her eyes. "Hello, Logan. I hope you're not bringing more bad news."

Logan suddenly felt guilty, the way he often did around the families of assault and murder victims, as if some irrational part of him believed that if he were a better law enforcement officer, he could prevent all such tragedies. He forced down the feeling and smiled back at the woman. "No, Miss Peyton, no more bad news. I just need to talk to Mrs. Litchfield."

"Bernice? Whatever for?"

"I really can't say, Miss Peyton."

"No, certainly you can't. It's none of my business. I'm sorry I asked." She stepped back, motioning him inside. "Come in out of the cold."

Logan stepped into the entrance hall, casting an appraising look at Joan. It had been less than a week since he'd come to this house to tell her about Rosie's body being found on Blaine's property. That night she'd looked harried—she was worried

about Rosie's disappearance—but otherwise she'd appeared very much as she had
fourteen years ago when he'd graduated
from high school. Now her skin looked dry
and bleached, emphasizing new lines
around her mouth and eyes. Even her hair
seemed to have lost its luster; it was carelessly pulled straight back with a silver bar-
rette to expose a quarter inch of gray
strands at the hairline.

"Bernice is upstairs with Mother," Joan
said. "Before I go get her, though, I'd like to
talk to you for a minute." Logan looked at
her inquiringly. "I heard about Rick Bennett
being taken in for questioning this afternoon."

"How do you know that?"

"I called to see if he'd come and check on
Mother this afternoon. Miss Roush told me
you'd taken him away."

"That sounds more dramatic than it was."

"Logan, please don't evade me. You don't
really think Rick knows anything about
Rosie, do you?"

"Well, yes," he said uncomfortably.

She looked at him searchingly. "What
does he know?"

Rosalind was Joan's niece, for all practical purposes her daughter. She had a right to the truth. "He admitted to being the father of her baby."

"What?" she cried, her hand flying to her throat. *"What?"*

"He was having an affair with her. It had been going on since midsummer. In the weeks before Rosalind's death, they were meeting at the Avery house because Blaine was at Cait's and the house was empty."

"I . . . can't . . . believe it." Joan walked shakily to one of the leather wing chairs and sank down. "Oh, my God," she moaned. "I can't believe it. Rosie and I were so close. How could I not have known? How could I have let something like this happen?"

Logan felt awkward in his pity. "I don't think there's much you could have done about it, ma'am. Bennett and Rosalind were very careful."

"Not careful enough to prevent pregnancy!" Joan suddenly stood up, her eyes blazing. "And to think I trusted that man, that I let him take care of my mother! My God, I invited a killer right into my very own home!"

"We don't know that he's a killer."

"You don't *know!* You mean you haven't arrested him?"

"No."

"Why not?"

"Because being the father of Rosalind's child isn't a crime. Besides, his alibi checks out."

Joan's eyes narrowed. "Don't *you* think he killed her?"

"What I think doesn't matter," Logan said. "Only hard evidence counts."

"How terribly fair-minded you have to be to do your job."

"You're the one who recommended back in high school that I'd be suited to this line of work."

The anger abruptly seemed to drain out of Joan, and she gave him a tired smile. "So I did. And I never told you how proud I am of you for getting your degree, did I? Well, I'm telling you now." She sighed and ran a hand across her forehead. Weak light bounced off her wide silver bracelet, and Logan noticed the beautiful sapphire-and-diamond ring she wore on her right hand. He remembered Rosalind's opal-and-diamond ring, which was originally to have been a birthday present to her mother. He wondered if this ring had been a birthday present for Joan. "How's Blaine taking all this?" she asked suddenly.

"As far as I know, she doesn't know. Why?"

"I was just thinking of how close she and Rick seemed to be getting." She sighed. "Blaine always was a kind and unselfish person. She reminds me of my sister." Her posture straightened, and Logan could almost feel her control returning. "I'll get Bernice for you now. Have a seat. Would you like something to drink?"

How many people would think to offer him refreshment at a time like this? Logan thought. But he remembered that even in high school he'd been sneakingly impressed with the elegant Miss Peyton's impeccable manners. "No, thanks, Miss Peyton. I'm just fine."

In a few minutes Bernice Litchfield appeared at the door to the library. In spite of her sixty years, she looked like a chubby, frightened little girl called to the principal's office. He smiled warmly. "Hello, Mrs. Litchfield. I appreciate your taking the time to talk with me."

"Mrs. Peyton's asleep. She's been so upset all morning, but I finally got her to sleep. Joan—*Miss* Peyton—is with her now."

"That's fine. Why don't you come on in and sit down? And close the door, please."

"Close the door?" Bernice repeated warily, as if she thought Logan was going to sexually attack her.

"I want to talk to you confidentially. You don't mind, do you?"

"No, I suppose not." Bernice shut the door and came to sit on the edge of a leather couch, her hands firmly planted on her big knees in their white hose.

"Mrs. Litchfield, you did private-duty nursing for Martin Avery, didn't you?"

"Yes, indeed. Poor man. Such a tragedy. First the paralysis, then . . . well, what happened."

"Yes. I understand that he sustained a broken shoulder as well as spinal damage in that car accident."

"Yes. *Bad* fracture, it was. Bad."

"Can you tell me what painkiller Dr. Bennett prescribed for him?"

"What painkiller Mr. Avery had?"

"Yes."

Bernice's pale eyes rolled to the ceiling for a moment while she thought. "Dilaudid."

"I see. How long were you with Mr. Avery?"

"From the time he got home from the hospital in February until he . . . died. In May. A couple of weeks later Miss Peyton came to me and said she wasn't real happy with the nurse she'd engaged right after her mother broke her hip. Seemed she got too snappy with Mrs. Peyton. You've got to have patience in this field, Sheriff. A *lot* of patience, particularly with the elderly, like Mrs. Peyton. This other woman, whose name I won't mention but I'm *sure* you know her—flouncy, undernourished little thing with fake blond streaks in her hair and skin-tight uniforms—anyway, she just wasn't a good nurse. Too young, I'd say. The young ones, they don't have the touch us older women do. Just don't have it. Besides, I'd taken care of Joan's sister, Charlotte, a long time ago, and I took care of Mr. Peyton last year right up until the week of his death, right before Christmas, so Joan knew I could handle the job."

"I didn't realize you'd been with the Peytons before."

"Oh, yes, sir. The Peytons always pay real good—and, well, frankly, I could use the money. Money's always tight, you know how it is. My husband was a good man, but he didn't believe in life insurance. Always said, 'Bern, why bet against yourself?' 'Fine for you,' I said right back. 'I'm the one that'll be left with the bills.' And sure enough, I ended up high and dry when he passed on."

"I'm sorry."

"I managed. Besides, I like it here."

"Did you like the Averys?"

Bernice's face stiffened. "Mr. Avery was real withdrawn. I think if he'd had a wife closer to his own age, someone he wasn't worried about losing—well, anyway, it was all right."

"Do you think Martin Avery was worried about losing his wife?"

"Well, of course! She was young, pretty. Made a big deal over him, acted like she was real concerned about him, but I don't think it would have been long before she'd have been looking around for a young guy. She acted awful friendly to Dr. Bennett, not that he encouraged her for a minute, don't get me wrong about that. Dr. Bennett's as fine as they come." Another Rick Bennett admirer, Logan thought dryly, wondering what Bernice would think about his affair with Rosalind. "Then there was that Sanders man. A teacher at the high school," Bernice went on. "He came to the house some, although he never paid much attention to poor Mr. Avery. There was also Blaine's brother-in-law, Kirk Philips. He was around a *lot*. All young, good-looking, *healthy* men. Poor Mr. Avery couldn't have helped being worried."

"Did he ever say so to you?"

"Well, no. He wouldn't. He was proud."

So what you actually *saw* was Blaine being solicitous of her husband and three younger men coming around, Logan thought. You *deduced* that Martin Avery was worried about losing his wife. "Mrs. Litchfield, when you were with the Averys, did you ever notice that any of Martin's medicine got lost?"

"Got lost?" Bernice echoed dubiously. "What do you mean, got lost?"

"Did you ever come up short?" Bernice stared. "Were you ever missing a vial of Dilaudid?"

"Do you mean, did someone take some of the Dilaudid away?" Logan nodded. Bernice's eyes grew guarded. "I know what you're getting at. You think I lost track of the medicine." Her voice rose. "What kind of nurse do you think I am?"

"A very good one, I'm sure, but I have to ask this. Please don't be offended."

Bernice's low brow was lowering even further, and Logan suddenly thought of a bull getting ready to charge. "Who says I'm careless with medicine?"

"*No one* has said you're careless with medicine, Mrs. Litchfield. I simply want a straight answer to my question. Did any Dilaudid turn up missing while you were taking care of Martin Avery? Yes or no."

"Absolutely not."

"Thank you," Logan said, wishing he felt relieved.

As he left the house and walked back to his car, all he could think about was the anxiety in Bernice's eyes.

3

Ashley strained against her leash, nearly pulling Blaine off-balance as she paid the bill at the veterinarian's office. Stuffing change and a receipt into her purse, she pushed the glass door open and the two of them burst out into the mauve light of the fading day. "*Okay*, Ash," she said as the dog plowed toward the car. "We'll go straight home. Robin will be back from Susie's by now, and you two can play ball."

Ashley was clambering into the front seat of Martin's Bronco when a car pulled into the parking lot, its horn honking. Blaine looked at it in surprise until the driver whipped it into a parking space next to the Bronco and climbed out.

"Logan!" Blaine exclaimed. "What are you doing here?"

Before Logan could answer, Tim jumped out from the other side of the car. "Hi! We were drivin' by and I saw you." He rushed over to Ashley, who had abandoned the car and stood looking at the little boy, her tail wagging furiously. "Ashley's not sick, is she?"

"No, Tim. She's just here for her yearly shots."

"Late Saturday afternoon?" Logan asked.

"This is the only vet in town who has Saturday afternoon office hours. It's because he takes off on Thursdays."

"Did the shots hurt, Ashley?" Tim asked. The dog licked his face and he laughed.

"She didn't even flinch," Blaine said.

"I'm so glad!" Tim rubbed the dog's ears. "When I saw you here, I made Daddy pull right off the road, didn't I, Daddy?"

Logan smiled. "Yes, you did." He looked at Blaine, his eyes growing serious. "Actually, I've been trying to get hold of you for a few hours."

"I had several errands. I've been out most of the day. Why were you trying to get in touch with me?"

"There's something I need to tell you."

Blaine felt color draining from her face. "Oh, no. What now?"

Logan turned to Tim. "Why don't you walk Ashley over to those pretty trees? You don't mind, do you, Blaine?"

"No," she said, her voice thick with worry. "Just hang onto the leash, Tim. We're out of town, and people travel pretty fast on this road."

"I got it." Tim looped the leash around his wrist. "But it won't do any good to send us away. Dogs have super ears. Ashley can hear everything you're sayin'."

Logan smiled. "But she can't tell you."

Tim led the dog over to two trees standing on the grassy plot beside the vet's office where they began an earnest search for sticks.

"All right, Logan," Blaine said, "please don't keep me in suspense any longer. What's wrong?"

"Today Rick Bennett confessed to being the father of Rosalind's baby." Blaine blinked at him, too surprised to speak. "They'd been having an affair for months. *He* took your key and had copies made, and they met at your house while you were in the hospital and later at Cait's."

"Rick and *Rosie?*" Blaine finally managed to say.

"Yes."

"Oh, Logan, there must be a mistake."

"Didn't you hear me? He *admitted* it."

A woman with a black poodle emerged from the vet's office and stared at them with unabashed curiosity as she stopped to let the dog urinate on the side of the building. Blaine forced herself to close her mouth, which she suddenly realized was gaping open. Logan smiled at the woman. She smiled back and finally pulled the dog along on its leash. Only after she'd gotten into her red Buick Regal did Blaine speak again. "Logan, I can't believe it!"

"You had no idea?"

"No idea? Of course not! I just can't take it in. Rick and a seventeen-year-old girl! And they were meeting in *my* house?"

"I'm afraid so."

"But he didn't say anything . . . not even when Rosie was found dead." She stopped, drawing in a deep breath. "Logan, you don't think that *Rick* . . ."

"Killed her?" She nodded. "He gave us an alibi. Stroud spent the afternoon working on it. It checks out, although there are a few holes. You see, he claims he was in Harry's that night. A lot of people saw him. But because a lot of people *were* there, it could have been possible for him to slip out."

"Possible? How about probable?"

"He would have had to work fast in order for his absence not to be noticed."

"Well, I guess that's one good thing," Blaine said, still feeling dazed. "There's little likelihood that he murdered Rosie."

Logan frowned. "I'm not so sure it *is* a good thing."

"What do you mean?"

"I mean that the alibi gets him off the hook. But he told me something else today that could mean trouble for you."

Blaine felt her breath coming faster. "Trouble for me?"

"Yeah. He wasn't trying to incriminate you, Blaine. He was simply answering my questions."

"Questions about what?"

"He told me that Martin was taking Dilaudid for his shoulder injury."

Blaine looked at him blankly. "Was he? I didn't know what drugs he was on. But what does that have to do with me?"

"We've ascertained that both Rosalind and Kathy were drugged with Dilaudid."

"They were?"

Logan nodded.

"I still don't see—" Her eyes widened. "Oh, my God. And *I* had access to Dilaudid," Blaine said slowly as the day grew darker and the net seemed to draw tighter around her.

15

1

Blaine drove through town, looking with un-
accustomed interest at the bank with its
smooth granite facade and glittering glass
doors, the graceful Colonial library surrounded by a black wrought-iron fence dating from the nineteenth century, the big
sandstone post office, the scattering of
stores, the movie theater which had once
been completely filled with water when the
Ohio River flooded in the thirties. In fact,
she'd seen pictures of the town during the
flood, when people had paddled up and
down the streets in boats and the marquee
had read "Gone with the Flood."

I feel like I'm seeing it all for the last time,
she thought in a combination of panic and
sadness. And maybe I am. Maybe within a
few months I'll be in prison for murders I
didn't commit. What malevolent force was

out there, she wondered, cooperating with a killer to make her look guilty?

When she finally got home, she left her car in the driveway and was surprised to hear music coming from inside the house. Robin had told Blaine she was spending the day at Susie's and wouldn't be home until six. It was only five-thirty, although darkness had already closed in. Blaine immediately felt apprehensive. She didn't like the idea of Robin alone in the house, with all that was going on. In fact, since Rosie Van Zandt's body was found, Sinclair had become like a ghost town after the sun went down. Apparently everyone felt safer behind locked doors at night.

Blaine felt even more apprehensive when she found that the alarm system hadn't been activated. But inside, Robin was peacefully playing the piano. She was safe, and Blaine decided not to lecture her on her carelessness.

She went immediately to the kitchen, fixed Ashley a bowl of water and herself a scotch and soda, and walked back to the living room to listen to Robin. The girl was rapt, her blunt fingers—the fingers of a true pianist—skimming over the keys with complete confidence. For a while Blaine thought Robin wasn't even aware of her presence, but when she finished, she turned around. "Know what that was?"

"Bach. 'Andante.' "

Robin smiled. "Right. And I didn't think you knew music."

"I don't, but I've been listening to you for three years."

"Listening closer than I thought."

"I always wanted to play."

Robin swept back her long, shining hair and looked at Blaine with interest. "I didn't know that. Why didn't you ever take lessons?"

"Rob, we hardly had enough money to pay the utility bills."

Robin's eyes dropped. "I forgot. You were on welfare when you were a kid, right?"

"No. That's what everyone thinks, but we weren't. Dad did yard work and all kinds of odd jobs. He refused to go on welfare."

"How could you live on such a little bit of money?"

"It wasn't easy. Mom worked at the bakery for a while, then she got sick of it. Believe me, she had no talent for cooking, and about all she got to do was clean the kitchen. When she quit, we had hardly anything. That's when she left. I was twelve."

"That must have been awful."

"I'm ashamed to say it wasn't." Blaine took a sip of her drink. "Mom and I fought constantly. I realize now it was partly because she was taking out her frustration about our poverty and Dad's drinking on me. Still, she didn't do much to help the situation."

"Because she didn't have a job anymore?"

"Because she never stopped nagging Dad about being a drunken failure, which made him drink even more."

Robin twined her fingers together and looked toward the fireplace. "My parents never argued." Blaine said nothing, although she knew the girl was merely parroting what she'd been told. "Daddy was so good to Mom. Daddy was great—at least until his accident. Then he was just so miserable."

"I know that, Robin." For the first time since she'd met Robin, she felt they were sharing a moment of closeness. The sensation was odd, but extremely comforting. What a time for this to happen, Blaine thought ruefully. Finally, when my world is falling apart, Robin opens up to me just a little.

The phone on the end table beside Blaine rang and she stared at it. "Aren't you going to answer?" Robin asked.

"Yes. It's just that after those weird phone calls . . . well, never mind. I can't cringe every time the phone rings." Hesitantly she picked it up as it shrilled a fourth time.

"Blaine, *what* is going *on?*" Cait blurted.

"What do you mean?" Blaine asked, trying to sound casual. Hopefully, Cait hadn't heard about Rick. She wasn't in the mood to explain his paternity of Rosie's baby to either Cait or Robin.

"I *mean* that I heard about Rick. Rick and Rosie. Is it true?"

"I guess so, but I'd rather not talk about it now, okay?"

Cait was silent for a moment. "Is Robin there?"

"Yes."

"And she doesn't know."

"That's right."

"Okay, I understand. But what's this I hear about a missing drug?"

"How on earth did you hear about that?"

"About three people have called me about it."

"Three!"

"Yes."

"How did they know?"

"I don't know, Blaine. I didn't interrogate them."

"But you're going to interrogate me."

"*You* are my sister."

"All right. Apparently Rosie and Kathy were drugged with Dilaudid, a drug Martin was taking, and since I found both girls . . ."

She was aware of Robin's eyes growing larger and Cait sputtering. She took another sip of her drink and interrupted her sister. "Cait. I hate to ask, but could Robin come and stay with you for a few days?"

Robin's eyes opened even wider, and Cait paused before saying, "Sure. But why? I mean, you're both welcome. I'd feel so much better if you were both here—why just Robin?"

"I have my reasons, Cait." For once Cait was silent. "So how about Robin coming over tomorrow, before noon?"

"That's fine, but—"

"Thanks a million, Caity. I really have to go now. Talk to you later."

When she hung up, Robin rose from the piano bench, looking at her furiously. "Why do I have to go stay with Cait?"

"Because too much is happening. I don't think you're safe out here, and besides, Cait lives two blocks from the high school. You won't have that four-mile drive morning and afternoon."

"I don't mind the four-mile drive. And did it ever occur to you to ask *me* if I *wanted* to move in with Cait and Kirk again?"

"No, because I knew what you'd say. But you're going."

Robin glared at her. "I *knew* you'd find a way to get rid of me after Daddy died! By next week I'll probably be in Florida with my grandparents."

"I'm not sure Florida is such a bad idea . . ."

Robin just stared at her. *"What?"*

"This has been such a terrible time for both of us. Maybe it would do you good to get away from everything for a few weeks—"

"You just want time alone with Rick, don't you?" Oh, Lord, Blaine thought. How wrong you are. "Or is it John Sanders? Who are you trying to get me out of the way for?"

"Robin, that is enough. I am not trying to 'get you out of the way,' as you put it. I'm trying to look after you."

"I don't need looking after!" Robin shouted. "I'm a grown woman!"

Blaine tried to act calm, although her stomach was tightening. She hated to argue with Robin. "No, you are not a grown woman. You are a teenaged girl who was friends with two other teenaged girls who were murdered."

"Oh, are you saying you think I'm next on the list?"

"Rob, please. I don't want to fight with you. I just want you to go to Cait's for a few days."

"And then on to Florida so you'll have the house and half of Daddy's money, and someone to fool around with!"

"Robin! Don't you *ever* say something like that again!"

"Why not? It's true. You've got it all now, don't you? All you need to do is get rid of me. Well, you're not going to find that as easy as you think!"

Robin stomped off to her bedroom, slamming the door so hard the whole house seemed to shake. Within a minute the stereo was pounding. This time it was too loud even for Blaine, who liked rock music. She walked down to Robin's door and knocked. When the girl didn't answer, she yelled, "Turn that down a decibel!" Nothing. Sighing, she went to her own bedroom, sat on the bed, and finished her drink. Then she lay down. Ashley jumped up beside her, and she rolled over, burying her face in the dog's golden hair. "At least you don't yell at me or ask a million questions," she murmured. "No wonder they say a dog is man's best friend."

She was surprised when the phone beside her bed awakened her. How had she actually managed to doze off, considering how upset she was, not to mention all the noise still thundering from Robin's room? Probably because she hadn't gotten a full night's sleep since Rosie was found. She glanced at the clock and saw she'd only slept about thirty minutes. She felt as groggy and heavy as if it had been three hours. The phone rang again, and groaning, she reached to pick it up. Cait, no doubt, wanting to drag more information from her.

Instead a fairly familiar voice said, "Blaine? Are you alone?"

Blaine frowned and sat up on the bed, flipping on the bedside light. "Bernice?"

"That's right. I need to talk to you. Are you alone?"

"No. Robin is in her room."

"Oh. I'll have to ask you to come out to my place, then."

Blaine rubbed her eyes and shifted the phone to her other ear. "Bernice, what do you want to talk to me about?"

The woman paused. Then she said, "Dilaudid."

"The drug Martin was taking."

"Yes."

Another pause stretched out, and Blaine finally said, "Bernice, I don't know anything about Dilaudid. I didn't even know Martin was taking it."

"No?" She was breathing heavily, and her voice sounded slightly slurred. "Sheriff Quint questioned me about the drug today. I didn't tell him anything. I was . . . scared. But I'm a truthful woman. I won't lie anymore."

Blaine's hand tightened on the receiver. "You won't lie about what?"

"About what I know."

"Bernice, will you just say what you

mean?" Blaine asked, both irritated and alarmed. She'd never liked Bernice's suspicious glances and malicious tongue, but at least the woman had never acted weird before.

"I don't want to talk about this over the phone. And I can't come there."

"Why not?"

"I'm . . . I'm having one of my headaches. My migraines. They're caused by tension. I've lived with a lot of tension the past few months. And today when the sheriff questioned me . . . well, this can't go on."

"*What* can't go on?"

"My silence. My silence about the Dilaudid. My silence about the afternoon Mr. Avery died."

Blaine felt as if her own breath had stopped. "The afternoon Martin died? You said you weren't here."

"I was afraid."

Blaine clutched the phone. "Bernice, *please*, this is cruel. What are you *talking* about?"

"Come to my home. You know where it is, don't you?"

"Of course, but I don't see why you can't just tell me—"

"Robin is in the house."

"So?"

"Come to my house, Blaine. I'll tell you everything, and maybe we can figure out something, some way to save her. After all, she's the same age as my granddaughter, Susie. That's why I haven't said anything before now. I knew how much she loved her daddy. But all these killings . . . And now they're onto the Dilaudid."

Blaine's hands turned icy. "Bernice, are you saying that Robin—"

"Just come to my house. If you aren't here in twenty minutes, I'm calling the sheriff."

The line went dead, but Blaine sat holding the receiver with stiff fingers. The doubt, the *fear* that had almost died in her mind during the past few months, had been fanned back to life by Bernice's cryptic comments. Robin, who had loved her father and looked with such desolation on his misery, his helplessness. Robin, who was supposed to have been with Rosie the afternoon of Martin's death. Could it be?

Blaine finally laid the receiver back in the cradle and stood up, running her hands through her hair. This was ridiculous, unthinkable. Bernice had simply . . . had simply what? Suddenly lost her mind? It was possible. She was obviously scared half to death about missing medicine. Maybe she'd be willing to throw blame on Robin rather than admit to incompetence on her own part. But that was rather extreme. What would happen to her if it were proved she *had* misplaced medicine? She'd lose her nursing license. Yet what if people took seriously the accusing finger she pointed at Robin? Hadn't Blaine had her own doubts about exactly what had happened the day Martin died, a day when he'd suddenly come into possession of a key to the gun case she'd so carefully hidden and retrieved a revolver he could hardly have reached without turning the gun case over on himself?

"I have to find out what she's going to tell the police," Blaine said aloud. "I have to decide whether she really knows something or whether she's just making insinuations because of panic. Either way, the repercussions could be disastrous. But what about Robin? I can't leave her here alone."

She called Cait, but there was no answer, which wasn't surprising. It was almost seven. She would be bathing Sarah, and Kirk was probably still at the shop, working. Rick was out of the question. The very thought of him being left alone with Robin sent shivers down her back, although she still couldn't imagine he was a killer. John? No, not after what Robin had said earlier about Blaine's wanting to get her out of the way so she could be with John. Besides, it was Saturday night. He always went out of town on the weekends.

No one. There was no one. "That's what you get for shutting yourself off from the world," she muttered. "You have four people you can call on for help, and they're either unavailable or unacceptable. There's nothing left but to go alone. I'll go and be back as fast as possible."

She hurried out of her room and down the hall to Robin's. "Rob!" she yelled above the sounds of Poison. "Robin!" There was no answer, and finally she turned the knob. The door was locked. Great, Blaine thought. She's gone into one of her colossal pouting spells. "Robin, please open the door." The door did not open. "Robin, I have to go out," Blaine shouted, determined not to get angry. She couldn't handle anger on top of everything else she was feeling. "I'll activate the alarm system before I go. Don't answer the door for anyone, okay?" Nothing. *"Okay?"* Damn that impossible girl! she thought. "I'm leaving Ashley here with you. I'll be back soon."

Hurriedly she checked all the doors and windows, even putting the lock panel on the dog door, slid into her coat, grabbed her purse, pressed the buttons to activate the alarm system, and ran outside. Then she went to her car and wheeled out of the driveway onto Prescott Road, heading north.

The temperature had taken an unusual rise during the day, but now it was dropping sharply again, causing the low-lying fog that had begun clustering in the trees thirty minutes before. It crept across the concrete, seeming to swallow the road, and Blaine put her headlights on low beam so they wouldn't reflect off the shimmering layers in front of her. She also turned on the wipers to keep the windshield free of the clinging mist. Already the countryside was taking on a blanched, dead look.

Bernice lived in an isolated, one-hundred-year-old farmhouse two miles from her. She had been there only once, on a morning when Bernice was having car trouble and asked Blaine to bring her to the Avery home, where she would spend the day with Martin. Blaine had been surprised at Bernice's home. Although she knew the house had been in Bernice's family since it was built, apparently Bernice had no love for it, because she'd done nothing to keep up its condition since her husband had died ten years earlier. Battered, spiky wicker furniture sat on the sagging porch, and the glance Blaine had gotten of the entrance hall showed her water-stained wallpaper and faded, frayed rag rugs on worn hardwood floors.

Blaine turned off Prescott Road onto a narrow dirt lane leading to the house. She slowed, avoiding ruts in the road. On either side of her lay pastures, once well tended but allowed to go to ruin long ago. The fog, growing thicker, hung over rough grass where Herefords with gentle-eyed white faces once grazed.

Abruptly the pastures ended and a stand of trees appeared, separating the pastures from the house. The trees loomed over the road, their bare limbs forming a skeletal canopy. This is like the woods behind my house, Blaine thought. I feel like I'm back in those woods where I found Rosie, where she was probably murdered . . .

Blaine slowed. What am I doing here? she asked herself silently. It's dark, it's isolated, and Bernice sounded so strange on the phone. But I have to find out what she was talking about. For Robin's sake, I *have* to find out.

She pulled up in front of the house, turned off the engine, and climbed the creaking porch steps. Bernice had at least left a porch light on for her, although it was a single, forty-watt bulb whose glow was nearly obliterated by the vast darkness and the fog. She knocked on the door. No answer. She knocked again, then stepped back. No light shone in the big front window. No noise came from inside. Bernice had said she was having one of her migraines. Had she taken something and then gone to sleep? No, certainly not after the insistent call she'd just made. Or had she been drinking? Susie had once mentioned being worried that her grandmother was drinking excessively, especially after Martin's death, then had begged Blaine not to repeat the remark. "I shouldn't have said that," Susie had fretted. "Mom and Dad would *kill* me. Besides, I don't know for *sure* that she's drinking, and I'm sure she doesn't do it on duty. It's just that sometimes when you call her when she's not expecting it, she sounds so *fuzzy*, you know, like someone who's had too much." Had Bernice "had too much" tonight? Was that why she'd sounded so strange on the phone?

Blaine turned the door handle. It revolved easily, but the door stuck. Obviously the wood was expanding in the dampness. She shoved, and when it wouldn't give, she stood back and yelled, "Bernice! It's Blaine Avery. Are you here?"

Still nothing. Blaine cursed under her breath. Here she was, trying to find out something vitally important about Robin, and Bernice was either asleep or gone. Gone where? she wondered. Gone to the police? It had taken Blaine a few minutes to lock up the house and try to get some response out of Robin. Maybe Bernice had decided she wasn't coming and had gone on to the sheriff's office. If so, there was nothing she could do to stop her.

Slowly she went down the steps to her

car, looking back at the house a couple of times for signs of life. But there was no indication of movement within. Reluctantly, she climbed in the car and turned the ignition key.

"Oh, for God's sake!" she shouted when the only response she got was the same clicking sound she'd heard the day of Rosie's funeral, when the car had been towed to Pearson's Garage. "They said they fixed it!" They also said to take it back to the Mercedes dealer, Blaine reminded herself. They said they weren't equipped to handle expensive foreign cars.

She tried a couple more times. Click, click, click. Hadn't she noticed something earlier? Hadn't the car seemed sluggish? And she'd ignored it. Stupid! She pounded the wheel in frustration, then reached for the car phone. Dead. Within the past few days, the phone company must have finally realized she hadn't paid her bill and stopped the service. What perfect timing! She put down the receiver, then laid her head on the steering wheel. "Why can't this sort of thing ever happen in your own driveway?" she asked aloud. "Why are you always *stuck* someplace?" Bernice, of course, had a phone, but she couldn't get Bernice's door open. At least not the front door. But there had to be other doors. At least one side door, right?

Blaine climbed out of the car and walked to the left side of the house, which faced a barn a few hundred feet away that Bernice clearly used as a garage because there was a gravel drive leading up to it. She impulsively walked to the barn doors first to see if Bernice's car was there, but they were padlocked shut. "Naturally," she muttered. Bernice was a fanatic about locks ever since the farmhouse had been broken into twenty years ago. The thieves had been a couple of teenaged boys who were breaking into houses all over the area and stealing jewelry. Bernice never tired of telling about losing her mother's cameo, which grew more valuable with every recitation of the tale.

Blaine looked around, spotting a narrow door at the side of the house. She hurried up splintery steps and pulled open a screeching screen door, reaching anxiously for the knob. But this door was definitely locked. She pounded on it for a minute, then gave up. She circuited the house. No other doors. "Did you really expect any?" she asked herself. "Did you really think that just because most houses this size have at least three doors, *this* one would?"

Blaine realized she was talking to herself out of fear. Bernice's call had shaken her to the core. Now she was out here in the middle of nowhere, stranded. There was only one solution—to walk back to Prescott Road and hail a car.

Glad she was wearing slacks and flat-heeled shoes, Blaine started back the way she had come. It wasn't far to the road, she told herself. It was just that the night was so ominously dark. Fog billowed out from the trees, and she suddenly thought of all those movies she'd seen about Jack the Ripper that habitually featured fog-enshrouded London streets. "Why don't you just make matters worse by trying to scare yourself?" she said furiously into the empty night. "Besides, this country lane doesn't look a thing like a nineteenth-century London street. Jack the Ripper wouldn't be caught dead here."

She had gone about a hundred feet when she heard a noise. Involuntarily, she paused. Fog distorted sounds, but she was certain

she'd heard a twig snapping in front of her
and slightly to the right, off in the woods. An
animal, of course. No cause for alarm. It
was probably something fairly small, like a
ground hog. Or maybe even smaller—a
skunk. Now wouldn't being sprayed by a
skunk finish off this perfect evening? she
thought, trying to laugh off her fear.

She took two more steps, then heard
measured, crackling sounds, the same
sounds her own feet made when she veered
off into the tall, crisp grass. Not animal
paws skittering through the woods, she
thought. Not even a deer timidly approaching. Calm, deliberate *footsteps*. Her heart
began to pound and she peered into the
woods, but it was useless. The world had
turned into a crawling mass of fog that even
extinguished the light of the moon. She felt
totally alone in this eerie mist—alone and
vulnerable. After all, two girls had been murdered . . .

She took another hesitant step forward
before a figure stepped out from the trees—
a bulky, coated figure that stood approxi-
mately ten feet in front of her. She gasped,
trying instinctively to make out a face in the
moment before a powerful flashlight was

shone directly in her eyes, blinding her. "Bernice?" she asked shakily, flinging up a hand to shade her eyes. The figure didn't answer. She heard gravel crunch as it began to move forward. Then she heard the distinctive sound of a revolver being cocked.

Blaine whirled and ran left into the woods that a few minutes ago had looked so menacing and now seemed like a safe haven. It was harder to shoot someone dodging through trees than someone running down an open road.

She heard footsteps pounding behind her, driving her away from Prescott Road, back in the direction of the house. *Concentrate*, she intoned silently. Don't think about who's following you or when he's going to shoot the gun. Just concentrate on not stepping in a hole or running into a low tree limb. *And don't look back*. You'll only slow yourself down.

Although Blaine was not particularly athletic, she normally was in good shape and had above-average stamina, thanks to triweekly workouts. But she hadn't really exercised since her illness, and her body felt sluggish.

The ground was covered with dried

leaves, and she cursed every one of them as they crackled beneath her feet. With all the noise she was making, she couldn't possibly lose herself in the woods, and she didn't dare stop for fear her pursuer would be on her in seconds. She had no choice but to go on.

She weaved around what seemed to be hundreds of trees, forcing her mind back to her flight. Briars grabbed her wool pant legs and she stumbled. Stopping to tear her clothes free, she heard feet thudding behind her, *close* behind her. Crouching low, she took off like a track runner. *Concentrate,* she told herself again. The ball of her foot slammed down on a sharp rock, sending a shock up her right leg to meet the pain in her right side. She gasped for breath in the cloying fog and knew that she couldn't keep on much longer. She already felt like someone running in a nightmare, legs pumping harder and harder and getting her nowhere.

Suddenly she broke out of the woods into an open field. Unless she'd managed to run in a circle, the house should be about fifty feet ahead, she thought. The house meant lights and locks and a telephone to save her from the stranger chasing her. Because her pursuer couldn't possibly be Bernice. The overweight older woman couldn't run that fast. And if Blaine couldn't get *into* the house? Well, she had to. The house was her only hope.

The fog had begun to swirl at an impossible speed, and she knew she was close to passing out. Oh, God, where was the damned house? She slowed, the stitch in her side becoming almost unbearable. She gulped air and tried to get her bearings. Was that a glimmer of light to her right? Or was it only a trick of the fog?

A shot cracked, and she was aware of a bullet whizzing just above her head. She let out a tiny, breath-starved scream and sprinted toward the light. A bulk materialized around it, and she realized she was seeing the weak porch light. She swallowed a sob, still listening for pursuing footsteps, still trying to concentrate all her energy on flight and not on whether the next bullet would find its mark.

She had reached the gravel drive and skirted around the house to the porch, leaping up the three steps and pounding across the old, unpainted boards. Another shot split the darkness with that odd snapping sound caused by the fog. Blaine grabbed the brass doorknob, turned it, and hurled all her weight against the door. It groaned, then opened, and she staggered into the dark entrance hall. She slammed the heavy door behind her and fumbled at the lock. But this was the original door, and the old-fashioned lock needed a key. Breaking into silent, wrenching sobs, she ran her hands up the smooth wood and found a bolt lock, which she shot into place. "Thank God," she rasped. Sagging against the door, though, she felt only a few seconds of relief. The side door was locked, but what about the windows? She would have to check before he found another way in. But the entrance hall was spinning, spinning . . .

2

Pain seared through Blaine's temples. For a few dizzy moments she had the impression her head had been pierced by something long and sharp. Then, slowly, reason returned. She felt her temples. Nothing, of course.

What she noticed next was the musty smell of rough fabric beneath her cheek.

That explained the pain—she had fallen and hit her head. The blow had been cushioned only by a thin rag rug.

Automatically, she glanced at her watch. Seven thirty-five. She had been unconscious only a few minutes at most. Her pursuer could still be outside, trying to find a way in. Or maybe he was *already* inside.

Her heart slammed painfully in her chest, and for a moment she felt paralyzed. If I could just disappear into this rug, she thought wildly. If I could just sink down inside where no one could see me . . .

Blaine clenched her hands into fists. Stop thinking like a terrified child, she told herself sternly. You can't disappear, but you *can* protect yourself. Slowly she sat up, looking around her. In a corner by the door stood a coat rack, and beneath it rested a long black umbrella. She scrambled to her feet, ran forward, and grabbed it, looking with satisfaction at its long metal point. It wasn't a gun, but it was *something*.

She didn't dare call out for Bernice. Raising her voice could give away her location if her assailant was in the house. Still, he must have seen her come in. And if he *was* in the house by now, would he have looked for her first near the front door?

She hovered in the hall, not knowing what move to make first. Should she hide? Should she make sure all the doors and windows were locked?

No. She should get to the telephone.

Clutching her furled umbrella, she crept forward to the edge of the living room, surveying it from behind the doorframe. Her eyes shot to the fireplace, where the remains of a fire smoldered, doing little to warm or light the big, high-ceilinged room, in which no lamps burned. Someone could be in there, she thought. Someone could easily be hiding behind some of that old furniture. She listened with hearing that in her terror seemed as acute as an animal's, but she heard nothing. No movement, no breathing.

Slowly she stepped into the living room, wishing desperately she could turn on a lamp, but the draperies were open onto the foggy night, and she didn't want to expose her location to someone who might be right outside, someone who could fire a gun through the big front window. No, she would have to search for a phone in the semidarkness.

She dropped down onto her knees to prevent casting a silhouette against the window, and began to crawl across a thick rug of some sort. She could smell the dust she was stirring up. She knew Bernice was fastidious in other people's homes and she couldn't imagine her being different about her own, but even a good vacuum cleaner would have been useless against this old, embedded dirt. Why on earth didn't Bernice fix up this place? Money? she wondered inanely, reaching forward to grasp the curved leg of a table. Slowly she raised herself up, running her hand lightly across the tabletop. A crocheted doily. A picture frame, which she knocked over but caught before it crashed onto the floor. A hurricane lamp that felt hand-painted. Leaves—a houseplant. No phone.

She dropped back down and continued her slow progress across an open expanse of rug. The fire was just about out now, and all she could see was vague shadows of furniture. To her right was a settee with pillows heaped at one end. In front of the settee was a coffee table, an unlikely place for a phone. Nevertheless, she swept her hands across it. Magazines, an ashtray, and a glass on a coaster. She picked up the glass, beaded with moisture from the ice cubes inside, and sniffed. Bourbon.

She crouched again. I will not give in to this impulse to shake and sob, she thought, although her legs were trembling and she could feel tears running down her cheeks. There has to be a phone somewhere in this house. My guess is that it's in the living room, and I *will* find it before *he* finds *me*.

Slowly, carefully, she crawled on, grasping her umbrella, listening for the slightest sound coming from the back of the house where another door might be unlocked. But she heard nothing. Finally she made out the form of what looked like a chaise longue with an afghan or blanket tossed on it. Beside it was a table.

She raised herself up again, feeling like a cat gently standing on its hind legs to begin a sniffing investigation of forbidden knick-knacks. The fire gave one final hiss and died. Now she was in complete darkness and she paused, momentarily overwhelmed by the sensation that someone was right behind her, reaching for her—a fear that since childhood had engulfed her whenever she was plunged into sudden darkness. She held still until the rush of panic abated, then forced herself to go on. Her left hand touched something glass—an ashtray. And there was a book of some sort, a fabric-covered book with tiny protrusions at each page. Index tabs. It must be an alphabet-ized address book. She drew in her breath, knowing what she would touch next—a telephone!

She sank down on the floor again and took the receiver off the hook. Light glowed beneath the buttons and relief flooded through her. So the phone lines hadn't been cut, as she'd feared. There was no 911 in this area. If she could only remember the number of the sheriff's office. Or maybe she should simply dial the operator. Punching zero, she leaned heavily back against the chaise.

A hand landed on her shoulder.

Blaine shrieked and leaped to her feet, feeling the hand trail down her back. Drop-ping the phone receiver, she whirled, back-ing away from the chaise. No movement. No sound except a woman saying "C and P operator" on the phone. But Blaine's eyes had become accustomed to the darkness, and she could see it. Barely. A hand hanging limply from beneath the afghan. A hand dripping blood.

16

1

A tremendous force seemed to be pressing on Blaine's chest. After her first scream, all other sounds caught in her throat. She felt as if she were choking. Then, finally, air rushed from her lungs and emerged in a long, rattling moan.

She couldn't run away. Who knew what terror could be waiting outside in the fog? Who knew what terror could be waiting in the *house?* She had no choice but to face what lay in front of her.

"Okay," she said softly. "Get hold of yourself. Just—get—hold—of—yourself." She took a couple of trembling steps forward, her eyes riveted on the shadowy, motionless hand. The *dripping* hand. Gingerly she lifted an edge of the afghan and pulled it back. The puffy face of Bernice Litchfield was angled toward the front window, as if she had wanted to snatch one last glimpse of the world before she died. Automatically, without thought, Blaine pressed her fingers to the woman's thick neck. At first she thought she imagined it; then she was sure. The faint fluttering of a pulse! Bernice wasn't dead.

Blaine shook off her coat, turned it wrong-side out, and used her teeth to tear two small holes in the lining. Starting with the holes, she ripped two strips of nylon lining from the coat, then picked up Bernice's right wrist. She took one of the strips and began tying it above the slash in the wrist, then stopped. There were bones in the lower arm that prevented her from tying the strip tight enough to form a tourniquet. Sweat popping out on her forehead in spite of the chilliness of the room, she moved the strip higher and tied the tourniquet above the elbow. Then she did the same on Bernice's other arm, thinking all the time of how cold the woman was. Shock, naturally. Blaine recovered her with the afghan, felt her way over to the settee, gathered some pillows, and put them under Bernice's feet. Finally she sank down on the floor, ignoring the blood that had seeped from Bernice's slashed wrists. The phone receiver lay at her feet. The operator's voice had been replaced by the noisy whine indicating the phone was off the hook. Blaine pressed the disconnect button for a moment, then dialed the operator again and asked to be connected with the emergency squad. Once she had given them the location of Bernice's house, she called the sheriff's office.

After she hung up, she crawled away from the chaise longue toward the fireplace. She withdrew a poker from the tarnished rack of tools beside the fireplace and huddled against the wall, too frightened to think about who could have done this to Bernice. If she could only hang on for a few minutes, she thought. If she and Bernice could both only hang on for a few minutes, help would arrive.

The phone rang and Blaine dropped the poker, looking at the telephone as if it were a living thing. But it wasn't. It didn't know it shrilled beside a dying body. It rang a second time. A friend of Bernice's, Blaine thought. Or maybe Susie.

The phone rang a third, then a fourth, time, and Blaine suddenly wondered if it was Logan calling. Maybe her message had been garbled. She hadn't been exactly articulate when she called the sheriff's office, and she hadn't talked to him. What if he was calling to confirm where she was? What if he didn't come, and the killer was still around?

She retrieved the poker, crept across the floor and picked up the receiver, managing a weak "Hello?"

A needle dropping down on a record. Oh, God, oh, no, Blaine thought. Scratching sounds. Then a strong male voice singing with reverence:

Rock of Ages, cleft for me,
Let me hide myself in Thee.
Let the water and the blood,
From Thy wounded side which flowed,
Be of sin, the double cure,
Save from wrath and make me pure.

2

She was vaguely aware of cars pulling up in front of the house, of footsteps crossing the porch, of the door being opened cautiously. Light flooded the entrance hall, then

Logan was calling, "Blaine? Where are you?"

"Here," she whispered, curled against the table, the phone receiver still locked in her hand.

"Blaine?"

More footsteps. Careful footsteps. Men with guns drawn, not knowing what they were walking into. How brave policemen are, Blaine thought vaguely. How brave to walk into such danger.

She was aware of shapes by the living room door. "There's no one in here but me," she said hoarsely. "I'm over here with Bernice, but she's dying."

A lamp flared. She heard Logan say, "Stroud, you and Clarke check the rest of the house, and be careful." Then he was beside her, his hand on her shoulder. "Blaine?" he said softly.

She looked up. Shadows hollowed his face with its chiseled features and prominent cheekbones, making it look slightly frightening. She swallowed. "I'm all right. But Bernice—her wrists—just like the others. Oh, Logan."

She couldn't look as he drew back the

afghan. "Did you put the tourniquets on her arms?" he asked.

"Yes."

"No one in the kitchen or dining room," someone said.

"Is anyone checking the upstairs?"

"Yes."

"Then you look outside. And let the EMS people in here now."

Logan knelt beside Blaine, put his hands under her arms, and drew her to her feet. "There's blood all over you."

"I know."

"Tell me what happened."

"She called me," Blaine replied as people entered and began working on Bernice. "She said she needed to talk to me."

"Talk to you about what?"

"I don't know."

"You don't *know?*" Logan prodded. Blaine shook her head, glancing away from him. "She just said she wanted to talk to you, and you came right out?"

"She sounded upset."

In the background Blaine heard someone say, "Blood pressure eighty over forty. Let's give her a vasopressor. Adrenalin, quick."

Logan held Blaine away from his chest,

looking at her intently. "Okay. Bernice was upset. What happened next?"

"I drove out here. She didn't answer the door and there weren't any lights, so I decided to drive home. But my car wouldn't start. The car telephone wouldn't work, either. So I started walking back to Prescott Road. Then someone stepped out from the woods. Someone with a gun."

"Who?"

"I don't know, Logan. He had a coat on with the collar turned up, it was foggy, and he almost immediately shone a flashlight in my eyes. Then he cocked the gun and I ran." Her breath quickened at the memory. "He chased me through the woods. When I made it to the yard, he shot at me twice."

"Twice?"

"Yes. I got inside and I passed out for a few minutes. I've never fainted in my life, but I was out cold for a few minutes—I'm not sure how long. Maybe up to fifteen minutes."

"Did you find Bernice before you passed out?"

"No. I woke up in the entrance hall. No lights were on in here, but I knew I had to get to a phone. Whoever chased me could still have been around. I crawled through the living room in the dark, and I found Bernice."

"No one upstairs." Blaine looked over to see Abel Stroud standing in the doorway. "Want me to turn on some more lights?"

"Please," one of the EMS attendants said. "It's pretty hard to work by flashlight."

"Go ahead," Logan said. He glanced down at the afghan that had been heaped over Bernice. "Did you cover her?"

"No. She was already covered. Completely. I only drew back the afghan from her face at first."

"Good thing you put on the tourniquets," one of the EMS attendants said. "You could have saved her life."

Blaine nodded. "I hope I did it right. I know how dangerous it can be to cut off the blood supply for an extended period of time . . ." She was aware of Clarke joining Stroud to begin a slow inspection of the living room.

"What did you touch in here?" Logan asked.

"All the tabletops. It was dark. I couldn't turn on any lights because I was afraid of making myself an easy target. So I crawled across the floor and fumbled my hands over the furniture until I found the phone."

"Where's Robin?"

Blaine tensed. "Oh, my God, she's alone at the house. I didn't even call . . ." Tears began to run down her face, and her hands trembled in nervous reaction.

The EMS attendants slid Bernice off the chaise longue onto a stretcher and headed outside, where revolving red lights splashed bloody color through the open front door and the uncurtained front window.

"Clarke, drive Mrs. Avery home," Logan said.

Clarke gazed at him in surprise. "*Home?* Not down to headquarters? I mean, this is the *third* time she's found a body—"

"I know exactly how many damned times it is!" Logan flared, causing Clarke to gape at him. "Just take her home for now, then stay with her. Abel and I have work to do." He looked at Blaine, and his words came out as a threat. "I'll talk to you later."

3

Ten minutes later Blaine braced herself when Clarke, nearly vibrating with suspicion and hostility, let her out in front of her house. She opened the box beside the front door, punched in the proper code to disarm the alarm system, then reached for her purse. She didn't have it. She must have left it in her car or dropped it in the woods; she couldn't remember now. She rang the doorbell, but there was no answer. Even outside she could hear music pounding from Robin's room, and she felt unreasonably annoyed. While she had been running for her life out at Bernice's farm, *because* of Robin, the girl had been here sulking and listening to music.

As Clarke stood by, quietly furious with the duty he'd been assigned, Blaine walked around the house to Robin's room and saw with horror that the bedroom window was up. "Robin!" she shouted. The girl didn't appear. "Robin, it's me."

Blaine stood on tiptoe and peered in. The room was empty and she felt a surge of anger, quickly followed by apprehension. "Robin! Robin, are you there?"

Nothing but the sound of Mick Jagger screaming about being between a rock and a hard place. Blaine ran back to Clarke, saying in a high, near hysterical voice, "Her window is open! Music is playing in her room, but she isn't there!"

For the first time Clarke's young face lost its angry look. "She wasn't planning to go out, was she?"

"No! She was here when I left. I told her not to let anyone in!"

Suddenly Ashley appeared at the front window, pushing aside the draperies as she barked. "Ash, where's Robin?" Blaine yelled without thinking, until she saw the deputy throwing her a dubious look. Obviously he was not one who talked to animals. "We have to get in through her window," Blaine told him, "but I'm not tall enough. Can you give me a boost into the room?"

At that moment Robin's blue Camero pulled into the driveway. Blaine nearly sobbed in relief, but when the girl stepped from the car, she demanded, "Where the hell have you been?"

Robin drew back slightly at the sight of the deputy. "I went out for a little while."

"Out where?"

"Just out. Driving."

"After I left? After I *told* you to stay here?"

The girl's eyes darted from left to right.

"Yes, after you left. I just needed some fresh air."

"You needed fresh *air*," Blaine said incredulously. "You needed fresh air so you went out—with a killer on the loose?"

Robin licked her lips. "Yeah. I don't see that it's such a big deal. You did it."

"Why is your window open?"

"Is it? I guess I forgot to close it."

Blaine's eyes narrowed. She took a deep breath. "We'll talk about this later. Just open the door, please. I seem to have lost my purse."

4

Thirty minutes afterward, the doorbell rang. "That's the sheriff," Clarke said, seeming relieved. Blaine and Robin had sat in steaming silence ever since they'd come in the front door. "I'll let him in."

Blaine picked up the framed photograph of her and Martin taken at Christmas last year. They were sitting in front of the Christmas tree, Blaine wearing a turquoise velour robe and the diamond-and-pearl earrings that had been Martin's present to her. Martin sported the red cashmere scarf that had been one of her gifts to him. He looked much younger than his years, his smile wide, his blue eyes reflecting deep happiness. A week later he would be lying in a hospital bed, paralyzed from the waist down, blaming her for his helplessness. I miss you, Blaine thought miserably. I miss the way you used to be and how secure you made me feel.

Logan looked tired to the bone. He needs coffee, Blaine thought, but I can't fix it. My legs are still trembling. "Robin, would you put on some coffee, please?" she asked finally.

"I make terrible coffee."

"Just put it on, Robin. I don't think any of us is that concerned about the quality right now."

The girl reluctantly left the room. Blaine turned to Logan. "Did you find any trace of the person who chased me?"

"No, Blaine. Nothing."

"*Nothing?* I was fired at twice. Didn't you find bullets lodged in anything, like the porch posts?"

"A cursory search didn't show anything. We'll need daylight to carry on a thorough search."

Blaine rubbed her forehead. No, of course there weren't bullets lodged in anything. That had only happened when Martin died, making her look guilty.

"Blaine, is there anything else you can tell me about tonight?"

"About being at the house?"

"Yes."

She stood up and walked to the fireplace. "The phone. I got a phone call."

"Before or after Bernice's call?"

"At Bernice's house!"

"You got a call at Bernice Litchfield's house?"

"That's right. It was like the other calls I've been getting—no one spoke, they only played a song. " 'Rock of Ages.' "

" 'Rock of Ages'? What does that have to do with Bernice?"

"She hummed it or sang it all the time. She nearly drove Martin to distraction with it. He spoke to her about it a couple of times, and she'd act hurt, and then the next day she'd forget and start singing it again."

Logan stared at her. "Blaine, how could the killer have chased you into Bernice's house, then called you? There aren't any pay phones nearby."

"The call didn't come immediately after I went into the house. As I said, I passed out for ten to fifteen minutes. Then at least another five went by before I found Bernice. Then I called the EMS, then the sheriff's office. The call came about five minutes afterward. That's almost half an hour later."

Clarke spoke up for the first time as Robin reentered the room. "How could a killer know you'd answer and not the police?"

"I guess he couldn't. He'd have to wait until he heard me say hello. Certainly if the police were there, one of them would answer the phone. If I answered, it meant I was there alone."

"Got this all figured out, don't you?" Clarke said.

"No, I don't, Deputy," Blaine said coldly. "But when I *do* get it all figured out, I'll let you know."

"Okay, let's get back to business," Logan said sharply. "You never explained to my satisfaction why you went to see Bernice."

"I told you—she called me. She was upset. She said she needed to see me."

"She was upset about *what*?"

"I don't know."

Logan regarded her sternly. "Blaine, you

did not go to that woman's house because she said she was upset. She didn't even like you—you wouldn't go out when a murderer is on the loose just to comfort her. What did she say?"

"A lot of gibberish. I think she'd been drinking. Look, Logan, I know she didn't like me, but she was good to Martin and—"

"And she knew something about the missing Dilaudid." A fresh tremor of apprehension ran through Blaine. Why did she always think she could hide things from Logan? It never worked. He pinned her with his gaze. "She denied to me this afternoon that she knew anything about some Dilaudid that was missing, but she did. She's not a good liar. Now that's what she wanted to talk to you about, isn't it?"

"Yes," Blaine said, barely above a whisper. "She wanted to talk about Dilaudid."

"What did she say about it?"

"Nothing, Logan. She'd been attacked when I got there, remember?"

"I meant over the phone."

"She just said she wanted to talk to me about it."

"That's all?"

"That's *all*."

Logan studied her, disappointment showing in his eyes. He knew she wasn't telling
the truth. His look hurt more than she would
have imagined, and she felt a terrible need
to restore his faith in her, but she couldn't
do that without endangering someone else.
Finally, Logan turned to Robin. "Clarke tells
me you were out this evening."

"Just to get some air, like I said."

"Where were you getting this air?"

Robin seemed too frightened to catch his
sarcasm. "Town. I drove downtown. I went
to the park, but I didn't get out of the car. I
just sat and looked at the river for a little
while. On the way back I had a flat tire.
That's why I was so late."

"Did you change the tire yourself?"

"Yes." She held out her arms, displaying
dirty smudges on the sleeves of her blue
sweater. "See? Dirt from the old tire. My
sweater's probably ruined."

"Where is the old tire?"

"In the trunk, of course. Where else would
I leave it? On the side of the road?"

"No one stopped to help you?"

"No. It was only a mile from here, and the
road was nearly deserted."

"Strange, we didn't see you when we were driving to the Litchfield place."

"I saw police cars and the ambulance go by, but everyone was going so fast. And I'd pulled off the main road. I was on that little side road leading out to the Dennis farm."

"So you were alone and no one saw you," Logan said slowly. "How interesting."

5

As soon as the sheriff and the deputy left, Blaine pounced on Robin. "*Where* were you earlier?"

"I told you—"

"I *know* what you told me. Now give me the truth."

"After you left, I got kind of scared here alone, so I decided to go for a drive—"

"Robin, stop it!"

Robin looked at her with wide, frightened eyes. "What do you mean?"

"On my trip to the bathroom a few minutes ago, I tried your door. It was still locked from the inside. Your CD player holds five discs. The last one was finishing just as we came in the front door, so you didn't have to go to your room to turn off the music. Lucky for you—you would have had a hard time explaining that locked door." Robin seemed to draw in on herself.

"I know exactly what you did," Blaine continued. "You put a piece of tape on the alarm switch on your window to prevent it from activating if I turned on the main unit before you got back. Then you used the music as camouflage and slipped out of the house through your window. You knew I was in my bedroom and wouldn't hear the garage door going up and down or your car leaving, and my car was in the driveway, so I didn't even see that your car was missing. You planned to come back in just as quietly as you left and sneak in your open window. Am I right?"

Robin's head dropped slightly. "Yeah, you're right."

"Where did you go?"

"To see Tony."

"To see *Tony!*"

"Yeah. I was upset about you sending me off to live with my grandparents. I needed to talk to him."

"Robin, Tony is possibly a killer!"

"He wasn't the father of Rosie's baby, Blaine. Honest!"

"I know. Rick was."

Blaine watched the girl's face closely. She looked genuinely shocked, then satisfied. "That's what Tony said. He thought Rick was the father, but I couldn't believe it."

"Why did Tony think Rick was the father?"

"Tony did odd jobs at the Peyton house. He said he'd noticed something between Rick and Rosie. Nothing definite, nothing he could tell the police, but *something*." Robin frowned. "Do the police know that Rick was the father?"

"Yes. Rick admitted it. You *really* didn't know? Rosie didn't tell you she was involved with Rick all summer?"

"Don't you think I'd have told the sheriff if I knew? I didn't have a clue. But I'm glad."

Blaine stared at her. *"Glad?"*

"Yeah. Now Tony's off the hook."

"Not quite. He *lied* about his alibi for the night of Rosie's death."

"But I know where he was," Robin said anxiously.

"Where?"

"It's a secret."

"Robin!"

"Why are you so anxious to blame Tony for everything?"

"I'm *not*. But you're being too vague. I don't think you really know where Tony was at all. I think you're only trying to protect him."

"I'm not!"

"Then if you like him so much, help him. Tell me where he was. Then tell the police."

Robin pulled a strand of her long hair around her throat, a nervous gesture Martin had said she'd had since childhood. "He'll never trust me with another secret."

"Oh, Robin, stop talking like a ten-year-old. Honestly, you and Tony don't seem to understand that we're talking about *murder* here, and Tony is eighteen—he's not a minor. Do you want to see him spend the rest of his life in prison?"

Robin looked frightened. She bit her lip. "Okay, okay, I'll tell you," she said reluctantly. "You see, his sister Sandra found a bunch of stuff in her son's room, little stuff that she knew he'd stolen. Her husband was out of town, and she freaked out. Didn't know what to do—whether to go to the police or try to protect the kid. So she called Tony out at Ron Gibson's. He went there and gave the kid a big lecture about what it's like to get busted for something. He told

Sandra not to go to the police, but Sandra was really worried about someone finding out that the family was in possession of stolen goods, so she swore Tony to secrecy."

"And she let him lie to the police to keep her secret? That doesn't sound like the Sandra I know."

Robin gave Blaine a defiant look. "Then maybe you don't know her as well as you think."

Blaine took a deep breath. "Rob, do you have *any* proof that what Tony told you is true?"

"I have his word for it."

"And that's enough for you?"

"Yes. I don't know why it's not enough for you."

"Because I'm not a seventeen-year-old with a crush."

"I'm not a child," Robin said through clenched teeth. "Anyway, I don't see what you're getting so upset about. Tony was with me this evening, so he can't be the killer."

"Will he go to the police and say he was with you?"

"Why should he?"

"Robin, do you know how ridiculous you sounded when you said you'd gone out for some air? Where did you get that line—a forties movie? Logan didn't believe it for a minute."

"I don't believe *you*. You're just trying to scare me. The sheriff seemed satisfied with my explanation."

"He left you alone tonight because he's focusing on me, but eventually he's going to ask where you *really* were."

Robin was looking less sure of herself. "Well, I didn't mean to be gone so long. I had a flat tire. That's true. And I did change it just where I said I did, by myself. Besides, what does it matter where I was?"

"Because that call from Bernice to me must have been made under duress. Someone was trying to lure me to that house."

Robin stared at her. "And you think it was me? Why would I do that?"

"You heard Logan—Bernice wanted to talk to me about the missing Dilaudid, the drug that was given to Rosie and Kathy and probably Bernice."

"Yeah. So?"

Blaine paced over to the French doors, staring out at the night. "Robin, were you with Rosie the whole afternoon of the day your father . . . died?"

"What? You *know* I was with Rosie!"

"Do I? You just lied to me *and* to the police about where you were tonight."

"But I knew you'd go nuts if I said I sneaked out to see Tony, and you want to send me away anyway, and—" Blaine turned and Robin broke off, her face paling. "You think I killed *Daddy?*"

"I don't think you killed him, Rob. But you knew how desperately unhappy he was. And suddenly he had a key that you saw me hide, and he was in possession of a gun he couldn't have reached without turning the gun case over on himself . . ."

Robin's mouth opened, closed, then opened again. "You knew *I* knew where the key was? You think I got the gun for Daddy so he could *kill* himself and make it look like suicide?"

"I would understand it, Robin. You loved him so much. He thought his life was over. He'd convinced you it was over, too. Maybe you thought you were doing the compassionate thing, like euthanasia. Maybe—"

"Maybe then you heard about the missing drug and figured Rosie had second thoughts about backing up my alibi the afternoon of Daddy's death, so I killed her with medicine I stole when Daddy was sick," Robin said in a hushed voice. "And then I killed Kathy because she saw something, and then I killed Bernice because she *knew* something . . ."

Blaine closed her eyes. "Robin, I went to see Bernice because she was hinting that she knew things about you being here the afternoon of your father's death and about the significance of the missing Dilaudid. I've *never* thought you capable of murder—"

"But you weren't sure, were you? At least that's what you're going to tell the police." Robin's voice rose. "You're going to say you thought *I* stole the Dilaudid and *murdered* those people!"

"Did I say anything like that tonight?"

"No, but you will if they back you to the wall! You didn't volunteer your little story tonight, so you'll look like you were protecting me. But pretty soon you'll tell it. And Logan Quint's in love with you. Anybody can see that. He'll try to protect you. He'll try to believe whatever you say! God, he didn't even arrest you tonight!" Robin raged on. "Anybody else would have arrested you!

You're going to go free and I—" She stood up, her fists clenched, her eyes blazing, and ran outside. Blaine heard her car engine roar to life and she screeched out of the driveway, leaving Blaine standing helplessly in the living room.

17

1

Sunday was a dreary, overcast day. The weatherman had predicted snow by evening, and Blaine could see the threat in the high, feathery cirrus clouds of early morning giving way to a thick, gray-blue cloud sheet that usually indicated rain or snow on the way.

She had awakened at six, and by ten o'clock she was so restless she put on her jacket and took Ashley out for a walk. They headed for the woods, and Blaine felt odd carrying the .22 automatic she'd taken from Martin's gun case. She remembered Martin teaching her how to use it. "Don't jerk, Blaine. Just *squeeze* the trigger. And stop closing your left eye. Keep both eyes open." She had tried, only to please him, not because she thought she would ever be carrying a gun. The idea seemed ridiculous at the time. But here she was, the gun tucked in the right pocket of her jacket, as she took what would once have been an ordinary walk in the woods.

She didn't know what drew her to the woods—maybe fear of them that she wanted to overcome. And Ashley was determined. She'd grown up running through the woods, sniffing out ground hogs and splashing through the creek. They went toward the trees automatically, just as they had done almost daily for nearly three years.

Blaine carried along a sack of food for the bird feeders Kirk had made. Perhaps if she set a task for herself, she thought, she wouldn't be overwhelmed with memories of finding Rosie's body. She took the elegant little red-and-gold pagodas off the low limbs and dumped in sunflower seeds, along with crumbled dog biscuits and some suet she knew wouldn't freeze. At least the few hardy, or maybe foolhardy, sparrows that had not flown south would have something to sustain them if the weatherman wasn't wrong in predicting a freakishly heavy, late November snow. But the day felt as if the prediction were accurate. She felt snow in the air, and suddenly she remembered her father telling her about twelve inches on Thanksgiving Day back in the fifties. He had made the whole event seem a magical time of snowmen and sleigh riding, instead of the dangerous weather disaster everyone else described. He would have been excited today, Blaine thought as she filled the last bird feeder, anticipating another huge snow like the one of his youth.

She was calling for Ashley, ready to head back to the house, when she spotted Logan on the path. She couldn't help the tremor of foreboding that ran through her when she saw him. "What in the world are you doing out here?" she cried as he drew near. "Has something happened to Robin?"

"No. But where is she? No one came to the door."

"Robin is at Cait's. We had an argument last night. She took off in a huff and I was a nervous wreck until Cait called an hour later to say Robin was there."

A brisk breeze lifted the dark hair falling across Logan's forehead. He wore jeans and a wool jacket over a sweatshirt, not his uniform, and he seemed troubled. "What did you and Robin argue about?"

"Oh, normal stepmother-stepdaughter stuff."

Logan looked at her sadly. "I wish you'd stop lying to me, Blaine."

She glanced away quickly. Should she tell him her suspicions about Robin? What if she was wrong. Could she risk ruining a young girl's life to protect herself? No. But what if she was right about Robin? Then the girl needed professional help, but she did not need the police thrust on her.

"Blaine?"

"I'm sorry," she said hastily. Ashley sat at her feet, looking at her expectantly, but she hadn't brought any sticks with her to throw for the dog. She stooped and patted Ashley's golden head. "How's Bernice?"

"Alive, but only by a fluke. It seems she was taking something for those migraine headaches she gets—I think the drug is called Cafergot. Anyway, it works by constricting blood vessels. Her doctor says she must have taken a dose before she was attacked, and therefore her blood flow was slowed. That, along with the tourniquets you applied, saved her. She's still unconscious, though."

"Good Lord," Blaine breathed. "But what about Dilaudid? Was she given Dilaudid?"

"Yes, but not a massive overdose, considering her weight. We found some on the floor along with the syringe. She must have put up a struggle, and the attacker ended up squirting a lot of the stuff out of the syringe. Finally our murderer screwed up."

"Our murderer," Blaine whispered, almost as if saying the words aloud would conjure up the person. "I don't suppose you found any signs of that person having shot at me out at Bernice's."

"No. So far we haven't turned up any slugs or cartridges."

"Oh. So I suppose you've come to arrest me."

"No. As much as the prosecutor wants you to stand trial, he can't sanction an arrest until there's some hard evidence, and there is none. We found the murder weapon—a dull kitchen knife. But there were no prints on it. None on the syringe, either, and you weren't wearing gloves." He looked down. "My men are still searching the woods and the house for gloves you might have worn and hidden before we got there."

Blaine swallowed. "No luck, I guess."

"Not so far."

"What about my car?"

"We had it towed in, but it's still being searched for evidence. Maybe you can get it back tomorrow. But you can have your purse now. That's what I came out to bring you. We found it last night."

He took her brown suede purse out of a bag he'd been carrying and handed it to Blaine. It had been her favorite, but now it was stained from lying on the damp ground for hours. "Look through it and see if anything is missing."

She crossed the path and sat down on an old oak log, sorting quickly through the purse. "Nothing. Keys. Billfold. All my money seems to be here. My driver's license and credit cards. Makeup."

"Not to mention the bag of M and M's."

Blaine smiled. "Crushed, but here."

"I remember that in high school you were always forgetting your keys, but you never forgot your M and M's."

"I still have my chocolate addiction."

Logan sat down beside her. "Has Bennett tried to get in touch with you?"

"No. Too ashamed, probably. He should be."

Logan picked up a twig and snapped it in half. "I guess you really loved the guy."

Blaine looked at him in shock. "No, I didn't love him, Logan. He was just a friend. It's true that he wanted things to be more serious—not an affair, but marriage. Now I know why. My money."

"I'm sure that's not the only reason."

"But it was the main one."

"Everyone I've talked to thought he was a great guy."

"Yes, he seemed to be." Blaine glanced at the decaying leaves carpeting the ground. "Obviously he wasn't, but I still can't quite believe he's a murderer."

"Well, this might help convince you. When his ex-wife heard he'd been brought in for questioning and might be arrested, she came flying in with a confession of her own. Back when they were married, Bennett was committing health-insurance fraud."

"What?"

Logan threw the twigs down and nodded. "She claims she kept quiet about it because he was her husband and she loved him, et cetera, et cetera. I think she was going right along with him until divorce time. Then she held the information over his head."

"She blackmailed him into giving her that huge settlement?"

"I'm guessing, but I think it's a good guess. I believe she thought that if he was arrested, he might tell us what really happened between them, so she decided to get to us first with her version."

"I always wondered why Rick gave her so much. I told myself it was because he just wanted her out of his life with no continuing battles over money."

"I don't think that kind of generosity comes naturally to Bennett."

"I don't think so, either. But considering what he had to lose, I'm surprised he did divorce her. Martin was still alive then. He couldn't have been planning on marrying me."

"Except that we're not sure Martin killed himself."

Blaine looked at him steadily. "Yes, he did, Logan."

"How do you *know* that? You weren't even here that afternoon."

"I thought you weren't sure about that, either."

"Your explanation that you suddenly decided to go shopping didn't ring quite true, Blaine. Even you have too know that."

"I *was* at the mall, Logan. I just didn't buy anything." She glanced up at the formation of Canadian geese flying overhead, squawking noisily. Ashley barked at them, then turned her attention back to the humans, who looked so serious. She moved closer to Blaine and laid her head on Blaine's knee, always a gesture of sympathy. "You're not arresting Rick, are you?"

"I don't have enough hard evidence."

"Oh. But the evidence keeps building up against me, doesn't it?"

"I'm afraid so. And you don't seem to care." Blaine flashed him a look of hurt and fright. "No, that's not right. You care, all right, but you're not doing anything to help yourself."

She lifted her hands. "I don't know what you expect me to do except say that I'm innocent."

"Can't you give me *something,* Blaine? Something that would help clear you?"

"For God's sake, Logan, I called you after every murder."

"You weren't alone when Rosalind's body

was discovered. You *had* to call after Cait and Robin had seen it. And in the case of Kathy, you were the last person to leave the gym because you had to lock up. You were in there *alone* with Kathy, which everyone knew. Arletta Stroud could testify to it."

"And I'm sure she'd love the opportunity. But what about last night? No one could testify that I was with Bernice."

"Blaine, your car wouldn't start. You *couldn't* get away. Even if you'd run, you would have had to leave the car behind."

Blaine put her head in her hands. "You're right. Everything points straight at me."

"Not everything," Logan said thoughtfully. "Tell me, did Robin know where the key to her father's gun case was?"

Blaine raised her head, her eyes opening wider. "W-what?"

"You said you hid the key to the gun case when Martin got so depressed. Did Robin know where it was?"

Blaine caught her lower lip between her teeth, then let out a long sigh. "No."

"You're lying to me again. *Why?* If she killed her father—"

"She *didn't* kill her father, Logan. She

didn't kill anyone. I just don't think she's capable of such a thing."

"You'd be surprised who's capable of murder," Logan said grimly.

"So you're hinting that she might be responsible for all the murders? Well, ask Tony Jarvis. That's who she was with last night when Bernice was murdered and she claimed to be out getting air."

Logan looked deeply into her eyes. "Tony Jarvis swears he was at home alone with his mother."

Blaine felt thunderstruck. Either Robin had lied to her or Tony had lied to the police, thinking that the only threat hanging over Robin was that of Blaine's anger at her for sneaking out. "Why did you ask Tony about Robin?" she finally managed, her voice thick with fear.

"He's a suspect in these murders, Blaine. Naturally I questioned him about his whereabouts last night. He said nothing about Robin. You're the one who just told me Robin was with him."

"Oh." Blaine felt as if she were struggling to get her breath. "Well, what about Rick?"

"Dr. Bennett could not be located this morning."

Blaine gaped. "He *couldn't?*"

"It's only eleven o'clock. Maybe he's in church."

In spite of her fear, Blaine couldn't help smiling in response to the quirk in Logan's expression. "Oh, sure he is."

"We couldn't find John Sanders, either."

"Well, that's no mystery. He must be in Columbus with Samantha."

"Except that Samantha is really Samuel." Blaine looked at him blankly. "*Samantha* was his alibi for the Rosalind Van Zandt murder. But further investigation showed the alibi didn't check out. When we questioned him a second time, Sanders said he'd lied—there is no Samantha Burton. The woman we talked to was his sister, Gail, covering up for him. He said he's gay, and the person he sees in Columbus is a man named Samuel Burleigh, a doctor. An *anesthesiologist*."

Blaine felt her face growing slack with surprise. "An anesthesiologist? Which means he has access to drugs . . ."

"Yes. Except that Dr. Samuel Burleigh is on vacation in Europe. We haven't been able to track him down, and when we do, we might find out he's not really Sanders's lover at all. He might just be an acquaintance Sanders is using as a smoke screen."

"Maybe," Blaine said slowly, suddenly remembering that during her years of marriage to Martin they'd invited John and "Samantha" to several weekend parties. But they'd never come. As far as she knew, no one in Sinclair had ever met the mysterious Samantha. "But I don't think so."

"You believe Sanders is telling the truth?"

"I don't know. But if he *is* gay, a lot of his behavior is explained."

"His behavior?"

"Just that he was so circumspect about his girlfriend. He never brought her here, which was odd, since they've supposedly been involved for years. And he's such a loner. I guess he thought he had to be. In this provincial little town, people wouldn't understand him. And I'm sure he'd lose his job if it became known he's homosexual."

"That's what he said."

Blaine frowned. "Oh, poor John, having to keep a secret life. He must have felt so alone here. He never even told me, although he knew I'd understand."

"Blaine, it may not be true. Maybe *that's* why he never told you. You two *were* pretty close. He must have known you'd be sympathetic."

Yes, John would have known that, she thought. So why had he kept silent? Fear that she would tell someone else who *wouldn't* understand or keep things confidential? Or because he would have been lying?

Blaine closed her eyes. Questions, doubts, ambivalence. What was the truth? How could they ever sort out the truth about these murders when everyone seemed to be lying? Rick, John, Robin. Even she herself. When she opened her eyes, Logan was watching her closely, his face full of compassion. "You think I'm innocent, don't you?" she asked suddenly.

"Blaine, I've known you since you were in the first grade and you toppled off the jungle gym and landed right on top of me."

She smiled. "And you're still trying to break my fall, aren't you?"

Their faces were so close Blaine could feel Logan's breath on her cheek. His dark eyes, which for the past six months had looked so remote, were now warm, almost caressing. He took her hand and squeezed it. His wedding band, cold from the brisk air, pressed into her skin. She stiffened, drawing her hand away, when what she really wanted to do was fling herself into his arms.

"I'm sorry," Logan said softly. "Sometimes I forget we're not still in high school."

"A lot of time has passed since then."

"And a lot of circumstances have changed. Not feelings, just circumstances."

Blaine felt her heart beating harder, her face growing warm with color, and she was glad Logan gazed off at the strong, old trees raising denuded limbs to the cobalt-blue sky.

"It's so beautiful out here," he said quietly. "You know, North American Indians were very religious, and they believed in a pervasive supernatural essence. The Iroquois called it *orenda*. It was personified as gods, demons, and creatures that sprang from natural features."

"Natural features like these trees?"

Logan nodded. "Right now I can't imagine anything but a benevolent creature springing from them. Then I think of Rosalind Van Zandt being killed out here . . ."

"And the trees seem full of demonic creatures."

He grinned. "Sounds nuts, doesn't it?"

"Actually, it sounds poetic. It also sounds frightening, because sometimes I get the same feeling here in the woods. I always have, but especially since Rosie's death. It's as if the trees possess some kind of intelligence, an almost human perception." She sighed. "I only wish they could tell us what really happened the night Rosie was murdered."

Logan looked down, twisting his wedding ring. "Blaine, none of this is what I came out here to say."

Blaine felt a chill run down her back. The warmth in his voice was gone. He raised his eyes and looked slightly past her, sitting a bit straighter on the log. "I'm turning this case over to the state police."

After the death of Kathy, she'd wondered why he wasn't asking for their assistance. But now, after being let go at the school, after finding out about the Dilaudid, after the episode with Bernice, she knew the danger she'd been in after Martin's death was only growing greater. Suddenly she felt forsaken, like someone trapped in a deep hole whose only hope has lain in a familiar if often distant and suspicious voice, a voice of authority, a familiar voice of someone she knew cared about her in spite of everything. A voice that would no longer be there.

"Why did you make this decision *now*?" she asked.

"Pressure from the public, pressure from the mayor." He shifted slightly, his dark eyes returning to hers. "And because I'm too close to the number one suspect."

"But we've hardly even seemed like friends anymore," she said faintly.

"I had a job to do, Blaine. I've tried to do it to the best of my ability. I *was* doing it to the best of my ability back when your husband died. But I'm not doing a good job anymore. I'm bending over backward to give you the benefit of the doubt, and it isn't helping you, it's hurting you. People say I'm shielding you because I'm still in love with you."

"But you're not in love with me," she said miserably. "Can't people see that?"

"Sometimes outsiders see things more clearly than the people involved."

"Then you *are* still in love with me?"

"I never stopped loving you, Blaine. But I'm married. And you're not over Martin. Besides, you don't need to be thinking about love affairs right now. You're in one hell of a mess."

"And you're abandoning me."

Logan pulled her closer to him, holding her while her sudden tears poured out on his wool jacket. "I'm not *abandoning* you, Blaine. Not in spirit, anyway. But this situation is out of my hands now."

"Because you want it to be."

"Because, unless I want people to be even more suspicious of you than they already are, I have to let go. I've done all I could, but you *won't* tell me the truth."

"So you think I'm a killer?"

"No. But you don't trust me enough to be honest. You're hiding things."

Blaine couldn't deny it. She'd lied about why she'd left the house the afternoon of Martin's death, and she wasn't telling him how worried she was about Robin's part in this whole mess. She bent her head, swallowing to stop the tears that didn't want to stop. He kissed the top of her head. "Maybe it's going to be all right, Blaine."

But she knew him too well not to hear the insincerity in his voice. He didn't think it was going to be all right, and neither did she.

2

The snow started around two o'clock. Blaine and Ashley stood at the French doors, staring at the lacy flakes falling with increasing speed. Within fifteen minutes she could no longer see the woods, and the ground was solid white.

Blaine turned away from the windows and wandered through the house, touching things, feeling an ache of tenderness for the home where she had once been so happy. Now Martin was gone, Robin was gone, and soon she would probably be gone, too.

She went into the little spare bedroom she used as a study. Her word processor had gathered dust in the past few weeks, and absently she traced her initials on the clouded monitor screen. *B.O.A.* She felt like a child and quickly wiped the initials away, turning to her filing cabinet, where a stack of student folders lay. Flipping through them idly, she remembered they were from the last class she had taught before she collapsed with pneumonia. Through the years, after arguing with students over grades they claimed she had recorded wrong in her grade book (always to their detriment), she had insisted students keep all their papers in a folder so they could be reviewed at the end of the year. This particular class had turned in its first assignment that unfortunate Thursday when Blaine had gotten sick, and she'd never had a chance to look at the folders. Robin had brought them home from her classroom and stacked them on her filing cabinet, where they'd lain untouched for weeks.

Rosie had been in that class, Blaine thought. Morbid curiosity made her sift through the pile until she found Rosie's folder with its reproduction of Whistler's *The White Girl* on the front. There she stood, in her long white dress, her dark hair flowing over her shoulders, her eyes both vulnerable and unfathomable. Had Rosie seen herself as the White Girl? Her resemblance to the portrait of Whistler's mistress, Joanna Heffernan, was remarkable. And Rosie, too, had been a mistress. The girl had always been intrigued with mysteries and cryptic messages. Was her selection of this folder for Blaine's class an irresistible urge to let someone know she was having an affair?

Blaine opened the folder, looking at Rosie's in-class essay on "The Legend of Sleepy Hollow." It was mostly fluff, but then, what could be said about the story except for its technical expertise? Blaine wasn't sure now why she had even made the assignment. Maybe just to make sure they'd read the story.

She was about to close the folder when a creased paper fell out of the side pocket. She picked it up, looking at it in confusion:

Rosalind Van Zandt
P. O. Box 94
Sinclair, WV 25561
September 12, 1991

Registry of Vital Records and Statistics
150 Tremont Street
Boston, MA 02111

Dear Sirs:
I would like to obtain a copy of the birth certificate of my father, Derek Garth Van Za

The partial letter had been typed on a dated, battered typewriter like the ones they had at school. Even the paper looked like the cheap copier paper provided in the typing rooms. Suddenly Blaine remembered

Robin mentioning coming upon Rosie typing a letter, which she'd torn out of the typewriter and stuffed in a folder. This had to be that unfinished letter. But why would Rosie have been requesting a copy of her father's birth certificate?

3

Tim sat in front of the television, lackadaisically doing his arithmetic. "Don't you think you could concentrate on your work better without the TV?" Allie asked.

"Nope. I hate arithmetic. It doesn't matter whether I'm watchin' *Magnum* or not when I'm doin' it. I'll still get a bad grade."

Allie bent over him, looking at the scrawled numbers on his notebook page. "Tim, I don't believe that. You aren't even trying. Look how messy this page is—you're certainly not going to turn it in to your teacher!"

"It doesn't matter if it's neat or not—I'll still get all the answers wrong."

His grandmother went over and shut off the television. "That is a rerun you've seen ten times."

"I still like it!"

"I know, but you have something more important to do. You should have done your arithmetic yesterday, not waited until this evening. Take out a fresh sheet of paper. You're going to start over and you're going to be neat. *And* you will get the right answers."

"Oh, Grandma!" Tim protested.

"You want to be a sheriff like your father, don't you?"

"Well, sure. That or a veternamariam."

"Vet-er-i-*n*ar-i-an. But you must be good in math to do either."

Tim looked disbelieving. "What's arithetic got to do with arresting people or giving dogs shots?"

"There is more to both jobs than you think. Now I must insist. I want you to start over. Then, when your father comes home, you can show him what a good job you've done. *He* was always good in math."

"He was?"

"Yes."

"Oh, okay," Tim said, reluctantly taking out a fresh page of notebook paper. "Maybe if my pencil was sharper I'd do better."

"I'll sharpen it," Allie said, reaching for the pencil, which showed teeth marks on the end. "Tim, when are you going to stop gnawing on your pencils? You aren't a puppy, you know."

Tim giggled. "When will Daddy be home?" he asked as his grandmother walked toward the kitchen door leading into the garage, where a pencil sharpener was nailed to the wall. She glanced at the kitchen wall clock. "It's ten till five. He promised to be home by six."

"You mean I've got to work on my arithemetic *that* long?"

Allie Quint made a sound of exasperation before she went out into the garage. Tim thought about turning the television on again, then changed his mind. Maybe if he acted like he was really trying with those subtraction problems, Grandma wouldn't make him work such a *long* time.

The phone rang and Tim ran to pick it up. "Sheriff Quint's house," he said importantly.

His mother laughed on the other end. "Timmy? My goodness, that was a formal greeting!"

"Mommy!"

"Did your father teach you to say that?"

"No, I made it up. Grandma and Daddy won't let me say it when they're around, but

Daddy's workin' and Grandma's out in the garage."

"Daddy's working, huh?" Dory said, some of the lilting charm leaving her voice. "Some things never change."

"There's been a whole bunch of *murders*, Mommy. Daddy and Grandma think I don't know anything about it, but I do. We're havin' a *crime wave!*"

"Murders? Of whom?"

"Oh, just some girls. Older girls, not ones I go to school with. Mommy, are you comin' home soon?"

Dory hesitated. "Actually, that's what I called about."

Tim's smile faded. "You're gonna be here for Thanksgiving, aren't you?"

"No, honey, I don't think I can make it. You see, I'm very involved with my work."

Tim paled. "When *will* you be home, then?"

"Well, I'm not sure."

"But Christmas is only a few weeks away. You're not gonna miss *Christmas!*"

"I'll try not to, but I'm just so *swamped* with things to do."

Tim heard a man in the background ask, "Who are you talking to, sweetheart?"

He could hear his mother put a hand over the phone and mumble something to someone. When she came back on the line, he demanded, "Who's that guy?"

"Someone who's going to help Mommy get her stories published. A very *nice* man, Timmy."

"He called you *sweetheart*."

"Well, it's just an expression. Anyway, I wanted to wish you a happy Thanksgiving. I might be taking a trip over the holidays, so I can't call for a while . . ."

"You said you had too much work to do to go anywhere!"

"This is only a short trip, not like coming all the way back to West Virginia."

"You're not comin' home at all, are you?" Tim asked stonily. "Not for Thanksgiving, not for Christmas."

"This is just such a bad time for me. Honey, try to understand . . ."

"Who are you talking to?"

Tim turned to face his grandmother. Tears ran down his cheeks, and he thrust the receiver into her hand. "It's Mommy."

Allie took the receiver and immediately said, "Dory? What did you say to Tim?"

Tim could hear his grandmother's voice

rising in the living room as he went into the front hall and opened the closet door. He could still hear her, now close to shouting, when he stepped out into the swirling snow.

4

The phone rang and Blaine tensed. What if she heard music? What if the killer had struck again? And here she'd been, alone all afternoon, with no alibi except for the police cruiser that came by every half hour.

Answer it, she thought. This call is coming to your home. You have Call Trace. Don't let nerves get the best of you and blow this opportunity to see who's calling. She picked up the receiver and uttered a careful "Hello."

"Blaine, this is Allie Quint."

"Mrs. Quint," she said with a mixture of relief and puzzlement. "What can I do for you?"

"It's Tim. He seems to have run away."

"Run away? In this awful weather?"

"Yes." Mrs. Quint's voice broke. "He got a call from his mother that upset him. It's not the first time he's run away because of her. I could just *kill* that woman. Oh, well, I got

hold of Logan—he insisted on doing paperwork at the office this afternoon, even
though it's Sunday. He's getting some men
together, and they're going to begin a
search of the woods between here and your
place."

"Why my house?"

"Because Tim was so taken with you and
Robin. And especially the dog. What's her
name? Ashley? Anyway, he's talked about
her incessantly."

"But I live over a mile from you—a mile of
solid woods. And in this snowstorm . . ."

"I know." Blaine could tell Allie Quint was
crying. "But we've looked all around the
neighborhood and checked with all of his
friends. I thought, just maybe, he'd gotten
to your place already."

Blaine pictured Tim with his sweet, hope-
ful face, his missing front tooth, his passionate attachment to Ashley. "I think you're
right," she said. "There's a very good
chance that if he's upset he'll try to come to
Ashley. She and I will go out looking for him
right now."

"I didn't mean you have to go out. I just
thought he might be there."

"I would have called."

"Yes, yes, of course you would. But maybe we should leave the search to the men."

Blaine had known Allie Quint since she and Logan were childhood friends. The woman had never been one to leave things *to the men*. She's afraid to have me search for the child, Blaine thought with a stab of pain. Like everyone else, she thinks I might be a murderer. Blaine abruptly closed her mind to the thought. Now was not the time to be concerned with people's opinion of her. "I'll call you back in half an hour, Mrs. Quint."

"Ashley," she called after hanging up. The dog, who had been napping under the dining room table, padded into the kitchen. "We have to search for Tim. Remember Tim? He's lost in the snow."

Lost in the snow. The words chimed in Blaine's head as, five minutes later, she and Ashley stepped into the white maelstrom that was the backyard. Snow lashed at Blaine's face. About three inches of it had accumulated on the ground in the past four hours, and walking was difficult, although she wore rubber-soled boots. She looked with concern at the dog, but Ashley seemed oblivious of the cold. Blaine stopped for a minute to look back at the house, where every light glowed, inside and out, hopefully as a beacon for Tim. She'd left the doors unlocked and the alarm system off in case he turned up while she was gone. She didn't feel good about leaving the house open like that, but in her pocket she carried the .22 automatic.

Blaine lifted her voice above the wind. "Okay, let's go, girl. I wish I had something of Tim's for you to sniff. You don't even know what you're looking for. But you didn't have a piece of Rosie's clothing, either, and still—"

She broke off. No, she wouldn't even think about that. Tim was fine. He was just lost.

They trudged across the back lawn toward the southern woods, the woods he would hide in. He was a smart little boy. He would know walking close to the highway would mean instant detection.

Wind howled across the open expanse of lawn. Blaine lowered her head and pulled the hood of her down parka tighter. She glanced back at the house and was disheartened to see that the illumination was swallowed by the churning darkness. Ashley was already completely coated with snow, but she plowed on, pulling at the leash as if she knew they were on an important mission.

They entered the woods and immediately the wind velocity dropped, although it still set tree limbs swaying. "Tim!" Blaine shouted. "Tim, where are you?"

Nothing, but then, her voice had been weakened by the cold and the strain of crossing the windswept lawn. "Slow down a minute," she told Ashley. The dog stopped in her tracks and began barking. "That's good. You're louder than I am. Maybe he'll hear you."

But Tim did not appear, and after a minute they started out again. Here in the woods the snow was only half as deep as out in the open, and the wind only a lonely moan through the tree branches. Still, if Tim was out here, he was in danger. If he fell and hurt himself, he could freeze to death. And if he wandered around lost for very long, he could suffer frostbite. Blaine and the dog walked and walked while she shouted for Tim until she was hoarse. Finally she paused, looking at her hands in their thin gloves and at Ashley, who had begun to shiver violently. "We've got to take a break, girl," Blaine said. "Maybe Tim is already *at* the house. If he isn't, we'll try again in a little while."

Ashley was dragging by the time they crossed the lawn again. The wind seemed even stronger now, and the snow was deeper. About four inches of it lay in a vast blanket of white. Blaine couldn't see prints she and Ashley had left earlier, and for a panicky moment she couldn't spot the outside lights at the house, either. Her sense of direction had always been poor, and she wondered if they'd taken a wrong turn in the woods and managed to go in a circle. But Ashley pulled determinedly on the leash, leading her forward, and finally the lights over the deck, which were usually too bright, shone dimly through the clouds of blowing snow.

"Thank God," Blaine breathed as they burst through the French doors.

She and Ashley staggered into the kitchen, both breathless and shaking with cold. Blaine shrugged out of her coat and thin, soaked gloves, throwing both on the kitchen table, and rushed into the laundry room to get a towel, with which she began vigorously rubbing Ashley's sodden hair. "I can't believe this weather," she muttered. "This storm has to be one for the record." She picked up one of the dog's snow-encrusted paws and began trying to dislodge ice clumps from between her toes when suddenly Ashley bolted away, barking furiously.

"What on earth?" Blaine exclaimed. "Ashley?"

The dog tore through the house, and Blaine started after her. She was in the living room when the phone rang. Mrs. Quint, of course. She picked up the phone and uttered a ragged "Yes?"

Immediately she heard an electric piano:

Blaine froze. "The Merry Widow Waltz." The music was so clear. And so was something else—the sound of a dog barking. A familiar bark. *Ashley's* bark!

Blaine uttered a strangled cry and

slammed down the receiver. The music was being played on Robin's portable electric piano. The call was being made from the phone in Robin's room.

18

A violent Tremor shook Blaine. "Ashley?" she whispered. "Ashley!"

The dog appeared, wildly agitated, and grabbed Blaine's wrist in her mouth, pulling her toward the door. Blaine went willingly. "We've got to get out of here," she murmured.

"Ring around a rosy,
A pocket full of posy;
Ashes, ashes,
We all fall *down*."

Dumbfounded, Blaine looked over her shoulder to see Joan Peyton standing behind her, singing, and holding a gun.

"Joan?" Her voice cracked. Ashley growled but stood still. She was not a trained guard dog—she was quick to let Robin and Blaine know when a stranger was around, but she had never been taught to attack. Blaine had no idea how the dog would react if her mistresses themselves were attacked.

"Familiar song?"

"Yes, Joan," Blaine said blankly, staring at the woman.

"Shut the dog in the kitchen," Joan ordered.

"I don't understand," Blaine faltered. "What are you doing?"

Something about Joan reminded Blaine of a coiled snake, her eyes cold and flat. "I said, shut the dog in the kitchen. I don't like to hurt animals, but I will if I have to."

Blaine looked at the gun. A .38 revolver pointed at Ashley. She led the dog to the kitchen and cast one longing glance at her jacket with her own gun in the pocket, thrown on the kitchen table nearly fifteen feet away. Too far away. If she made a dash for it, Joan might shoot her. "Stay," she told Ashley, then quickly stepped out of the kitchen and shut the door. Ashley immediately began scratching at it. Although she had been shut in the kitchen a few times, she had sensed Blaine's fear.

"Okay," Blaine said shakily. "Are you going to tell me what this is all about?"

"It's about death." Joan's long black hair,

usually pulled back in a sleek French twist, now hung in damp, curling strings. The iron control she was so noted for had finally snapped. She looked wild, almost feral, and very frightening.

"Joan, obviously you're upset." In spite of her fear and shock, Blaine almost burst out laughing at the inanity of her comment. Joan, however, was watching her carefully. "Do you think I killed Rosie? Is that what this is about?"

"Everyone thinks you killed Rosie. Even Logan Quint isn't going to be able to protect you much longer."

Ashley was scratching furiously at the door now, and suddenly Blaine knew the dog *would* help if she could, but she was trapped. Even the lock panel was in place on the dog door.

"No, he isn't. He's turning the case over to the state police," Blaine said, mesmerized by the gun pointing at her. "You don't have to jeopardize your own welfare to see that I pay for Rosie's murder."

Joan stared at her for a moment. Then, amazingly, she threw back her head and laughed. "My God," she gasped. "You really don't know, do you? How *can* you be so stupid?"

"Stupid?" By now Ashley had stopped scratching at the door and lapsed into barking. "I don't know what you mean by stupid, Joan."

Joan wiped tears away from her face with her left hand. "I knew everyone else doubted you, but I thought you'd have sense enough to figure it out . . ." She shook her head. "And I thought there was actually a brain under all that red hair."

Oh, God, Blaine thought. Yes, there *was* a brain now quickly putting all the pieces into place. "You're not going to try to convince me that *you* killed Rosie," she said, badly simulating shock. "I don't believe it."

"Try."

Blaine's voice emerged small and breathy. "*Why* would you kill Rosie?"

The weird, flat eyes narrowed. "I knew every move the girl made. I knew all about her and Rick."

"And you thought her having an affair was worth *killing* her over?"

"Yes."

Blaine forced herself to take a deep

breath. "You knew Rosie was meeting Rick out here that night, didn't you?"

"I *told* you I knew every move the girl made. Even if I hadn't noticed the change in her behavior, I would have seen her pulling her car out of the garage and heading down the alley two or three nights a week. I'm not blind. I even knew the exact time she was to meet Rick that night. I overheard her talking to him on the phone. So I met her here earlier. She tried to hide when she realized I was outside, but she wasn't the only person with a copy of the key to this house. I had one made from her own copy."

"And you implicated me in her murder by putting her things behind my furnace. *Why?*"

"You were a bad influence."

Blaine stared at the woman, her determination to be passive suddenly overcome by an awful realization. Without thought she blurted, "That's not true. I had *no* influence over that girl. You killed her for another reason. What was it? Jealousy?"

Joan looked at her stonily. Ashley had abruptly stopped barking, and the house was frighteningly silent for a full minute. Then Joan gave her a cunning smile.

"So you *do* have a mind—a better one than I thought." She stepped nearer. "Did you ever meet my sister, Blaine?"

"Once or twice, when I was a child."

"But you didn't really *know* her. Oh, what a treat you missed! Charlotte." She laughed again, a harsh laugh full of bitterness. "My parents thought she walked on water. *Her! I* was beautiful. *I* had a four-point average at Radcliffe. *I* was Miss West Virginia. But who did my parents love? Charlotte. She wasn't smart. She wasn't even pretty. But she was *sweet*. That's what they always said. I tried so damned hard, but all *I* ever got from them was restrained admiration. Even when I was a kid, I brought home straight As from school and they said, 'Fine job, Joan, keep up the good work.' If Charlotte managed to bring home straight Cs, they practically threw a party."

"Maybe that's why they fussed over her so," Blaine ventured. "Because she *didn't* have your gifts, they had to make her feel special."

"Oh, I've heard that one before," Joan scoffed, shrugging her wide shoulders, the shoulders Blaine suddenly realized were so strong because of Joan's daily workouts. "A psychiatrist gave me that rationalization once. But that's all it is—a rationalization meant to make me feel better. Do you know what my father said to me when I was sixteen and, on one of those rare occasions when he allowed himself a drink, he had too much scotch? He said, 'Joan, you're so damned perfect, it's hard to love you. But Charlotte is *human*. That's what makes *her* lovable.' Can you believe that? They loved her because she was so *ordinary*."

Blaine remembered Ned Peyton, a man born in a two-room shack who by tenacity and native intelligence had amassed a small fortune but remained a simple person with bad grammar and crude tastes. And then there was Edith Peyton, reared with material advantages her husband had never had, but daunted by a strange, almost monkeylike face. They must have been intimidated by Joan, their beautiful, brilliant, elegant daughter. Charlotte, on the other hand, had been average in every way. She hadn't intimidated anyone.

Blaine's hands were icy, and she was beginning to tremble all over, but she tried to keep her voice casual. "You always hated

Charlotte. That's why she had so many accidents when she was growing up, isn't it?"

"Very good, Blaine. And do you know, the stupid thing never realized what was going on. She thought she was just clumsy."

Blaine looked directly into the woman's expressionless eyes. "Then you really weren't Rosie's mother, were you?"

"I knew you thought that!" Joan crowed. "Half the people in town think I was. She looked so much like me, and she was born in Boston when I was living there. And, of course, no one ever saw her father." She sighed. "But no, she was Charlotte's."

Blaine asked slowly, "Joan, where *is* Charlotte?"

"Why, dead in Brazil, you know that."

"No, I don't think so. You've got nothing to lose now. Why don't you tell me the truth? Considering what you've put me through, I think I deserve it. And it's not as if I'm going to be alive after tonight to tell anyone."

Joan appeared to be considering. "No, I guess you won't be, will you? And there's only one other person I told how I managed everything so brilliantly. I *am* a brilliant woman, you know."

"Yes, I do know that."

"I was wasted at that high school."

"I always thought so."

"I only came back here because of my parents."

"That was very kind of you, very unselfish."

Joan nodded as if pleased, so lost in her own world she seemed unaware of Blaine's insincere tone. "All right. I'll tell you the whole truth, and nothing but the truth." She giggled, and Blaine suppressed a shudder. "During my years in graduate school, when I was living in Boston, Charlotte followed me there. You see, she *loved* me. Isn't that ironic? I told you she was stupid. Anyway, after my marriage broke up, I came home, but Charlotte stayed. She told me she was in love with someone, but she couldn't tell me who because he was married. As if I cared *who* it was! I was just glad she had a reason for staying."

She sighed again. "Things were wonderful when I came home. Charlotte was gone. I wasn't competing with her anymore. I felt so peaceful. Then Charlotte arrived with a baby. She'd written home a few months before that she was married, but it was a lie.

Charlotte told my father the whole story of her affair, and do you know, he accepted the situation! That staunch Baptist! My God, if it had been me, he would never have spoken to me again. I can't tell you how furious I was, but I bided my time. Charlotte said in a few weeks she was going back to Boston—her lover was getting a divorce. But then she changed her mind. Just about the time for her to go, she told me she wasn't going to be responsible for breaking up a marriage. The relationship was wrong, she'd told the man it was over, and she was going to remain at home with Rosie." The dead violet eyes sprang to life. "Stay at home! Just when my parents were starting to really love me. Or at least depend on me. And then there was *him*. He was the real reason she was staying, I *knew* it. The man I wanted, that's what she really wanted—to take one more thing away from me. I couldn't let that happen. I just couldn't. So I killed her," Joan ended simply.

Blaine's throat tightened, although she'd already guessed the truth. "You killed Charlotte?"

"Yes. I took her for a ride and shot her in the woods. I don't remember exactly where now. A few miles north of town. I buried her there." Her forehead puckered with the strain of remembering, then quickly smoothed as she gave up the effort. "Before she died I made her write a note saying she'd gone to Europe and didn't want the baby of a man who'd decided to stay with his wife. The note said that every time she looked at Rosie, she'd see him, and she hated him." Joan's eyes narrowed to dangerous slits again. "She fought me about that note, but I told her if she didn't write it I'd go home and kill Rosie, too."

Blaine stifled her desire to call the woman a monster, and Joan continued in a calm voice. "I was glad later I didn't have to kill Rosie, because my real revenge wasn't murder, it was theft. Charlotte took what I wanted most—my parents' love, the interest of the man I wanted—so I took what she wanted most—her child. And Rosie showed great promise. She was so lovely, so intelligent." Joan looked perplexed. "You know, I've always wondered who her father *really* was. Not someone common, I'm sure. No, it must have been someone extraordinary to counteract Charlotte's genes."

Ashley's paws stabbed uselessly under

the kitchen door a few times. "Then Rosie's father's name wasn't Derek Van Zandt?"

Joan shook her head. "That was Charlotte—considerate to the end. She used a false name on the birth certificate to protect the father. I think she'd read that name in a romance novel. It was *my* father who invented the story about Derek Van Zandt being an engineer from a wealthy Boston family. He told it around town when Charlotte had the baby. The dashing *Derek* was in Brazil building a bridge—that was the explanation for why he didn't come home with Charlotte when Rosie was five months old, you see."

"Did your mother know?"

"Oh, yes, although she convinced herself later there really had been a Derek." She frowned. "You know, I think Mother might have always been a little unbalanced."

"But recently Rosie began to suspect the truth, didn't she? That's why she wrote to Boston asking for a birth certificate for Derek Van Zandt."

"You knew about the letter?"

"A partial rough draft was in her folder. I just found it today."

"How careless of her. But, yes, I'm afraid

she did get suspicious and confirmed her suspicions by writing to Boston. Then she was silly enough to confront me with what she'd found out—that there was no Derek Van Zandt born in Boston. She loved mysteries, you see, and she began wondering why she'd never seen any of her father's relatives. She was told they were all dead, but as she got older, she began to doubt that *all* the Van Zandts had suddenly dropped dead, or that her father didn't even have any friends who were curious about his child. Then she started wondering about that big monument my father had erected. She knew how devoted to Charlotte he was—he would have had her remains shipped back from Brazil if there were only enough to fill a matchbox."

"Did your father know what *really* happened to Charlotte?"

"He never said he didn't believe Charlotte had run off to Europe because she didn't want the child, but I think he guessed the truth after a while when he never heard from her again. I think he knew she was dead, and that I'd killed her." Her face turned hard. "Do you know I was left out of his will? He even appointed his lawyer as executor, not me. Oh, yes, I think he knew."

"But he didn't do anything."

"What could he prove? Nothing. Absolutely nothing. I was very careful. Besides, do you think he would have wanted the whole town to know his daughter was a murderer? He would have been afraid of what the scandal would do to *Rosalind*, his darling. Oh, no. He went along when I told him we should say Charlotte died in Brazil with her husband. It was so far away, no one would ever find out, and if Charlotte ever came back, I explained, we could claim there had been a horrible mistake about her death. But he changed toward me after that." She smiled. "He never spoke to me unless he had to. In fact, as he got older, he acted almost *frightened* of me. It was very satisfying. At last I had the upper hand."

"But when Rosie confronted you about there being no Derek Van Zandt and you told her the same story—that her mother had run off to Europe and abandoned her— she didn't believe you, did she?"

"No. I guess everyone had done too good a job brainwashing her about what a wonderful person Charlotte was. She didn't believe her mother would have left her."

"But there was something else, wasn't there? Something that made her *afraid* of you?"

Joan's tongue darted out, wetting her dry lips. "It was Rick. She was very intuitive. She knew that I . . . cared for Rick."

For a moment Blaine's fear vanished with her shock. "You *did?*"

"Yes. Is that so hard to believe?"

"Well, no, I guess not."

"I'm only a few years older than he. And for a while he seemed interested in me, too. And then he found out that I had no money except my salary at school. Father left me only enough money to buy Rosie a car on her seventeenth birthday, *which* I dutifully did. And *Mother*, God bless her rotten little soul, was leaving everything to Rosie."

"Everything?"

"*Everything*. And if by some chance Rosie predeceased her, everything went to Baptist charities. Father had instructed her to do this, and although she didn't know why she was doing it since she didn't have a clue about how Charlotte had really died, she went right along with him. She didn't put up one word of argument in my favor. You see how much she loves me?"

"Joan, I'm sorry," Blaine said sincerely, for the first time realizing the depth of the Peytons' disregard for their elder daughter and understanding a little better what the tremendous pain of being deprived of their love had done to Joan and how she'd learned to turn her tremendous anger and hurt onto others.

"I was sorry, too," Joan said bitterly. "And when Rick found out, he turned his attentions to you, the very woman who married Martin Avery."

"Martin?" Blaine said blankly. Then something clicked in her mind. "You said that when Charlotte was home, she captured the interest of the man you wanted. Was it Martin?"

"Of course. I was dating Martin—oh, casually, but I knew I could win him over. He was so handsome, Blaine, even handsomer than when you married him."

"I know," Blaine said slowly.

"Oh, yes, you would. You did yard work here, didn't you?" she sneered. "He married the woman who once mowed his grass. Good God!"

Even under these circumstances, the old feelings of embarrassment and resentment flared up in Blaine, but she concentrated on keeping herself calm, on keeping Joan talking. "Joan, you claim there is one other person who knows what happened to Charlotte."

"There *was* one other person."

"Martin."

She nodded. "He called me one Saturday afternoon. He said he had to talk to me because he'd been doing a lot of thinking. A *lot* of thinking since his accident. And things didn't fit together. Things about Charlotte."

Blaine felt as if she couldn't get her breath. "That was the afternoon of his death."

"Yes. I came out as he asked. He told me that he'd staged an argument with you— even thrown an ashtray at you to get you out of the house. He had to because you were always hovering over him. Then he called Bernice and told her not to come. We were alone for the afternoon. Then he started talking about Charlotte. He said he'd never been able to stop thinking about her. He'd loved her, you see, and he'd never gotten over her."

Blaine felt a dull hurt, but she wasn't surprised. She'd always known there was someone in Martin's past he couldn't get over, but she'd mistakenly thought it was his wife, Gloria.

"Charlotte had nearly obsessed him since the car wreck, he said. He didn't know why. He'd been recalling how she looked, acted, little things she'd said. He'd been trying to straighten it all out, writing it all down in journals."

The journals in which he wrote for hours shut in his study, Blaine thought.

"He said he knew what happened. Just like my father, he figured it out. He knew I'd killed Charlotte."

"Then why didn't he go to the police?"

"Martin's mind wasn't functioning up to par." Joan gave her superior smile. "He was obsessing on the past, while the present was losing reality. Just like an old person. I didn't know if anyone would take him seriously or not, but I couldn't take the chance."

"So you shot him." Joan nodded. "But the locked gun case . . ."

"Robin told Rosie where you'd hidden the key shortly after Martin's accident. Rosie and I still had a good relationship back then—she confided in me about things like that. After I left Martin on the deck that afternoon, I simply went in your room, found the key, got a gun from the case, went outside, and shot Martin in the head. Then I fired a second shot with the gun in his hand." She frowned. "You see, I really *wanted* that one to look like suicide. I didn't want a police investigation, because I wasn't sure who else he'd told his theories about Charlotte to. Then I put another cartridge in the gun, came in the study and got his journals, and burned them."

"Because if they'd simply vanished, then questions *would* have been raised about the possibility of an intruder in the house. Burning the journals seemed like something Martin might do before he killed himself."

"That's right. I also thought the police might check your phone record, and I knew they'd find a call to my home just shortly before Martin died. So I made up the story about him calling to see when Rosie and Robin would be home."

"Are you the hit-and-run driver who rammed our car last New Year's Eve?"

Joan looked affronted. "I'm smarter than that. I could have been injured or unable to get away from the scene. *That* was an unfortunate accident. The rest of it—all that was in my control—all had been carefully planned. I thought of everything!"

"Except that the second shot you fired hit that tree in the backyard."

Some of the glee faded from Joan's face. "You know, I was so nervous, so afraid you or Robin was going to walk in, that I didn't even realize that shot hit the tree. As I said, I *wanted* it to look like suicide." She shook her head. "But then Logan Quint and the prosecutor decided it was murder made to *look* like suicide. So when it was necessary for me to eliminate Rosie, I decided to follow what the police thought was your pattern."

"And if they hadn't suspected me?"

"I was prepared to tell them about Rosie's affair with Rick, the man so *many* people think you're involved with. I was going to say that Rosie was afraid of you. After all, she didn't come out here to visit Robin anymore, did she? It would all look quite plausible, especially since I'm such a good actress. That was my talent in the Miss West Virginia contest, you know. Acting. I'm wonderful."

"You've certainly had *me* fooled for years," Blaine said dryly.

"Yes, I knew I did. Anyway, after what I told the police about Rosie and Rick, they would have to proceed with a murder investigation that would point right at you."

"So why didn't you do it?"

Joan brushed at her forehead. "I didn't want to do it unless I was forced to. I wanted to appear your loyal supporter. That made me seem more sympathetic, don't you see? *The woman who believes in Blaine Avery no matter what the evidence*. That's how the police would think. It would keep their attention away from me, just in case Martin had babbled his *deductions* about Charlotte to anyone else. Besides, other problems came up. There was so much to think about. Like Kathy Foss. The girl knew something. I didn't know how dangerous she might be, so I had to get rid of her."

Blaine couldn't help noticing the strange grinding noises coming from the kitchen. Teeth on wood. What was Ashley *doing*? "How did you know Kathy knew something?"

"You forget—even though I was on leave, I had a direct line to the school. Susie saw

Kathy collapse and wake up babbling about Rosie and seeing something and being afraid. Susie called Bernice every day. She told her about it, and Bernice told me."

"And Bernice?"

"She knew about the medicine," Joan said casually. "Not your Martin's medicine, like Logan Quint thought. My *father's* medicine. He, too, took Dilaudid when he was dying of cancer last year. Everyone forgot about that. You see, I had a fantasy about giving both him and Mother overdoses—of course I would never have done such a thing, but it was fun to imagine. It gave me such a sense of power. So I started sneaking small quantities of Dilaudid out of the vials and replacing them with water. Then it got to be a game—exactly how much Dilaudid could I steal without Bernice noticing?

"Well, finally she did. Sort of. She said Father was in so much pain, the medicine just wasn't working, and she didn't understand it. Then once I got careless, and she told me there was less Dilaudid in the vial than there should have been. But she wasn't *totally* sure, so she never said anything to the doctor. She was always afraid people were going to think she was incompetent, find out about her drinking. But when Logan came to the house asking about Dilaudid, I could see the wheels starting to grind away in that dull brain of hers. Pretty soon even *she* would have been forced by conscience to go to the police and tell them about the Dilaudid that seemed to have disappeared a year ago."

"So *that's* the medicine you've been using," Blaine said. "And you saved empty vials from that time to store it in. One of them was found at the high school."

"Exactly. And that was no accident. I wanted the police to know what the girls had been given. Then someone, probably Rick, would tell them Martin had been on Dilaudid. My only mistake was in hiding the vial a little too well. I wanted it found immediately."

"But what made you think I'd go to Bernice's last night?"

Joan gave her a sage look. "I know people, Blaine. I've known *you* since you were a smart-aleck little girl who never knew her place."

The eyelashes! Blaine thought in ironic astonishment. She's hated me ever since I was six and told her the false eyelashes didn't look good on her.

"I knew that if stupid Bernice called and threatened you, you'd probably tell her to take her hints about the missing Dilaudid to the police and be damned."

How wrong you are, Blaine thought. I've been frightened to death of spending the rest of my life in prison ever since Martin's death.

"But if she threatened Robin, well, that would be another matter. Martin told me that. He said to me during those last days, 'Do you know that Blaine still loves me? In spite of everything, she still loves me. And she loves Robin. Oh, they may spat, but there's feeling there. Yes, Blaine will always protect my girl.' "

"Martin said that?"

"Yes. You see, he didn't resent you as much as you thought he did. At least not when he was himself, not consumed with self-pity. He did leave you in his will, didn't he?"

"Yes," Blaine said softly, feeling as if a tremendous hurt were easing. Martin hadn't hated her after all.

"But just in case he was wrong about how

much you cared for Robin, and Bernice's insinuations didn't work, I took along a
bracelet of yours. I got it from your jewelry
box the day I found the key to the gun case.
A cheap little bracelet, but one that had
your initials inside."

"The bracelet my father gave me when I
graduated from high school! I've looked
everywhere for it!"

"How touching. Anyway, if you didn't
show up at Bernice's, I was going to drop it
there. As it turned out, that would have
been the wisest course," Joan said thoughtfully. "That way Bernice *would* have bled to
death, and I would have avoided that awful
run through the woods."

"And what about the phone calls? Why
did you keep calling me and playing music?"

"I thought it was a nice, macabre touch."

"You wanted to torment and frighten me."

"Oh, yes. You deserved it for marrying
Martin. Besides, you told people about the
calls. Thanks to Arletta and Abel Stroud,
half the town knows about them. People
think you're crazy, claiming to get calls like
that. Crazy enough to commit murder."

Blaine closed her eyes. When she opened

them, Joan was withdrawing a multi-dose vial from her coat pocket. "I have plenty of Dilaudid left."

Blaine's mouth felt full of sand. "I thought the idea was for me to be charged with all these murders."

Joan frowned. "Well, it was. And I just about made it happen. But Bernice was my downfall. She lived. When she regains consciousness, she'll tell who tried to kill her, so my plan won't work now. I'll have to kill you myself."

"And what about you?"

"I'll leave the country. I think I'll go someplace warm. Some place where they don't have an extradition agreement with the United States. Yes, that would be best." She smiled. "Won't Mother be in a fix then? No Bernice, no Joan."

"But if Bernice regains consciousness soon, you won't make it out of town."

"Oh, yes, I will. I'm driving my father's old car. They won't be looking for it. They won't even know it's missing. I'll drive to Columbus to catch a plane and be gone before they know what happened."

And she could get away with it, Blaine thought in horror. The chances of Bernice coming to and talking coherently within the next few hours were frighteningly slim.

Something hit the French doors, and they both jumped. Ashley suddenly began to bark again. "What is it?" Joan demanded furiously. "Who's out there?"

Logan, Blaine prayed. But Logan wouldn't fling himself against the doors. Peering into the snow, she saw a small figure that scratched on the glass. "Mrs. Avery?" it called weakly. "Mrs. Avery, help me!"

19

Blaine's heart seemed to drop into her stomach. It was Tim. So all along he'd been on his way to her house, where he thought love and safety awaited him.

"Open the door," Joan ordered.

"Oh, Joan, please. It's Logan Quint's son, and he's only seven."

"I said, open the door!"

"He'll go away if we just ignore him."

Joan looked at her stonily.

"Joan . . ."

"*Open it!*" Joan shouted.

Blaine's jaw clenched. "I won't."

"Then I'll shoot you right now, and shoot him through the glass before he has a chance to run. Do you prefer that option?"

And she will, Blaine knew. What's one un-planned murder to her? Rigidly, feeling frozen, she went to the door and opened it. Tim almost fell into the room.

Blaine knelt and held him to her. His little

face was swollen with cold, his eyes and nose were running, his black hair was soaking wet. He was shivering violently.

"I d-didn't think I w-was gonna m-make it," he managed through chattering teeth. "I g-got lost."

"Oh, Tim," Blaine moaned, holding him against her.

"So you're Logan Quint's child," Joan said easily. "It's hard to tell much about your looks in your present condition, but I'd say the Indian blood is quite prominent."

Tim looked past Blaine at Joan, his face puckering. "Who're you?"

"A friend."

Ashley was back at the kitchen door, her paws stabbing through the crack at the bottom as she barked ferociously. "How c-come Ashley's in t-there?" he asked.

"Because I don't want to shoot her," Joan said.

Tim's eyes widened, and Blaine knew they'd fastened on Joan's gun. "You're g-gonna *shoot* us?"

"No. I have something much more fun in mind. Blaine, stand up."

Blaine touched Tim's cold face, tried to smile reassuringly, and stood, never turning loose his hand in its wet leather glove. "All right, Joan. What now?"

"Now I think we'll take a little walk."

"But there's a *blizzard*," Tim cried.

"*You* made it through the snow, didn't you?"

"But I got lost and I kept fallin' down." He looked imploringly at Joan. "Please don't shoot us, and please don't make us go back out there."

"Pretty please with sugar on it?" Joan asked sweetly.

"Sugar and a cherry on top," Tim said fervently.

Joan's smile faded. "Request denied."

As Blaine had listened to this bizarre interchange between Joan and Tim, she had been aware that Ashley was no longer barking. Now she heard a noise in the kitchen, like wood hitting linoleum. At the same moment that she realized what had happened, Ashley appeared outside the French doors, barking frantically.

"How did she get out there?" Joan demanded.

Blaine swallowed. "She must have chewed the knobs off the lock panel of the dog door leading outside."

"Ashley, help us!" Tim yelled.

The dog hurled herself at the glass, which shuddered but didn't break. Her lips disappearing into a slit, Joan aimed the revolver at the doors. Blaine and Tim both screamed as a shot shattered the glass. The dog yelped and was silent.

"I didn't want to do that," Joan said regretfully.

Tim burst into tears. "You . . . you *witch!* My daddy's gonna get you! My daddy's gonna hang you from the highest tree for what you did, you horrible, big, ugly, *mean*—"

"Timmy, don't," Blaine said, pulling him against her.

"But she *killed* Ashley!"

"And now I'm going to kill the two of you," Joan said calmly. "Outside. *Now.*"

So this is how it's going to end, Blaine thought distantly. A string of violent murders to end with the deaths of Tim and me.

Blaine felt tears sliding down her face as, coatless and still clutching Tim's hand, she stepped out into the frozen night. The end, the end. Is this all life was? A little, innocent boy dying because he happened to come to the wrong house on the wrong night?

Then her eyes shot around her. There was no body of a golden retriever. Blood dotted the snow where Ashley had stood when Joan shot him, but it wasn't a lot of blood. For some reason, Blaine's heart soared. Ashley was alive. And if Ashley had made it . . .

Tim tugged at her hand and murmured so softly that Joan, walking behind them, could not hear. "Ashley's okay." Blaine nodded. Then Tim whispered, "Don't worry. I'll get us out of this."

Blaine almost laughed at this dear little boy with his fierce loves and his emotional strength. Already his tears had dried, and despite the snow beating their faces, Blaine could see his determined expression. At that moment he looked exactly like Logan.

Clad only in boots, jeans, and a loose-knit sweater, Blaine was immediately freezing. Her hair blew wildly in the wind, sometimes lashing painfully against her face. Tim squeezed her hand. "It's gonna be okay."

"Go *on*," Joan shouted above the wind. "Into the woods."

The hem of Blaine's jeans was soaking, and she was shivering almost uncontrollably. And what about Tim? she wondered.

He'd been outside for at least an hour. Thankfully, he'd remembered to wear his gloves, but his face could already be frost-bitten. What could his mother have said to upset him enough to make him run away on such a godforsaken night as this? she thought, trying to fill her mind with something besides fear. Allie Quint hadn't said why he'd run off, but instinctively Blaine knew something disastrous was happening in the marriage of Logan and Dory. Dory. Cait had seen her once at a library reception. She'd told Blaine that Dory was blond and beautifully fine-featured, although a petulant mouth and restless, troubled eyes had somewhat ruined the effect.

Your thoughts are rambling, Blaine told herself. You have to concentrate, just like you did when Joan was chasing you through the woods at Bernice's house. Concentrate on what you're doing and how you're going to save Tim, even if saving yourself is impossible.

Trees suddenly rose in front of them. In the swirling snow they had missed the entrance to the path, and Blaine paused, knowing that the floor of the woods here was a mass of vines. "Go *on*," Joan snapped.

Blaine pushed her wet hair back from her face. "This isn't the path. Don't you want to find the path?"

The gun pressed into her back. "I don't give a damn about the path. Stop stalling. *Walk*."

The vines were frozen talons that grabbed at their shoes. Tim fell once and Blaine heard a tiny sob escape him before he quickly clambered to his feet and controlled himself again. He isn't going to let Joan know how terrified he is, Blaine thought. He doesn't realize she isn't even aware of our emotions anymore. She glanced back to see Joan smiling crookedly, her eyes glazed. Somehow the sight was more frightening than the gun aimed inches from her back.

Finally they reached the path, but Joan ordered them to cross it and head back into the woods again. She's taking us to the creek, Blaine told herself in despair. She's going to kill us by the creek, just like she did Rosie.

They staggered over the snow and the vines. If only she'd fall, Blaine thought furiously. *Why* can't she fall? Then I could get the gun. But Joan seemed remarkably sure-footed, much more so than Blaine and Tim, who kept tripping and clinging to each other for balance. Blaine was no longer trembling—she was numb. Probably too numb to even grab the gun if Joan did drop it.

"I really must apologize for this weather," Joan shouted. "The night Rosie died out here was just beautiful."

She sounded so matter-of-fact, as if she were discussing a social event. Blaine felt Tim shudder as he clung more tightly to her hand, but his eyes stared straight ahead as they crunched over the frozen vines and zigzagged around huge trees laden with snow.

Suddenly there was a rushing noise behind Blaine, followed by a stabbing pain in her arm. She shrieked and whirled, but it was too late. Joan had already plunged a syringe into her upper arm. Dilaudid, Blaine thought as Joan drew back, aiming the gun at her again. The syringe, more than half empty, still hung in Blaine's arm and she tore it loose, letting it drop on the ground.

"What did you do to her?" Tim screamed.

"Took her by surprise," Joan said pleasantly.

"You gave her a shot and she's *bleeding!*"

"Just shut up and keep walking."

They plodded on again, but within minutes Blaine felt the drug coursing through her, slowing her down, blurring her vision. Tree limbs groaned above them, battered by the unrelenting wind, and somewhere off to the right she heard a loud cracking. No doubt it was a sumac with its weak wood. The wind must be tearing a limb from it, or perhaps the whole tree was going to crash down. A night of death and destruction, Blaine thought.

And then they were at the creek bank. Blaine stiffened as she looked down into the dark, cold water.

"End of the line,"Joan said grimly. Tim looked up at Blaine, this time unable to keep the fear from his brown eyes.

"Now what?" Blaine asked, noticing that her voice sounded slightly slurred. She wanted to lie down in the snow and go to sleep.

"Well, I've been thinking about that all the way here," Joan said. "I think simple death is a little too good for you, Blaine. So I've decided to kill the boy while you're still conscious. I want you to die with the horrible image of him being murdered dancing in your brain." She looked at Tim kindly. "It won't hurt, honey, really. Don't be afraid."

"I'm *not* afraid of you!" Tim shouted.

"Of course you're not," Joan said in a patronizing tone. Then she looked at Blaine. "Tell me, are all children such habitual liars?"

"I really wouldn't know," Blaine answered. "But I *do* know that he's afraid. He's terrified."

Tim's eyes blazed up at her. "I'm *not!* I'm not a bit—"

Blaine squeezed his hand so hard he winced. Then, with her head turned slightly away from Joan, she winked at Tim. He frowned, and she wasn't sure he realized she was winking, or if he thought she'd simply developed a twitch from the cold. "Admit it, Tim. You're scared to death, aren't you?"

Tim hesitated. She held her breath, releasing it only when he said, "Well, kind of."

"And you're going to do whatever this lady tells you, *aren't* you?"

Blaine's heart beat in heavy thuds coming

too far apart. If she could only make him seem weak and cooperative, maybe Joan would take her eyes off him long enough to let him get away. It was already too late for her. In a couple of minutes she wouldn't be able to stand. Another excruciating five seconds passed while Tim looked at her. Then his face suddenly puckered in a good imitation of sobbing. He turned to Joan. "Yeah, lady, I'll do anything. Only *please* don't hurt me!"

"That's better," Joan said. "That is much, much better. I'll tell you what I want you to do. I want you to sit down by that tree over there."

Tim stood absolutely still, and Blaine could feel fright rushing through him. "Do as she says, Tim."

"B-but she's gonna *kill* me!"

"Just do as she says, and she might change her mind."

Tim looked at her imploringly. "Mrs. Avery?"

"Don't call her that!" Joan snapped. "She's plain old Blaine O'Connor, nothing but trash."

"Huh?"

"Never mind. Just go ahead," Blaine said,

nudging him. Joan stood about two feet behind her and she staggered, as if the drug were having an even more profound effect on her than it was. Joan tensed as Blaine regained her balance nearly six inches closer to her, but Blaine kept her eyes on Tim. "Go on, Timmy. Go stand by that big oak."

Tim released her hand and with dragging steps walked to the tree. He looked so small against its wide trunk. He stood with his back to them until Joan said, "Turn around, little boy. I don't want it said that I shot someone in the back. Besides, I want Blaine to see your eyes when you die."

Joan took a step forward. Blaine's breath labored in her chest. She closed her eyes for a moment, trying to refocus. And she prayed for strength.

Very slowly, Tim turned around. His hands were clenched; his swollen face was defiant. Blaine felt rather than saw Joan aim the gun at Tim before she hurled herself to the left.

A shot exploded as Blaine and Joan both crashed to the ground. "Tim, *run!*" Blaine screamed, not knowing whether or not the little boy had been hit.

"Mrs. Avery!" he yelled.

"Run!" she screamed again as Joan cursed and threw Blaine off her. Blaine toppled sideways, her face pressing into the snow. "Where is it?" Joan shrieked. "Where *is* it?"

The gun, Blaine thought. I knocked the gun out of her hand. And then she saw it lying in the snow near her left foot. She could never raise herself up, grab it, and shoot Joan. She just didn't have the strength to sit up or to hold onto the gun if Joan fought her for it. Instead she flung out her leg. Her booted foot connected with the gun and sent it skittering a couple of feet through the snow and over the bank into the dark waters of the creek.

"You bitch!" Joan gasped as she crawled toward Blaine. "You think you've won, don't you? But you haven't."

Suddenly Blaine felt Joan's strong hands on her shoulders, lifting her, dragging her through the snow toward the creek. Blaine kicked weakly, trying to struggle, but her strength was almost gone.

Joan rolled her over the bank of the creek. Blaine landed faceup, swallowing dirty, frigid water. Gagging, she managed to raise her head out of the shallow water and draw a breath, although her lungs felt as if they didn't really work anymore. The drug was slowing her respiration. Her head went under again, and this time she held her breath as long as she could before weakly lifting it once more. Joan pounced on her like a cat.

"Drown, dammit!"

Blaine's hands sank in the dirt of the creek bottom. She raised them and tried to claw at Joan, but all she managed was weak flailing. She gasped frantically, but there wasn't enough air. But there was sound. Was that a dog barking? Blaine wondered foggily as Joan pushed her head under the water again. No. It must have been her imagination. Everything was such a horrible jumble. All that existed was black, foul-smelling water. Hands on her face. Knees on her chest. Her lungs screaming for air.

Blaine swallowed more water. She was losing consciousness. For just a moment her father's face flashed before her eyes. Then Martin's, Logan's, Robin's, Tim's, Ashley's . . .

Suddenly strong arms were pulling her

out of the creek. She heard screaming, a dog barking, someone ordering, "Blaine! Blaine, *breathe!*" But she couldn't. If they would stop pounding on her chest, she could tell them that, she thought irritably. If they would just stop pounding—

Abruptly she convulsed, rolled onto her side, and began spewing water. "Come on, Blaine! That's it!" someone shouted. "You can do it, Blaine!" Logan? But it couldn't be him. It was all a dream—a dream of being saved.

She was rolled onto her back. She was cold and sick and unbearably sleepy, but she looked up. It *was* Logan. Somewhere far off she heard a woman shrieking. A dog was alternately licking her face and whirling to bark at the screaming woman. And a little face appeared over her. She blinked repeatedly until it came into semi-focus. It beamed down at her. "Ashley found Daddy and a bunch of men in the woods looking for me. She led them here. She *tracked* us." Tim? He gazed triumphantly up at his father's anxious face. "You see, Daddy, my dream was right? I *told* you a big gold dog was gonna save me!"

And then she slept.

Epilogue

"The woods don't seem haunted anymore," Blaine said. "If there is an *orenda*, or some kind of spirit animating the trees, it's no longer trying to tell us something."

Logan smiled. "I'm surprised you can come back here at all after what happened. If the search party hadn't been so close to your house when Ashley found us, if she hadn't been so good at tracking you through the storm, if we'd been two minutes later pulling Joan off you, if the emergency squad hadn't been so quick—"

"I spent two days in the hospital imagining all those horrible things that might have happened, then I decided such thinking is useless. Everything turned out okay for Tim and me. That's what I try to keep in mind."

The day was bright and dry as they strolled along the path, listening to Tim and Robin up ahead, laughing as they tossed a frisbee for Ashley to catch.

Logan looked at her closely. "Are you sure you're all right now?"

"I'm more all right than I have been for a year. I finally know Martin didn't hate me for the accident. You know, Logan, I always thought he killed himself, but I was afraid he'd deliberately fired into that tree and replaced the cartridge in the gun so that it would look like murder and I'd be a suspect. I did him a terrible disservice, but it's over. And Robin and I have finally made peace."

"I guess when she realized the hell you'd gone through in the summer over Martin's death without ever mentioning to the police that she knew where the key to the gun case was, she had to know you cared about her."

"Yes, it made a difference. I guess we've both been blind."

"And how were you blind?"

"By not thinking about how often Joan came out here to see Martin before his death. They hadn't seemed so close before. I think she got a sick thrill out of seeing him so helpless, as if it were a punishment for loving Charlotte and later marrying me instead of her. And I should have realized that, considering the eagle eye Joan kept on

Rosie, she would have known about her affair with Rick." Blaine sighed. "What's going to happen to Joan?"

Logan looked troubled, almost haunted, and Blaine remembered how much he had always liked the woman. "I've heard she spends most of the day grooming herself, or pretending she's winning the Miss West Virginia pageant, or having imaginary conversations with her parents and with Martin and Rick. In her mind, they all adore her. And she sings. 'Ring Around a Rosy' seems to be her big favorite. It's my guess she'll spend the rest of her life in an institution."

Blaine dug her hands deeper in her pockets. "You just wonder how someone like that can function normally in society for so long."

"We all wear masks sometimes. Joan managed to wear one *all* the time. She fooled everyone—everyone except her father. And, unfortunately, Rosie near the end. If only the girl had kept her suspicions about the mythical Derek Van Zandt to herself."

Blaine frowned. "I have a feeling none of that really made any difference. Rosie's death warrant was signed when she became involved with Rick."

"Love seems to get a lot of us in a hell of a lot of trouble." Logan reached over and took Blaine's hand out of her pocket, holding it tightly. "I've agreed to give Dory a divorce. I should have insisted on it months ago, but I thought keeping the family together for Tim was best. But it wasn't. He almost died that night because of her."

"That night wasn't exactly Dory's fault," Blaine said. "But you're right—Dory apparently doesn't want to be a mother, and Tim shouldn't be subjected to her unhappiness. How does he feel about the divorce?"

"I've done my best to explain things to him. And he'll be spending a certain amount of time with Dory each year, although she doesn't want joint custody." He smiled ruefully. "Too much responsibility for her. But Tim will adjust. He's a tough little guy."

"You're telling me!" Blaine laughed. "You should have heard how he tried to stand up to Joan."

Ashley bounded back to them, bandage on her side where Joan's bullet had nicked her, orange frisbee in her mouth. Tim and Robin were close behind. As usual, Blaine was startled by the change in Robin's appearance. She looked flushed and lovely, the tension that had turned her face surly for almost a year now finally gone. She knew her father hadn't killed himself, nor had Blaine killed him. And she was dating Tony Jarvis, who it turned out had been lying about being with his mother the night Robin claimed to have met him, all to protect her.

"We keep telling Ashley she's supposed to bring the frisbee to us," Robin said, laughing.

"But she just *won't* do it!" Tim knelt beside the dog and gave her a fierce hug. Ashley dropped the frisbee and licked his face.

"I guess you'll just have to come out and work with her regularly," Robin said.

"Oh, I will!" Tim answered fervently. "I've heard Grandma say you can't teach an old dog new tricks, but *I* can. Besides, Ashley's the smartest dog in the whole world. *And* the bravest, don't you think, Robin?"

"I certainly do."

Logan had dropped Blaine's hand, and he looked at Tim. "I suppose it's time for us to go home, son."

Blaine saw mixed emotions pass over the child's face—hope, reluctance, a little anxiety. But he said cheerfully, "Yeah. Mommy said she'd call me to talk about the di—di . . ."

"Divorce," Logan said.

"Yeah. Besides, I've got to do arithmetic. I've *always* got to do arithmetic!" Tim's arms fell away from the dog, and he gazed up at Blaine. "I had a real good time today."

"So did we. How about coming back next Saturday to continue Ashley's frisbee training?"

Tim brightened. "Can I, Daddy?"

"Sure, son. You can come anytime you're invited."

"Am I invited?" Tim asked Blaine.

"I told you before—you have an open invitation. Come out anytime you want."

"And Daddy?"

Blaine smiled into Logan's eyes. "The open invitation goes for him, too."

As Logan and Tim walked across the wide back lawn, leaving Blaine and Robin standing on the path, Robin put her arm around Blaine's shoulders. "So what's going on between you two?"

"A very wise young lady once told me that love might be put on the shelf for a while, but it doesn't die."

"And what do those wise young lady's words mean to you?"

Blaine smiled. "At this moment, they mean I get all my satisfaction out of being alive and having you and Ashley. As for the future . . ."

Suddenly Tim turned around, flashed them his wide smile with its missing front tooth, and called, "We'll see you real, *real* soon."

"As for the future," Blaine continued, waving to Tim, "I'll be here waiting."